THE CLIFFS

THE CLIFFS

J. Courtney Sullivan

ALFRED A. KNOPF · NEW YORK 2024

THIS IS A BORZOI BOOK
PUBLISHED BY ALFRED A. KNOPF

Copyright © 2024 by J. Courtney Sullivan

All rights reserved. Published in the United States by Alfred A. Knopf,
a division of Penguin Random House LLC, New York, and distributed
in Canada by Penguin Random House Canada Limited, Toronto.

www.aaknopf.com

Knopf, Borzoi Books, and the colophon are registered
trademarks of Penguin Random House LLC.

Library of Congress Cataloging-in-Publication Data
Names: Sullivan, J. Courtney, author.
Title: The cliffs : a novel / J. Courtney Sullivan.
Description: First edition. | New York : Alfred A. Knopf, 2024.
Identifiers: LCCN 2023028063 | ISBN 9780593319154 (hardcover) |
  ISBN 9780593319161 (ebook)
Subjects: LCGFT: Novels.
Classification: LCC PS3619.U43 C55 2024 | DDC 813/.6—dc23/eng/20230717
LC record available at https://lccn.loc.gov/2023028063

Jacket photograph by Pat & Chuck Blackley / Alamy
Jacket design by Jenny Carrow

Manufactured in the United States of America
First Edition

For DONNA LORING,
with gratitude and admiration

And in memory of
DEANNE TORBERT DUNNING

THE CLIFFS

Prologue

THE HOUSE, long abandoned, had stories to tell. The house was a contradiction. Clearly well-loved at one time, but left to rot.

Jane first saw it from the water. She was seventeen, narrating a sunset cocktail cruise aboard Abe Adams's lobster boat.

Three months earlier, on a Friday in late April, she got called to the principal's office for the first time in her life. Heart pounding, she walked the empty halls. Her shoes echoed against the linoleum no matter how softly she stepped, mortifying her. Jane was in the habit then of taking up as little space as possible. Her cheeks grew hot as she tried to imagine what she had done wrong.

The receptionist, plump and frizzy-haired under fluorescent lights, was grinning from behind her desk when Jane entered the room. She gestured toward the open office door with enthusiasm, and Jane wondered if she took some sadistic pleasure in hearing teenagers receive their comeuppance through the flimsy wall.

Across from the principal sat Jane's English and social studies teachers. All three of them were grinning too. They had summoned her, they said, with excellent news. Jane was one of twenty-five honors students in the state of Maine selected to be part of a summer program at Bates College. Very prestigious, they said. An incredible opportunity. It would set her apart on her applications next year. She would get to take a seminar for college credit, immersing herself in a topic of her choosing at a level not possible in even her most rigorous AP classes. That day or the next, they said, her mother would receive a letter with more details. But they couldn't wait to tell Jane in person.

Jane's first thought was that she wished she could tell her grandmother. Instead, she went home and waited for her mother to bring it up.

Five days passed without a word on the subject. Jane sifted through the already-opened mail on the kitchen counter when she got home from school each afternoon, but found no trace of the letter. She had visions of her mother hiding it, burning it, throwing it away.

When Jane couldn't wait any longer, she asked her mother flat out if she had gotten the letter.

"Yeah," her mother said, all casual. "I don't know, Jane. It sounds expensive. It sounds like a scam."

Jane explained that the program was free, the books and everything, even transportation.

"Nothing's ever really free," her mother said. "They're using you."

"For what?" Jane said, indignant.

"You'd still have to have a summer job," her mother said. "You can't skip out on that."

"When have *I* ever skipped out on anything?" Jane said. Under her breath she added, "I cannot wait to get out of this house."

"Where do you want to go?" her mother said. "Grab me a pen. I'll draw you a map."

Jane went to the room she shared with her older sister and slammed the door. Holly was in there, reading a magazine in bed. She didn't look up.

JANE'S BEST FRIEND, Allison, baked her congratulatory brownies and bought her a set of her favorite rollerball pens at CVS. Allison's friendship was proof that much of life came down to luck. She would have had no reason to speak to Jane had they not been assigned a shared locker freshman year, the year Jane's grandmother died and Jane moved with her mother and sister into her grandmother's house in Awadapquit.

Before that, they had been living in a rented apartment in Worcester, Massachusetts, with her mother's ex-boyfriend. An awkward arrangement. They had broken up months earlier, but neither one wanted to move out. Jane and Holly had to tiptoe around him on the sofa, where he seemed to be twenty-four hours a day. Their mother was relieved to escape that situation, but even so, she seemed to resent the house. A gift she couldn't refuse that nevertheless held her hostage in her hometown when she had meant to be gone for good.

Jane didn't know what possessed Allison to draw her out, to ask her so many questions, to invite her over. Everyone at school had known one another since birth, it seemed, and everyone wanted to be Allison's best friend. But for some reason, she chose Jane, the nerd, the new girl, the one who read novels at the bus stop before school because she liked reading novels, but also because she hoped it might disguise the fact of how alone she was.

Allison's parents ran an inn. They sat on every local council and committee. They called Tuesday night bingo at the fire station and volunteered at pancake breakfasts in the school gym in winter. Her dad coached baseball and hockey. They were busy. But they always acted happy to see Jane. They asked her about herself, especially Allison's mom, Betty, who seemed proud of Jane in a way her own mother was not.

In the three years they had known one another, Jane had eaten more dinners at Allison's house than she had at her own. They never spent time at Jane's house, an unspoken understanding for which Jane was deeply grateful.

Jane's mother always claimed to be overwhelmed, though by what, Jane had no idea. She seemed unable to deal with the details of life that other adults just handled. Whenever anyone asked what her mother did for work, Jane lied. She would say her mom was a book-keeper, which she had been once, years ago, a time before memory. She still talked about that job sometimes, as if she might be headed back any day.

Her actual job, if you could call it that, was going to yard sales and reselling what she bought later for slightly more than she had paid. She shopped on Saturdays and Sundays. On Mondays, she brought her finds to various local consignment stores and individuals and tried to make a profit. The rest of her hours at home were spent talking on the cord-

less phone to whichever guy she happened to be dating, while drinking a beer, and circling addresses and times for upcoming yard sales
in the newspaper. Or else sifting through junk at the kitchen table.

All the worst stuff, the stuff she couldn't sell, remained in their
kitchen and living room, cluttering every available bit of space. The
countertops were crowded with bowls full of old campaign but-
tons, clip-on earrings, baseball cards, batteries, and power cords
that didn't correspond to any known device. On the front lawn, blue
plastic tarps covered three-legged coffee tables and bicycles with no
chains and God only knew what else.

ALLISON RODE THE BUS to Bates with her the first day,
because Jane was so nervous. After that, every weekday in July, she
made the ninety-minute trip alone to the stately campus, all redbrick
buildings and leafy green trees. Jane read the whole way there and
back, pride radiating from within so intensely that she sometimes
worried strangers could sense it on her like a smell.

The seminar she chose was called Early Women Writers. The professor, a sixtyish woman with bobbed hair, wrote on the board during the first class meeting: *Most Lives Will Be Lost to Time.* She spoke the
names of women from as far back as the sixteenth century who wrote
down their life stories when no one thought it appropriate for women
to write at all. By doing so, they endured. Jane's brain lit up at the
idea. She devoured the poems of Lucy Cavendish and the detailed
diaries of Anne Clifford.

On the Wednesday night of her fourth week of class, there was
a massive thunderstorm. Jane loved thunder and lightning. She was
under the blankets in her bed, reading until midnight, listening to
the rain. Happy. Twice, the power went out, but popped back on a
moment later.

On her way to the bus stop the next morning, she saw several
fallen tree limbs, evidence of the weather. But the sky was a blazing
blue, like the storm had never happened.

She got to Bates early that day. As she approached the classroom,
Jane overheard the professor talking to someone.

"This one girl, Jane, she's smarter and more curious than most of

7

my sophomores and juniors," the professor said. "I'm really impressed by all the kids in the program. I'm glad I signed on to do it. The whole thing is about giving some early college exposure to high-achieving, at-risk kids, so that hopefully they'll be the first in their families to finish college. Break the cycle, you know."

No one had said anything to Jane about that. She wanted to challenge the statement, to tell her she was wrong, to demand to know in exactly what way she qualified as at-risk. But she knew. She had a single mother with a drinking problem and no money. An older sister who had landed on the evening news for getting wasted and stealing a boat with a group of guys, an incident Holly swore she did not remember when she woke up in a jail cell the next morning.

Jane had thought this summer program was evidence that she had successfully set herself apart from them. Now she realized the opposite was true. The family she came from defined her and always would.

She didn't read on the bus that afternoon, just stared out the window. The worst part of it hit her then: her mother knew why Jane had been chosen. That was why she hadn't mentioned the letter. Jane felt guilty for putting her mother in the position of having her failings pointed out to her like that. And furious at her mother for being such a failure in the first place.

She went home and cried in the shower until the water ran cold. Then she changed into her work uniform—khakis and a white button-down shirt. As usual, she showed up at the dock five minutes early for the seven o'clock cocktail cruise and greeted her boss, Abe, with a smile.

The previous two summers, Jane worked days, welcoming parents balancing strollers and sunblock and coffee to-go as they and their excited offspring climbed aboard. Jane spoke cheerily into a scratchy corded microphone, spouting the same set of facts four times daily, receiving near identical responses from every group.

Jane would say: *Awadapquit's pedestrian drawbridge is the only one of its kind in the United States.* The passengers would nod at others in their party—hmm, interesting.

She would say: *Lobster was once so plentiful in Maine that they fed it to prisoners for every meal. Reformers railed against the practice, calling it cruel.*

To this day, by law, prisoners in Maine can only be fed lobster twice a week. At this, the passengers would chuckle, since they themselves had, within the last day or so, doled out almost twenty dollars for a boiled one and a quarter-pound hard-shell.

When the boat got far enough offshore, Abe pulled up one of his traps and Jane plucked the most impressive lobster out for all to see. She waved the slippery creature, legs and antennae writhing, in the faces of children aboard. They in turn either grabbed the lobster eagerly or shrieked and hid in their mothers' shirts. There was no other possible reaction.

That summer, because Jane had class during the day, Abe offered her the coveted evening tour, on which the tips were better and neither lobsters nor children were present. Instead, couples sipped weak vodka-cranberries out of clear plastic cups and Abe hewed close to the rocky coastline so they could ogle the area's grandest oceanfront properties, the ones set far back from the road, hidden behind tall trees and long, winding driveways, visible only by boat.

That night, fifteen minutes into the trip, the sky turned an astonishing shade of orange, and Jane obsessed over what the professor had said about her.

Outwardly, she went through the motions.

As she did every night, she directed the crowd's attention to a tiny island, maybe a quarter mile from the cliffs, where harbor seals rested on the rocks. Technically it was named Saint George's, but Jane had never heard anyone call it that. The island didn't seem big enough for a name. In a bad storm, the whole thing disappeared beneath the waves.

"The island to your left was christened Saint George's by the British explorer Archibald Pembroke when he discovered this part of the world in 1605," she said.

Jane wasn't sure this was true. At some point she had seen a map of Pembroke's journey, and his final destination appeared to be a spot some three hundred miles south. She had brought this up with Abe, who said Pembroke had possibly landed in several different places. Jane suspected Abe didn't want to probe further, as doing so might require changing the script.

Whether or not Pembroke had actually set foot there, in 1930 the local antiquarian society had erected a small stone monument on the island to commemorate the three hundred and twenty-fifth anniversary of his voyage.

The monument still stood. From this distance, it was nearly indistinguishable from the natural rocks on either side, but for the fact that it alone was plagued by a barrage of seagull droppings, which rained down upon it like so much white paint, obscuring the inscription on its face.

As Jane mentioned the monument to the passengers now, a woman in the front row nudged her husband and pointed in the other direction, up toward the cliffs.

"That one gives me the creeps," she said.

Her voice was loud enough that Jane stopped speaking and turned to see what she was pointing at. Jane's eyes anticipated what she was used to seeing across from the island—a spot where two giant pine trees stood, right where the land jutted out into the sea, with overgrown hedges running along the cliffs on either side.

One of the trees had fallen in the storm. She could see its roots reaching up toward the sky like long, grasping fingers. It had left a gap, through which Jane glimpsed a house, pale purple, very old, with turrets and elaborate trim painted green in some spots and blue in others. One upstairs shutter dangled precariously. The window beside it had been smashed. A white curtain billowed out from within.

The woman was right. The house was creepy. Jane had the strongest urge to go there and explore. She was drawn to deserted places. Those patches of the world where you could feel the life that had been lived there and was no more. New England was full of them. Boarded-up factories and state mental hospitals. An abandoned amusement park, where she and her sister once climbed the rungs of the flume ride, all the way to the top.

Jane considered herself law-abiding in the extreme. She would never shoplift or run a red light. She had never had a sip of beer. But to her, trespassing in such places didn't feel like a crime. It felt like honoring whatever came before.

———

THE NEXT MORNING, as Jane got ready for class, she thought of the purple house, and how nobody would know or care if just that once she didn't go to Bates.

In the living room, her mother was asleep on the couch, the TV still on from the night before, four empty Bud Light cans on the table. Jane had heard her come in late.

She watched her for a moment. She was beautiful, but not, Jane thought, in the way a woman her age ought to be. She wore the same low-cut tops and push-up bras as the twenty-two-year-olds who bartended at Charlie's Chowder House. She used too much eyeliner and pink lipstick, and she smoked, which gave her skin a crepey quality.

Not for the first time, Jane imagined some sort of Freaky Friday scenario, in which her mother switched places with Betty Crowley, Allison's mom. That one morning Jane might wake to find her flipping fried eggs in a tasteful sundress and Dr. Scholl's sandals.

Her mother stirred.

Jane got her backpack and her bike and was off.

She coasted down Shore Road, sneaking up each private drive until she spotted some sign of life—a station wagon or a woman crouching in her garden—and then rode quickly back the way she came. There was no way the purple house was occupied.

She found it after forty minutes of searching. She had missed the turnoff at first. A rusty mailbox at the corner of Shore Road was the only indication that there was a house there at all. Jane followed a long dirt path beneath a canopy of trees that blocked out the daylight, until she emerged onto a large plot of land, right on the cliff, overlooking the ocean. There was the purple house, and a barn painted to match. The lawn had been allowed to turn wild. The rhododendrons in front of the house covered everything, up to the second-story windows.

Jane had the wonderful childlike sensation that at any moment, someone might pop out from behind a tree. A fear that electrified her, even as she knew there was no real danger.

She walked onto the front porch, careful to avoid the rotten boards.

There was a historical plaque beside the door, printed with the name of the original owner, dating the house to 1846. Jane peered through a window into a living room. Abstract paintings hung on almost every available bit of wall. There was a portrait of two sour-looking young women above the fireplace. A pair of green velvet couches atop a fancy rug. A child's dollhouse in the corner.

Through a window on the other side of the front door, she saw a dining table and chairs, a crystal chandelier. She could make out the entryway too. The upstairs banister had fallen down into it, looking like a railroad track across the floor. A floor-to-ceiling mural of a sunset over the ocean had been painted directly onto the wall.

Jane walked the grounds awhile. In a grove of pine trees to the side of the house, at the far edge of the property, she discovered a small cemetery, just a handful of graves, old and crumbling.

Later, she sat with her back against the fallen pine on the grassy promontory that jutted out over the water like a fat thumb and took in the view of the island, St. George's, directly across. So close she could swim there if she wanted. She ran her hands over the universe of roots. She thought there was something sacred and sad about such a tree falling. Imagine what this tree had seen in its lifetime.

Jane pulled a book from her backpack and started the reading assignment for the next day's class. She stayed all afternoon. In the weeks that followed, she read every title on the syllabus that way, sitting in the grass at the purple house until it was time for work. She never went back to Bates.

By the time Jane brought Allison to see the house, she had discovered that the back door was unlocked. Emboldened by her friend's company, she dared to go inside for the first time.

"I've been dying to see the upstairs," Jane said. "But I was afraid I might fall through the ceiling and break my legs."

"And my being here makes that less likely . . . how?" Allison said.

"It doesn't," Jane said. "But at least you could run for help."

"This may be your worst idea ever," Allison said.

But she followed Jane inside and together they started opening kitchen cabinets. Dishes were neatly stacked. There was food that had expired in 1968, twenty-five years earlier. Animals had chewed through boxes of cereal and rice and tins of coffee and cookies. The cupboards were littered with droppings and shredded paper and crumbs.

In a pantry off the kitchen, the shelves were full of crystal and glass objects in every imaginable shape and size—bowls and goblets and platters and salt shakers.

"This place is spooky," Allison said. "Let's go back outside."

"Please, let's go upstairs first," Jane said, whispering for some reason.

"What happens if we *both* fall through the ceiling and break our legs?" Allison said as they walked into the entryway, where the wooden banister lay on the floor.

Jane hadn't thought about that. They went upstairs anyway. All that remained of the banister there were the bottoms of the spindles, cracked and splintered. There were marbles everywhere in the hall, and shattered shards of glass.

"What in the hell," Allison said.

They entered a bedroom. The bed was unmade. Clothes hung in the closets. A hardcover book lay folded open on the nightstand and a pile of *Life* magazines sat on the floor.

The owner must have died suddenly. But why had no one come along since? Her professor's words echoed in Jane's mind: *Most Lives Will Be Lost to Time.*

"I can't believe you've been coming here alone," Allison said. "There is some kind of weird energy here, don't you feel it?"

Jane didn't. She felt at peace there in a way she hadn't since her grandmother was alive. Watched over, somehow.

As with most differences between her and Allison, Jane chalked this up to a deficiency in herself. Maybe it didn't feel weird to her because the alternative was her own house—loud and cramped and unpredictable. The absolute opposite of this place.

The size of Jane's house forced her into an unwanted sense of intimacy with her mother and sister. From any spot in any room, you could hear the TV, the buzz of the refrigerator, phone conversations, and whatever was going on in the bathroom. If her mother cooked bacon, the smoky scent of it clung to Jane's clothes for days.

SHE MADE THE MISTAKE of bringing her sister to the purple house only once. They sat together on the bluff and Holly kept saying how cool it was that you could see all of town from this distance, but no one could see you. It occurred to Jane then that that's how she always felt in Awadapquit.

Holly mentioned the house at home later that night, and their mother snapped, "Do not ever let me catch you going out there again, do you hear me?"

She made a face like Jane had gone specifically to hurt her.

"Why not?" Holly said.

"Just don't."

Jane didn't believe she had a reason. That was just how her mother was. She could manage to find fault with anything Jane did. Or maybe she was picturing wild parties, the sort of thing she herself would get up to in a house like that.

Jane ignored her. She went back, all through fall and spring of senior year, and in the summer that followed. Sometimes with Allison, to talk where no one could hear them. But Allison had started dating Chris by then. More often, Jane went by herself. She went to read in peace, to escape whatever drama was unfolding at home, to watch the ocean. She knew of course that the place did not belong to her, but felt all the same that it did.

Jane left Maine for college the following September. For many years, she forgot about the purple house. Even when she went home for a visit, she never thought to go. It wasn't until she met David that she remembered and wondered if anyone had ever bought the house, if it was still standing.

JANE WENT TO Wesleyan in Connecticut for undergrad, where her eyes were opened to the realities of inherited wealth; where she read George Eliot and Virginia Woolf and Shakespeare; where she developed a taste for bourbon and red wine and started drinking every night. Though not in the way her mother did, because unlike her mother, Jane knew how to stop before things got messy. Most of the time, anyway.

After college, she got her master's and PhD at Yale. She worked as an assistant at Emily Dickinson's homestead in Amherst, Massachusetts, and later, as a junior archivist at the special collections at Wellesley College. At twenty-eight, she landed her dream job, at the Schlesinger Library at the Harvard Radcliffe Institute in Cambridge.

Jane had friends, she socialized, but she was a very independent person, as she always had been. She preferred to live in a tiny studio, rather than have roommates. She went out to eat alone all the time, sitting at the bar, bringing a book, even on a Saturday night. ("I could never," Allison said when Jane told her this.) When she had finally saved enough money to travel through France and Spain, Jane went by herself, and felt lucky not to have to worry about what anyone else wanted to do or see.

Throughout her twenties, she occasionally went on dates, most of them bad and made bearable only by copious amounts of alcohol. A few times, she woke up in some stranger's bed, unsure how she had gotten there. Such behavior was slightly worrisome, she realized. But she was young. Unencumbered. Most young people she knew were like that. Jane never missed a single day of work or even arrived late. She was never so hungover that she couldn't run three miles the next morning. This was how she knew that she had everything under control.

She had one serious relationship, at twenty-seven, with a chef named Andre. He was sexy and fun, but when she was with him, Jane found herself behaving exactly as her mother would. This alarmed her. This was her greatest fear. Some people took *What Would Jesus Do?* as their guiding principle. Hers was *What Would My Mother Not Do?* And yet she and Andre developed a false sense of closeness fast, over too many tequila shots and late nights out in bars. Jane moved in with him six months after they met, even though they fought constantly. Three months later, she moved out. An explosive drunken goodbye scene ended with Andre sobbing as Jane threatened to set his childhood teddy bear on fire.

After they broke up, she felt devastated. It was a feeling she had never experienced before, and yet it was familiar. Romance had always caused her mother harm in the end, setting her life back. Jane decided then that the safest thing, the smartest thing, was to be alone. To never dip her toe into those waters to begin with. She liked herself best when she was controlled, composed, invulnerable. That was the woman she wanted to be.

Jane hadn't been expecting David.

They met a few months before her thirtieth birthday. Her boss at the Schlesinger, Melissa, set them up. Jane looked up to her, and so this meant the world. David was a good friend of Melissa's. An economics professor, four years Jane's senior.

"He is such a catch," Melissa told Jane before the first date. "If I were straight, he's one of about three men on the planet I'd consider dating. He's kind and funny. He runs marathons. He loves kids. Jane, he *bakes* to relieve stress. Seriously, David is like the male version of Pearl."

Pearl was Melissa's wife, a social worker who was dedicated and hardworking and yet knew how to enjoy life in a way most people didn't. Every year the two of them threw a big Christmas party at their house in Jamaica Plain. Jane marveled at how appealing the house was. Not at all stuffy or showy, just homey and warm and well-appointed. A home that exuded contentedness.

"Be gentle with him," Melissa said. "David's been through a lot. His ex-wife had an affair. She was constantly lying to him. He knew it, but it was like he didn't want to know. And then it all blew up in his face. It was a nightmare."

"Poor guy," Jane said, but she was thinking, *Mayday, damaged goods.*

David turned out to be exactly as Melissa had described. And he was so handsome. He reminded Jane of Robert Redford in *The Way We Were,* with his dreamy smile and shaggy blond hair. It was true, he was a catch, and Jane felt honored that Melissa had thought her worthy of him. Lurking below that was a more self-defeating thought: that Jane had tricked them both, that *she* was the damaged goods and it was only a matter of time until David realized it.

Almost from the start, they spent every free second together, alternating between sex, naps, and walks along the Charles, where they talked for hours. David's apartment had floor-to-ceiling bookshelves, every inch of them filled. Jane loved reading all the spines, getting to know him in that way. She wondered sometimes how many of the books had belonged to his ex-wife. Jane found herself irrationally jealous of this woman she had never met for having gotten to live with him. And grateful to her too, for letting him go.

On a Saturday, Jane and David might not leave his bed until four in the afternoon, when they suddenly realized they were starving. They would go to the French bistro down the block for cheeseburgers and chocolate cake and a bottle of wine, as if bulking up for hibernation. Jane would look around at married couples not talking to each other, staring at their phones, or parents of young kids, arguing, or two people clearly on an awkward first date. She felt sorry for them all. Certain that none of them—maybe no one on earth—had ever felt so perfectly matched with another person as she did then.

David wanted her to bring him home to meet her family at Thanksgiving, three months after they met. Jane proposed several alternative scenarios—*Thanksgiving in the Caribbean! Thanksgiving in New York!*—but he insisted. When she finally agreed, he made a pumpkin pie from scratch, so she couldn't change her mind at the last minute.

The whole ride up to Maine, a thought kept coming into her head: *He will know the real you now.*

As they sat in traffic, Jane told David about Thanksgivings past.

There was the year when she and Holly were small and their mom passed out drunk on the sofa by noon and they decorated her with feather boas and sparkly stickers, taking pictures with a disposable camera, until their grandmother caught them and made them stop.

The year their mother got into a fight with her loser boyfriend while they were all watching the Macy's parade. The boyfriend got up, presumably to use the bathroom but, in fact, to leave. For reasons unknown, he took the turkey and the roasting pan. They never saw him again. Jane's mother spent the rest of the day in bed. Jane and Holly ate toaster waffles with mashed potatoes, and watched *Fatal Attraction* on VHS. ("Ahh, that old holiday classic," David said.)

There were two Thanksgivings—Jane's senior years of both high school and college—when their mom was in rehab and Jane went to

Allison's house and got to experience the real-life equivalent of the holidays in those old Folgers commercials.

Holly went to rehab over Christmas once, the year her son Jason turned three. Jane wasn't sure why these things always happened at the holidays, but in that case, Jason had been young enough that they simply pretended it was Christmas Day after Holly returned home in early January, dragging a neighbor's half-dead Christmas tree into their house from the curb.

None of it was remotely funny at the time. But Jane had become an expert at shaping the small traumas of her past into amusing anecdotes.

She was trying to warn David, to prepare him for whatever horrors and humiliations awaited at her mother's house. The only time she brought her ex, Andre, home, they had arrived to find her sister and her mother, side by side on the driveway, sanding an old dresser in their bathing suits. Not realizing it was Jane's house, Andre said, "Check out the Playboy bunnies." Things devolved from there.

Jane had long thought of her mother and grandmother as foils of one another. Her grandmother, widowed at thirty-five, never went on a single date as far as Jane knew. She didn't drink. When they stayed here in Maine with her every summer before she died, she made Jane and Holly eat vegetables and go to bed on time and say their prayers and attend Mass on Sunday mornings. She was what a child wanted their caretaker to be. Reliable, steady, with no apparent yearnings of her own. Jane wished she was there to meet David, to represent some other, better aspect of her family.

But that first visit home with him went better than expected.

Jane's mother and sister were on best behavior. By then, Holly had joined their mother in her resale business, which over time transpired less at yard sales and more online, so that they no longer even needed to leave the house to do their work. Holly made them cards and a logo. Their website was called Trash to Treasure.

("Because just Trash doesn't have a good ring to it," Jane said to Allison.)

In recent years, the house and yard had been even more full of junk than before. But when Jane and David arrived, for the first time ever, the tarps and piles had been cleared away. Probably moved into one big pile in the garage, but still. Jane was touched that they had made an effort.

David was kind and polite, as always. He looked past her mother's recycling bin full of empty wine bottles and the near-hoarding and the occasional bickering. He complimented the gravy from a can and later, when Jane teased him for it, swore he genuinely thought it was delicious.

Her mother was charming, but not overly flirtatious. They all drank too much wine, even David, but no one behaved badly as a result. Jason was eleven then and obsessed with basketball. David, it turned out, had played in high school. They both loved the Celtics. They talked players and stats over dinner, and went out and shot hoops in the driveway the next morning. Jason beamed, and all three women smiled happily, because if there was one thing they all cared about it was the family's only child.

"This is nice," David said as they were leaving, running his hand over the driftwood sign by the front door, hand-painted with the word *Flanagan*. It had been there since Jane's grandmother lived in the house. She liked that he noticed it.

That afternoon was Jane's reward—a visit with Allison and Chris and their new baby. They talked about Chris's job managing a high-end restaurant in town and how, at their Thanksgiving dinner, Allison's parents announced their plan to retire in a couple of years and hand the inn over to Allison and Chris to run.

Chris and David had nothing in common, but they got along well, laughing easily. When the baby fussed, David offered to pace the house with her until she calmed down, a trick he said he had learned when his nephews were little.

"Oh my God, you're a natural," Allison called after him.

"He really is," she said to Jane.

"I know," Jane said. "He loves kids. He's great with them."

Allison grabbed Jane's arm and said, "If you don't marry this guy, I will."

Jane smiled. Allison's approval meant everything to her. So why did the comment freak her out?

Allison claimed that Jane was scarred by her previous relationship, but that it was totally different from what she had with David, because Jane was younger then, and Andre was legitimately an asshole and the whole thing was doomed from the start.

"David is a million times better," Allison said. "And he's clearly crazy about you."

That's how unbroken Allison was, Jane thought. She believed that if a man was good enough, his love could fix what was broken in Jane, could transform her into something other than the emotional delinquent she had always been.

Jane didn't know how to explain to her friend that there was within her an almost violent ambivalence. When she was with David, she wanted to lean fully into him and a life together. But part of her resisted all of it in the extreme. When they were apart, her thoughts spun out. She felt certain it couldn't work. That she wasn't made for that and would eventually have to let him go. Jane was always, privately, trying to discern which part of her was right. She never said a word about these thoughts to David for fear that they might hurt his feelings, when truly, they were not about him.

As they headed out of town on the way home to Cambridge, on a whim, Jane directed David to the purple house.

"I want to show you my high school hideaway," she said.

The place looked much the same as it had the last time Jane saw it, if a bit worse for wear. The barn roof had caved in. There were signs of new life layered on top of the old. Squatters had left behind food wrappers and beer bottles and playing cards. A sweatshirt, a sneaker. Needles in a coffee can on the porch. Her beloved old fallen tree was gone. Removed by the town, maybe. The grass had been mowed.

"I'm getting a strong *Grey Gardens* vibe off of this place," David said. "It's kind of cool, though. And that view. Wow."

They walked to the edge of the cliff, hand in hand, pretending the property was theirs. He said they would have to put up a fence, or else their kids would end up going over the edge, especially at the narrow headland jutting out, begging to be jumped from.

Jane told him that had been her reading spot when she was a teenager, and she expected their kids would use it in the same manner.

"Maybe Eleanor," he said. "But the twins? Chad and Brad? Forget it. Those two are monsters."

Jane raised an eyebrow.

"Chad and Brad, huh?" she said. "Clearly we are not putting you in charge of names."

He grinned.

"Clearly," he said.

He kissed her.

All of this felt predetermined. They were joking, and yet they weren't. They barely knew each other but could see into their future together. It seemed like everyone could. Even so, part of her said it was too soon for them to be talking this way. She needed to be careful. A fear tugged at Jane's pocket, whispering that she had only wandered temporarily into somebody else's lovely life.

TEN YEARS LATER

2015

1

Genevieve

ASCENDING THE STAIRCASE and switching on
the light in the upstairs hall, Genevieve noticed a crack in the freshly
painted wall outside Benjamin's bedroom door. It was jagged, deep,
maybe six inches long. Further proof of what she had sensed in the
weeks since they moved in: that despite her efforts, a house as old as
this one could never be conquered. Every flicker of the lights, every
leaky faucet, felt like a fresh reminder that she had been foolish to
assume otherwise.

Paul would accuse her of being dramatic, but when you thought
about it, a house was a foreign object, invasive to its surroundings.
Nature would keep trying to assert its dominance, to force its way in.
Walk the aisles of any hardware store and you would know this. Row
after row of poisons, traps, and tools, designed to beat back what
rightfully belonged.

Even after she installed French drains at great expense, water
pooled in the basement. When the pools dried, mineral deposits like
white fur remained around the edges. A brown spot appeared on her
bedroom ceiling, alarmingly soft to the touch, like the top of a newborn baby's head. She heard scratching sounds from inside the attic
walls at night—squirrels, most likely, the exterminator said. One
afternoon, several bricks fell out of the just-repointed chimney and
landed a few feet from where she and Benjamin stood, pulling bun-
dles from the car. More than once, she had the unpleasant sensation
that the kitchen floorboards were moving, only to realize a moment
later that what she had seen was a cluster of sugar ants seizing upon
a crumb.

When they had people up from Boston on a Saturday, gathered on the patio to watch the sunset, or sipping cocktails around the white marble kitchen island, only then did she experience the house as she had imagined it in the beginning. Everyone marveled at how she had pulled it all together, how beautiful it was.

Paul liked to show them photos. The before and after. He did not mention the in-between. The months they spent arguing about the cost of backsplash and cabinets and hardwood floors and whether to tear down the antique wallpaper in their bedroom or go through the complicated process of having it restored. Genevieve always advocated for the most expensive option, privately believing that the higher the price, the better the quality. She was forever asking his opinion, though she knew what she wanted. She just didn't always trust her own judgment. Paul, on the other hand, knew precisely what he disliked but was unable, most of the time, to articulate what he might prefer.

On multiple occasions over the last year, Genevieve had gone to bed without saying good night, having sunk into a rage over his disinterest in their family's summer retreat. This place was meant to be the answer to the question of why he worked so much; compensation for the lack of each other's company all those years while he was building his business. It was here that they were supposed to make up for lost time, to *reconnect*. Yet her husband could not be bothered to look up from his phone and tell her whether he preferred a bold yellow or a classic beige for the custom patio cushions, so what possibility was there that he would ever look up, in the larger sense?

She never said any of this to the guests, of course.

Please don't go to the dark side in front of our friends, Paul would say when the doorbell rang.

And she would say, *I wouldn't. I won't.* Anyway, they weren't her friends. They were guys her husband knew from college and their wives. They were Paul's clients and colleagues. Men he met on a golf course somewhere.

Genevieve ran her finger along the crack in the wall. She had spent weeks deliberating over the color, finally settling on a shade of light gray called Shadow. In every space, there came the moment of truth—revealing, once the paint had dried, whether she had chosen wisely.

The seafoam green in the guest bath had been a disaster. So bad that she had it covered over in white after a week. In the case of the upstairs hallway, she had been pleased with her choice. Now what would she do? It would take weeks, maybe months, to get the painter to come back for a crack like that, and she didn't dare try to patch it herself. She added it to the mental list of things she had already fixed that needed fixing again. A list she suspected would never be complete.

Her son's tiny room was behind a hidden door, which, when closed, blended completely into the wall—no trim, no doorknob. They had several other bedrooms, far more spacious, but Benjamin insisted on that one. He liked the coziness, she thought. And the novelty.

Standing there now, she heard his sweet voice. A balm.

Genevieve took a deep breath.

"And what did she tell you?" she thought Benjamin said.

After a pause, he giggled.

She had left him half an hour ago, slowly unfolding her body from her spot on the twin bed, careful not to wake him. Benjamin couldn't fall asleep without her. Paul said this was indulgent, that a four-year-old boy should be expected to soothe himself.

Who really cared, was what Genevieve thought. Who did it harm? A few years from now, Benjamin wouldn't want to talk to her, let alone sleep beside her. Half the time, she fell asleep too, waking at dawn, having left all the lights on.

Tonight she had possessed an unusual amount of energy once he was asleep. Plus the knowledge that the cleaning ladies were coming tomorrow and she needed to tidy up ahead of time, or else face their silent criticism upon finding the toy room a mess, the sink full of dishes.

They were always going on in Portuguese and laughing. At her, she assumed.

The boss, Cathy, was the only one who spoke English.

"Such a big house for just you and your boy," she said when they met.

"And my husband," Genevieve said. "He comes up on weekends, mostly."

Cathy made a face, which Genevieve could not interpret. Was the woman pitying her? Judging her?

Who gives a shit, Paul would say. And it was true. She had always cared far too much what other people thought.

Benjamin kept talking, so softly that she couldn't make out the words.

Usually, if he woke up alone, whatever the hour, he ran through the house calling out for her until he found her, downstairs watching television or asleep in her own bed. Never before had Genevieve come upon him at night, awake and alone, but sounding cheerful, unafraid.

She had read somewhere that mothers mourned past versions of their children. It was impossible to know if it was the last time you would ever change a diaper, or rock your baby to sleep or carry him from one room to the next, until you were on the other side of it. Sometimes the child who greeted you in the morning was somebody altogether different from the one you kissed good night.

"I did that once," Benjamin said now, his voice growing louder. "I did!"

Genevieve pushed the door open gently. She was trying to go unnoticed, but Benjamin's head snapped to attention.

"Mama. You scared me."

He looked toward the window, beyond which lay the flat black sky, the black ocean, glinting gold.

"Who you talking to?" she said. She was joking. She expected him to laugh.

But Benjamin looked confused. He glanced back and forth from Genevieve to the window, then said, as if it should be obvious: "Her."

There was a pause before he added, "She's come in here the last few nights. She doesn't stop talking. She's keeping me up."

Genevieve wasn't sure what to say next. Strangely, she decided on, "What does she look like?"

Benjamin pointed. "She's right *there.*"

His tone said *See for yourself.* It seemed to dawn on him then that Genevieve couldn't. That's when he grew hysterical.

The sound of Benjamin's screaming. Genevieve would never forget it.

It took half an hour to settle him. She had been able to do so only by promising he could sleep on the couch, with the TV on, and that he could have a cup of chocolate milk.

She sat beside him and petted his head.

"There really was a girl there," he said.

Genevieve said, "I believe you," and, as she said it, realized that she did.

She had chosen to ignore certain signs. Moments that made no sense. Once she closed a window against the rain and swore she felt someone else's hands lowering it. The lights flickered, in the living room, in Benjamin's room—but only when Benjamin was there. Was that right? Or was she imagining this detail now, after the fact?

Certainly she had not imagined the marbles, inexplicable, everywhere, all over the house. Cloudy glass orbs, blue and red and green, something old-fashioned, something no one had ever given Benjamin or any child of his generation. She found one on the white tile in the master bath when she stepped out of the shower. Another on the rug beneath the dining room table. Four or five in a row under the TV stand. Paul said the only explanation was that the marbles had been there all along. The house was old. The floors sloped. And so a marble rolled out from under something every now and again.

JUST AFTER ELEVEN, Genevieve left Benjamin asleep on the sofa, angelic beneath a knitted blue blanket. She went to the kitchen, poured a large glass of vodka over ice, and called her husband. He let it go to voicemail. She pictured him at home, watching the news or baseball highlights, seeing her name on the screen and deciding not to pick up.

She called again. This time, he answered.

After she told him, Paul said, "That kid's got a wild imagination."

"It wasn't that," she said.

"You think it was, what? A ghost?" he said, and scoffed.

There were moments when his maleness made her feel almost murderous.

But then, she hadn't told him what she had done.

An image came into her mind and she closed her eyes tight to will it away. But there he was, that sinewy young man. The last thing she saw of him as he walked away from the house was the tattoo on the back of his neck. A solid red star. It looked like the stamp they pressed into a child's hand at a petting zoo, to signal that admission had been paid.

"Can you come up for the night?" she asked Paul. "I'd feel better if you were here. I know it sounds silly, but the whole thing was really upsetting."

Paul reminded her that it was a ninety-minute drive and he had to work in the morning. He said she should take a Xanax.

But what if Benjamin needed her, what if he cried out and she didn't hear him? She had never seen him so terrified.

"He wasn't making it up," she said.

"Gen——" Paul said, with an air of warning. "I told you you weren't going to like being up there alone. It's messing with your head. You need company. Why don't you call that innkeeper friend of yours, and invite her over for a drink. You said she was nice."

The innkeeper, Allison, had only been nice because Genevieve was a paying guest who returned every summer for a week and always reserved the most expensive room. That much had been made clear when Genevieve stopped by the inn to tell Allison that she and Benjamin would be here all summer. She showed Allison pictures of the renovation on her phone.

"I know that house," Allison said, but she didn't elaborate.

She was sweeping breakfast crumbs on the inn's wide front porch, where white wicker tables were already set for lunch.

Allison ended the conversation abruptly, saying, "I'm sure we'll be seeing you around. You have my number, right? Text me if you need anything."

Genevieve had texted, to say it was nice to see her again, and to suggest that they should get together, maybe with the children.

A month passed with no reply.

She had never had a knack for women. The way they told secrets, their own and other people's, as a form of currency. Her mother was reserved, believing that one kept her problems to herself. From a young age, Genevieve learned to be that way too, so that once she got to Bryn Mawr, she often found herself passing through a hallway full of girls in pajamas, going on about boys they had crushes on or some professor who was having an affair, and thought, *I have nothing whatsoever to add.*

There was a girl her sophomore year whom she drove to chorus rehearsals each week. Genevieve thought they were friends. But one night, rounding the corner into the dining hall, she heard the girl say, "Poor Genevieve's stuck so far up her own ass, she hasn't seen daylight for months."

Genevieve met Paul shortly before graduation, at a party off campus. He was several years older than her. She liked his outsize personality, his confidence. Her mother was impressed by his name. She had read about his father in *Time* magazine.

"The family came over on the *Mayflower*!" she said.

Genevieve would want for nothing, her mother told her, married to a man like that.

AFTER PAUL HUNG UP, Genevieve brought her drink to the patio, switched on the outdoor lights, and went to the railing. She looked out over the rolling lawn and the cliffs and the water, the cove lit by streetlamps, and the town of Awadapquit in the distance. The view was what had seized her when she first discovered this spot.

Their land could only be seen from the ocean. A quarter mile of pine trees stood between it and the main road. She must have passed the turnoff a hundred times without knowing it was there. Who knew what made her turn that afternoon last August? Benjamin had fallen asleep in the back seat after a morning at the beach. She decided to keep driving.

When she spotted a rusty mailbox at the edge of Shore Road, she turned right on a whim and followed a dirt path, darkened by trees. Reaching the end, emerging into sunshine, had been an astonishment. She found there an expanse of overgrown grass, dried to a wheat-like gold, and beyond it, the ocean. On a small island across the way, seals sunned themselves on the rocks.

A sagging, uninhabitable Victorian with peeling violet paint sat on the property. Genevieve left Benjamin sleeping in his car seat. She went right up and peered inside. Making plans. As if it were already hers.

The house was fully furnished. It looked like someone had taken a walk decades ago and never returned.

There was no other home in sight. Just trees surrounding the land on three sides, and the ocean on the fourth.

What she felt that day was a form of lust. Genevieve had to have it.

When she brought Paul to show him, he pointed out the broken windows, and the ones that had been left wide open to the elements for who knew how long. Ceilings were caving in in some of the rooms. The upstairs banister had collapsed down into the foyer. A wall on the sunporch had buckled. Every inch of the mansard roof was covered in moss. Off to the side of the house was a barn that had sunken in on itself like an old pumpkin.

"Money pit," Paul said, dismissing the whole fantasy in two words.

"Obviously it's a teardown," she said. "But look at the view. I'm telling you, this is a real estate unicorn."

"There has to be a reason it's sitting here, unoccupied," he said.

"Because it's been waiting for us."

"Hey, Sam Littleton, your place is a dump," he said.

She stared at him blankly. "Who?"

Paul pointed at a small white plaque with black letters beside the front door:

CAPTAIN SAMUEL LITTLETON HOUSE
c. 1846

Genevieve had seen the name Littleton on other buildings in the area.

"Historically significant," she said. "That's worth something."

When Paul asked if it was even for sale, she knew she was making headway.

His lawyers tracked down the owner. Some old woman in Philadelphia. Even though she admitted she hadn't laid eyes on the property in decades, getting her to agree to sell took more persuading than Genevieve could have imagined. But everything had its price.

Had it been up to them, they would have leveled the house and started over. Genevieve had in mind something three times the size, with cedar shingles, and windows everywhere. A summer home should be airy and bright. But it turned out the house was on the historic register, which meant they could not tear it down or make changes to the façade.

What you could see on the surface was bad enough. The unseen was worse. The home inspector pointed out asbestos in the basement and the old knob and tube wiring, which would need to be ripped out and replaced to avoid them burning the house down, which Genevieve wasn't certain was the worst idea. The previous owners never shut off the water. The pipes had frozen and burst. Most of the downspouts were long gone. The wooden gutters were clogged full of leaves and needed to be replaced. Weeds were now growing in them as if they had been planted there. The foundation was cracked. An awful smell turned out to be a dead raccoon decomposing in the chimney.

She hired a landscaper to strip away all the overgrowth—to mow the massive lawn, and rip out the dead hedges that lined the cliff, and the pine tree that stood there, limboing dangerously over the water. They lost privacy this way, but they gained a far more dramatic, unobstructed view.

Genevieve paid a junk guy with a pickup truck two thousand dollars to take away the contents of the house. His name was John Irving.

"Not *that* John Irving," Genevieve had said the first time they spoke on the phone. She was met with silence at the other end of the line.

He did not seem to know that there was another, greater man who shared the name. Was it possible no one had ever made him aware of this?

John Irving and two young assistants made a dozen trips. Most of what they removed, she assumed, would go straight to a dumpster. Every so often, he held up an object—an old silver set, a mirror in an ornate gilded frame—and said, "You sure you don't want to keep this? It might be worth something."

The idea that any of it might be worth something was what had led the woman in Philadelphia to amass so much junk that it eventually overtook her.

"You keep it," Genevieve said.

John Irving gave her the number of a local salvage place that would haul away the old marble mantelpieces and the leaded windowpanes so that they might be repurposed elsewhere, but the company couldn't come out for a month and she was eager to move as fast as possible.

She found a gifted contractor who ripped out all the dark, dinky spaces on the first floor—*the parlor, the sitting room*—and made it open concept. (What he did with the leaded windows and the mantelpieces, she had not a clue.) The walls turned out to be full of wire lath and horsehair plaster, far harder and more costly to take down than she ever would have imagined. But what a difference it made.

The contractor built the biggest addition the town would permit at the back of the house, which wasn't very big but it was something. In the kitchen, he installed sliders with a view of the water. He built a second full bath upstairs and a half bath in the front hall.

He recommended an interior designer. She and Genevieve agreed that the downstairs walls should be white, with a slightly lighter shade of white to cover over all the heavy wood trim. This brightened the house tremendously. They added a whimsical, flamingo-printed wallpaper in the powder room. A kitchen island painted navy.

The designer sent emails at all hours. It was madness, but Genevieve enjoyed the flood of choices only she could make. All the attention, the anticipation, reminded her of her wedding—experts bombarding her with updates, a flurry of action punctuated with setbacks and surprises, that would culminate in a thing of beauty, with her at its center.

When the renovation was done, she felt immensely proud of herself. Most of the work of her life was invisible—she made the doctor's appointments and gave Benjamin his nightly bath and remembered to send flowers on her mother-in-law's birthday. Tasks no one took any notice of if you did them properly. Only if you didn't. But now she had made manifest something concrete, something special.

The designer called all excited one morning. *Maine Coast* magazine was considering Genevieve's house for its summer issue. The designer knew an editor there, who told her they had narrowed their search down to Genevieve's house and two others. They wanted to highlight an old home, one whose owners were focused on honoring local history.

"She did say that the other two houses preserved a lot more original detail, but neither is on the water," the designer said. "So to clinch the deal, I floated an idea by her and she loved it. There's this old hippie in Awadapquit who sells rare Indian antiques. Thomas Crosby is his name. He used to have a gallery in the seventies, but now he only sees people by appointment. He has a basket made of braided sweetgrass and ash, from the 1850s. You don't usually find them that old. It's museum quality, in perfect shape. Impossible to know exactly where it was made, but he's pretty certain it came from one of the local tribes. I'm sure you know the town name means *where the beautiful cliffs meet the sea* in the language of the Abenaki who once lived there. Your house is built on the beautiful cliffs they were talking about! I told the editor if they chose you, you would have the basket in your house and they could write about it."

"Sure," Genevieve said. "A basket sounds good."

"But here's the thing. The cost is eight thousand."

Genevieve paused. "For a basket."

"It has the original handles, perfectly intact. That's very rare, apparently."

"Could we just borrow it from the dealer for the photo shoot?"

"No, I'm afraid not. But also, the splints in it are a gorgeous marine blue, so it goes with the rest of your décor."

Genevieve couldn't tell Paul. He would lose his mind.

When the basket arrived, she was surprised by how small it was. The base only five inches in diameter. It widened in the middle and was most narrow at the top. The designer placed it on the glass coffee table in the living room.

One day Genevieve discovered to her horror that the cleaning ladies had started using the basket as a catchall for things they found that had no designated place—loose change and matchbox cars and pens without caps.

"That's a very expensive antique," she said. "Please never touch it."

They looked at her like she was crazy, but they didn't go near the basket after that.

Maine Coast agreed to come shoot in March, as soon as the infinity pool was installed at the edge of the property. The final touch. Which was nothing compared with the rest, Genevieve thought then. A matter of downing some trees and digging a hole.

John Irving had a chainsaw. One gray February morning, he and his assistants arrived to clear beach roses and several pine trees off to the side of the house, to make room for the pool. Genevieve felt a bit bad about chopping the trees down. They were over a hundred feet tall and a hundred years old. She drove up from Boston to make sure they removed only as many as were absolutely necessary.

"We found a surprise," John Irving said when she got out of her car.

He led her to the spot where the beach roses and pine trees had been, shocking now in its bareness. There they were. White headstones, covered in a layer of electric green moss.

Three of them were very small. There had once been names carved there, but they had worn away with time.

The other two were twice the size. One had a crack down the middle. The words were so faded she would not have been able to decipher them had she not known the name from the plaque by the door—*Samuel Littleton.*

Next to him was Hannah Littleton. *Beloved Wife,* her epitaph read, above dates of birth and death. She had outlived him by forty-six years.

There was one more grave, different from the others. Instead of a slender slab, it was just a rock. Round and uneven, about the size of a basketball. There were no dates listed. Only the words *Sister Eliza* carved crudely by someone who clearly did not carve headstones for a living.

"Those tiny little graves, those were for babies. So many didn't survive long in those days," John Irving said. "I don't know how people could bear it." He shook his head. "A lot of these old homes have family cemeteries on the grounds. I think they're kind of charming. The past bleeding into the present, that kind of thing."

So the junk guy was a poet. Fabulous. Fuck.

"But we were planning on a pool there," Genevieve said.

"Right. Well."

The property wouldn't make any sense without a pool. She had torn a page from a design magazine years ago, and held on to the vision, the fantasy. If she ever had a beach house, it would have an infinity pool, from which you could watch the ocean by day and the stars at night. Tiled in the exact tranquil shade of blue she once saw at a hotel pool in Marrakesh.

"There's nowhere else to put it, the rest of the yard slopes," she said. "Isn't this just my luck?"

One of the young assistants stared at her. He wore a T-shirt, even though it was freezing. His brown hair was pulled back in a ponytail.

Genevieve held his glance for a long moment, then looked away.

Paul's mother told her once that she couldn't imagine living in a house some stranger had lived in before her. Paul grew up in a sprawling custom home, built to his parents' specifications the year before he was born. He was not the sort of person to describe a cemetery in his own backyard as charming. Neither, for that matter, was Genevieve.

"I don't understand," she said. "How did the inspector not see this? Shouldn't the seller have disclosed it?"

He shook his head. "I—don't know."

Genevieve remembered then. They had agreed to take the property as is. The inspection had only been for their education.

Paul would want to sell. After all the work she had done.

The junk man left. One of his assistants rode with him in the truck.

The one in the T-shirt had come in his own car. He lingered. He watched the truck disappear down the dirt road, then said, quietly, without meeting her eye this time, "I can help you out. My buddy has a Bobcat. It wouldn't take more than half a day to get rid of all that."

"Even," she began, unsure how to put it.

"Yup," he said, matter-of-fact.

He wanted to be paid in cash. She could tell when he named his price that he thought he was getting one over on her, but she would have paid far more.

Genevieve didn't ask questions. She told him she was going straight home and wouldn't be back until the weekend, when the pool company was scheduled to come. He said it would be taken care of by then.

She went into the house and took the money from the safe in the bottom drawer of her husband's desk, reminding herself to replace it before he noticed.

Then she went back outside and handed over the stack of crisp bills. He counted them, nodded at her, and walked away toward his car. Hair pulled up off his neck. Red star tattoo a shock against paper white skin.

GENEVIEVE WAS STILL AWAKE when the sun rose and the view from the living room window turned from pure blackness to soft blue morning. She sat in an armchair directly across from her sleeping son, not wanting to let him out of her sight.

She felt wired, and jumpy at the slightest sound. She had her computer in her lap, attempting to google her way to resolution.

According to the search results, you could often rid a home of an unwanted spirit by telling it firmly to leave. If that didn't work, you could burn sage and mugwort in every room, wash the floors with a concoction made of bay leaves and boiling water, sprinkle pink Himalayan sea salt on the threshold. Genevieve bought all these ingredients online.

She practiced in her head what she would say when Benjamin woke. Calmly, she would ask him if the girl in the window had told him her name.

"Could it have been Eliza?" she would say, sounding casual, almost indifferent.

It couldn't have been the other one, Hannah. She died in her eighties. The children who died were babies. Benjamin had called the ghost a girl.

For the first time, Genevieve wondered where the bodies had gone. What did the kid with the ponytail find beneath the earth when he dug down? Would the family have been buried in wooden caskets? Would anything of them remain?

One thought cascaded into the next. It was like a series of questions Benjamin might ask—how does hot water get to the shower—it comes through the pipes—and how does it get there—it comes from the hot water tank—and how does it get *there?*

Really, she wasn't to blame. The junk man's assistant made it seem like no big deal, an act he had carried out a hundred times before. Had he not offered, she never would have suggested it. What would she have done? Moved? Planted some arborvitae and pretended the graves weren't there?

She needed to find him, because then—what? Genevieve didn't know the answer. And she didn't know his name. She could ask John Irving, but wouldn't he find that suspicious?

Was what they had done illegal?

She did an online search for *disturbing a grave, jail time,* then thought of the killers on *Law & Order,* who stupidly left online trails of their misdeeds. To the words she had already typed into the search bar, she added *TV miniseries about.*

She had promised herself she was never going to tell Paul, or anyone. Doing so now would cause problems. But he was right. She didn't want to be alone here. Maybe she should take Benjamin to the inn in Awadapquit until Paul returned. He would never have to know; he never looked at credit card bills. Case in point: he still didn't know about the basket.

Yes, she would go to the inn. She could make a plan there. Catch her breath.

Feeling somewhat relieved, Genevieve closed her eyes and sank back into the chair, exhausted. For several minutes, there was no sound but the whirring of the central air. She was falling asleep when she heard what sounded like footsteps in the hall. Her chest tightened. Was she losing her mind? But no, they were coming closer. She looked at Benjamin and wondered whether she could somehow scoop him up and carry him to safety. She tried to telegraph to the ghost that she was sorry. She would make it right.

A voice whispered her name. "Genevieve. Genevieve."

She didn't move.

The cleaning lady stepped into the room, vacuum in hand.

"Morning, Genevieve," she said.

2

Jane

THE ROOM SMELLED like popcorn and hot dogs.

Fifteen rows of folding chairs had been arranged on either side of an aisle, down which the winners ran as if this were an episode of *The Price Is Right* and they had just been given a new car. They hooted and hollered and high-fived when their numbers were called. Chairs went askew from the nonstop jumping up, the shimmying past protruding knees and bulging purses to get to the front and claim what was theirs. It was all crap, but never mind. People loved to win.

A group of individuals got together and decided something was fun. That was what made it so.

So thought Jane, bad sport, hater of crowds, from her spot in the last row.

Maybe she would have found the evening enjoyable under different circumstances. If she could have had a drink or two beforehand. If she wasn't in Awadapquit indefinitely, staying by herself in her mother's house, for the first time since her mother's death. If this were just a regular weekend visit and David was here to laugh with her about the fact that the big winner so far got a volleyball printed with the name of a local Realtor, a five-dollar gift card to the Pancake King, and a bar of soap shaped like a seashell, and that had been enough to provoke suspicion among a few vocal attendees that the whole thing must be rigged.

For much of her life, Jane had been intimately familiar, even comfortable, with loneliness. But after ten years of David's companionship, she had lost her sea legs. David had been her armor out in the world. A certain degree of protection came from being his. Even when he wasn't with her, Jane never felt alone.

Throughout their marriage, she had maintained the independent core of herself, which was possible with David in a way she didn't think it would be with many partners. He understood why she never wanted to merge their finances, why she cared so deeply about her work, why she enjoyed socializing only under the right conditions and even then got depleted by it and needed to go off for a bit and be alone. He understood why she was scared to have children, even though a huge part of her wanted them. Jane was known and accepted by him in a way she didn't think she ever would be by any other man.

The words spoken on their last night together echoed in her head: *I think we should take some time apart. This isn't working anymore.*

Such a generic, boilerplate way of ending what had been a singular love.

As if sensing her gloom, Allison shot her a huge smile from up front, where she stood churning raffle tickets in a drum. Jane smiled back. There was no one else in the world for whom she would have attended the Awadapquit Rotary Club's annual two-cent sale.

Allison knew this. For her last birthday, she sent Jane a mug printed with the words *Sorry I'm Late, I Didn't Want to Come.*

About tonight, Allison had said, "It'll be fun! Okay, it won't be that much fun, but we need to get you out of the house."

Awadapquit had a year-round population of just over a thousand people, most of whom avoided the beach and the downtown area in the high season. They were teachers and farmers and contractors and nurses and police officers. Retirees fulfilling their dream of living by the ocean.

The town center was made for vacationers. Art galleries and artisanal ice cream shops and so many stores selling caftans and sandals and overpriced tote bags made of recycled sailcloth. Jane often wondered how they all managed to stay in business.

Just beyond that, along Route 1, were motels and motor lodges, their neon signs flashing NO VACANCY. There was a trampoline park, two mini golf courses, a shop made to look like a giant log cabin, with a fake totem pole in the parking lot, and a sign that read 10,000 GIFTS! Jane had never once set foot inside.

The two-cent sale was the rare summer event that wasn't for summer people. It was held each year on the last Saturday in June at the town hall, a one-story brick building wedged between the post office and the municipal parking lot. The odd out-of-towner might wander in, seeking a glimpse of the locals in their natural habitat or hoping to get a deal. But they would soon realize that the friendly townspeople didn't want to chat with them tonight, and that the prizes weren't worth having, and then they would back out of the room slowly and head to Skip's piano bar or to the tired old sofa in whatever cottage they had rented for the week.

Allison had already gone through three rounds of tickets, calling out thirty prizes per round. The crowd showed no signs of fatigue.

One of Jane's tickets had been a winner, fetching her a jar of home-made red pepper jam. Because she had not been paying attention, she didn't realize until Allison called the number out a second time and, when no one claimed it, shouted, "I assume it's Jane. Jane, I'll hold this up here for you."

People turned to see who Jane was. A few of them recognized her from high school and nodded hello. A few recognized her from high school and did not nod. The rest just looked away.

In Jane's social circle in Cambridge, great attention was paid to the idea of the many elsewheres from which they all came, and what it said about them that they left those places behind. Jane spoke of spending her teenage years in a seaside tourist town; used its folksiness to her advantage. The city was the harder place, the more important place. It would seem only logical then that it would be easy to return home after living there so long. But it turned out the city spent much more time thinking about its own relative importance than anyone else did.

Here, success was measured by one's house and one's children. Jane's accomplishments didn't translate. No one would ever know or care that six months earlier she had won the Women's Studies Section Award from the Association of College and Research Libraries, though it had been a major happening in her world.

A common refrain throughout her adulthood was that it was tedious, the way strangers at cocktail parties asked what you did for work. Now she wished anyone would ask her that. Instead, trying to place her, they asked whether she had kids, and when she said no, they excused themselves as if this was the result of a curse that might be catching.

Allison called out yet another number, this one attached to a coupon for ten dollars off a brake job at the garage in town. The winner was a man in his seventies. Short and squat, with wispy silver hair. Jane remembered him. He ran a junk hauling business and had the preposterous name of a famous American novelist. John Updike? John Steinbeck? He used to move heavy furniture hither and yon for her mother in his pickup truck, in exchange for a smile, an expression of amazement over his strength, a beer with her on the back deck.

When Allison declared a fifteen-minute break for refreshments, Jane noticed a trio of guys about her age huddled together in a corner. The tallest one poured a Coke into three Styrofoam cups. Another looked around, pulled a flask from the pocket of his hooded sweatshirt, and tipped it into each of the cups.

Maybe everyone here was three sheets to the wind. No wonder they were enjoying themselves. Jane wasn't judging. She was jealous. She watched that amber liquid flow from the flask—whiskey, she figured. She could taste it. The burn on contact, the velvety feeling of it slipping down her throat, making a night like this one more palatable.

She hadn't had a drink for three months. The first thing she did when she got to her mother's house a month prior was empty the contents of the liquor cabinet into the sink. She stood pouring several bottles of cheap cabernet, then gin, then vodka, then bourbon, then scotch, not in the least bit tempted by any of it. Jane had thought in that moment that maybe she had killed her desire to drink once and for all, but apparently not. Right now, she wanted to walk over to those guys in the corner and down the contents of all three of their cups before they could say a word.

Instead, she went to the refreshments table in search of something sweet. This was the way of things now.

The bakery in town was right next to the wine shop. Her new, ill-advised ritual was to walk the aisles of sauvignon blanc and cabernet, debating which one she might have bought were she still allowed to drink, until she could no longer stand it. Then she would go next door and buy half a dozen éclairs, and eat three of them in the car before she even got home. This, clearly, was the sort of behavior a therapist would call deranged, which was why Jane did not go to therapy.

She bought a can of Coke and a brownie, which she ate in two bites, then wandered over to the table at the front of the room where one could bid on silent auction items. These were the big-ticket prizes, the ones Allison said might fetch a hundred dollars or more. A one-night stay at the Saint Aspinquid Inn, courtesy of Allison and Chris. A forty-five-minute massage from someone calling himself Hans of the Healing Hands. A two-year supply of mulch.

Jane lifted a pen from the table, drawing circles in the air, trying to find something worth bidding on. She didn't want any of it, but Allison had put a lot of work into this. She should be supportive.

A few hours earlier, Jane had helped transport various donated gift baskets here from Allison's kitchen table.

"It's all total shit," Allison said then, in a panic. "Debbie Mahoney took four paperbacks off her bookshelf, wrapped them in cellophane, and now she's bragging that she sponsored the Book Lovers Bundle. And that weirdo Hank, I swear he filled a basket with leftover Halloween candy. What's wrong with everyone? This is for a good cause."

The proceeds would go to the Rotary's scholarship fund. Jane herself had been a recipient back in the day. Allison's mother, Betty, headed up the Chamber of Commerce then, and she had made sure of it. The money hadn't been much. Enough to cover her books for a semester. But it meant something to Jane that this town was behind her, or at least Allison's mom was.

Betty's absence here tonight felt palpable. People kept asking Allison how she was doing, in a manner that gave away the fact that they already knew.

"She's hanging in there," Allison said again and again.

The mulch seemed to be the hottest item, with five bids already placed. Jane increased the highest by ten dollars and wrote her name beside it. She could gift it to her sister if she won, or maybe her mother's yard needed mulch; she had been staying there for a month now, but she had no idea, mulch being a topic she knew nothing about.

When she was done, only five minutes of the fifteen-minute break had elapsed.

Jane took her phone out of her bag. What did socially awkward people do in group settings before cell phones? she wondered. Just stare into space?

She looked at it, as if someone had sent her the most shocking news and she had no choice but to engage.

In reality, the screen didn't contain anything new. No one had tried to reach her since she last looked. Maybe it was the signal. There were lots of dead zones in town. Sometimes when her phone seemed particularly quiet and her anxiety about this mounted, Jane drove out to Route 1 to see if David or her boss, Melissa, had texted or called.

Melissa hadn't been in touch yet since Jane left Cambridge. Any thought of her brought back the memory of what happened, a searing sensation like putting her hand on a hot stove. Jane actually winced each time.

Occasionally, she did have a voicemail from David. They had agreed to talk as little as possible this summer, but there were sometimes practical matters that one or the other of them needed to discuss.

Before, in the course of an average day, they communicated a dozen times or more, sending links to articles that reminded them of some shared trip or memory or conversation, never needing to provide context. They sent recipes and book reviews and movie trailers. They sent a thousand texts that read Thoughts on dinner? All the things that added up to a shared life.

Now anything that reminded her of him did only that and no more. The impulse to share, that dopamine hit of knowing she had found something David would like, ran straight into the brick wall of reality: they were no longer speaking.

From across the room now, Jane saw Abe Adams waving at her. His already substantial belly had grown since she saw him a year ago, at her mother's funeral.

Abe was talking to a thin, balding man whose back was to Jane.

Jane went toward them to say hi, realizing too late that Abe's companion was Daniel Canavan, the asshole who had strung her mother along for a year, claiming he feared commitment, only to dump her on Christmas Eve and move to Florida with some other woman, whom he married immediately.

Jane and David had never trusted the guy, but her mother didn't want to hear it.

That had been what, five years ago? Six?

"Dan. You know Jane Flanagan," Abe said now.

"Of course," Canavan said. "How's Shirley? I'd love to see her while I'm here. Make up for lost time."

He gave a lascivious raise of the eyebrows. Jane hated him. He was smarmy and overly confident and wearing too much cologne. Exactly her mother's type.

"She's dead," Jane said.

"Jesus," Canavan said, clutching his chest. "Really?"

"I'm pretty sure," Jane said.

Abe gave her an amused look as Canavan excused himself.

"Poor bastard's third wife just left him," Abe said as they watched him walk away.

"I can't imagine why," Jane said.

He laughed. "How are you, kid?"

She was always happy to see Abe.

It had been twenty years since Jane worked alongside him on the boat. She still remembered the script. Bits of it came to her every so often, when she was lying awake in bed, or brushing her teeth. Recently, she recalled saying, *Only fifty percent of female lobsters are capable of producing eggs,* her voice cheery, upbeat. *We mark those ones and throw them back. They're too valuable to eat. The female lobsters that aren't capable of reproducing are the ones that end up on your dinner plate. They serve no other purpose.*

How did the passengers react to that? She didn't remember now. Filtered through the lens of a childless, recently separated thirty-nine-year-old woman, it felt aggressive. Mean. It was a wonder no one had ever told her to go fuck herself.

"Just up for the weekend?" Abe said.

"Actually, I've been here almost a month," she said.

"A month! How have I missed you?"

Because I almost never leave the house and I've been actively avoiding every-one, Jane thought.

"I've been so busy," she said.

"I haven't been around much myself," he said. "Been visiting the grandkids. I open for the season on Monday. So what brings you here for such a long stretch?"

"We've been meaning to get my mom's place ready to sell. It's been sitting empty. I have this break from work for a while, so I'm just tackling the clean-out now. Not sure how we've gone so long without dealing with it."

He nodded, somber.

"When Helen died, it took me four years before I could bear to let her sister empty her closet," he said. "She kept saying she knew some-one who could make a quilt out of Helen's old clothes, like that was an exciting substitute for my wife."

Jane smiled, sympathetic, sad. She remembered Allison telling her Helen had died. Jane had wanted to attend the funeral, but she had a conference in Phoenix. She sent flowers. Nice ones. When she received a note a month later, written in Abe's manly scrawl, thank-ing her for the "over the top arrangement," Jane burned with shame.

"How's your husband?" Abe said. "Remind me of his name."

"David."

"That's right. How's David?"

"He's good," Jane said, looking just past Abe. She thought she might burst into tears and tell him everything if she met his eyes. *He's good, especially now that he's rid of me, the terrible wife who got blackout drunk at a work event and made out with an assistant in front of her boss, who happens to be David's best friend. Yes, that's right, I managed to ruin my marriage and my job in one fell swoop.*

Jane wondered, if she said this, whether Abe would believe her. She imagined probably, like most people who knew her, he wouldn't think Jane capable of such a thing.

"Is David here with you for the summer?" Abe said.

"No, unfortunately. He has to work."

She took a deep breath, tried to center herself, so she wouldn't cry.

The pain of losing her mother was in large part about potential. All the conversations they had never gotten around to having and now would never have. The pain of losing David was material. With him, Jane had had something close to perfect.

"I guess having summers off is a nice perk of being a professor." Abe said it proudly, as if Jane were his own child.

Jane wasn't a professor and she didn't have summers off. David was, and did. But she didn't correct Abe.

She had tried and failed many times to explain her job to her mother. The closest her mother ever got was that Jane was a librarian. At some point, she just started telling people, "Jane works at Harvard," because, as her mother put it, even the biggest idiot on the planet knew what Harvard was.

After a while, Abe got pulled away, and Jane was once again on her own. But then along came Allison, putting an arm around her. Jane was instantly at ease.

"You won something," Allison said.

"Was it the basket of stale Halloween candy?"

"Nope. It was in the silent auction. We just took final bids."

"Oh, the mulch!"

"No. The gift certificate for a reading with a psychic medium."

Allison handed Jane a slip of paper.

"I didn't even see this. I definitely didn't bid on it," Jane said, wondering if she had done so by accident, and strangely disappointed about not getting the mulch.

"Technically, I bought it for you," Allison said. "I need you to accept it, as a favor to me. No one else was bidding on it and I don't want to hurt the medium's feelings. I would take it myself, but then she'd know, since I'm the one who asked her to contribute. Obviously, you're not the type and it's probably bullshit. But you are in pain. Maybe it could be good for you and your mom to connect."

Jane looked around, as if searching for someone to bear witness to the absurdity of this idea. She tried to come up with a witty reply, but all she could manage was, "What?"

"Please accept it," Allison said. "For me?"

Jane nodded, knowing this was something she would simply never do. The gift certificate would sit in her wallet so long that eventually its edges would soften and disintegrate, like the Velveteen Rabbit.

As if reading her mind, Allison said, "She can only do it on the second Tuesday in July, at nine in the morning. I'll give her your address. Promise me you'll answer the door."

3

THE MEDIUM'S NAME was Clementine.

Of course it was, Jane thought.

On the morning she was due to visit, Jane was awakened by the sound of her mother's dog, Walter, whining at six o'clock.

This was the hardest part of every day now. Waking up. Remembering where she was and why.

Walter was a four-pound Pomeranian, an orange powder puff of a thing. Every time Jane looked at him, she was reminded of one of those fox stoles women wore draped over their shoulders in old movies. He shed constantly. His fur was everywhere. On her pants, on the sofa, on the rug, in clumps in the corners of every room not five minutes after she vacuumed.

Her mother had doted on Walter, treated him better than she had her own children. Jane was pretty sure she loved him more too. After dinner, her mother would lay the plates on the floor and let Walter lick them clean before putting them in the dishwasher. Jane remembered David one Easter, having to look away so he wouldn't gag.

When Jane and David visited, her mother would say, "Jane, take your brother out, please."

And Jane would say, "That dog is not my brother."

Walter barked at every passing car, every delivery person, every jogger who dared cross his path. He was six years old. The average Pomeranian lived to be fifteen. Jane had looked it up.

She had always figured that, having nothing to give, her mother would leave her nothing when she died. But Walter was so much worse than nothing. Her mother hadn't technically left him to Jane, or to anyone. She didn't have a will, even though she knew for months before her death that the end was coming.

Jane's sister said she would gladly take Walter if it weren't for the fact that Max was deathly allergic.

"Who's Max?" Jane had asked at the time.

"Jason's friend," Holly said, as if Jane ought to know. "He's living with us for a while."

Since Jason's early teenage years, Holly had been that laid-back mom who took in all the misfits. The kids who didn't get along with their parents, the kids no one wanted at home anymore. Jane thought it was admirable, sort of. Though there was no structure in Holly's house. She was not a shining example of responsible adulthood. But then maybe that's what made her the right person for the job.

Jason was twenty-one now. He worked at a bar. He still lived with Holly and she still housed various wayward friends and acquaintances of his for a few days or weeks at a time. But Jane didn't believe for a second that Max's allergy was the reason Holly couldn't take the dog. It was far more likely that, like Jane herself, Holly just didn't want to.

There was no one else. So after the funeral, Jane and David brought Walter back to Cambridge with them, even though their building didn't allow pets. They had to smuggle him in and out for walks.

Walter had been elated when Jane brought him back to Maine with her after all those months away. He ran through the rooms of the house, spinning around in circles, and Jane took actual pleasure in it until she realized that he was expecting to find her mother. *His* mother, as far as he was concerned.

Jane tapped the mattress now, suggesting that he jump up beside her. She didn't love sharing her bed with Walter, but she could sometimes squeeze an extra half hour of sleep out of him that way. Not today. Walter's whine turned to an incessant bark.

"Fine," Jane said.

She didn't change out of the sweatpants and T-shirt she wore to bed. She put on a bra and sneakers and off they went.

It was a gorgeous morning. The sun already strong in the sky. Most of the other houses on her mother's street were summer rentals, with different families checking in each Saturday and leaving the following Saturday with precision, from mid-June until Labor Day. These people were always friendly. They nodded hello when she saw them, maybe commented on the weather or asked her opinion of the best restaurants in town, and that was it. This level of intimacy with her neighbors suited Jane.

None of them were outside now. They were still sleeping. They were on vacation.

She walked to the corner, crossed Shore Road, and went up a paved incline on the other side.

The town name, Awadapquit, meant *where the beautiful cliffs meet the sea.* The phrase had become a motto. You saw those words all over—on the sign welcoming you to town, on every brochure and tourist map. In addition to the cliffs, Awadapquit boasted a range of natural wonders. Woods, river, and ocean. Sand dunes and three flat miles of beach. Mount Mekwi rising above it all.

When she was young, Jane had never thought of it as special. But now, having traveled the world, seeing so many places, she realized that the view from the top of this hill was, in fact, extraordinary.

The hill dropped down to a rocky footpath that ran along an inlet, where two dozen empty lobster boats and sailboats bobbed in shallow water. A footbridge connected the path to the cove on the other side, with its neat rows of shops, and beyond them, the ocean.

The cove was quiet at this hour, but for the lobstermen in their orange rubber coveralls. On the patio at Charlie's Chowder House, umbrellas were still closed, chairs taken in for the night. In a few hours, teenagers in crisp white collared shirts would rush around serving fried clams and rum punch and tourists would pack in with their strollers and wagons full of beach gear.

A hundred and twenty years ago, the cove was where the fishermen lived. Now the small shake-shingled buildings housed art galleries and stores selling overpriced pottery, Christmas ornaments in the shape of lighthouses and lobster traps, T-shirts with bad beach puns printed across the front.

There was a light on in the candy shop. The smell of chocolate wafted out as she passed. Inside, on the far wall, was a window with the best ocean views in town, flanked on either side by bins of saltwater taffy, arranged by color, all soothing pastels in wax paper.

On the doormat of a seafood shack sat a gray plastic box of live lobsters. It reminded her of the loaves of bread bakers left on the stoops of Cambridge restaurants sometime in the predawn hours, there when she and David set out on an early-morning run and taken in by the time they returned.

Jane hadn't gone for a run for more than a year, but she still thought of herself as a runner, still considered the possibility each day. She wasn't sure why she didn't go. To an extent, she thought the dog was to blame. Certainly, when she was still working, his daily morning walks made a morning run impossible. But now Jane had all the time in the world, and she still didn't go.

Since her mother died, she had felt almost disembodied. She kept up with her work, until she didn't. And now with what needed to be done at her mother's place. But that was all she seemed to have the energy for. Jane was a brain floating through space, subsisting on caffeine and sugar, pushing down the more complicated emotions that lived inside of her, to be considered at a later date.

At the edge of the cove was the entrance to the Cliffwalk, a mile-and-a-half paved stretch along the ocean that connected this spot to town and the beach. Jane was hit with the smell of salt air, a cool rush of it on her cheeks.

She and Walter wound along the path, no one else in sight. By late morning, it would be so crowded, impossible to move at anything resembling a normal pace. But for now, they had it all for themselves. Walter lifted his leg to pee on a patch of grass. Jane looked out over the sea and then closer, at the white surf smashing against the rocks, the tide pools full of barnacles and swaying seaweed, entire universes that had formed overnight and would vanish by afternoon.

They walked on, pausing at the spot the locals called Little Beach, a sandy patch that appeared between cliffs at low tide. She could remember sitting on a red and white striped towel beside her grandmother on that slip of sand the summer she was fourteen, and the novel each of them was reading, and how later that day when they finished, they swapped. The memory of that last summer with her was so clear. It seemed impossible that her grandmother was no longer present. Not on this patch of sand. Not on this earth.

Jane's grandmother's love of Awadapquit was what brought the family here. She moved to Maine shortly after her husband died, when Jane's mother was ten.

Jane had always admired her grandmother's strength. Thrust into single motherhood with no support at a time when such things were unheard of. Later, she went back to school and became a teacher.

When Jane asked her once how she managed, her grandmother shrugged. "What choice did I have?" She paused, then added, "I knew God would provide."

She didn't have much family of her own. Her husband's family had money but they shut her out after he died. She decided to move with her daughter to Awadapquit because it was her favorite place in summer and it was cheap to live there year-round. She cleaned houses for a living then. She could do that anywhere.

The house she rented and later bought was simple, small. Built as a summer cottage in the twenties. It was identical to all the others on the street and so close that through the open window you could hear your neighbor's breakfast fork clanging against his plate.

The front door opened straight into the kitchen/living room. Beyond that were two bedrooms and a single bathroom. The view out the front windows was of tall pine trees, but if you looked to the right, you would be staring straight into the parking lot of the Tides Motel. Jane's grandmother adored the house. It was modest, but it was hers.

When Jane was a sophomore in high school, she went looking for something in the kitchen junk drawer and found a copy of the mortgage for the house, folded up and tucked into a small white envelope. It was signed not by her grandmother, but by a man and woman whose names she didn't recognize. When Jane asked her mother who they were, her mother sighed.

"They were nobody," she said. "They were summer people whose house she cleaned. I assume she paid them back over time, but she didn't have the funds for a down payment or the credit for a mortgage."

"She didn't have enough money to borrow money," Jane said.

"That's right," said her mother.

Jane thought about it a lot over the years. She imagined the scene, her grandmother having to push past her pride and ask these near-strangers for help. People whose toilets she scrubbed. It made Jane want to cry. It made her want to seek out the family of her long-dead grandfather and demand to know how they could have treated her sweet grandmother the way they did. But they were all gone now too, probably.

The house had meant different things to Jane at different points in her life.

Jane and Holly visited their grandmother there every summer as kids, the highlight of Jane's year. Jane had never seen her mother read anything longer than *People* magazine, but her grandmother always had books on the shelves and a fresh stack from the library on the coffee table. She gave Jane her passion for history, taking her on day trips to see E. B. White's farm and countless small museums around the state.

Jane remembered stepping inside the house for the first time after her grandmother died. How wrong it felt to be there among her belongings without her.

By the time she left for college, Jane had lived in that house longer than anyplace else. Her mother remained there for the rest of her life. It was the first and only home she ever owned.

Now Jane was living in the house again. Temporarily, but still.

She didn't know how it happened that when her life fell apart, she decided to come here. To the town she thought of as home, sort of, but not in a way that conjured memories of warmth and love and comfort. In crisis, Jane had acted on instinct. That was all she could figure out.

The house contained so much of her mother and grandmother, their overlapping lives evident in her grandmother's white Pyrex bowls and her mother's Tupperware; her grandmother's china tea set mixed in with her mother's coffee mugs on the shelf; her grandmother's red plastic rosary beads in the junk drawer, alongside her mother's pink plastic cigarette lighters.

On the kitchen windowsill sat her grandmother's dusty collection of seashells and two dried starfish, perfectly intact, and a sand dollar, which her grandmother claimed to have found on Awadapquit Beach early one morning at low tide, though Jane had never seen a sand dollar, outside of the gift shops on Main Street.

Whenever Jane and David visited, they rented a cottage on the opposite side of town from her mother's place. This always offended Jane's mother, even though she was the one who had turned Jane's old bedroom into a storage space for secondhand furniture she planned to sell eventually.

"There's a perfectly good bed in there somewhere," she would say. "Just move a few things around."

A month ago, when Jane went to hang some clothes in the closet in that room, she found it full to bursting with old dresses of her mother's. The smell of her was still there.

And so, for now, she was living out of a suitcase, trying to be at peace with her mother's clutter until she could make sense of it all.

It was the nature of her work that she often dealt with the belongings of women who were approaching the end of life. Jane took this responsibility seriously. But she had seen how people got too attached to things, bogged down in ephemera. She was ruthless in her own apartment—donating clothes if she hadn't worn them in a year, clearing out the fridge every week, making sure the countertops were bare before she could sleep at night, and never allowing junk mail to travel any path other than straight from the mailbox to the recycling bin.

The home she shared with David was spare and tidy, every piece of furniture carefully chosen, nothing of that make-do feeling with which she had been raised.

On the Cliffwalk now, and every time, she could hear the sound of her own teenage voice, amplified through the tinny microphone on Abe Adams's lobster boat. *These rocks are some of the oldest in the world, dating back five hundred million years. The spot where Awadapquit's famous Cliffwalk now stands was once under thousands of feet of water.*

So hard to contemplate. The dark cliffs were threaded in places with white quartz. Flecked in others with pale gray that told the story of the earth's crust forming, of lava pushing through, turning to stone.

Her grandmother had seen the ocean as a constant, as reassuring, in her eyes, as Jesus Christ himself. But the warming planet, the erosion here and all the way up the coast, made it so that, for Jane, even this view—Jane's favorite in the world, her mother's favorite, her grandmother's favorite—could no longer be relied upon for comfort.

One morning years ago, Jane's mother had looked out over these cliffs, at the sparkling sea, and declared that she wanted her ashes spread here when she died. It was a happy declaration. Like she was planning a vacation that would simply never end.

They hadn't done it, sprinkled the ashes. Not yet. They were wrapped inside clear plastic, inside a metal box, inside a green paper bag, inside her mother's bedroom closet. Jane felt a dull nagging guilt every time she saw them. She rarely went in there. Her mother had died in that room.

Remembering, reflexively, Jane took a deep breath.

She watched her mother gasp for air at the end, and told herself she would never take the ability to breathe for granted. Jane was used to walking down a crowded city street and noticing other people for what they wore on the surface. A coat she admired, a full head of flowing hair, a face too full, jowls drooping. But after her mother died, it was like she could see through people, and she thought it a miracle to consider in, say, a packed movie theater or a traffic jam, the collection of beating hearts all around her, kidneys flushing out toxins, synapses firing just as they were meant to. Everything working in perfect order, for the moment.

From this distance, Jane could make out a few surfers in wetsuits in the water down at the beach. A handful of old men waved metal detectors over the sand.

A month after they were married, she and David came for the weekend, stayed at the Saint Aspinquid. David got up early one morning and took a swim. At breakfast, he realized his wedding band was gone. Jane told him it didn't matter; they would get him another. But David was despondent. He returned to the beach at sunset and offered these men with their detectors a reward of one thousand dollars, twice what the ring had cost. The old men tried, but it never turned up. The ring must have been swept out by the tide, or maybe tossed into some child's plastic bucket. At the time, it had seemed like an actual loss.

ARRIVING BACK to the cove twenty minutes later, Jane noticed big hot pink letters written on the chalkboard sign in front of the trendy new coffee shop that offered vegan muffins and foam art and struck her as out of place in Awadapquit, yet always had a line out the door.

Jane went closer to see what the sign said today: YOU ARE STAND-ING ON STOLEN ABENAKI LAND.

Recently, she had begun to see land acknowledgments used at conferences and museums in Canada, where the movement for Indigenous rights was far ahead of that in the US. But Jane was surprised to find such a thing here.

There were lots of nearby spots named for Indigenous people and tribes. In the case of natural locations, like the Mekwi River, and the town of Awadapquit itself, this seemed right. Honoring the names Indigenous people had given.

But Jane had often raised an eyebrow driving past the Abenaki Office Park in Winston. And the old Shawmut Bank, founded by white men, its logo a bust of Chief Obbatinewat. Allison's parents had named their inn after Saint Aspinquid, a seventeenth-century chief of the Pawtucket tribe, and a local folk hero, to whom they had no particular connection, and whose very existence many people doubted.

Some instances were worse than others. Whenever she drove up to Maine from Cambridge, Jane passed through Saugus, Massachusetts, where a school gym on the side of Route 1 was decorated with enormous letters spelling out SAUGUS: HOME OF THE SACHEMS, over a red illustration of a Native man in a headdress, several stories tall.

It seemed to her that whenever New Englanders attempted to honor the legacy of Indigenous people, the story was told in past tense. The sign in front of her now went a step further than mere acknowledgment. Rightly so, it made an accusation of theft. But what did it mean to acknowledge that this land had been stolen, when no one had any intention of giving it back?

Jane had debated this with Melissa and David in the context of

Harvard, where last year a group of students had requested that the school adopt a formal land acknowledgment for the first time. Melissa and David were of the mindset that this was, at least, a meaningful gesture, a step in the right direction. While Jane thought that at Harvard in particular, such a thing felt insufficient, given the university's fraught history with Native Americans, dating back to its founding.

A few years ago, anthropology students began excavating the foundations of the 350-year-old Indian College in the middle of Harvard Yard, which had primarily served as a means of indoctrinating the sons of Indigenous leaders with Puritan values, in the hopes that they would spread these ideas among their people.

Louis Agassiz, nineteenth-century Harvard professor and founder of the school's natural history museum, was a devotee of craniometry, the study and measurement of human skulls as a means of assessing intelligence. The skulls in question often belonged to Indigenous people, acquired by scientists and military men who thought nothing of pillaging their graves. Agassiz argued that the range of skull capacities between people of different races proved that not all human beings were descended from Adam and Eve. Only Caucasians, Agassiz claimed, were created by God.

The very category of race and the way it had been used against people of color ever since began with Agassiz and his peers. Their findings were used to justify slavery and the genocide of American Indians. They set off a terrible legacy at Harvard, and every other major university and museum in America and elsewhere, of white men digging up Black and brown bodies in the name of research.

Since 1990, federal law had mandated institutions to catalogue human remains and sacred funerary objects in their collections, as a first step toward returning them, if they could be identified as originating with one of 574 federally recognized tribes. The onus was on the tribes themselves to prove that items belonged to them and that they were truly sacred. For those whose tribes had been decimated and no longer existed, there was no recourse. Harvard was still in possession of something like seven thousand human remains, two-thirds of the original collection, mostly held at the university's Peabody Museum of Archaeology and Ethnology.

To this day, Agassiz's name was carved above the front doors of the Harvard Museum of Natural History. Inside, in glass cases where stolen sacred items, since returned, had once been, there were now blank white spaces with signs explaining the absence. There was something ghostlike about them, Jane thought. Without asking outright, they raised the question at the heart of why so many institutions were reluctant to part with what they had taken: *If we give these things back, what will we replace them with?*

Of course, this was even more the case when talking about the land on which it had all been built.

Jane snapped a picture of the chalkboard sign with her phone, and on instinct opened a text message to send it to David and Melissa. But then she thought better of it. She put the phone in her pocket and walked on.

A S   J A N E   A P P R O A C H E D   her mother's house, she noticed a small red car in the driveway. There was a woman behind the wheel.

She had the windows rolled down. One bare, fleshy arm rested in the open space.

The woman's eyes were closed, her mouth slightly agape.

"Hello?" Jane said when she reached her, unable to think of precisely what question she should be asking.

The eyes snapped open.

"Jane?"

"Yes?"

"Clementine. I'm a bit early."

She was almost two hours early.

Jane glanced down into the car. The passenger side floor was covered in crumpled fast-food wrappers and paper cups and black-and-white map printouts. On the seat above that was a balled-up sweater, a crushed straw hat, a roll of paper towels.

"We don't have to start yet," Clementine said. "But if you don't mind me just coming in for a minute—I very much need to pee. I've been in the car for three hours. I got on the road at four a.m."

"Wow," Jane said, wondering why.

"I like to see the sun rise," Clementine said. "And I was nervous about traffic, but it was a breeze. Yay. But now, like I said, I have to pee. Oh, I can just hear my mother, telling me I should have gone at the rest area in Kennebunk. Well, Mother, I didn't have to go then!"

Jane stared at her. She wanted to know if this was a figure of speech or if Clementine really did think she heard her mother telling her that she should have used the rest stop bathroom.

It was an imposition. Jane hadn't showered yet or checked her email or made coffee. She was still wearing the sweats she had worn to bed.

She had planned to call Allison before this woman arrived. She wanted to know exactly what and how much Allison had told her. Jane didn't know the protocol. Was she supposed to tip? Was a psychic medium who made house calls like a food delivery person, a gig worker who relied on the generosity of strangers to get by? Or was she more like a master plumber, who came to your home to perform a vocation and would therefore be insulted by a gratuity?

Allison had sent Jane a link to Clementine's website. The fact of her having a website seemed antithetical to clairvoyance, though Jane couldn't quite say why.

In large letters on the home page were the words Clemetine Wembley, Certified Medium and Psychic.

Certified by whom? Jane wondered. Also, Clementine's name was misspelled.

She clicked on a page of testimonials and then a menu of services and their corresponding prices:

Reading. $100 (30 min)/$180 (60 min)

Pranic Healing. $125

Hypnotherapy. $75

Bachelorette/birthday parties. $300, plus gas and tolls
(up to 10 people, 120 min)

Schlocky as it was, Jane hadn't said no. She was doing this as a favor to Allison. Like all future events she dreaded, she had just pretended the moment would never come.

Now here was Clementine, getting out of the car. She was probably five-foot-ten and was full all over—her bosom, enormous, bobbed free beneath a formless purple dress. Her stomach and arms spilled out. Her hair was red. Her skin as white and unblemished as a glass of milk.

Clementine said, "Hi there, you!" like she was greeting a friend.

She wasn't looking at Jane. Oh God, was she addressing a ghost? Jane couldn't take it.

Then she realized Clementine was talking to Walter. The dog sat, head in the air, looking almost regal. Jane had never seen him encounter a new person without losing his mind, darting this way and that, yapping his head off.

She led the way inside, and pointed toward the bathroom.

"Just over there," Jane said.

From her spot in the kitchen, she heard Clementine lock the bathroom door. She heard the stream of piss hit the water. All the while, Clementine hummed to herself.

The toilet flushed, the sink turned on and then off, the bathroom door opened. Clementine came out and showed no sign of leaving.

"Sorry the house is a mess," Jane said reflexively.

"Don't feel bad. I know how it goes."

Jane wanted to point out that the house wasn't half as messy as Clementine's front seat, and that she would have tidied up had this stranger done what a normal person does when they arrive early, and just driven around town or taken a walk. Also, it wasn't her house. She said none of this.

"It was heaven driving down here on a Tuesday," Clementine said. As she spoke, she walked around the room, touching small objects, picking them up and turning them over like she was browsing in a gift shop. It must be lovely to be a psychic; people just expected you to be strange.

Jane wondered what she was looking for. Some lingering energy of her mother's, alive in her belongings? Most of them were secondhand. In lieu of family heirlooms, the Flanagan women possessed an assortment of items other families had sold for a dollar. Did that mean they would contain her mother's energy or someone else's?

This, Jane thought, was where belief in the occult lost her. The details couldn't stand up to scrutiny. It was like when they told Jason heaven was a place up in the clouds when he was four, and he very wisely asked if anyone ever fell out and landed on somebody's head.

"Most clients want me to schlep hither and yon on a Saturday," Clementine said. "It's a real help that you could see me during the week. What do you do for work, Jane? You must be self-employed."

"No. I work at the Schlesinger Library at Harvard. It's an archive dedicated to the history of American women."

If Clementine were truly psychic, she would know that Jane no longer worked there. That she had been fired. Well, *put on leave* was how Melissa phrased it on that last, awful day, but Jane feared then and now that it was merely an attempt to soften the blow.

Clementine gave her a sympathetic look that made Jane wonder if maybe she did know, and she too was being polite.

Just in case, Jane added, "I'm taking a leave of absence this summer."

"You ought to come to Camp Mira," Clementine said. "That's where I live in the summer months. It's on a beautiful private island off Bar Harbor."

"Camp Mira," Jane repeated.

"Yes. It was one of the first Spiritualist gathering places in the country," Clementine said. "The camp has a fascinating history. It would make a great addition to your archive. I'd be happy to tell you the whole long story sometime, show you old diaries and photos and posters. We have loads of memorabilia."

"I'd love that," Jane lied.

She had lost count of the number of people who, hearing what she did for work, claimed that their grandmother was a pioneer in the field of law or pie-baking or landscape architecture, and should be considered. Everyone thought their own story worthy of preservation.

"Can I get you something? Coffee? Water?" Jane said, hoping to change the subject.

"No thanks," Clementine said. "Shall we begin?"

Jane considered sending her back out to the car until the appointed hour. But she knew she would spend that time worrying about what was to come. Best to get it over with and get on with her day.

They sat on opposite sides of her mother's small kitchen table. The top was a cheap brown laminate, meant to look like wood. Jane hated that table. It was one of those yard sale finds that her mom kept only because no one wanted to buy it.

Clementine pulled three pink crystals, the size of golf balls, from her purse. She set them on the table, at the feet of Jane's grandmother's kitchen Madonna.

Jane looked back and forth from the statue to the stones. She was an equal-opportunity skeptic. As disbelieving in the faith in which she was raised as she was in the stranger sitting across from her.

The Catholic Church was the one thing Jane and her grandmother ever argued about.

All the terrible revelations about priests molesting thousands upon thousands of children that surfaced after her grandmother's death made Jane wonder if they would have swayed her, or if she would have continued to turn up at Saint Anthony's every Sunday for the eight o'clock Mass, as some people, inexplicably, still did.

Jane thought she knew the answer, but maybe it was only what she hoped the answer would be. This was the trouble with the dead. Eventually they became someone else's invention.

"Your friend Allison told me a bit about your situation over the phone," Clementine said. "Your mom passed to spirit last year, is that right? Remind me of her name."

"Shirley," Jane said.

With just that one word uttered, she felt exposed.

"How does it work, exactly, what you do?" Jane asked Clementine.

She had learned somewhere along the line that asking people questions about themselves was a surefire way to get them to stop asking about her.

"I hear a faint ringing sound," Clementine said. "If I choose to tune in to it, more information comes. Voices. Messages from spirit."

"Do the dead ever speak to you when you're not seeking them out?" Jane said. "Or can you turn it on and off?"

Clementine gave her a look like she had asked whether rain was wet. "They're like inconsiderate relatives, Jane. They show up unannounced whenever they feel like it. I can try to tune them out. I do try, most of the time, or else I'd never have any peace. But they come anyway. At all hours."

"Have you had this ability your whole life?"

"I was eight when I met my first spirit guide. I would tell my parents about her and they'd laugh at me," Clementine said. "They started getting angry, though, when I talked about her at school and my teacher called the house to ask if anything funny was going on at home. Which in fact it was, which made them want me to shut up about it all the more. Right?"

Jane nodded. She didn't really buy any of the spirit world stuff, but she was curious to know what the something funny was.

"Children are more receptive to ghosts," Clementine said. "They're more open than adults are. We drill it out of them, in time. We tell them the person they see is their imaginary friend, and later, that's what they believe too. There's some interesting research that suggests maybe it has to do with the way children under five can see parts of the electromagnetic spectrum that other people can't. Evidence shows it's possible spirits are only visible in ultraviolet light and only the youngest children can see that with the naked eye."

"Interesting," Jane said, wondering what exactly Clementine meant by *research* and *evidence*.

Research conducted by the person who certified mediums, perhaps.

Clementine inhaled deeply, closed her eyes.

"First I ask my spirit guides to help me invite the spirits into the room. Well. That was fast. She's here. A plump woman, right? *Jolly* would be a better word for her. Always smiling. Silver hair."

Jane shook her head. Her mother looked nothing like that.

"You've had her protection for a long time," Clementine said.

Jane opened her mouth to disagree, to point out that her mother had been dead for only a year, and most of it had been a total disaster.

But Clementine continued. "Mary? Or Marie?"

"Mary," Jane said. "My grandmother."

She felt some wall of doubt within her crack open, a light shining through, while at the same time her brain whirred into high gear to disprove it. Weren't most people's grandmothers plump and gray haired and called Mary? Clementine could have gotten the name online. Probably from the obituary Jane herself had written for her mom. *She is preceded in death by her mother, Mary Flanagan.* Clementine had thrown in that "Or Marie?" to make it seem as though she wasn't sure.

"Mary is always with you," Clementine said. "Have you ever had a time in your life when you felt guided? When you made some major decision and it was like it was being made *for* you? Someone nudging you toward the right choice? That was her."

What came immediately to mind was when she went to Wesleyan her senior year of high school for the accepted students weekend. Jane's heart pounded for forty-eight hours straight. Her palms were sweating. She willed people not to shake her hand. She didn't belong there, among the private school girls, and the outspoken radical activists with the shaved heads who acted as if they had known each other all their lives. And yet she felt a thrill at the idea of living among them. She knew somehow that even though it felt impossible, she would do it.

Meeting David had felt that way too. Returning home from their first date, dinner at a tapas restaurant in Kendall Square, she was overcome with the certainty that he was her person. When he reached out the next day, it was not to ask her to dinner the following week (though they did that too) but to invite her to a one-night showing of *Indiscreet* at the Brattle Theatre, two months hence. No question in either of their minds that they would still want to see each other then.

Clementine said, "Your mom wants you to know she's here. She's sitting next to Grandma. There's a third person coming through too. A teenager, I think. No. Younger than that. She's sitting in your grandmother's lap. She's giving me the letter *D.* A name that starts with *D.* Does that mean anything to you? Is she a member of the family?"

Jane tried to think, but nothing came to mind.

"Deirdre, is it? Or no, that's not it. She's here with your grandma."

"Sorry," Jane said. She felt like she had failed a test.

"Your mom thinks we should go sit out back. She says you need to sit out there more often."

"Probably true," Jane said.

She paused, unsure whether they were meant to obey this order.

Clementine stood up. "Is it through here?"

Jane followed her. They sat on the deck in green plastic Adirondack chairs. Her mother had loved sitting out here, watching for hummingbirds in the morning. Jane had never seen one until this past month, and now she saw them all the time. She thought of her mother whenever she did.

Her mother sat out here in the evenings too, smoking, listening as animals moved through the brush, a bottle of wine at her side.

Sometimes she would spy a family of deer or wild turkeys. It happened much more often these days. It seemed like condos and developments were being built on every inch of land in the area. The animals had nowhere to go but into people's backyards, where they would be remarked upon, photographed, at first. Then later seen as a nuisance.

"Yes, this is much better," Clementine said. "Okay, so Mom is telling me she lived here with you at the end?"

"She lived here all the time. This was her house," Jane said. "And yes, at the end, I was here with her."

"But you didn't grow up in this house," Clementine said, not so much asking a question as seeking confirmation.

"Not exactly. We moved here when I was a freshman in high school. This was my grandmother's house and after she died, we moved in."

Clementine nodded. "Yes." She laughed. "Your grandma says she hated it when you all painted the kitchen cabinets green. She says what were you thinking."

Jane wondered if she was making it up. If she was, what kind of life was that, going around telling people their dead grandmother didn't like the paint they chose? Searching for details and seizing upon them.

When Jane didn't respond, Clementine said, "You were a family of strong women."

"Sure," Jane said. Had Clementine ever told anyone they came from a family of weaklings?

"Strong-willed women too," Clementine added. "Often at war with each other."

"Yes," Jane said.

"There was love, of course. There almost always is. But I can feel the hostility, the power of the harsh words that got thrown around here," Clementine said. "A loss of control."

"My mother was an alcoholic," Jane said. "She could get really nasty when she drank."

Jane was familiar with the brand of sympathy engendered by saying you were raised by an alcoholic. It was too easy, in a way. Not fair. Since the statement implied that she herself was different.

Inside the house, the dog started barking like mad. Probably a car had driven past, or he'd seen an ant, or his own shadow.

"Sorry," Jane said. "He's nuts. He barks at everything."

Clementine nodded. "Animals can sense the presence of spirits."

Jane blinked. This was not at all what she had meant, of course, but it didn't seem worth saying.

"So you lived here, just the two of you," Clementine said. "You and your mom."

"And my sister, Holly."

"Okay, yes. Your grandmother says your mother and sister were two peas in a pod."

"They were," Jane said.

She thought of how they even wore their hair the same way, and both dyed it an identical shade of blonde.

"And you felt left out?" Clementine said.

"No," Jane said. "Not really."

If anything, Jane felt grateful to stand apart from them.

"You've always been the good one, the obedient one," Clementine said.

"Yes," Jane said. Privately she thought, *Yes and no.*

Then Clementine said, "You've worked hard to give the appearance of being good, anyway."

Jane startled, because this was exactly true. She wondered if Clementine was really psychic, or if she just had a strong sense of human nature. Maybe they were the same thing in the end.

It had always mattered a great deal to Jane that her marriage to David was different from anything her mother had ever had or even wanted to have with a man. It was calm and reasonable and based on trust. Yes, they loved each other, but more importantly, they liked each other. Their marriage was stable ground on which to stand. Until it wasn't.

Clementine tipped her head to the side now and bounced it up and down like she was trying to shake water out of her ear.

"Jane, sorry, but D wants to come through again. The young girl. She's desperate for you to get a message to her mother. She says it could be her only chance."

"Who is her mother?" Jane said.

"I have no idea. But D is saying she needs you to tell her that it wasn't her fault. Tell her she's at peace in the water. She's not at Lake Grove anymore."

"Lake Grove? You mean the country club?"

Clementine shrugged. "I'm not familiar with this area."

"But why would the girl be coming through to me?" Jane said.

"Any number of reasons. Maybe no reason at all."

"That's helpful."

Clementine blinked. "Think of me as a telephone line. I just transmit messages, I don't always know what they mean."

"Sorry," Jane said.

"It's frustrating," Clementine said. "Believe me, I get it. Some of what I say here today won't make sense right this minute, but hold on to it. Later, it might."

Jane tried to picture Clementine in a house somewhere, cooking dinner, or watching TV. Did she have a husband? Children? Had she ever had a normal job? Was this even her job, or something she did on the side? Jane imagined her into various roles—teacher, pharmacist, usher in a theater. She couldn't envision her doing anything but this.

"The main thing Mom wants to say to you is that despite whatever happened, she really did do her best," Clementine said.

Jane bristled. That was something her mother said all the time, whenever Jane tried to talk to her about things that went on when she was a child. It drove Jane crazy. There was no more effective way to shut down criticism than *I did my best*. What could a person ever say in response?

And had she, really? If she had and it was never good enough, was that her daughter's fault?

Over the years, their phone calls sometimes ended with tension, even the occasional hang-up, especially if they spoke in the evenings, once the wine was flowing. After the fact, her mother never apologized. Communication resumed only via the buffer of the family group text. Jason would send a funny anecdote or a photo of his math test with a big red *A* at the top, and they would both weigh in and, in that way, be reunited.

When her mother died, things between them went from unresolved to unresolvable. For months, Jane walked around so full of anger about this. She woke drenched in sweat from dreams in which she screamed in her mother's face to come back; they weren't finished. David always tried to soothe her after.

Sometimes Jane allowed him to, grateful for his embrace. Other times, she felt smothered. She went and slept in the armchair in the living room. She wasn't good at being comforted by someone else. For most of her life, she had done that for herself. She knew she was safe with him, but could never quite manage to flip the switch on the instinct that told her David would harm her if she wasn't careful. Her mercuriality wore them both down. It was exhausting. Jane knew this.

"Your mom wanted the best for you, but she was jealous too," Clementine said.

Jane thought it was true. Sometimes she felt sad about how small her mother's life was compared to her own. But when she tried to broaden it, her efforts never went over well. She invited her mother to join her on a business trip to Rome, all expenses paid, and her mother said she was too busy with work.

While visiting Awadapquit once, Jane asked her mother to dinner, just the two of them. There was a new farm-to-table place she had heard was great, so she suggested they go there. When she was in high school, not a single restaurant in town stayed open in the offseason or offered anything fancier than lobster rolls. There were now a handful of fine-dining options within a few miles. The one Jane chose boasted on the menu that the kitchen used only organic produce from local farms. Not just corn and tomatoes, but ramps and kale and fiddleheads. The entrees included duck breast and wild-caught salmon and handmade gnocchi.

Jane thought everything was delicious.

Her mother acted weird and suspicious the whole time.

"The chef is from *Portland*?" she whispered when she heard a waiter say as much. "I should have known. This place is so pretentious."

She left half the food on her plate.

"There's a girl at Camp Mira, Evangeline, who does past-life regression," Clementine said. "She believes parents and their children choose one another. The choosing isn't always about being content. Sometimes it's a means of working through conflict, or having something to teach the other person. Evangeline told me my mother and I were unhappily married in a past life."

"To one another?"

Clementine nodded, casual, like she had just told Jane the two of them both wore a size eight loafer.

Jane's earliest memories of her mother were good ones. She remembered her mother turning cartwheels across the living room when the Patriots won a big game. Her mother letting them stay up to watch *Dynasty* with her, all three of them falling asleep in her bed. Having dance parties, serving frozen waffles with whipped cream for dinner if Jane and Holly begged enough. How she looked when she was newly in love and hopeful. How she would kiss them, leaving lipstick prints on their cheeks on purpose, and spritz them with her perfume before she walked out the door to a date.

But more often, she was moody and hungover and some guy was not living up to expectations. Or not calling when he said he would, in which case she locked herself in her room to stew, oblivious to what her children were doing. As an adult, when Jane observed friends' kids complaining about having to go to bed or turn off the television or brush their teeth, she wanted to squeeze their cheeks and tell them how lucky they were that someone cared enough to make them do such things.

When her mother was diagnosed with lung cancer, stage four, a year and a half ago, Jane and David jumped into action. He had a friend of a friend who was a top oncologist at Dana Farber. People came from all over the world to see him. David called in a favor. The doctor said he would take her on and get her into a cutting-edge clinical trial.

Jane's mother said no. She didn't want to travel to Boston; she didn't want to spend her final months sick from chemo. When Jane said she could stay with them, her mother said, "I wouldn't be comfortable."

"But you have to do something," Jane said over the phone.

"Just let it be," her mother snapped.

A few days later, on the phone with her sister, Holly said, "Mom is doing research online to an obsessive degree. She keeps texting me links at three in the morning."

Jane was surprised, relieved. She herself was also in research mode—at that very moment, as they talked, she was writing down every item on a list of twenty cancer-fighting superfoods and trying to devise ways of sneaking them into baked goods without her mother knowing.

"What is Mom researching?" she asked.

"Things to do in Vegas," Holly said. "And hotel deals and stuff."

"Excuse me?"

"Didn't she tell you? She wants us all to go. She's pouring every ounce of energy into planning the trip. This was what she wanted to do for her seventieth birthday, and since she's probably not going to make it to seventy—" Holly couldn't finish the sentence.

"That is absurd," Jane said. "And so bad for her health. Doesn't everyone smoke everywhere in Vegas?"

"What difference does it make?" Holly said. "That ship has sailed. Plus, Mom smokes."

"Not anymore, she doesn't," Jane said. "She's on oxygen, for God's sake."

This was met with silence.

"Christ, Holly, you're kidding me."

"Honestly, I think a trip is a good idea," Holly said. "It gives her something to look forward to."

And so they went. Holly and Jason, David and Jane, and Shirley. For three nights, they gambled and ate at buffets and laughed and drank and went out of their way to get along. They didn't talk once about cancer. Jane watched her mother flirt with strangers and throw back cocktails and dress up in short, spangly dresses and dance and smoke like a chimney.

On the flight home, Jane scrolled through all the pictures she had taken on her phone during their stay. She knew she would never set foot in Las Vegas again. It occurred to her then that there were a few things her mother was a lot better at than she was, including having fun for the sake of it. Enjoying herself.

When Jane looked up from her phone, her mother was watching her from across the aisle. They exchanged a smile that felt as close as they would ever get to understanding.

Five months later, her mother was dead.

She had wanted to die at home. Jane came up to Maine for the final days to help Holly make it happen.

Jane had been sending a weekly grocery delivery, heavy on the produce. She found all of it in her mother's fridge when she got there, in various states of decomposition. Shriveled peppers and tomatoes. Dark green spinach liquefied at the bottom of a flimsy plastic bag.

Later that night, she found a book about the history of antique collecting, autographed by the author, which she had given her mother the previous Christmas. It was tucked between the window and the sill in her bedroom, used to prop the window open, its pages warped from rainwater.

For the last few days of their mother's life, she lay flat in bed, head thrown back, eyes unfocused. They could never be sure whether she saw anything. She was in severe pain. She moaned for hours on end. They placed morphine pills under her tongue, sometimes far more of them than the doctor had advised.

They changed her diapers, they washed her, they administered suppositories and sponged water onto her cracked lips. They moved her every so often to prevent bedsores, but she still got them. It all felt unreal to Jane. She and Holly drank the entire time, round the clock. No other way to get through it. Empty wine bottles lined her mother's dresser and the floor below.

Once a day a hospice nurse arrived to check in and take her pulse. These visits only ever lasted five minutes, but they were the thing that kept Jane and Holly sane, reminding them that a world still existed out there, that contrary to how it felt, they were not murdering their mother. This gruesome process was what it meant to die peacefully at home in your own bed, surrounded by family, as the obituaries so often read.

In the middle of it all, the power went out. Their mother hadn't paid the bill for months.

"Feels like old times," Holly said, sitting there in the dark.

During their childhood, they were never not worried about money. Jane could never understand why her mother wouldn't just get a proper job. A steady stream of collection notices arrived, and calls during dinnertime. Occasionally, a landlord banged on their door, furious that she had paid the rent with a bad check, or not at all. They moved a lot.

Jane swore she remembered them going to pick up donated food from a church basement, but Holly was fairly sure it never happened. They agreed on the issue of their mother's pride, how she might order McDonald's hamburgers, five for a dollar, and if they asked for theirs with cheese, she would say, "We have some at home." Not for their benefit—they all knew it wasn't true—but for the sake of the pimply teenager in the paper hat on the other side of the counter.

The fear of scarcity followed Jane into adulthood, into her marriage. It popped up at odd times, surprising her. She panicked when they were low on groceries, even though they could go out and buy more whenever they wanted. When David turned the heat up to seventy. When he left a light on just in case he felt like walking back into that room at some later point in time. When they went to his parents' house for Christmas and Jane saw the living room, like a scene in a movie—a tree as high as the ceiling, surrounded by presents wrapped in red and silver paper.

Money was one reason why Jane was scared to have kids. In those middle-of-the-night moments of panic, she pictured some reversal of fortune by which she and David would be unable to support their children and have to turn them over to the state, even though she knew it would never happen.

Holly, as an adult, had gone the other way. She believed she deserved the best, and no momentary financial reality could dissuade her. She leased a Lexus. Despite what she did for work, she would never let Jason wear anything secondhand; it was a point of pride with her.

Jane looked at Clementine now, sitting in what used to be her mother's chair. The thought that Jane, reincarnated from some other realm, had chosen this inheritance was preposterous.

"We are almost out of time," Clementine said. "But before I go, one more thing." She smiled conspiratorially. "Is there any chance you're pregnant?"

Jane sputtered.

"No chance," she said.

This subject, which had been a regular part of her thoughts and discussions until just a couple of months ago, now felt so removed from her reality that the mention of it was jarring.

"You might want to take a test to be sure. Your grandmother keeps saying something about a baby. She's singing lullabies!" Clementine said. "She's saying she's thrilled to have a great-granddaughter on the way. Might your sister be pregnant?"

"God, I hope not."

"Could be a crossed line or something. Sometimes that happens and we—oh dear, sorry, Jane. It's D again. She's repeating herself. They do that. It's the thing about getting the message to her mother. Sorry. I don't mean to burden you. Maybe just write it down. She's insistent. Lake Grove. She says you'll know."

Jane typed the words into an email on her phone: *Lake Grove. She says you'll know.*

Clementine leaned on the arms of the chair to push herself up to her feet. She looked around the yard. It was small, but pretty and private. Over the years, Jane's grandmother had planted blueberry bushes, tomatoes, basil, white roses and peonies, a dogwood tree.

"I can see why your mother wanted us out here," Clementine said. "You know, Jane, if you ever want to talk to them directly, you can. Sit right here when you do. The tranquility, the quiet, helps when you're trying to make contact with the spirit world. You'll see."

Jane felt strangely regretful to see her go.

She realized then that she had been waiting for Clementine to say something about David. Jane wasn't wearing her wedding ring. If she had been, maybe Clementine would have taken it as a clue. She regretted this now, in a way. She would have liked to know what the spirits had to say on the matter, even as she told herself that this was all make-believe. If Clementine needed a ring to know Jane had a husband, it only proved her suspicions.

"You really should come up to camp and see us before summer ends," Clementine said again as Jane walked her to her car. "I think you'd find it an interesting place."

She hugged Jane goodbye.

When they embraced, Clementine jerked away as if Jane had given her an electric shock.

"Oh, Jane," she said. "You're in pain."

They were the exact words Allison had said after the two-cent sale. It made Jane feel as if they had been talking about her behind her back.

"This isn't about your mother. This is about you, Jane. Something you did," Clementine said. "You have to face that. It's going to pull you under if you don't."

4

"SO? HOW WAS IT? Tell us everything."

"It was interesting, I guess. It was weird."

Jane sat across from Allison and Chris at a table on the front porch of the Saint Aspinquid Inn. Chris had set out a pitcher of lemonade and three glasses. In normal times, the glasses would have contained white wine. Jane would have brought a bottle. She told Allison not to abstain from drinking on her account, but Allison said she didn't feel like drinking, truly, it would only make her tired. Secretly Jane was relieved.

To passersby, they probably looked like tourists having a relaxing afternoon chat. In reality, every few minutes they were interrupted by a guest in need of fresh towels or a restaurant recommendation or help with the air conditioner in room five.

Chris jumped up to take care of each problem in turn. This was Allison's hour to herself. They each held tight to any speck of free time allotted by the other, the only line between work and life that existed for them. They lived with their two kids in the owners' quarters where Allison's parents had raised her, and kept to the same schedule they'd had. Up at five each morning to make the coffee and the scones and the scrambled eggs.

"Some of what she said was off the mark," Jane said. "But a few things were really accurate."

"*Yeah,*" said Allison. She had demanded the highlights via text hours earlier. "Her knowing what your grandma looked like, and her name. That's nuts. Plus, she knew you all fought all the time. Most mediums would just say, oh, your mother loves you so much."

"How much did you tell her about me?" Jane said.

"Just that your mom died and that you probably wouldn't believe anything she said, so apologies in advance if you were rude."

Jane laughed.

"Can we talk about D?" Allison said. "*I'm not at Lake Grove anymore.* What did that mean? I looked online to see if there had ever been a murder up at Lake Grove Country Club, but I didn't find anything. So then I called Teddy McCarthy, who's been the general manager there forever."

"Of course you did," Jane said.

"Teddy said there had never been a murder or anything like that, as far as he knew. But then he called me back and said there was a girl who died. A cocktail waitress. She accidentally ate shrimp and she was deathly allergic. Her throat swelled up. She dropped dead right there in the lounge. But her name was Ann Johnson. So that doesn't solve for D. But who knows? It's entirely possible that D was killed and buried on the golf course, and no one knows about it."

"I think we need to cut back on your *Dateline*," Chris said.

"Isn't it kind of an imposition on Clementine's part to make this my problem?" Jane said. "Like, really? I'm the only one who can get this message to D's mother? Even though I don't have a clue who she is?"

"I'm not sure I'd call it an imposition," Allison said. "A medium can't choose who speaks through her."

"True," Jane said. "If only I hadn't sought out the help of a medium. Oh wait, I didn't."

"I'm sorry!" Allison said. "How was I supposed to know this would happen?"

"Clearly *you* are not psychic," Chris said.

"Even if I could figure out who D is, who's to say that her mother would want to hear from some random woman that her daughter's ghost has a message for her?" Jane said. "And by the way, why is it that dead people always come back to tell their loved ones, 'I'm at peace'? Why is it never, 'This absolutely sucks, get me out of here'?"

"I just come back around to—if you're a psychic, why aren't you a millionaire?" Chris said. "Wouldn't you know what the winning lottery numbers will be on any given night?"

Allison looked at him hard. "Chris."

"What?"

"That is like seeing a really tall guy in the street and asking him if he plays basketball."

He cocked his head. "Is it?"

When Allison and Chris got married years ago, Jane had had her doubts. Allison was funny and smart and vibrant. Why did she want to tie herself down to a boy she had known since kindergarten? It seemed like she was headed for a life so small, so underwhelming. But they were still in love, still laughing together now.

"I saw the ghost of my great-uncle one Christmas when I was a kid," Allison said. "He showed up during dinner at my grandma's house. He was mad that my great-aunt brought a date."

Jane and Chris exchanged a look.

"It's true!" Allison said.

"How is it possible we've never discussed this?" Jane said.

"I don't know. It's not such a big deal. That kind of thing happens all the time, especially with kids. Children see ghosts much more easily than adults do. Everyone knows that."

"Yeah, Jane, everyone knows that," Chris said.

Jane grinned.

"Clementine said something about that. Oh, and she was talking about past lives, and she said this thing about how parents and their children choose each other. Like, as a means of working through relationship issues from their past lives."

"I believe that," Allison said.

"You do?" Chris said.

"Having children has made me more open-minded to the notion of the full spectrum of life, including the before and after."

"What does that mean?" Chris said.

"It means once you meet your kids, it's hard to imagine their existence as some random act of biology," Allison said. "As individuals, they seem destined for you. Don't you think?"

"I guess so," he said.

"It's possible to imagine, then, that the unknown places that precede life and come after it are two points on the same circle."

"You've lost me now," he said.

"When I was pregnant with Amelia and Oliver, I used to walk in that old cemetery just past Main Street, looking for baby name inspiration on the gravestones. I had never paid any attention to it before."

Chris nodded. "Creepy," he said.

Allison gave him a playful shove.

"Jane, have you ever noticed that it's always women who believe in the unseen? Men might believe in God, maybe even heaven, but they're not willing to believe in ghosts. Life after life. I think it's because they have no concept of life *before* life, how it feels to imagine a person and then bring that person into existence."

Jane felt a pang in her chest. When she gave Allison the highlights of her session, she had not mentioned the part about Clementine asking if she might be pregnant. It was embarrassing, how much she wanted it to be true when she knew it couldn't be.

"So to be clear, you believe in ghosts?" Jane said.

"I don't not believe," Allison said.

A tall, skinny guy walked up to them on the porch now. His dimensions made Jane think immediately of Abraham Lincoln, though he was wearing a short-sleeved plaid button-down shirt, khaki shorts, and flip-flops, and holding a laptop.

"Hey there," he said, sounding friendly, apologetic. "Sorry to bug you."

"Not at all," Chris said. "That's what we're here for. How can I help?"

"I think the Wi-Fi's down. I've been trying to send an email for ten minutes."

Chris stood up. "Excuse me, ladies," he said. "Follow me," he said to Abe Lincoln. As they went inside, through the open front door, Chris said, "Hey, I'm curious—did you ever play basketball?"

A smile spread across Allison's face. She shook her head.

"You know, certain guests, staying at an old inn like this, are disappointed if it *isn't* haunted," she said. "When my brother and I were babies and business was slow, my mom made up this story to tell people who asked, about past residents and creaking floors. She always said what's the harm? The story got more and more detailed over time—there was a ghost known as 'the General.' He had stayed here along with George Washington, something like that. Then a reporter from *The Boston Globe* wrote an article about haunted places in New England. Unbeknownst to my mom, he had been a guest here and asked about ghosts and she told him the whole ridiculous made-up story. It ran in the paper! Afterward, she was terrified some history buff would write a letter to the editor saying the General never existed. She went to confession over it, she made a donation to the Sisters of Saint Joseph, and promised to make it an annual thing if God would let her get away with this one white lie."

"Ha," Jane said. "That is so your mom."

A moment of silence then, as there always was now when Betty came up in conversation.

"How is she?" Jane said. A stupid question, but she couldn't not ask.

"The same," Allison said.

"And your dad?"

"You know. He hates to see her in that place. But he's always there. He says it's lonely at their house now. He misses her. Even though she isn't really her anymore."

Allison's parents had been the type of happy couple other married people envied. Richard and Betty ran a business together day in and day out. They had two kids. And after forty years, they still seemed to like each other a lot. There was so much easy laughter in their home. In high school, Jane would watch them talking while they made dinner, or side-by-side under a blanket on the sofa, each reading a book. At every school event, there they'd be, holding hands. Their quiet, steady love was a revelation.

"Oh, by the way, my dad wanted me to thank you for the beer-of-the-month club you signed him up for," Allison said now. "It gives him something to look forward to. And the beers are really good, apparently."

"I'm glad," Jane said.

Ever since Betty got sick, she had tried to make an effort for Allison and her dad. Jane had dinner delivered to the inn from Allison's favorite restaurant on nights when she knew Allison had been with her mom all day and would be too tired to cook. After they moved Betty into the nursing home eight months ago, Jane started sending flowers to her room on a weekly basis, always including yellow roses and sunflowers, since these were Betty's favorites. Allison was so appreciative, but Jane felt guilty that she hadn't yet gone to visit Betty in person.

She wasn't sure she could face it.

As long as Jane had known Betty, Betty had taken care of her. She sent Jane tins of cookies in the winter. She emailed Jane and Allison links to articles about the importance of getting enough sleep and the best vitamins for bone health and recipes for thirty-minute dinners and the new novel they should be reading.

Jane texted Betty questions from time to time. Things her own mother wouldn't know or care about, or else things she didn't feel like asking her own mother. Like the best way to roast a chicken, or how to keep hydrangeas from wilting, or when it was time to switch from a regular moisturizer to the anti-aging kind.

Betty always had the answers. Until, one afternoon three years ago, she forgot where she parked her car at the mall, and security had to call Allison to come get her. That was weird, but everyone was prepared to chalk it up to a bad day. Two months later, Betty took Amelia and Ollie to the playground and came home with only Ollie in the stroller. And so they took her to the doctor. And so began this hellish phase of Allison's life. And Betty's.

Three years on, Betty no longer recognized her husband, children, and grandchildren. Allison said Betty's personality had changed too. Betty was mean and bitter when she had always been sweet. She lashed out at everyone—the staff at the nursing home, and the family when they visited. Richard and Allison both went several times a week, even so. Allison was never sure whether or not it mattered to Betty. Her father, she said, got so depressed every time that he ended up crying in his car in the parking lot after.

For a second now, Allison looked like she might cry, but then her phone lit up and she smiled instead at a picture someone had texted her. She held the phone out for Jane to see.

"From Amelia and Ollie's babysitter," she said. "They're clamming in the river."

"Clamming in the river," Jane said. "It sounds so wholesome. When I was their age, I spent summer afternoons watching *General Hospital* with my grandmother."

Allison made a sad face. "I don't know," she said. "I feel guilty sometimes. The kids get so little of my attention, especially in the summer. I don't know how my mom ran this business and took care of us at the same time. I wish I could ask her."

"Kids didn't require as much supervision back then," Jane said.

"We never even had any babysitters," Allison said. "We went to summer camp at Saint Anthony's, which my brother and I both hated, but that was maybe three hours a day, twice a week."

Allison's family had attended the same church Jane's grandmother used to drag her to on Sundays when she was visiting during the summer. Their lapsed Catholicism, their distrust of organized religion in general, was one of a few strong beliefs Jane and Allison had in common. Or lack of belief, as the case may be.

Jane wondered sometimes if she and Allison had ever made bored eye contact in the pews as children, years before they met. Jane used to smuggle in Baby-Sitters Club books and hide them in the missal. She and Holly invented a game where they counted random things on the bodies of people standing in line for Communion—red shoes, black purses, warts. Anything to pass the hour.

It had been decades since Jane had entered a church. "When we were young, Saint Anthony's had so much power over me," Allison said now. "Over every aspect of my family's life. Now, when I drive by, my kids yell, 'Look! A castle!' They have no idea what's inside. That always makes me feel like I'm doing something right. But of course I also feel guilty, because what would my mother think?"

The Catholic god did not stick to them, but the Catholic guilt was another matter. Allison got married in the church to please Betty. Jane would never have considered doing that, but her guilt manifested in other ways.

"It's funny," she said. "Thinking about Clementine on the way here today, I had these words from the Nicene Creed running through my head: *We believe in one God, the Father, the Almighty, Maker of heaven and earth, of all that is seen and unseen.* Something about that seen and unseen bit."

"Hmm."

"Irish Catholicism is rooted in paganism," Jane said. "Whether they like to talk about it or not. I guess it's all more connected than we tend to think. Is the idea of being able to communicate with spirits really any more bonkers than a virgin birth and an ascension into heaven?"

"Much less bonkers, I'd argue," Allison said.

Two figures, an adult and a child, appeared in the doorway to the inn. The woman, around their age, wore a pink Lilly Pulitzer dress and white sandals. She had the toned arms and calves achieved only by yoga teachers and wealthy housewives.

The boy at her side looked about Ollie's age.

"Allison!" the woman called from where she stood, instead of walking over.

Allison didn't respond.

Chris returned, squeezing past the woman and child.

"Allison!" she called again.

Jane watched as Allison's and Chris's eyes met, and Chris said, "Genevieve? How can I help?"

"I was hoping to talk to Allison," she said, and came to the table, the child trailing after her.

Chris, from behind them, shrugged and went back inside.

"Hi, Genevieve," Allison said.

Jane detected a hint of annoyance in her friend's voice. It shocked her. She so rarely saw Allison acting anything but pleasant toward anyone.

"I was wondering if you know of a place where I can buy Benjamin a good pair of sneakers. He'll need to be measured. I swear his foot got two sizes bigger overnight."

"Sure," Allison said. "There's a children's clothing store in Portsmouth called Lollipop. They have a good selection of shoes."

"Great. Thanks."

Normally, Allison would have turned this into a good-natured chat about the speed at which boys outgrew their clothes, or offered some witty anecdote about the shopkeeper in question. But now Allison swiveled her head back toward Jane to signify that the conversation was over.

When, after several moments, Genevieve hadn't left, Allison said, "This is Jane, my best friend since high school. Jane, Genevieve is one of our guests. She comes every summer."

"Didn't think we'd be back this year, though," Genevieve said.

Jane looked at her, confused.

"Because we bought a place."

No one said anything for an almost unbearable amount of time. Genevieve seemed to want Allison to explain. Allison was, for some reason, unwilling.

It was so uncomfortable that Jane had the urge to laugh.

Finally, Genevieve said, "We have a squirrel problem. The exterminator recommended we leave for a bit while he does his thing." She sighed, a tad overdramatic, Jane thought.

"I swear, we've owned our house in Boston for over a decade and not had as many issues in all that time as we've had in this summer house in the past few weeks," Genevieve said.

"You live in Boston," Jane said.

Genevieve nodded. "Beacon Hill."

"I love Beacon Hill," Jane said.

It was her favorite neighborhood in the city. The sloping cobblestone streets, the gorgeous old brownstones with their historical details: boot-scrapers and lavender windowpanes, gas lanterns lining the sidewalks instead of streetlights. There was beauty and history everywhere you turned in that part of town.

The women of Beacon Hill had an outsize presence at the archives, especially those who lived there in the second half of the nineteenth century. Louisa May Alcott. Harriet Beecher Stowe. Sarah Orne Jewett. Rebecca Lee Crumpler, the first Black woman doctor in America, who started her practice to provide medical care to freed slaves after the Civil War.

Every time Jane found herself strolling through the area, she felt them around her, more real than the tourists with their Dunkin Donuts coffee and their selfie sticks. Nowadays the women of Beacon Hill were mostly investment bankers and partners in law firms, or else they were married to men who held these positions and did not work at all. Genevieve looked like she fell into the latter category. *Our house,* she had said. Not just an apartment in Beacon Hill. A house. A person would have to be unspeakably rich for that.

"Jane lives not far from you. In Cambridge," Allison said. "So she can be close to her job. At Harvard."

She sounded so self-satisfied that it was as if she had just said Jane played first base for the Red Sox.

"Jane runs the Schlesinger Library at Radcliffe," Allison went on. "You've probably heard of it. They have the archives of famous women. Amelia Earhart, Rosa Parks, Julia Child. Jane is highly respected in her field. She just won a huge award a few months ago. She has a PhD in American history from Yale."

Jane gave her a look.

"So," she said. "You bought a house here in town?"

"Just outside of town," Genevieve said. Absentmindedly, she ran her hand through her little boy's thick, dark hair. Again, Jane felt a pang and thought about what Clementine had said. Could she be pregnant? No.

"Genevieve bought your purple house," Allison said.

"Wait, what? Your house?" Genevieve sounded alarmed.

"Not really hers," Allison said. "It's kind of an inside joke."

Coupled with the hand in the hair, maybe, Jane felt flattened. As if she had been about to make an offer and Genevieve had swooped in and stolen the house from under her. It stood abandoned for so many years that Jane had long since stopped worrying that someone might buy it.

Whenever she and David came for a visit, they went to check on the property. One year, they arrived to find that someone had ripped the kitchen appliances out of the walls and taken them—where? Why?

Two summers back, they had a picnic on a blanket in the grass. They made love, brazen, unafraid. That was the last time Jane was there. The last time it would be theirs.

She felt bereft.

"What do you know about the house?" Genevieve said.

"Nothing, really," Jane said. "Just—I've always admired it."

"Did you know the previous owners?"

"No."

"It was a wreck when we bought it," Genevieve said. "You should come see the renovations sometime. Actually, I wonder if you might be interested in helping me with some historical research. I'm dying to know more about the house's original owners. As far as I can tell, there was a couple. There's a plaque for him, Captain Samuel Little- ton. Another woman, named Eliza, lived with them. I'm not sure how she was connected. I'd love to know anything at all about them. The ultimate would be to find a photograph to display in the house. To honor their memory."

A touching idea, Jane thought, just as Allison said, "I doubt Jane would have time. Her job is very demanding."

"Of course. I'm sorry," Genevieve said. She sounded chastened, but then added, "I would pay you whatever you think is fair."

The boy tugged at her dress.

"We better get going," Genevieve said. She reached into her purse and scribbled something on a piece of paper, then handed the paper to Jane. "If you change your mind and feel like a project."

Genevieve and her son walked the length of the porch, down the stairs and toward the sidewalk, where they disappeared behind the tall hedges.

"I loathe that woman," Allison whispered.

"I know."

"You could tell?"

"Uhh, yes. What was that?" Jane said, incredulous.

A certain type of Mainer, including a surprising number who worked in hospitality, approached tourists with an air of annoyance, even disgust. But, like her mother before her, Allison was the fur- thest thing from that. Guests returned to the Saint Aspinquid year after year because she had a gift for making them feel welcome.

"No one but me or Chris would ever be able to tell," Jane said. "Your coldest, bitchiest self is still way nicer than most people."

"That woman is the worst guest we've ever had," Allison said. "Impossible to satisfy. She's been coming every summer for five or six years. She spends the entire time complaining. And then she comes back! Why? To torture me. She called a couple of weeks ago at the crack of dawn, because a squirrel had gotten into her attic and somehow made its way down into a bedroom, so she needed to flee. Which, first of all—give me a break, it's a squirrel. In what, a seven-bedroom house?"

Jane thought she too would most likely have fled if a squirrel popped out of the ceiling, no matter how many bedrooms she had, but she let Allison go on.

"I so wanted to say we didn't have a room for her, but I couldn't lie. So now she's back, and she says she doesn't know how long she'll stay. She's got all the time and money in the world."

"Cheer up. That kid has to go back to school sometime," Jane said. "What, early September?"

"Don't even joke about that," Allison said. "The first time she stayed, she called down to the front desk and tried to order room service for dinner. Chris explained that we're a bed-and-breakfast, we don't have room service. I was in the kitchen and I could hear him very politely repeating this. I knew exactly who he was talking to too, because when she checked in, she asked to switch rooms twice, wanting the best possible view, when they are all the same. Anyway, Chris hung up the phone and the next thing, I swear to God, he comes into the kitchen and makes her a club sandwich."

"What?"

"Yeah, I don't know. She just has this entitled rich-person ability to get what she wants. When she told me she bought your purple house, I was so mad. Chris thought I was losing it. I was ranting on about why is it always these wealthy outsiders who get to have the gorgeous homes they will probably only use for a week each summer, and don't even love? Last month, she texted me to see if I wanted to get together with the kids," Allison said. "No thank you. I didn't even reply. Then two weeks ago, there she is again, asking me to go for drinks. I made an excuse, but didn't she just find her way in. Now she keeps trying to talk to me all the time. Like she owns me because she booked a room. I half want to tell her to quit acting so smug about her oceanfront property and remind her that it will probably be under-water in ten years."

"I don't think I've ever heard you so negative about a person," Jane said. "You sound like—me."

Allison reached over and plucked Genevieve's phone number out of Jane's hand.

"That was so like her. I tell her you're a renowned archivist, and then she asks you to do this dumb personal project for her."

"I'm not even remotely a renowned archivist," Jane said. "In fact, right now, I'm an out-of-work archivist."

"That's temporary," Allison said, as if willing it to be so. In a softer tone, she added, "Any word from Melissa on when you can go back?"

"*If* I can go back," Jane said. "And no, not a peep."

Melissa had been Jane's mentor. After she set Jane and David up, they became friends as well. On occasion, Jane and David would go on double dates with Melissa and her wife, Pearl. Out to dinner, or to see a show. Pearl and Melissa rented a house on Martha's Vineyard every summer. The last three years, Jane and David had gone to stay with them for a long weekend each May, so Jane and Pearl could run in an annual Memorial Day 5K.

On the night Jane lost everything, Pearl was there. She had just invited Jane and David to come to their house for Easter dinner. She was planning to make lamb and mint jelly and string beans and au gratin potatoes, she said. David said he would bring dessert, maybe try a strawberry shortcake recipe he had come across online that used banana bread in place of angel food cake. Melissa and Jane joked that they would bring their lovely selves. There was no warning sign that the bottom was about to drop out of her life.

And now, silence. It was possible that all that was over.

With each day that passed without a resolution, Jane was more certain that she would not be returning to her job. She missed work-ing. She missed office chatter, and the way her Sunday night melan-choly could be wiped away by the bustle of a Monday morning. She missed the energy of being on that campus, surrounded by bright young people from all over the world.

Above all else, she missed the work itself. Her days at the Schlesinger were full and busy. She developed exhibits and oversaw six junior archivists, as well as the student workers and interns. She was out of the office maybe a third of the time, meeting with prospective donors for lunch at one of the cafés near campus, or at their homes, where they sifted through old treasures together.

She would give anything now to do the very tasks she and her colleagues always complained about—to experience the itchy eyes and runny nose brought on by the dust and cigarette ashes and mouse droppings that collected in family albums and boxes of papers. Even to listen to some stranger drone on over the phone, insisting that her entirely mundane family member's story was riveting and deserving of a place on their shelves.

Melissa hired Jane eleven years ago, shortly after she herself was named executive director. From their first meeting, Jane was in awe of her. She was the first Black woman to hold the position. The first openly gay woman too. Like Jane, she had not been born into rarefied academic circles, but unlike Jane, she carried herself with such assurance and was so obviously brilliant that you would never know. Since then, Melissa had promoted Jane twice, most recently to the role of the collection's lead archivist.

In its early decades, the Schlesinger amassed a collection of mostly white, upper-class women's papers. But since the seventies, they had been at the forefront of inclusive collecting, with a focus on representing the lives of women whose voices had not yet been documented in any archive. The library did a series of oral histories, recording the stories of minorities and recently arrived immigrants who had no formal collections to share, but were nonetheless an essential part of the American experience.

Melissa's mission was to raise up even more voices. She never stopped probing the question of whose stories were told and by whom. Melissa wanted the archive to be a living organism, a gift they could take out of those temperature-controlled rooms and bring to girls in communities and families like the ones she grew up in. To educate and inspire.

In an oft-repeated speech to potential donors, Melissa said, "In

New England, everyone's crazy about documenting who founded a place, who got there first. We name everything for them, and they are, invariably, white men. The towns, the streets, the schools. But what about the ones whose names we will never know? How do we go about learning their stories and passing them on? I want girls of every race and creed and background to look up and say, 'Her. She looked like me and she accomplished the extraordinary.'"

Melissa's passion was contagious. Jane had always felt honored to be a part of the work they were doing.

"Can we go back to Clementine for a sec?" Allison asked, pulling Jane to the present. "She didn't say anything about David?"

"Not directly. She said she could tell I was in pain, that I did something terrible I need to face. Something like that."

Allison's eyes went wide. "She knew that? Dammit, Jane. You always bury the lede."

"That's not burying the lede," Jane said. "Burying the lede would be not telling you how she said I'm pregnant."

"Stop. Are you serious?"

"Yes. I mean, I'm not pregnant. But yes, she said that. She said my grandmother told her that either I was pregnant, or Holly was."

"Are you sure you're not?"

"I haven't seen David in four weeks," Jane said. "I had my period a week ago. So no, unless it's one of those cautionary tales you used to read about in *YM* magazine in the nineties—a sperm got trapped in the elastic band of some girl's underwear and activated later, that sort of thing."

"So then, maybe," Allison said.

Jane loved her. This friend who wanted her happiness so much that she was willing to believe in magic if it might be so.

"I think I still have a couple of old pregnancy tests lying around," Allison said. "Hopefully they're not expired. Come inside real quick."

Jane shook her head, but she followed.

She waited in the lobby while Allison went to look.

The last time they had an in-depth conversation on the subject of Jane having a baby was just a few months ago. It was astonishing, how quickly your whole life could change.

At that point, Jane was preparing to go off the pill, and having a small freak-out about it.

"I'm excited, I'm hopeful. I'm afraid," she said to Allison over the phone.

"Afraid it will be hard to get pregnant?"

"Yes, that. And also I don't know what to do with kids."

"You're great with my kids," Allison said.

"Yeah, I can do a few hours of Legos and Disney movies. I can order a pizza. But I don't know what to do with kids I can't return at the end of the night. Or, you know, ever."

"No one does until they have them," Allison said. "You'll figure it out."

"I can get my head around school days, school nights. But what am I going to do with them on weekends?" Jane said. "When it's just us. My mom used to leave Holly and me locked in the car for hours on end, listening to Jimmy Buffett tapes and eating Pop-Tarts while she was at estate sales."

"Well, you won't do that," Allison had said. "Because it's illegal now. But also, you just won't. Plus it won't be only you and them, like it was for your mom. You'll have David. He's going to be an amazing dad."

The only other time Jane tried to quit drinking (half-heartedly, but still), she and David had been married for a year, and everyone assumed she was ordering seltzer because she was pregnant. It made the real reason feel all the more shameful. That's where they were supposed to be at their age, as a married couple. Jane had fucked up the timeline. It was extra painful because she knew how much David wanted a child, and what a wonderful father he would be.

She wanted a child too. But everything Jane loved and longed for terrified her. She hated this about herself. Several times during her marriage, she had gone off the pill, and then, panicked, she went right back on. Then off again, then on. Her mother's death had set them back even further. David was patient. They agreed to put the baby thing on the back burner, as if they were unaware of how biology worked, or the fact that if they waited too long, the decision would be made for them.

A few months ago, finally, at thirty-nine, Jane woke up one morning and felt ready. Truly ready. After years of indecision, she was flooded with clarity. David was overjoyed. She began timing her ovulation, a step she had never taken before. She took several pregnancy tests, all negative, but that didn't upset her. Jane hadn't been trying long enough to get discouraged when everything fell apart.

Allison returned now, waving a stick wrapped in hot pink foil.

"My last one!" she said. "Maybe it's meant to be."

Jane rolled her eyes as she took hold of it, and went into the small bathroom by the front desk. But she felt a fluttering in her chest, a sense of excitement, in spite of herself.

She closed the door, and allowed herself to imagine that maybe she really was pregnant. What if fate had thrown her a bone? What if the ghost of her grandmother had interceded on Jane's behalf in fixing a miracle?

In that blue-and-white nautical-themed bathroom, Jane peed on the plastic stick, set it on the back of the toilet, and waited. For two minutes, she fantasized about what she would do if it was positive. She would call David immediately. She would go home to him and they would start again.

Jane was a striver, a self-made woman, who had never faced a test she could not pass if she put her mind to it. So despite all scientific evidence to the contrary, by the time 120 seconds were up, she believed.

But no second line appeared. Of course it didn't. There were no such things as miracles.

She stepped out of the bathroom, shook her head. Allison looked as disappointed as she was.

"So Holly's pregnant then?" Allison joked.

"Can you imagine?" Jane said. "Holly having two kids, twenty-one years apart? Actually, that does kind of seem like something Holly would do."

They laughed.

Allison hugged her.

"Sorry," she said.

"It's okay, I knew I wasn't," Jane said.

She inhaled deeply, stuffed the disappointment down.

"Speaking of Holly, I should get going. She's coming over in a bit so we can go through my mom's bedroom. That woman had so much stuff. It's insane."

The first things to go had been the massive pieces of furniture that were never intended to stay in the house but, rather, bought for resale.

"Mom didn't get how tastes have changed," Holly said to Jane soon after Jane arrived in Maine, as they were surveying the house and its contents. "We have to gear the business more toward high-end clothing and repurposed antiques. I kept telling her that. People don't want their grandmother's hope chest anymore. They want to buy trendy, flimsy furniture online for two hundred dollars so they won't feel bad switching it out for something else in five years. But I have the solution for that: sponge paint and Mod Podge. Your grandma's old crap, made over."

"Now that's a tagline," Jane said.

"If I'm honest," she said now to Allison, "I definitely thought Holly would do the cleanout if I waited her out long enough. Does that make me a bad person?"

"Kind of, but I won't tell anyone," Allison said.

Jane smiled.

"She lives so close. And she's not really doing anything else. Besides selling things on eBay that she just bought on Craigslist and watching *Days of Our Lives,* or whatever it is she does. But she seems content letting me do ninety percent of the work now that I'm here," Jane said.

She had made progress on their old bedroom. Enough so that she could sleep in there now. And in the kitchen and bathroom.

But their mother's room felt more *of* her than the rest of the house. Jane thought Holly should be there for this part. Earlier, she had moved their mother's ashes from the closet, knowing the sight of them might be too much for her sister.

"I guess I don't have anything better to do either at the moment," Jane said. "No husband, no job, no wine. What's left but decluttering?"

"Is it hard, the no wine part?" Allison said.

"Yes and no," Jane said. "Some nights it's really hard. Some nights I barely notice. I keep thinking the other shoe is about to drop, but so far, so good."

"I'm really happy you quit," Allison said. "I've been meaning to say, the AA meeting at the Presbyterian church is supposed to be great. It has helped a lot of people I know. I'd be happy to check it out with you if you want."

"My mom used to go to that meeting," Jane said.

"Oh."

"My sister too."

On and off over the years, Jane watched them use the program like someone who never goes to the gym but feels virtuous nonetheless for having the membership card in her wallet. They dropped in and out. Sometimes her mother went straight from an AA meeting to a bar.

Holly might stay sober for a few months, talking constantly, self-righteously, and exclusively about her sobriety, before unceremoniously starting up again.

Jane didn't want to be her mother, the one who tried every method of getting sober without success. She wanted to be her grandmother, the one smart enough not to drink in the first place. Though of course, that train had left the station long ago.

Jane and David used to walk home from work together when their schedules allowed. They passed a church at the edge of Harvard Square, with a sign out front announcing Tuesday night AA and Al-Anon meetings.

Jane had looked into Al-Anon. A twelve-step program for the relatives and loved ones of addicts.

Once, walking by that church, she half joked to David, "I should probably start going, huh?"

"To AA?" he said.

She swore he sounded hopeful. This made her feel ashamed, and then, for some reason, angry.

"I really don't think I need AA," she said to Allison now. "Truly. I'd go if I did. But quitting hasn't been that hard for me."

"Well, good," Allison said. "I was worried, obviously. I'm proud of you, Jane."

Something about this embarrassed her. Various bad nights flashed across her mind. Nights when she had been with Allison, or called Allison—in tears, or full of drunken laughter at a bar, singing loudly into her voicemail at one in the morning because a song they liked in high school was playing.

After the rehearsal dinner for Allison and Chris's wedding, Jane stayed out at an Irish pub with the groomsmen. The next morning, she was due at Allison's place at seven o'clock to help her get ready. Even with a hangover that made it feel like someone had her skull in a vise, Jane was there five minutes early with coffee and egg sandwiches. But Allison looked pissed.

"My brother told me he had to carry you home over his shoulder," she said.

Jane, amused, said, "He did?"

"You were flirting with some married guy. He was going to take you out on his boat. You were yelling at my brother to leave you there with your new friend, making a big scene."

Jane laughed. "Oh my God."

"It's not funny," Allison said. "Something really bad could have happened to you."

It had always mortified Jane, the way her mother grew more flirtatious when she drank, but Jane was like that too. Intimacy and alcohol were two parts of life with which she struggled, and when she combined them, trouble ensued.

Likewise, when Jane was young and her mother claimed not to remember the worst of what she'd done while she was drinking, Jane had never believed her. In time, she came to understand that as well.

She told Allison every absurd detail of her dating life as soon as it happened. The stories were meant to be entertaining, mostly. But once in a while it became clear to Jane that Allison was concerned. When David came along, Allison seemed happy to believe that Jane's wild days were behind her. Jane herself felt the same way.

After that terrible night three months ago, she confessed to Allison right away, and Allison was nothing but supportive. But her shock and her sadness were clear. Her inability to find a silver lining made it that much more obvious that Jane had dug herself a hole she could never get out of.

"I ruined the best thing I ever had," Jane said now.

"You're owning it," Allison said. "That's worth something."

"Really? Owning that I'm a broken fuck-up is worth something?"

"You're not broken. You're just—slightly damaged."

"Gently used," Jane said.

"A floor model," Allison said.

"Unfortunately not one in like-new condition," Jane said.

"Definitely not. But still plenty of use left in it. Sold as is, of course."

"Of course."

Allison cast her eyes down at the tabletop.

"Okay. Serious question. Do you think you did it on purpose to push him away?" she said.

"No," Jane said. "I don't know."

"You're both incredible people and you love each other. You'll find your way back to one another," Allison said.

But Jane could tell she wasn't entirely convinced.

5

AN HOUR INTO sorting through their mother's room, Jane hadn't found a single thing she felt like she needed to keep. Holly, meanwhile, had filled four large moving boxes with stuff. She was their mother's daughter.

Jane was a minimalist. Her mother knew this about her, and yet every time Jane and David visited, she had sent them home with some yard sale find she had been saving. It was always completely wrong. A collection of *Star Wars* figurines for David, who had never expressed a shred of interest in *Star Wars*. Assorted military paraphernalia. For Jane, there were loud blouses, two sizes too big and smelling of some stranger's sweat, and Beanie Babies, including one called Princess Diana, which was, for some reason, a bright purple bear.

"They're making a comeback," her mother said. "That will be worth thousands one day. Do not take the tags off, whatever you do."

At the end of every trip, Jane and David took whatever she had given them to the Goodwill in Portsmouth before they got on 95 South. Jane felt slightly guilty, but they couldn't bring these things home, where they would only take up space in corners and drawers.

When her mother died, Jane felt overcome with remorse. She had the strongest, strangest urge to go to Goodwill and search every rack and shelf until she found whatever was left of her mother's terrible gifts. She would buy them all back, keep them forever.

That urge had passed. Now she wanted only to see this house emptied out, put in order.

Tonight they had started with their mother's dresser, Holly reaching into a drawer and removing several sweaters, holding each one up, then putting them all in a box.

The sweaters were pilled and old. Half of them were speckled with moth holes.

"Do you actually want any of those?" Jane had said.

"I want all of them," Holly said.

"Why?"

Holly shrugged. "I just do." Quietly, she added, "They smell like her."

Jane could have cried then. For her sister's devotion, for her own inability to feel much at all. Instead she soldiered on, opening a drawer stuffed full of socks and mail—unopened bills and ten-year-old Christmas cards and a spring circular for a small department store that no longer existed.

"Who shoves their mail in a dresser drawer?" Jane said. "Jesus."

"It makes me really sad to think of throwing all this away," Holly said. "It's the stuff of her life, you know?" She teared up, sniffled, wiped her eyes. "But okay, fine."

The top of the dresser was loaded with tchotchkes. Holly took four porcelain cardinal figurines and a mug their mother had used as a pen holder, along with the cheap Bic pens inside it. She kept a makeup mirror, and snow globes from various European cities their mother had never even been to.

Jane wondered if Holly would ever open the boxes, or if she just could not bring herself to let these last bits of their mother go. In which case, what? All these remnants would someday become Jason's problem?

"The snow globes? Are you sure?" Jane said. "Some of those don't even have water in them anymore."

"I know, but the day she got them, we were at the Brimfield antiques show and we had the funniest time," Holly said. She started to laugh, thinking of it. "There was this old Irish guy hitting on Mom. His name was Bertie Flaherty, but when he said it with his strong accent, it sounded like he said *Bertie Farty*. We were laughing so hard, I peed. I just want to remember that, you know?"

"You'll remember it, with or without the snow globes," Jane said. "Keep them if you want. I'm just saying."

"I get it," Holly said. "You don't want to be dragging my body out from under an avalanche of old junk when it all falls down on me."

"More or less," Jane said.

A bottom drawer was full of back issues of *Allure* magazine and old Mega Millions tickets. Even Holly could admit there was nothing worth keeping there. Or, almost nothing.

She placed a single magazine on top of everything else she was taking.

"Why that one?" Jane said, amused.

"It has an article about brow shaping I want to save."

Jane nodded. "And you remember that, twenty years later."

"I do," Holly said. She flipped to the page to prove it. "Actually, on second thought, I could probably make a few bucks from these."

With that, she moved all the magazines to her pile.

Jane said not a word.

Beneath the magazines in the drawer there was an old yellow Walkman with a tape inside. Holly pressed play. The thing still worked. They each held one end of the rounded headphones to one of their ears.

It was a recording of the two of them, Jane and Holly, doing a pretend radio show.

"DJ Jane and Hare-brained Holly coming at you live," a child version of Holly said. She was maybe ten. Her voice had a squeak to it that made her sound even younger.

Jane, who would have been eight, spoke next. "Our sponsor today is Dave Dinger Ford. How does Dinger do it? Come and see. Come to Dave Dinger Ford in Braintree."

A song came on, half over. Jane remembered. To give the illusion of a real radio station, they recorded whatever was playing on the alarm clock radio and turned down the volume when they wanted to speak.

On the tape there was some whispering, followed by Jane saying, "And here comes 'Can't Fight This Feeling' by Chicago."

More whispering.

"And here comes 'Can't Fight This Feeling' by REO Speedwagon," Jane tried again.

Jane and Holly locked eyes and smiled. Then the sound squiggled to silence, the tape snapping midway through.

"Oh no," Jane said.

Holly wrapped the headphone cord around the Walkman and slipped it into her purse.

"You can't be serious," Jane said.

"What?"

"It's broken. It's a hundred years old!"

"Jason might be able to fix it, I don't know."

They moved on to the closet.

The first thing Holly pulled out was a slinky blue cocktail dress.

"You should keep this, it would look great on you," she said. "I don't have the curves for it."

Jane raised an eyebrow. "You know I'm almost into my fourth decade of hiding under tops that can double as two-man tents," she said.

"You should bring back that XXL Ani DiFranco concert tee you wore all of senior year of high school," Holly said. "It was so flattering."

Jane grinned. "Shut up."

She tossed the blue dress into the box marked *Donate, Goodwill*, knowing her sister would likely fish it out before the night was over.

Holly dragged a few shoeboxes to the rug. Old sneakers with holes in the toes and scuffed-up pumps in various sizes. Yard sale busts, Jane thought. She started pulling hanging items out and tossing them onto the bed.

After a minute, Holly said, "Holy shit."

From one of the shoeboxes, she had produced a diary. Leather-bound, pocket-sized, with a lock. They stood looking at it for a long, long time.

"Should we read it?" Holly said at last.

"Yes," Jane said. "Wait. No. Yes?"

"It's locked," Holly said.

"Those old locks are easy to break," Jane said. "Here, give it to me."

She was able to pop the book open with one clean tug on its covers.

"Well done," Holly said.

"Thanks."

"Do you think she wanted us to find it?" Holly said.

Diaries were among the most frequently donated materials at the Schlesinger. This was a question asked by so many donors. Were they honoring a legacy or violating a loved one's private thoughts when they handed a diary over?

What was the point of leaving such things behind if you didn't intend for anyone to read them? That's what Jane told those people when they asked. Privately she believed that in many cases, whoever wrote the diary had probably not expected to die before she could decide what to do with it; had kicked that particular can down the road until it was too late.

"I don't know," she said now. "It doesn't seem like something Mom would do."

"I need a drink," Holly said. "Want one?"

"No," Jane said. "Actually, sorry, there's nothing to drink in the house. I'm on the wagon."

"Oh. How long has that been going on?"

"A few months."

"Well, that's okay, I have wine in my car," Holly said.

Car wine. Of course.

Holly disappeared, and returned two minutes later with a giant wineglass filled to the brim.

Jane watched her take a long sip and felt envious. Had things been different, she too could be taking the edge off this discovery with alcohol. She didn't want to drink, exactly. But she thought about it every night around this time. Had to make the conscious decision not to, which for some reason required imagining the smell and the first taste, as well as playing the scenario out to its worst possible end.

"Here goes nothing," Holly said.

She opened the diary and cleared her throat, as if preparing to read aloud in front of an audience.

Jane covered her face with her hands.

"I feel like Mom is going to come in here and catch us," she said.

"Me too," Holly said. "My heart is racing."

She held out the book so they could both look. The cover page was printed with the words "This Diary Belongs To." Under them, their mother had dutifully written in by hand, *Shirley Flanagan.* Something about that made Jane ache.

"Turn the page," she said.

They read in silence.

Half a grapefruit, she had written. *Cottage cheese on toast. Black coffee, two cups.*

"What she had for breakfast that day," Holly whispered, as if deciphering some complicated code.

The rest of the book was blank.

"Shocker," Jane said, her immediate disappointment turning quickly to annoyance.

True, she herself had started many a journal with the best of intentions only to stop writing after an entry or two. But this felt personal. Like her mother saying once more, this time from the great beyond, that Jane would never really know her.

Women (and some men, but mostly women) came into Jane's office week after week with stories of their foremothers' achievements. Sometimes they were there to speak of their mothers or grandmothers, by whom they had been raised. But sometimes they went further back. A great-great-aunt or a great-grandmother they had never met but grew up hearing about. They had such tales to tell about these women. Not all of the stories they'd been told were true, but that was another matter.

Jane's family had no such stories. When she asked her mother about previous generations, her mother said, without curiosity, "We don't have any family."

"Everyone has family," Jane said.

She eventually pieced together their family tree. Her great-grandparents on her mother's father's side came from the west of Ireland and settled outside of Boston. Her grandfather survived the Battle of Okinawa only to die of a heart attack at forty-one. But that was just the bones. Jane had nothing to hang on them, no color with which to fill them in, to make these names and dates and places come alive.

She held this against her mother. Jane felt certain her grandmother would have told her all the things she wanted to know. Not only that, but she would have understood why Jane wanted to know them. About Jane's grandfather, her own father, Jane's mother said she remembered very little.

"He was really funny and sarcastic, like Jane," she told Jane and Holly once, when she was newly in love and in a radiant mood. She never knew how much that detail mattered to Jane, how Jane clung to it like a precious keepsake, how much it would have meant to hear more.

Their lack of relatives added to the sense Jane had of being alone, always. Throughout her life she had seen how having family added a fullness, an interconnectedness, to other people's experience of the world. It seemed every conversation Allison had with a stranger ended with the two of them realizing that her second cousin was his child's third-grade teacher; that her uncle had gone to prom with their aunt.

Holly interrupted Jane's thoughts now, saying, "My friend's friend Lauren Murphy is a killer Realtor. She said it's important to list a cottage like this while the summer people are still around. No one would consider it as a year-round home. Besides our family, of course."

Jane had been after her sister for months about selling. But now she worried about where she would go if they sold the house too soon. Renting someplace on her own, actually signing a lease, made her marital struggles feel far too real, and permanent. She was most comfortable floating in exile or purgatory or whatever this was, for the time being.

"I probably need another couple of months at least before any Realtors come in here," Jane said. "To get everything ready."

Neither of them stood to gain much from the sale. Their mother owned this house in name only, she had refinanced so many times. Until now, Jane cared about selling only because she was the one stuck paying the mortgage and the property taxes and the homeowner's insurance.

Having consumed half the wine in her glass, Holly went back to the kitchen and filled it to the top, then hoovered up as much as she had just poured. This time, she brought the bottle into the bedroom with her when she returned.

Jane wished David were there. His presence made everything easier, better. Especially around her family. Before she knew David, she might go a year without seeing them, making her excuses at the holidays. But he made them more bearable. Maybe because they no longer felt like all she had in the world. He was her home now. Or had been until recently.

Jane thought about the pregnancy test, and how reckless Clementine had been to put the idea in her head. She had sounded so sure of it too.

"Is there any chance you might be pregnant?" Jane blurted out, when she hadn't meant to mention it at all.

"What?" Holly said. "*Christ.* No. Why? Do I look bloated?"

"No! No. It's a long story."

"Well now you have to tell it."

"Did I tell you I was having this meeting with a medium?"

"A medium."

"Yeah. A psychic medium."

"Uhh no."

"Allison asked me to do it as a favor. Long story. But the medium came this morning and she said Mom and Grandma were here and Grandma said I was pregnant. Or maybe you were? Which I was pretty sure was bullshit."

"Wait. You had a medium come here? To Mom's house? And you didn't tell me?"

Jane paused, suddenly aware that she had messed up.

"It didn't occur to me that I should," she said. "I'm sorry."

"There's no way Grandma would speak through a medium," Holly said. "Even if that stuff was real, she wouldn't talk on principle. She hated that shit. It was against her religion. Plus there was the thing with Mom calling some TV psychic and running up a crazy bill when we were kids."

"I don't remember that."

"It was when we were here with Grandma for the summer," Holly went on. "Mom was melting down over some guy. She must have spent the entire time we were gone chain-smoking and calling that one-nine-hundred number. Grandma was furious. At Mom, but also at the company for preying on vulnerable women."

"Which guy was it?" Jane said.

"I don't know his name. He was married. It was a whole mess."

"Grandma told you that?"

"No, Mom did. She said it was one of the few times ever that Grandma didn't get on her case, because Grandma had her own thing with a married guy once. Well, you know about that."

"What?"

"Mom said Grandma told you. And something about you sort of rubbing it in Mom's face that you knew."

"I have no idea what you are talking about."

"Grandma was crazy in love with him," Holly said. "Mom was a kid at the time. She said Grandma would bring this married guy around and sometimes she would make Mom go to his house and sit there while they were in the other room. A couple times Grandma didn't even come home and Mom was here all by herself, terrified. She had just lost her father and been moved to a place where she didn't know anyone."

"That didn't happen," Jane said, indignant.

Their mother was the one who did that kind of thing. She left Jane and Holly alone all the time. She sometimes didn't return until morning, and they'd be so scared, up all night worrying that she was dead and they were now orphans, like Punky Brewster. She told them not to call their grandmother, but occasionally they did—when a door-to-door salesman wouldn't stop ringing the bell, when a storm knocked out the power and they started telling each other ghost stories by flashlight and scared themselves to death.

Holly shrugged. "I'm just telling you what Mom told me. She said Grandma came home one night completely hysterical, ranting on about what a bad person she was. Mom was pretty sure something awful happened with the married guy, but Grandma never said what. Mom was only like ten or eleven. It was super trauma-tizing, as you can imagine. After that, Grandma never mentioned the married guy again. To the point where if Mom mentioned him, Grandma would pretend she didn't know who Mom was talking about."

"Because Mom made the whole thing up," Jane said.

When Jane was a kid, her mother sometimes said, "My mother was no picnic to live with when I was growing up. You think she's a saint. You have no idea."

She was threatened by how much Jane loved her grandmother. She wanted to change Jane's high opinion of her, but it never worked. Jane needed her grandmother to be her constant, even after she was gone. Even now.

The year her grandmother died and they moved into this house, Jane started reading all the books on the shelves, title by title, in order of where they sat. She finished each one, even when they were totally inappropriate or over her head—*1984, Persuasion, Valley of the Dolls, The Complete Stories of Flannery O'Connor, The Grapes of Wrath,* and everything Maeve Binchy ever wrote. Jane didn't come to the end of them until she was eighteen. Upon finishing the last book (it was *Love in the Time of Cholera*) she felt bereft. But the sight of the books on the shelves remained a comfort. Sometimes she pulled one out because she knew her grandmother had jotted down her grocery list or a phone number inside its back cover.

When Jane returned home for Thanksgiving break her first year at Wesleyan, the books were gone. Her mother, in a rare fit of tidying up the house, had sold them. Jane felt in a way that her grandmother had died all over again. She wept.

Her mother claimed not to understand.

"But you'd already read them," she said. "They were just taking up space."

Space that she had filled back up with lightly chipped Hummel figurines. A commemorative plate from the JFK inauguration suspended on a stupid metal stand. A Wade Boggs bobblehead in a protective plastic cube.

Jane could never decide if her mother sold the books out of subconscious spite or if she really didn't know what they meant to her.

Either way, she took the whole episode as proof that her mother didn't understand her at all.

Her mother felt bad. She tried to buy the books back. The hardcovers were easy, still right where she'd left them. But the mass-market paperbacks with greasy sunblock stains were gone. She had sold them for a nickel apiece to the secondhand bookstore in Winston, where they were scooped up by tourists, for whom the books' appeal was that no one would mind if they accidentally got left behind on the trolley or if a wave washed over them when the tide reached their blanket sooner than expected. Those were the books Jane cared most about. The ones her grandmother wrote in and stuck old receipts into. The ones that showed signs of her. To this day, the sight of Maeve Binchy's name made Jane's stomach drop in despair.

Because she did not wish to think about this anymore, Jane told Holly about D——the ghost girl sitting in their grandmother's lap, who kept interrupting. How the medium had told her to find D's mother and pass along a message.

"Why was she sitting in Grandma's lap?" Holly said.

"I don't know."

"No way," Holly said. "Don't do it. Do not reach out to the mother."

"I never said I was going to. I don't even know who she is. If she's even real, which she isn't."

"You won't be able to resist scratching the itch," Holly said. "I know you. You get obsessed. But seriously, Jane. Don't. It's a trap. Didn't you watch *Debunked*?"

"No," Jane said.

"This woman named Amy Jackson is the host. She started a firm for debunking."

"A firm for debunking."

"Yes. They did a whole season on psychics. Amy has a staff and all these volunteers. They spend months making fake Facebook profiles for people who don't exist. They create a backstory. They put in a mix of really somber, personal things, like today is the anniversary of my father's death, but then also links to macaroni-and-cheese recipes and inspirational quotations and pictures of cats. Then they sign up for a public event some famous medium is doing, under the fake name.

These mediums pull details right off the fake social media pages. Like once Amy went, using the name of one of her fake Facebook personas. A made-up woman whose made-up daughter, Penny, died of cancer. And the medium stood on that stage and said, 'Someone in here lost a daughter.' Amy raised her hand. The medium told her, 'I have Penny here with me.' Fucked up, right?

"There was one episode about all the times Sylvia Browne went on the Montel Williams show to talk to people whose loved ones had disappeared."

"Who is Sylvia Browne?"

Holly looked at Jane like she was painfully stupid. "She's one of the most famous psychic mediums of all time."

"Okay. Go on."

"She always led people in the wrong direction. Remember the girl who was chained up in that guy's basement in Cleveland for all those years? Sylvia Browne told her mother she was dead. The mother died believing it. A few years later, her daughter escaped. Oh, and there was this grandmother who vanished. Her whole family was on *Montel*. Sylvia told them the initials of the guy who abducted her. She said the grandmother was still alive. Sylvia shook hands, on camera, with this woman's son-in-law. And guess what."

"He killed his mother-in-law," Jane said.

"He killed his mother-in-law," Holly repeated, in such a way that Jane could not be sure whether her sister knew she had just said that exact thing. "Sylvia set the investigation back by years and never even apologized," Holly said. "I don't know. That stuff freaks me out. If something bad is going to happen, let it happen. I don't need to know in advance."

"You just spent five minutes telling me why you don't believe in any of it," Jane said.

"Frauds exist in every profession," Holly said. "That doesn't mean you discount the whole thing. This medium you talked to. Did she say anything that rang true?"

"She knew you were Mom's favorite. And that Mom hated me."

"She didn't hate you, Jane. She just—felt like you looked down on her."

"Well, I didn't."

That was a lie. She did.

"But come on, she was proud of you," Holly said. "She loved you. You know that."

Jane was skeptical of declarations of love. They were too easy; they could absolve a person of too much.

"I only lived in Cambridge," she said. "It's not even two hours from here. She never once came to campus to see my work or to our apartment."

"You didn't invite us to your wedding," Holly said.

"I eloped!"

Holly put her hands up. "I'm just saying, it went both ways with you two. You never really got one another."

Hours after their mother died, Holly posted a picture online of the two of them out to dinner somewhere, with their identical smiles, faces pressed together. Holly captioned the photo Me and you against the world, Mom. RIP.

Where did Jane fit into that?

She loved you, Holly said. But what did love even mean?

When their mother drank, especially in their adolescent days, it was Jane who got the worst of her outbursts. She hurled insults. She once fell down drunk and, when Jane reached out an arm to help, accused Jane of pushing her. Her mother might act sheepish the next morning but otherwise it was as if none of it had happened, and they moved forward, moved on, having no other choice.

Remembering this now, Jane felt a flare of regret. She had always wanted to know why she was the object of her mother's fury. Her death had not been sudden. Why hadn't either of them tried harder to connect at the end?

Holly poured herself more wine, took a sip, placed the glass on the nightstand.

She flopped onto their mother's bed, and lay flat on her stomach, knees bent, feet in the air, like she used to when she was twelve. She started scrolling through her phone.

She had to be well beyond tipsy at this point. She wasn't even attempting to pace herself.

"Have you eaten today?" Jane said. "Why don't I order a pizza."

Holly wrinkled her nose without looking up from the phone. "Too greasy. I prefer to drink my calories."

That was something their mother would say. That was something their mother *did* say.

Since Holly wasn't paying her any attention, Jane took out her phone too. No texts.

Out of habit, she checked her work email, though Melissa had instructed her not to reply to any messages that came in during her leave. An automated response alerted the sender that Jane was not checking her inbox, with instructions for whom to contact instead. At first, there were dozens of messages each day. It felt like a punishment watching them arrive, unable to reply. But recently they had reduced to a trickle, which was its own kind of torture. Things at work, it seemed, were going fine without her.

Friends and colleagues had stopped reaching out after she canceled all future dinner plans without explanation and stopped replying to their texts and calls. It wasn't that Jane didn't want to speak to anyone; it was just that she had no idea what to say. How to explain what happened. And so much of her social life revolved around people who were close to both her and David. She was paranoid about how much any of them already knew.

At the top of her inbox now was a message from a Genevieve Richards with the subject line Great to meet you today!

Yes, Melissa had said not to open emails, but this one didn't count. Jane clicked on it.

Hi Jane, It was so nice to meet you at the inn. I hope you don't mind, but I looked up your contact info. I just want to reiterate that I would love to talk to you about maybe doing some research on the former owners of my house! At the very least, you should come for a drink. Please let me know when you might be available. Yours, Genevieve

Jane put the phone down.

"What are you doing?" she said.

"Looking at guys on Tinder," Holly said.

She scrolled her finger across the screen.

She held the phone out to show Jane a picture of a good-looking guy, vaguely familiar.

"This motherfucker," Holly said. "I met him the normal way."

"What's the normal way?" Jane said.

"In a bar," Holly said. "We slept together twice and then he ghosted. Then I see him on here and he swiped left on me. Not interested. Now that's just rude."

Jane read his profile. Please be chill. If you love drama, keep moving. Codependent? No thanks. I'm a professional, kind, fit, fun-loving guy looking for great times. ENM

"What's ENM?"

"Ethically non-monogamous," Holly said.

"Eww."

Jane couldn't think of anything encouraging to say about Tinder, so instead she asked, "Do you talk to RJ much these days?"

RJ was Jason's father. A pretty good guy, Jane thought. A fisherman from a long line of fishermen. He was gone for long stretches, all through Jason's life. But when he was around, he was a decent-enough influence. He took Jason to Portland Sea Dogs games and out for ice cream. He seemed more like an uncle than a dad, but Jane had always had a soft spot for him. Every time she saw RJ, she could tell he still had feelings for her sister. Holly had dismissed him as a viable option when they were young and she got pregnant, assuming someone better would come along.

"I can't just recycle my high school boyfriend," Holly said now.

"Why not?" Jane said.

Holly groaned. "You are so lucky to be married, I cannot even tell you."

It was true, Jane thought. She was lucky she didn't have to deal with this stuff. So lucky to have David. Then came that horrible stomach-dropping-out feeling of remembering that she didn't.

When Jane arrived here in May, she told Holly she had the summer off and had decided to use the time to get the house ready to put on the market. Jane didn't tell her the rest, and Holly didn't ask. They had never had the sort of sibling relationship where they told each other much of anything personal.

But now, from a place beyond her control, Jane started to cry. It felt like an actual nightmare imagining having to start her whole life over without David. How did people do that? She could not begin to envision having to meet men online. If such a thing was hard for someone as naturally social and confident as Holly, Jane herself was doomed.

"Jane?" Holly said, jumping up and coming to her side. "Oh my God, are you okay? I'm here. I'm with you."

Jane took in huge gulps of air. She couldn't catch her breath.

"Sit down and put your head between your legs," Holly said. She rubbed Jane's back. "Breathe. Just breathe."

Jane did as she said, focusing on the inhale and exhale. After a minute, she felt better.

"Thank you," she said, wiping her eyes with the tips of her fingers.

"What was that?" Holly said. "I think you had a panic attack."

"The thing is," Jane said. "David and I——"

She started to cry again.

"He left you," Holly said, as if she had been expecting it. Not because of anything particular to Jane and David, Jane thought, but because this was what men did in their experience.

"No," Jane said. "I left."

"Why would you leave David?"

"I didn't leave David, I just——it's hard to explain. He needed to be free of me."

"He said that?"

"No. It was my decision."

"So you're happy about it?"

"No, I am miserable."

Holly looked confused, like she wanted to ask more questions. But instead she hugged Jane tight, for a long time.

Maybe Jane had underestimated her sister. Maybe she had been wrong not to trust her sooner with the truth.

Pulling away, Holly said through a burst of wine breath, "Can I say something?"

"Yeah," Jane said.

"You know I love David, but I always found his blond hair suspicious. I don't trust blond men. A man should not be blond unless he's a literal baby. Right?"

"What?" Jane said, incredulous.

She started laughing and could not stop.

FORTY MINUTES LATER, Holly had crossed a line from pleasantly drunk to complete trainwreck. She was slurring her words; her eyes were glassy. There was only maybe an inch and a half of wine left in the bottle.

Jane said she would drive Holly home. Holly scoffed and said that was ridiculous, she was fine to drive, she only lived five minutes away.

This conversation. It was exhausting. It was boring. It was horrifying to look at her sister and know that she had been in Holly's shoes, many times.

They went a few more rounds, then Holly twisted on the cap of her wine and put the bottle into one of the boxes she was planning to take. She got to her feet, lifted the box, and promptly stumbled forward, losing her balance.

Under the table, Jane texted Jason to ask him to come pick up his mother.

She felt bad for doing it. As a teenager, she was on the receiving end of more "Come get your mother" calls than any young person should have to be.

Jason texted back a thumbs-up emoji.

"I'm going," Holly said, reaching for her purse. She took the box and started toward the door.

Jane followed.

Outside, Holly set the box down on the step, then started digging through her purse for her keys.

Jane's heart pounded, knowing Jason was in a race against the clock. If Holly found the keys, she would go. How far was Jane willing to take things? Would she wrestle the keys away, throw them in the bushes? She had done this to her mother in the past, on multiple occasions. David had done it to Jane once too.

A couple and their two young kids walked by eating ice cream cones. Jane gave them a big smile. *Nothing to see here.*

Just as Holly said in a bratty voice, "Found 'em," and jingled her keys in Jane's face, their mother's red Toyota Camry pulled up. For an instant, Jane thought it *was* their mother. She thought this every time. Jason had taken her car when she died. It made sense. He needed a car and there was one in the family, just sitting there. But Jane wished he would trade it in for something else.

Jason reached over and opened the passenger-side door.

Jane all but shoved her sister into the car.

"Sorry, bud," she said. "Thanks for doing this."

"Don't act like Jason is doing you a favor. He's *my* son," Holly snapped. She narrowed her eyes at Jane.

"She hasn't eaten anything," Jane said.

"Don't talk about me like I'm not here, Miss High and Mighty," Holly said. "Seriously, like you're any better?"

She wouldn't remember any of this in the morning.

Jane slammed the car door shut. She watched them pull away, realizing too late that after all that, Holly hadn't taken the boxes.

Jane reached down into the box at her feet and picked up the wine bottle. She twisted off the cap, breathed in. She held the bottle to her lips, considering, before dumping the contents into her grandmother's azaleas. Back inside, she went to the freezer and pulled out a pint of mint chip.

Two nights ago, she had impulse-bought a chocolate birthday cake at the grocery store. A small one (*serves 6–8,* the label read), decorated with puffy frosting balloons in primary colors. A kid in a hairnet wrapped it up, and asked if she wanted anything written on top. Jane briefly considered asking him to pipe out *Jane, You Are an Idiot* or *Quit Stuffing Your Face* but she demurred.

She ate the cake alone, straight from the box, straight from the knife, one sliver at a time, telling herself that she was done, then going back for more. By the time she went to bed last night, the whole thing was gone.

Now she removed the lid from the ice cream and stood watching it soften, before digging a tablespoon in. The thought of using a bowl crossed her mind. She dismissed it.

Jane ate half the pint, then put the rest in the freezer, proud of her restraint.

She felt a lingering gloom from the scene Holly had made. There were many ways to define what it meant to be an alcoholic, but for Jane it was when drinking changed your personality. When it made you mean. Her mother had been like that. Her sister was like that. Jane was like that too.

She dropped into bed without washing her face or brushing her teeth.

As soon as she laid her head down, the events of the day came flooding back. It felt like weeks ago that Clementine showed up at her door.

All the conversation about dead people, with Clementine, with Allison and Chris, with Holly, had not seemed particularly heavy in the light of day. But now Jane felt scared. It embarrassed her, this childish instinct that nighttime was inherently more sinister. But it felt true, imposed as it was in the minds of girls and women everywhere.

In their apartment building in Cambridge, she had refused to go down to the laundry room after dark. Only David walked the dog alone at night. When she was single, she slept with a giant knife under the bed. Life held the threat of so many horrors. Murderers. Lost souls. Jane thought about D. The weight of a missing child who wanted to tell her mother something. Missing, how? Kidnapped? Trafficked? There were dark corners of this world that everyone knew existed and yet couldn't, or didn't, do anything about. When Jane imagined a child killed in a situation like that, the only relief was in knowing that whatever the suffering, it had ended. But if what Clementine had said was true, death wasn't the end.

An unexpected aspect of her work at the archives was comforting the bereaved, who were handing over their loved one's papers and possessions. Jane wasn't very good at it at first. She didn't know what to say. But over time, she realized that for those people, sad as they might be, the process accomplished the impossible—it gave them one more experience with their lost loved one.

Jane didn't believe in ghosts or heaven, but she believed in the power of stories, written, told, and handed down in the form of objects left behind.

What if D's mother was like that? A person for whom only Jane could provide solace.

She knew it wasn't true. Jane wasn't pregnant. There probably was no such person as D. It was all nonsense, but she couldn't stop thinking about it.

Jane missed David. The way he took care of her. The way he understood her strange impulses, most of the time. She wanted to call him. To tell him all the crazy details of her day. Maybe even about the pregnancy test, how sad it made her when it turned out to be negative.

It had been weeks since they stopped talking on a daily basis. That had been her choice. But she was finding it particularly agonizing tonight. Nothing ever felt quite real until she shared it with David.

She wanted to see him, to smell him, to hold his hand.

She imagined asking him to meet her, just for the night. Maybe midway between them, a nice hotel on the coast, where she could sleep in his arms, the way she used to every night, and they could wake up together, themselves again.

Instead, she tried to focus on the novel she had been attempting to read for a month, but she couldn't pay attention. She could always lose herself in a book until recently. Being unable to do so was a shock to the system, a greater surprise than the fact that she and David were apart, that she was living here, that the job she loved was most likely no longer hers.

Her laptop was on the nightstand. She opened it.

In what had become a pathetic ritual since she left, Jane went to his Facebook page. David never posted. He had used the same profile picture for years. But it was the one she most wanted to see, the two of them on their wedding day, smiling goofily at one another, so in love.

Memory had taken on new meaning for her these past months. She thought so many times each day about the thing she had done to ruin her life, but she could not remember it.

That night was far from her first blackout. But it was the first that made her fully aware that she was capable of doing things she wouldn't recall the next day, that could fundamentally change how the person she loved most saw her. She didn't remember the events that had severed their marriage. How could that be? Where was she, Jane, in that moment?

Where was her mother now, her body in ashes? Why would her grandmother care whether or not Jane knew that she hated the green kitchen cabinets? Did the living matter as much to the dead as the dead did to the living?

Jane had tried, at some desperate point with David, to blame what happened on grief. Grief for her mother that she wasn't even sure she felt. She felt it now in some new, unbearable way. Tangled up with her regret over him. Sometimes the tragedies of a person's life didn't happen neatly, single file, one at a time, but all at once, so that it was impossible to know how you felt about any part of the whole.

Jane stared at their wedding photo. Was it meaningful that David hadn't changed his profile picture? She knew it wasn't. He probably hadn't looked at Facebook for months.

She had left for his sake. To make herself better for him, or to give him space to decide he was better off without her. But she didn't know if this had been the right thing to do, or what move she ought to make next.

Just to feel something, anything, else, Jane clicked back to her email inbox. Genevieve's message was still at the top. **Great to meet you today!**

She believed Allison about Genevieve. Jane knew the type. They had patrons like that at the archives, entitled rich women who felt they were superior to everyone else, and needed to be indulged.

But Jane knew how to manage women like that. It didn't much matter to her whether or not she liked Genevieve. It was a job. A job that would give her an official reason to explore the house she had loved and wondered about since she was seventeen.

Genevieve couldn't be all bad. She was going to lengths to honor the former occupants of her home. Wasn't it a good sign, that upon buying an old house, she had immediately gotten curious about its original owners?

Jane replied with a quick note saying she was happy to take on the project.

To her surprise, Genevieve wrote back immediately, asking if Jane might be able to complete the work in two weeks' time, at which point she could come to the house to show her whatever she'd found.

Jane responded that the timeline sounded fine, but she would love to visit the house sooner, as soon as possible, to look around.

Two weeks it is! Genevieve replied. **Come to the house then, not sooner. I'm worried about the squirrels and the exterminator and all. Let's wait. Okay?**

Sure, Jane wrote. She didn't know what dangers an exterminator could possibly cause her, or why he needed two more weeks. But no matter. She would wait.

She closed her laptop.

She longed to sit beside her grandmother on the sofa, head on her shoulder, as her grandmother stroked her hair, and told her what to do.

Clementine had told Jane to go out in the backyard and the voices would come. Wisdom, there for the taking.

An hour earlier, she was afraid. What if she decided not to be? To take the risk, to walk down the alley alone. To do that, she supposed, you had to have reached a point of feeling like you had nothing to lose, which conveniently, was exactly how she felt at this moment.

Jane went out in bare feet. Even as she reminded herself that she did not believe in what Clementine said, she stood on the deck listening for a long, long time.

She didn't hear a thing, besides the wind in the trees.

6

FOR THE NEXT TWO WEEKS, unable to face her own problems, Jane lost herself in the puzzle of Genevieve's house.

Allison told her she would come to regret accepting the offer, and that whatever Genevieve was paying her, it wasn't enough.

For once, Jane thought, Allison was wrong. Genevieve was paying her the equivalent of a month's salary at the Schlesinger. And the research assignment was a welcome distraction. There was something intoxicating about finding a clue that led to another and another and another. This was the one thing Jane had ever done that could make hours feel like minutes, could help her forget the troubles that might otherwise sink her.

She logged on to various genealogy sites and property databases using her work credentials, grateful that no one had changed the passwords. In minutes, she found the records for Genevieve's house. The land had been handed down from a descendant of one of the town founders in 1843 to his grandson, the ship captain Samuel Littleton, whose name was on a plaque by the house's front door. According to the land records, the home's construction began in 1846 and was completed two years later.

Jane was shocked to see that the 1860 census listed Samuel as deceased and his wife, Hannah, as head of household. A maid, Eliza Green, lived with the family by then.

She found a record of death for Samuel. He died at thirty-four, a year before the Civil War began. How strange, Jane thought, to miss the event that defined your generation. His cause of death was listed as drowning.

Samuel's wife, Hannah, lived to be eighty. Three of their five children—Alfred, Polly, and William—died in infancy.

Through some strange alchemy, Jane felt Hannah's sorrow. There was something profound about holding it up to the light, remembering what the woman herself no longer could. Jane imagined her, already bereaved on account of her children, and then widowed, alone at such a young age. Hannah never remarried, having had, Jane supposed, her fill of heartbreak for a lifetime.

On Monday night, she read everything she could find about Samuel Littleton's ship, the *Providence*. The Maine Maritime Museum had included it in a 1996 exhibit about the state's famously turbulent seas. There was still a description on the museum's website.

The *Providence*'s entire crew was lost on what should have been the final day of a three-year voyage. Entering the tidal passage from the ocean to its hometown shipyard, the *Providence* met with stormy seas and went down less than an hour before it was meant to reach the harbor. The community was devastated. The sailors' loved ones saw the whole thing happen from the shore, but were powerless to help. It was somehow worse than a ship going down far away, in open water.

How had Jane never heard the story before? She called the museum as soon as it opened the next morning to ask if they had more information. The man on the phone was kind, and happy to help. He emailed her pictures of paintings of the wreck from the museum's collection, and a letter Samuel Littleton wrote to his wife on his last, fateful journey. She had had a child while he was away, a son he was eager to meet. He wrote that he could not bear to be apart from Hannah any longer. He had arranged for her and the children to come with him on his next voyage, a three-year journey to Indonesia that was never to be.

Jane wrote it all down for Genevieve. She thought about the *Providence* as she walked Walter along the craggy coastline at sunset, imagining the boat's shape out on the water. She imagined Hannah Littleton, eager to see her husband again. Excited to go with him on that journey to a part of the world she had never seen. Her life, her children's lives, might have been so different in so many ways had Samuel not died.

Once Jane knew about the Littletons, she couldn't help but imagine them at the house, populating spaces she had previously thought of as her own. She pictured Hannah and Samuel on the porch, taking in the view. Hannah alone there, looking out at the sea, worried for her husband during long voyages. And later, as an old woman, thinking back on her life and losses.

Jane envisioned the children reading on the window seat in the living room, or running barefoot through the grass, maybe daring to climb down the cliff ledge when they got a bit older and their mother wasn't looking. She saw the maid, Eliza, standing tiptoed on a chair, cleaning the glass transoms above the doors, or down on her knees, buffing the hardwood, dreaming of a day off at the beach with her beau.

Jane searched for contact information for the house's most recent owners, the people who sold it to Genevieve. She figured maybe they knew something of its history. Marilyn and Herbert Martinson had divorced almost fifty years ago. He had since died.

She still lived in Philadelphia. Jane looked her up online and learned that Marilyn had been a painter of some renown in the sixties, though she hadn't done anything since. She read an appreciative blog post about how Marilyn vanished from the art scene and how it was a pity because she was so full of promise.

Marilyn would now be eighty-eight years old. She had a landline listed in the white pages online. Jane called her twice, leaving a message both times. She was fairly sure she had the right number. The voice said, *We aren't home right now,* but Jane knew that was something women of a certain age who lived alone said on their outgoing voicemails. Years ago, her grandmother had done the same on her answering machine.

BY WEDNESDAY MORNING, she had taken her research as far as she could on her own. Jane crossed the bridge over to Abe Adams's lobster boat at ten o'clock. She knew he would be in the cove, between tours. Since running into him at the two-cent sale, Jane often saw Abe in the early mornings while she was out walking the dog, but she usually just waved hello and kept going.

"What's up, kiddo? You looking to get your tour guide job back?" he teased when she approached.

Abe was dressed in his usual uniform: a bright blue polo shirt, with the name of his boat—*The Great Escape*—embroidered over his chest. Bright orange rubber bib pants, held up with black suspenders. A worn Red Sox cap.

He opened the bed of his blue Dodge pickup and placed a pile of brochures there, securing them under a rock.

"Maybe," Jane said. "You hiring?"

"I'd hire you back in a second," he said. "The kids I have now, ooh, they're sloppy. No fear, either. They show up late. They don't memorize the script, they just read it. Or worse, make things up as they go along."

Jane thought of Allison's mom, her invention of a Revolutionary War ghost. Visitors to Awadapquit had been getting a miseducation from the locals for decades when you thought about it.

"I'm helping a friend gather information about the original owners of her house," Jane said. "It's one of those big old houses up on the cliffs."

She pointed off into the distance.

"Lucky friend," he said. "Nice of you to help her investigate."

Jane didn't say that Genevieve wasn't really her friend. That Genevieve was paying her. That she was doing this to distract herself from the fact of having crashed her life.

She liked talking to Abe. He was someone she had never disappointed. He still saw her as the high school version of herself. A good girl.

"The man who built the house was captain of a ship called the *Providence*," she said. "I guess it was a pretty famous shipwreck at the time."

Jane couldn't help but tell Abe the details, even as she wondered if she ought not to, if they might upset him.

Abe nodded along as she spoke. He didn't seem bothered.

"Oh yes," he said. "I remember hearing this story as a kid. I don't think anyone's mentioned it to me since."

It never failed to astonish Jane that an event, a local tragedy, could shape an entire generation and then be forgotten. It was no one's fault. There was too much history to contain. Down through the ages, men had tried by agreeing on what was important—wars and explorers and kings. But where did the rest end up? What was it worth?

The longing for answers to these questions took on many forms. It was religion, it was mediumship, it was what Jane had dedicated her career to. How many times had she been called upon to sift through the rubble of some semi-noteworthy woman's attic after she was gone, facing down the travel photos and the tiny boxes of baby teeth and the bad landscape paintings and the love letters, charged with trying to make order or meaning out of it all?

Abe told her about the *Liberty*, a Revolutionary War–era sloop that had washed up on the beach in nearby Winston and was buried completely. Once a decade or so, he said, a storm came through and whipped up enough sand to expose what was left of it. He pulled a cell phone from his pocket and showed her pictures. A ship's hull and planks emerging as if from nowhere, the boardwalk in the background—the arcade, the bars, the burger joints—boarded up for winter, covered in snow.

"This was what, seven years ago? February '08," he said. "Remember that big nor'easter? Some kids were playing on the beach. The waves were huge and sand and snow were flying everywhere and all of a sudden, this ship appears. Scared the crap out of them."

Jane laughed.

"You should talk to Lydia Beazley," Abe said. "She runs the town historical society."

"I didn't know Awadapquit had one," Jane said. "Where is it?"

"It's in the back of what used to be Lydia's camera shop, which is now Lydia's toy store. Up at the head of the beach road."

"Ahh."

She had been picturing something more formal, something official.

"Yeah, I wouldn't get too excited if I were you," Abe said. "But tell her I sent you. I think you'll get a kick out of each other."

———————

BY THE TIME Jane arrived at the shop ten minutes later, Lydia was expecting her.

"Abe called ahead," she said. "Come on through."

Lydia had shoulder-length silver hair, with heavy bangs cut straight as a yardstick. She wore a fitted khaki skirt, with a hem that skimmed her knees, a crisp gray cardigan set, and canvas slip-ons.

Jane followed her through two rooms full of racks and shelves displaying every toy a child could want. A section of baby dolls in pink boxes, and accessories for the dolls—miniature strollers, high chairs, plastic bottles of fake milk. A section of board games. Picture books and puppets and water guns and beach toys. Puzzles and crafts and dress-up for rainy days. A whole wall of stuffed animals.

"Your shop is adorable," Jane said.

"Thanks. Do you have kids?"

"No."

"Me neither. I used to sell cameras and run a one-hour photo here," Lydia said. "Photography is my passion. Really, I'm not big on children. If you had told me twenty years ago that I'd run a business catering to them, I would have told you you were crazy. But then, if you'd have told me I'd be out of business because by now everyone would just take pictures with their telephones, well, that would have sounded even crazier."

Lydia led Jane into a dim back office full of silver filing cabinets. So different from the rainbow of good cheer on the other side of the door. There were piles of books and papers everywhere. Built-in bookcases on one wall held old, dark leather-bound volumes. On another, wood-paneled, hung framed black-and-white photographs of what Awadapquit looked like a hundred years ago. Unspoiled by the condominiums to come. One lot where now there were six or seven. Jane stared at the pictures, projecting herself into that other version of this place.

"Sorry it's such a mess," Lydia said. "This was supposed to be temporary, but—" She shook her head. "Oh, don't get me started."

Jane didn't say anything, but Lydia continued on as if she had been begged to.

"Years ago, the town council voted to fund a dedicated space for the Historical Society, but it never happened. We even found the perfect spot. The former Elks lodge with the big green yard out back on Elm Road. Totally flat yard, would have been ideal for outdoor events. At the last second, the select board voted to turn it into a senior center with lawn bowling instead. Idiots."

"That's a shame," Jane said. "It would be great if the town had a place like that."

"It's embarrassing that we don't," Lydia said. "Most people don't even know all this is here."

Jane told her about Genevieve's house, how Genevieve wanted to honor its past.

"My house was built in 1753," Lydia said. "My ex-husband had to duck whenever he was on the second floor, the ceilings are that low. It's not something I was willing to change. That house will outlive us all. I'm not an owner, only a caretaker."

"Absolutely," Jane said.

"I wish more people understood that," Lydia went on. "It can be frustrating to dedicate time to preserving the past when it seems like nobody cares. I was in charge of organizing all the In Memoriam benches on the Cliffwalk, dedicated to various interesting people who've lived here or visited. But does anyone ever look up the names to learn who they were, or even bother to read them?"

"I do," Jane said.

Lydia smiled.

Jane knew exactly what Lydia meant. There were people who wanted history honored, preserved. And there were people, far more of them it seemed to Jane, who didn't see the point. History could only ever be as meaningful as those alive were willing to make it.

She remembered going along with David on a work trip to Nashville. While he was at the conference, Jane visited Andrew Jackson's homestead, because this was what she did whenever she went someplace new—sought out the nearest historical home or museum or walking tour. A busman's holiday, her grandmother would have said.

Given Jackson's legacy on this former slave plantation, she hoped to find a tour that was somber, reflective. The guide was a young kid with pimples all over his cheeks. The group was comprised of high school students on a field trip and tourists killing time until the Grand Ole Opry started. None of them seemed to question the guide's assertion that many of Jackson's slaves remained loyal to him after the Civil War, because though Jackson was harsh, he loved them like he loved his own children. When the guide spoke of slaves who attempted to escape and had dogs sent after them, dogs that took chunks out of their calves, half the teenagers grimaced like they were watching a car crash in a movie. The other half stared at their phones. As they walked into the former slave quarters, two women in the group were loudly debating where to go for barbecue after.

The detail that got the biggest response was the revelation that in Andrew Jackson's day, many people washed their hair only once a year. All assembled, young and old, exclaimed in horror at that.

Jane was not exactly surprised by these reactions, but she still found them depressing. At the hotel bar that night, she railed on to David about how most people were, when you got right down to it, pretty terrible. They got more worked up about last week's episode of *The Bachelor* than they did about living in a country built by slaves and founded by slaveholders.

Or maybe that was too harsh. Maybe it was more a function of education, of learning *how* to see. Jane had been raised in a household where topics like politics and social justice were never mentioned, and considered almost frivolous compared to the demands of every-day life. But then she had gone to Wesleyan, where so many of her classes focused on marginalized voices. They were talking about rep-arations and allyship and gender fluidity twenty years ago. She had seen things through this lens ever since.

David pointed out how lucky Jane was to work among people who insisted upon wrestling with and digging into the past, even the ugli-est parts, and the unknown parts.

He was right. She felt grateful whenever someone walked into the Schlesinger wanting to know about a woman lost to time. They had over four thousand archival collections. Every week she got requests for Angela Davis's papers, and Julia Child's. But Jane loved when a patron inquired about someone she herself didn't know was there. Most of the papers were archived off-site. She felt so pleased for them when they got to make a special trip to the library.

A few months back, a young woman had asked to see the files of Dorothy Dignam, who was part of a rarely visited collection about the history of women in advertising. Jane watched as she sat for hours, riveted, carefully turning each page. At one point, the young woman gasped. She had opened a diary and the dried-up petals of a hundred-year-old wildflower had fallen out and onto the table.

Jane wanted to tell Lydia about her work at the Schlesinger. She thought Lydia would appreciate it. But she didn't want to get into why she wasn't there now. So instead she told her about Samuel and Hannah Littleton. Lydia knew the story, vaguely.

"Your friend's house—it's that big Victorian, the pale purple one, right?" she said.

"Yes!" Jane said. "I've always loved it. A million years ago, when I was in high school, I used to go exploring there."

"What a property. I'm glad your friend is giving it a new life. It's a crime that the last owners let it fall into disrepair the way they did."

"Did you know them?" Jane said.

Lydia shook her head. "Out-of-towners. Came for the summer, brought every person they had ever met, and kept to themselves out there. One year they just walked away from it. Never came back. Apparently they didn't give a damn about leaving the house to become an eyesore for the rest of us. I heard they had a nasty divorce and the house got tied up in that. There was talk at one point about the town seizing the property. The Littletons were a big family around here. Still are, if we're talking real estate. They own most of the buildings in the cove to this day, even if lots of them have moved away. I know a few who are still around. I can put you in touch if you like."

"Thank you," Jane said. "That would be great."

"Ethel Troy was part of that family," Lydia said. "Littleton was her mother's maiden name."

Jane made a face that indicated she didn't know who Lydia was talking about, and Lydia added, "Ethel lived in that house too."

Lydia went to the bookshelf and pulled down an old-fashioned looking volume, with a green leather cover.

"Here's Ethel," she said. "Take a look at this. There are a couple other things I want to find for you. I'll keep looking."

She handed Jane the book she was holding. Embossed on the front were the words *A History of Awadapquit, Maine, by Ethel Troy.*

The book was published in 1949 by a small press in Kennebunkport.

The introduction laid out the facts. *Awadapquit, which means "where the beautiful cliffs meet the sea" in the Abenaki language, was settled in 1642. Shortly thereafter, an Englishman named Ephraim Littleton was given a grant of 100 acres in order to build a sawmill on the Awadapquit River. I am a proud descendant of this great man, who made shipbuilding the main way of life in our town.*

Jane wrote down Ephraim Littleton's name. He was related to Samuel, clearly, though she couldn't work out how exactly.

The book went on to list the names of the next ten men to build sawmills here. Six of them were Littletons too.

I swell with pride when I think of these brave ancestors, forging ahead in a new world despite the perils that lay just out of sight. Vicious redmen knew the woods, knew where to hide, and when to pounce on these honest workers and their families. The savages claimed many innocent lives in the early years, including that of Ephraim Littleton himself. His home and sawmill were burned simultaneously and he is believed to have been inside one or the other structure on that fateful day.

Again, Jane made a note: *Samuel descended from town founder, who was killed in a raid.*

She thumbed through a chapter about Awadapquit's first court, established in 1644. An early order held "that any wife who shall speak of her husband in a dishonorable manner may, at his discretion, be held in the stocks for three hours, and subsequently whipped."

In 1658, the town erected a "ducking stool" as a means of punishment for the same offense, "for the administration of the husband at his will and pleasure."

Ethel Troy had outlined, without commentary, precisely how it worked—the offender was strapped to a chair, which was connected somehow to the end of a pole, and then submerged into the frigid water below as many times as the wronged party deemed fit.

Essentially, if a man didn't like what his wife had to say, he was legally encouraged to waterboard her.

"Jesus," Jane said under her breath.

She read on.

Legend has it Awadapquit was first sighted by the British explorer Archibald Pembroke in 1605. The voyager made many stops up and down the coast on that consequential journey, and returned to England with a handful of savages, as instructed by his bene-factor Sir John Fernsby. The captive redmen were ordered to describe the location from which they came. Fernsby was taken with their detailed descriptions of a fertile and beautiful land, rich in resources. He immediately financed further exploration of the area, leading to the arrival of some of New England's first colonists a few short years later.

Jane felt a jolt of recognition. Archibald Pembroke. He was the one rumored to have landed on the island across from Genevieve's house, for whom there was once a small monument, though it had since washed away in a storm. The story went that he had christened the island, as well as many other landing spots up and down the coast, just as Ethel described. How many times had Jane mentioned Pembroke's name on one of Abe's tours? And yet she had never heard about any captives. She wondered now what happened to those men.

She also wondered about the source of Ethel's claim that Pembroke landed here at all. It was entirely possible she had made it up and, with the passage of time, her version of events had become the one trusted and shared by people like Abe Adams. Lydia had said Ethel lived in Genevieve's house at some point. Perhaps that explained why she had chosen the island directly across the way for her story.

Jane reread the passage, noting but not surprised by the words Ethel had chosen: *Redmen. Savages.* Reading something from a decade ago could make clear how the culture had evolved, or not. Something from almost a century ago, all the more so. Language conveyed whatever the author was trying to tell but also, unintentionally, the attitudes and prejudices of a person, a time.

When Jane turned the page, there was a photo of the monument to Pembroke, alongside two other pictures of signs of the same size, their letters engraved in a single coordinated font. All three signs were dated 1930. Jane looked closer. One was located a few miles south, in York. It read: IN MEMORY OF THE WORST INDIAN ATTACK IN AMERICAN HISTORY. ON CANDLEMAS DAY 1692 ABENAKI INDIANS LEFT THEIR SNOW-SHOES ON THIS ROCK AND IN THE DAWN OF A JANUARY MORNING CREPT INTO YORK AND CAPTURED OR MURDERED THREE HUNDRED SLEEPING INHABITANTS.

The third monument, according to the book, was in Winston, the town just north of Awadapquit.

WINSTON'S LANDING. IN 1630, THE INDIANS SOLD THEIR LAND NEAR THE MOUTH OF THIS GREAT RIVER, AND REMOVED TO TERRITORIES NORTH.

A caption stated that all three signs had been paid for by the Maine Antiquarian Society, part of a statewide "Indian landmark trail."

One told a story of murderous violence unleashed upon innocent colonists in their beds. Another, of a peaceful and willing handing over of land. Jane assumed neither was accurate, which made her want to know the true version of events.

She opened her mouth to say something about this to Lydia, just as Lydia shouted, "Here it is!"

She handed Jane a booklet, held together by two staples.

The Homes of Awadapquit, Maine. (1952)

It was a collection of brief histories of the oldest houses in the area.

Jane found Genevieve's house on page 47. There, in brief, was the story about Captain Littleton, killed at sea, and his wife, Hannah, left behind to raise her two children on her own.

She turned the page to a black-and-white sketch of the house, with a dozen wicker lawn chairs arranged on the grass.

A fine example of the early Victorian style. Currently owned by Ethel Troy and occupied by Ethel and her sister Honey, since 1916.

Ethel Troy again. And now, her sister Honey. Jane made a note about them, then turned the page.

The Troy sisters have welcomed boarders to the Lake Grove Inn for many years. They have room for up to fifteen guests.

Lake Grove.

Jane thought of Clementine, of D, for the first time in days.

A boardinghouse was exactly the kind of place where a girl might have met with foul play. She might have been anyone passing through. D was not necessarily of this town, probably not someone whose mother Jane could find if she tried.

Jane wanted to share the whole story, to tell Lydia how a girl named D had insisted via a medium that Jane should let her mother know she was no longer at Lake Grove. But she sensed that she shouldn't. You could tell who was up for woo-woo and who was not. Lydia, with her salty matter-of-factness, didn't seem the type.

Instead Jane said, "It says here the Troy sisters called the house the Lake Grove Inn. I've been trying to locate someplace called Lake Grove for this other project I'm doing. I wonder if this was it."

"I think there have been a few places around here that have been called by that name," Lydia said. "There's the country club. And—what else?"

"But where is Lake Grove? I mean, the actual lake. There isn't one, is there?"

"I never thought of that," Lydia said.

Reading on, Jane learned that the sisters had modernized the house, adding indoor plumbing and electric lights. They ran a highly successful business for nearly three decades, remaining afloat even through the Depression. During World War II, the US military commandeered the property. Guests were no longer allowed. The sisters themselves were pushed out for a time and had to live in a small rented apartment in town. A radar station was built in the yard, and manned every hour of the day by soldiers on high alert for German U-boats.

Jane pointed this out to Lydia, who said, "Now, isn't that fascinating?"

The doorbell rang, twice in a row.

Lydia groaned.

"Come with me, we can talk out there," she said. "Bring the books."

Two families had entered the store. A dad in swim trunks and flip-flops with three small boys in tow. And a pair of women with a little girl, who was older than the other kids, though Jane could never say how old children were. Was she maybe nine or ten?

Lydia greeted them all. She was friendly enough, though she did not attempt to muffle the sigh brought on by the three boys knocking a bunch of miniature monogrammed license plates off a spinning wire rack and onto the floor.

Jane was still thinking about D, and how Lydia might help her. Genevieve's house was the former Lake Grove Inn. Was it the place D referred to? Maybe Jane had been called to do this research, drawn to the house itself all those years, for a reason.

The fact of having had such a thought alarmed her slightly. Her meeting with Clementine must be rubbing off.

They stood behind the counter. Jane said in a low voice, "This will probably sound weird, but a girl died. Her name started with the letter D, I think. She died at Lake Grove."

"The country club? Or the inn?"

"I'm not sure."

"When was this?" Lydia said. "What happened to her?"

"I don't know, exactly."

Jane thought she sounded insane, but Lydia didn't seem to notice.

"There was that triple homicide out there at a house right next to the club, in the eighties. A young lobsterman and his fiancée and a friend of theirs. It was a stabbing. Drug-related. Crackheads, you know."

The adults in the shop all shot her a look. Lydia wasn't bothering to keep her voice down.

Jane quickly searched online for mention of the murder. None of the victims had names that started with *D*. And it hadn't happened at a house near the Lake Grove country club, but at a house adjacent to the public golf course across town. It surprised her how much she had wanted it to be D, so that the puzzle would be solved. Maybe also because if Clementine was the real deal, that meant that somewhere out there, Jane's mother and grandmother actually had gone on living, in a way.

LATER THAT AFTERNOON, Lydia forwarded Jane an email from one of the people she'd reached out to on Jane's behalf, a Rose Littleton, who lived in town and was distantly related to Samuel's branch of the family. She had attached hundreds of pages of Littleton genealogical records, and said that while she had no information specifically about Samuel, she was fairly certain the Maine Historical Society in Portland did.

Jane sent an email to an acquaintance from grad school who worked there.

She had last seen Evan three or four years ago at an archivists' conference in Miami focused on adapting to changing technologies, a frequent discussion topic and cause of concern in their field. So few people today wrote, never mind saved, letters. They took a thousand pictures a month but didn't bother to print them. They clicked a button and a year's worth of correspondence over text was deleted forever.

But all the anxiety assumed that this was a new problem, when in fact the vast majority of women's writing—their love letters, their diaries—had always been discarded. Burned by the creator or her children, thrown away, lost.

At the Schlesinger, they endeavored to find out what women of the past truly did and thought and felt, while also understanding that you could possess volumes of someone's autobiography and still not know any of that. It was an utterly modern idea that one's diary should be a confessional. Jane believed people were now leaving more honest chronicles of their lives behind than ever before. They existed on blogs and social media, in emails. The challenge was how to capture them.

Evan responded to her message after just a few minutes, saying that he wasn't sure whether he had anything on the Littletons, and inviting her to come in person the next day so they could search together. After that, he would be launching a big new exhibit that he had spent months working on. After *that,* he was taking a weeklong vacation with his husband and kids, in part to make up for all the late nights he had spent on the exhibit.

Jane went, happily, grateful for the change of scenery. She liked Portland, with its bustling streets and active seaport and charming old redbrick houses. The museum itself spanned three buildings, one of which had been the childhood home of Henry Wadsworth Longfellow.

As she parked her car, it dawned on Jane that someone had probably told Evan what happened with her job. Theirs was a small world. A small, gossipy world. She wished she had thought of this sooner. She wouldn't have come.

Evan greeted her in the lobby. He had put on maybe twenty pounds since grad school, and now had an endearing bald spot forming at the back of his head.

He asked how things were at the Schlesinger.

Jane assessed his tone. It sounded genuine. She was fairly sure he didn't know.

"Great," she said. "Busy."

This was the week she was meant to present a paper at an annual women's studies conference in London. Jane had been working on it, almost finished, when everything fell apart. One area of discussion at the conference would be how archives historically dedicated to women could and should adapt to a nonbinary world. This was something they talked about often at the Schlesinger. She had been eager to discuss it with colleagues from various cultures, to hear their ideas and bring them back to share with her team.

Melissa was supposed to go with her. Jane was looking forward to spending time one-on-one, to long dinners together, just the two of them. Trips like this were how they had gotten to know each other well in the early years of working together. Melissa maintained a healthy professional distance in the office. But a location change made things looser, more spontaneous.

Jane wondered if Melissa had chosen to bring someone else in her place. She swore to herself not to check the conference website later, though she knew she likely would.

She wondered if David was still meeting Melissa and Pearl for dinner sometimes, if they sat around talking about what a mess Jane had turned out to be, how she had fooled them all into thinking she was normal.

"So this ship captain you're interested in," Evan said. "Is that work-related?"

"No," she said. "Just something I'm investigating for a friend."

He brought her back into an enormous research library.

"I looked," he said. "I found a couple of things."

They were the same newspaper articles Jane had already read, about the shipwreck.

She tried to hide her disappointment.

"Thanks for meeting me when you have a new show going up tomorrow," she said.

"Of course."

"What is it, by the way?"

"It's incredible," Evan said, his face lighting up the way Jane's did when she was excited about some new endeavor at work and had the chance to tell someone about it. He sounded almost giddy, like a kid with a crush. She missed that feeling.

"It's all about the history of the Wabanaki, the Indigenous people of Maine," Evan said. "As told by Wabanaki people themselves. We wanted to center Indigenous Mainers instead of othering them, basically. An effort toward decolonizing the museum experience. Since, as you know, in most museums, the best-case scenario for depictions of Native Americans is like a life-size diorama of a wigwam, with mannequins in loincloths holding spears and killing a taxidermied buffalo."

Yes, Jane thought. And the worst-case scenario was the situation at Harvard, where human heads were kept in drawers.

"I'm certain decolonization will be our generation's contribution to the field, as much as some previous generation's was to amass the stolen goods and create all the stereotypes in the first place," he said.

Jane thought of the photographs she had seen in Ethel Troy's book, of monuments erected by some long-ago antiquarian society.

"I hope you're right," she said.

"It was one of the reasons I left HHNE—they weren't getting this message," he said. "Of course now that I'm gone, they're all over it. New director is all about inclusion and telling a broader story. Not that I'm bitter. Okay, maybe a little."

HHNE, or Historic Homes of New England, was where Evan had worked before he took this job. A smallish org with a big budget and an exceedingly wealthy board that bought historic properties in Maine, New Hampshire, Massachusetts, and Vermont and turned them into museums.

"Do you want to come check out the exhibit?" Evan said. "It's almost done. You'll be one of the first to see it."

"I'd love to," she said. They walked together down a long corridor.

"So how did this all start?" Jane asked.

"We have a beaded purse from 1863 in our permanent collection," Evan said. "The label on it says *A pocket book made by Mollocket, the last of the Pequawkets.* Ever heard of her?"

Jane shook her head.

"A bit farther north, her name is all over. They call her Molly Ocket. There are schools and businesses named for her. A holiday in her honor in Bethel. That label, though. It just bugged me every time I saw it. She's famous, partially anyway, for being the last of her people. It's such an outdated, dangerous idea, you know? Indians were here, but now they're gone. There's this Australian historian, Patrick Wolfe, who says settler colonialism is a structure, not an event. It's ongoing, and part of what keeps it that way is the idea that Indigenous people aren't here anymore. When they're very much here. If you want to fight colonization, you can start by telling the stories of the people we've been taught to believe went extinct long ago. I got really inspired by a trip to the Abbe Museum up in Bar Harbor. Have you been?"

Jane shook her head.

"It's an entire museum dedicated to the history and culture of the Wabanaki. It tells the story in all its difficulty, but it's a joyful place too. I wanted a similar feeling here, for this. I know this brilliant Penobscot woman, Naomi Miller, who has done some work with the Abbe. So I reached out to her. We got her a grant to come on board as a cultural advisor to the project. She brought in a bunch of other great people. And this is the finished result."

Jane recalled the story she had read the day before, about the Indigenous men captured by Pembroke and forced to educate his benefactor on the virtues of their homeland. She mentioned it. Pembroke's name didn't ring a bell for Evan, but he said he would go back to the research library and check to see if they had anything.

They stopped in front of a set of double doors. A sign out front read WABANAKI VOICES: PAST, PRESENT, FUTURE.

"Go ahead in," Evan said. "I'll meet you in there."

There were a dozen or so people working quietly. Two guys up on a lift, hanging a massive canvas. A pair of women reading over something on a piece of paper.

Jane knew how busy they were, how much there was to do at the eleventh hour before a show like this. She tried to stay out of their way.

The first section gave an overview of the Wabanaki confederacy, comprised of four federally recognized tribes—the Maliseet, Mi'kmaq, Penobscot, and Passamaquoddy—as well as others whose tribes had been decimated, and for whom no official tribal land existed.

There were once twenty tribes at least in what was now called Maine. An interactive map of the state allowed you to click on any town to see which people had originated there.

Questions to consider, read the screen. Where are the descendants of these people today? Were they forced to relocate? Where did they go? . . .

Jane clicked on Awadapquit and a text box popped up on the screen: For ten thousand years, this was the land of the Pennacook/ Abenaki. In the wake of settler colonialism, in the late seventeenth and early eighteenth centuries, the members of these tribes who had not already been annihilated by war and disease mostly fled to Canada, allied with the French. There are today two Abenaki reservations in Quebec, but not a single one in Maine. The Abenaki are not officially recognized as a tribe by the United States government.

Next was a section on how this came to be. It contained a page from the journal of the Reverend Thomas Smith, eighteenth-century Unitarian Universalist minister, pastor of the First Church, in what was now Portland. In 1755, he wrote of organizing a posse to round up, murder, and scalp Wabanaki men, women, and children, after the lieutenant governor issued a proclamation that bounties would be paid as followed: 50 pounds for every live male above the age of twelve, or 40 for his scalp; 25 pounds for any live female or boy younger than twelve, or 20 for his scalp. Smith wrote that he received 198 pounds, "my part in scalp money."

In the description below this it was written that the Indigenous people who were captured alive as a result of these roundups were most likely sold into slavery in the West Indies. And that to this day, there remained in that church, right beside the pulpit, a plaque honoring Reverend Smith, its longest-serving pastor. Meanwhile, in the 1880s, the federal government tried to ban Native rituals, calling them "repugnant to common decency and morality." The legal prohibition on practicing their religion lasted until 1978.

There was a quote from Thoreau, regarding the Penobscot people of Maine: "The ferry here took us past the Indian island. As we left the shore, I observed a short shabby washerwoman-looking Indian; they commonly have the woebegone look of the girl that cried for spilt milk . . . This picture will do to put before the Indian's history, that is, the history of his extinction."

There were documents about state hospitals in New England carrying out forced sterilizations, forced abortions, on Indigenous women. And parents forced to separate from their children, who were taken away to federal boarding schools to be "civilized" and often ended up abused, neglected, or dead.

DID YOU KNOW THAT IN THE 1960S, AROUND A THIRD OF ALL NATIVE AMERICAN CHILDREN IN THIS COUNTRY WERE TAKEN FROM THEIR FAMILIES AND PLACED IN THE FOSTER CARE SYSTEM? read one sign. CONSIDER HOW THE REPERCUSSIONS OF THIS ARE STILL FELT IN FAMILIES TO THIS DAY.

One section told of how the Penobscot Nation and the Passamaquoddy Tribe fought on the side of the Americans in the Revolutionary War, how George Washington promised them aid and protection for their land for these efforts, because without Wabanaki people, the Americans could never have held the territory that later became Maine. But once the war was won, none of the assurances were granted. Washington became one of the richest landowners in America by dispossessing Native people of what was rightfully theirs.

For the next two hundred years, the Penobscot and Passamaquoddy people lived in poverty, under the control of state-appointed Indian agents. Indian Island, the Penobscot reservation, didn't have running water until the late nineteen-sixties. Indigenous people weren't allowed to vote in state elections in Maine until 1967.

In 1980, as part of the Maine Indian Claims Settlement Act, the federal government paid the Maine tribes just over 80 million dollars as compensation for stolen land, after a yearslong legal battle between the state and the tribes. Though the money was welcomed, many now believed that the specifics of the state's requirements related to the act had only served to thwart the realization of sovereignty for the tribes, cementing the state's paternalistic relationship to them.

The exhibit came right up to the current moment, offering glimmers of hope. One section detailed possible amendments to the Settlement Act. Another was all about a growing movement based on following Indigenous values in order to heal the earth and fight climate change, viewing the land through a lens of kinship, rather than ownership. There was a mention of land acknowledgments, not as a matter of placation but as a call to action. The United States could return national parks to the appropriate tribes if it wanted to. Greater commitment could be made to support tribal sovereignty.

The Penobscot River had been polluted by industrialization since colonizers arrived. At one point, the river was so overwhelmed with sawmills that logs covered the water from shore to shore, making it impossible to navigate by boat. The English dammed the river to prevent fish from spawning, in order to starve the Penobscot. In more recent years, illegal waste from a paper mill had poisoned the water, making fish and plants that fed off of it toxic for human consumption.

To combat this, the Penobscot Nation, in their tribal census, had recently granted personhood and citizenship to the river. For thou-

sands of years, the Penobscot River had been a source of nourish-
ment, spirituality, medicine, and culture for their people. It was their
means of traveling for hundreds of miles in any direction. The river,
they wrote, was an ancestor to every member of that tribe. As such,
the river had "all rights, powers, duties, and liabilities of a member
of the Penobscot Nation by birth." They would protect and honor it,
just as they would anyone else who was their kin.

Jane moved on to the final section, a collection of photographs of
contemporary Indigenous leaders and innovators in Maine and the
rest of New England taken by a young Mi'kmaq photographer. There
was a picture of a woman named Jessie Little Doe Baird, a citizen of
the Mashpee Wampanoag nation in Massachusetts. A typewritten bio
explained that her ancestors were the ones who greeted the *Mayflower*
upon its arrival. In the 1990s, in her early thirties, she began dreaming of these ancestors. They were speaking to her in their native language, which she did not know. No one had spoken it in 150 years.
She was a social worker, a mother of five. She took it upon herself to
revive the language, with the help of an MIT-based linguist. She now
ran an immersion school on Cape Cod.

In the next photo was a striking Passamaquoddy named Geo Soc-
tomah Neptune—tall, with a shaved head, tattoos, vibrant makeup,
and a feathered headpiece. The plaque read INDIAN TOWNSHIP,
MAINE, MASTER BASKETMAKER, DRAG ARTIST, ACTIVIST, TWO
SPIRIT.

Jane fished around in her purse for a notebook. She wrote the
names down. Already, wheels in her head were turning.

All this was happening just a couple hundred miles north of where
she grew up, but she hadn't known any of the details. There was
almost no Native presence in the part of Maine where her family
lived, as far as she knew. For the first time, she wondered about the
Littleton family and their role as town founders, as they were always
called. As if no one else had been there before them.

She was just approaching a black-and-white photograph of a woman
in a blazer, with short, dark hair, when Evan came up behind her and
said, "She's a badass."

Jane was embarrassed to admit she had no idea who the woman

was. She looked closer at the name printed beneath the frame. STATE REPRESENTATIVE DONNA LORING.

"She's brilliant," he went on. "She was a senior advisor on tribal affairs to the governor for a while, and a tribal representative of the Penobscot Nation in the state legislature. Not to mention, the Penobscots' first woman police chief. She served in Vietnam. She's been fighting for tribal sovereignty for decades. And she's responsible for the state law that says public schools have to include Indigenous history and culture in the curriculum."

"Wow," Jane said. "I didn't know about that. That was definitely not the case when I was in high school. I'm pretty sure the only time Native Americans got mentioned was on Thanksgiving."

"Yeah," he said. "Apparently the implementation of the law has been hit-or-miss so far. But still, it's major progress, right? And she's one of the people who pushed for the new law that prohibits Native American mascots in Maine public schools. You know, teams called the Indians, or the Chiefs or whatever. Maine's the only state in the country to do that so far."

He sounded proud.

Evan held forth a book. "Okay, I may have kind of struck out on your Captain Littleton, but this is interesting," he said. "A few of those early explorers left behind entire books detailing their journeys. In this case, it looks like just one letter survives. It's a long letter, though, written by one of the men on board Pembroke's ship in 1605. It was written to the guy who bankrolled the voyage, and it mentions the kidnapping a few different times." Evan opened the book to where he had placed a yellow Post-it. "See here? Tricking those men is described as 'a matter of great importance for the full accomplishment of our voyage.' It was totally premeditated, of course."

Jane took the book from him and read the page.

There were details of how the sailors got the men to come aboard under the guise of friendship, then forced them belowdecks. Five or six white men attacked each of them. Surprised by their strength, they dragged them down by their long hair. They tied them up, and took them away.

The letter described the hostages as "specimens," but they were also mentioned by name. Jane wrote each of the names down in her notebook, for purposes that were not entirely clear to her yet. This was often how it went with her work. Important stories had a certain shimmer around them, and she knew to tuck them away for later, when she would better understand why.

As they went to leave the room, they crossed paths with a tall woman in a navy blue pantsuit who looked to be in her fifties, her long black hair tied back in a ponytail.

"Here's the genius behind a lot of this show," Evan said. "Let me introduce you. Naomi Miller, meet Jane Flanagan. Jane and I went to grad school together. She's been checking out the exhibit. She's impressed."

"I'm blown away," Jane said.

"Thank you," the woman said.

"You two should know each other," Evan said. "Jane, Naomi is a citizen of the Penobscot Nation. Grew up near Indian Island in central Maine. She's the one I told you about. She has a consultancy. She's providing an antidote to what our collection lacks. She's doing this work here and elsewhere. Helping us fill in blind spots. Naomi works with the Wabanaki Nations to repatriate photographs and audio recordings, all kinds of things. And then deepen the stories of those objects. Like all these museums and collectors have the objects, but they have no idea about the meaning behind them or the people who made them or why. Naomi's work is about connecting those dots."

"That's fascinating," Jane said to Naomi. "I'd love to hear more. We should have coffee sometime, if you ever have time."

"You should say yes, Naomi, because Jane works at Harvard and they desperately need your help, and also they have deep, *deep* pockets," Evan said jokingly. "Also, I just think you two would like each other."

Evan seemed a little punchy. He probably hadn't slept, given the exhibit was opening so soon.

"I'd be happy to," Naomi said.

"Jane's a Mainer, too," Evan said. "She grew up in—was it Awadapquit?"

"That's right," Jane said. "Good memory."

"Where the beautiful cliffs meet the sea!" he said.

"Now you're just showing off," Jane said with a smile.

Evan gave her a conspiratorial look.

"In other news," he said. "Naomi just got engaged."

"Congrats," Jane said.

Naomi shook her head, dismissing Jane's enthusiasm.

"We're not having a big wedding or anything," she said. "It's my third marriage. What is that old line? *Remarriage is the triumph of hope over experience.* You might say that's my mantra."

She smiled wide.

Jane smiled back. She was pretty sure Naomi was doing the thing she herself often did—getting to the painful punch line about her own failings so that no one else could get there first. Or as a means of letting everyone know that she knew what they were thinking, even if they weren't.

A couple of feet away stood a girl holding a clipboard. She looked about twelve years old. She piped up then, in what sounded to Jane like a child's voice: "Triumph of hope over experience. Sounds like the tribes' relationship in trying to work with the state of Maine."

"Ha," Naomi said. "Nice one."

Naomi's whole body seemed to relax. Jane liked her. A woman who was far more comfortable talking about her work, her calling, the world—maybe anything—than she was talking about her personal life.

"Jane, my summer intern, Loreen," Naomi said. "Loreen was a fellow at Harvard last year."

So this was not a Take Your Precocious Child to Work Day situation. This child was in fact an adult.

"Jane's at the Schlesinger," Evan said.

"Oh!" Loreen said, lighting up. She had that look of someone preparing to ask, *Do you know so-and-so?*

Jane felt like a fugitive about to be caught.

"You should come to the opening tomorrow," Evan said. "Donna Loring is going to speak. And there will be this incredible drum ceremony."

Jane froze. "I wish I could, but—"

Evan waved his hand in the air as if to say he required no explanation.

Jane congratulated them on the exhibit and said she had to get going.

Out in the hall, she thanked Evan. When they hugged goodbye, she felt sad to leave him, even though she hardly knew him anymore. But Evan was one of her own. She was used to spending all her time with such people. Margot, her office mate, whose hobby outside of work was leading marathon sessions building Wikipedia pages for minor female historical figures. Melissa, who read two books a week for fun. David. Their intellect, their shared curiosity was always where the two of them connected with the greatest ease.

On her way out of the museum, Jane stopped into the gift shop. There was already a table set up for the new exhibit. They were selling baskets and miniature canoes and drums and moccasins, all handmade by Native Maine artisans. Jane bought several of the books on display—Donna Loring's book, *In the Shadow of the Eagle.* A book specifically about repatriation called *Plundered Skulls and Stolen Spirits* by Chip Colwell, curator of anthropology at the Denver Museum of Nature and Science. She bought a book of poems by a contemporary Wabanaki poet named Jason Grundstrom-Whitney, and *Dawnland Voices,* a thick anthology of Indigenous New England writers.

She was buzzing when she got back to the car. She thought of what Evan had said, about places that needed to update their understanding of this piece of history. Jane thought of the Awadapquit Historical Society, with its books about dusky redmen. They desperately needed something like this, though in truth they needed lots of things, up to and including a location that was not in the back room of a toy store.

She thought of the Harvard Museum of Natural History, with its strange empty glass cases.

She thought of the Schlesinger, which had pledged years ago to abide by a set of best practices for culturally responsive use of American Indian archival material held by non-tribal organizations. But which, to date, did not have any American Indian archival material.

This was not for lack of trying. In part, it had to do with the reality of some tribes wanting to keep their own papers, or else donate them to the National Museum of the American Indian. From an Indigenous perspective, access was not meant for all people in all circumstances. This went against the general belief among archivists that the information they gathered could serve its highest purpose by being accessible to the greatest possible number of researchers.

It was problematic that the only mention of Indigenous women at the Schlesinger existed in the archives of white women. While they dealt in firsthand accounts, some of these inevitably included stories of other, often less powerful, individuals, which complicated matters. They were well aware of this. They had reached out to several prominent Native women, but so far, none had agreed to have her papers housed there.

Without thinking, Jane dashed off an email to Melissa, recommending she check out Naomi Miller's work and the Portland exhibit. She suggested they think about approaching one or more of the Indigenous women featured in the exhibit to see if they might want to have their papers housed at the Schlesinger.

When Melissa hadn't replied by the time Jane got home, Jane realized she never should have written her. Melissa had made this clear when last they spoke. It was just that Jane had gotten carried away, caught up in the old excitement of a big idea. Briefly, it had made her forget about her circumstances.

It was a strange feeling, to hope with everything she had that she would be allowed back into her own life.

EARLY THAT EVENING, back at her mother's house, Jane's phone rang. A Philadelphia number. At first, not recognizing it, she didn't pick up.

She was in the midst of packing the contents of her mother's linen closet into garbage bags. One for Goodwill and one for the trash. Her sister still hadn't been by to pick up the things she left behind. Nor had she apologized for her behavior.

The phone kept ringing. At the last second, Jane remembered. The woman who sold Genevieve the house lived in Philadelphia.

She answered just before the call went to voicemail.

"Hello?" Jane said.

"Jane Flanagan? This is Marilyn Martinson."

Her voice was clipped, to-the-point.

"Hi!" Jane said, with a bubbliness that was not her own, as if to make up for Marilyn's lack of enthusiasm. "Thank you for getting back to me."

"I only have a few minutes."

"Got it," Jane said. "I'll get right to it, then. As I said in my message, I'm doing research on your old house in Maine for the current owner. Genevieve Richards. You sold her the house."

No reply.

"Hello?" Jane said, thinking maybe they had been disconnected.

"I'm here," Marilyn said.

"Okay. Great. Well."

"What do you want to know about us?" Marilyn said.

Jane reminded herself that this woman was close to ninety. She was probably used to fielding calls from fifty scam artists a day, telling her she had won a free cruise or that she owed back taxes or that her nonexistent grandson had been kidnapped for ransom. Of course she was wary.

"Actually, it's the original owners I'm trying to learn about," Jane said. "The Littletons."

"I see." Her voice seemed to soften. "You're writing an article?"

"No, it's just for Genevieve's personal knowledge. It's important to her to honor the people who built the house. She always says you don't own an old home, you just take care of it."

Actually, Lydia Beazley had said that. Jane wondered if it had been the wrong thing to say. Marilyn hadn't taken care of the house, after all.

"It's an interesting story," Marilyn said. "He was a ship captain. His boat sank off the coast of Awadapquit the day it was due to return home."

Jane was afraid that if she said she already knew this, some spell would be broken and Marilyn would stop talking. She remained silent, until Marilyn said, "I still have some of Hannah's letters somewhere. I could see if I can dig them up. They weren't from Samuel. They were from her brother, written during the Civil War."

"I'd love to see those," Jane said.

"Yes, and I took home a silk bonnet that was probably hers. And a photograph of her with Samuel."

"Really!" Jane said. "That's just what I've been looking for. Do you think you could text me a picture of the photo? Do you still have it?"

"Yes," Marilyn said. "I have the photo. I'll send it. If I find those other things, I'll send them too. Give me your address."

Jane did so, eagerly.

"I always felt as if I knew the Littletons," Marilyn went on. "I felt especially attached to poor Hannah. She just looked so happy and in love in the picture. No idea what was coming her way. She went through hell. I swear there's some kind of curse about that house. All the women who move there end up alone."

"Do they?"

"Yes. Hannah, of course. Me. Buying Lake Grove led directly to my divorce, though that was no great loss, believe me. Still. I heard a story once about the sisters who lived there before us. I don't know if it was true or not. But someone told me the house was purchased by one of their fiancés, who ran off the night before they were supposed to move in."

Jane thought of Genevieve, wondered what this meant for her.

"You called it Lake Grove," Jane said.

"Yes. That's what we always called the house," Marilyn said. "There was a sign when we moved in that said Lake Grove Inn on it. Those sisters who owned it before we did ran it as a boardinghouse and that was the name."

"Right," Jane said. "I saw a picture of what it looked like then."

"Did you?" Marilyn said. "I would imagine the sign is still in the basement if the new owners want it. We—didn't take much with us when we left."

Jane thought of the mural of a sunset in the front hall and wondered if Genevieve had left it up. She hoped so.

She asked Marilyn now if she had been the one to paint it.

Marilyn said no, the mural was her ex-husband's work.

"Was it because of your divorce that you stopped going to the house?" Jane said. She couldn't help herself. She wanted to understand.

"Yes," Marilyn said. "I didn't want to go back, but I wouldn't sell.

Herbert, my ex, he begged me to. I knew keeping the house would cost him. And I wanted him to pay."

Jane was taken aback by the frankness of this admission. She decided then to push just a little harder.

"Did you ever know anyone named D who lived there? Or a girl whose name started with the letter *D*, I guess."

Jane wasn't sure if Marilyn heard her. She could make out another voice in the background.

"I have to go now," Marilyn said. "We'll have to pick this up some other time."

7

Marilyn

MARILYN DIDN'T PAINT anymore. Hadn't in years. She wanted to, more than anything, but her hands shook terribly. Her arthritic fingers bulged as if she were a witch in a fairy tale. She had wasted so much time in the middle of her life, not painting. Sunk deep in despair. She regretted this, but she could do nothing about it, then or now.

At first, when Caitlin suggested including some of Marilyn's work in a show, Marilyn dismissed the idea.

"I have nothing new *to* show," she said.

Caitlin explained that it would be a group show, a look back at the work of several women artists. Caitlin had a rather important job at a rather important art gallery. Marilyn couldn't remember what the job was exactly, and it felt impolite to ask, this far into their friendship. Suffice it to say, Caitlin had the power to make a show happen if she wanted to.

Though it embarrassed her—she had accomplished so little—Marilyn said yes. She felt perfectly safe with Caitlin. Caitlin wouldn't have suggested it if it was a bad idea. Marilyn's life had not been easy, but along the way angels had emerged and saved her. Caitlin was one of them.

They had lived across the hall from one another for two years.

Early on, running into each other by chance, they had two or three long conversations about art, standing in the hallway between their locked apartment doors. Then Caitlin and her husband, Josh, invited Marilyn to dinner. Ages since anyone had done that. She went to the Italian bakery beforehand and stopped in front of the glass case of beautiful desserts that she so often admired but never had a reason to buy. She selected a key lime tart. She told the boy behind the counter, "I'm taking that to a friend's place tonight. Little dinner party." He didn't care, which was fine.

During dinner, Caitlin thrilled to every mention of some minor painter Marilyn had crossed paths with in the fifties and sixties. She knew all their names, wanted details about what they were like. Josh was very friendly, but he wasn't at all interested in art. He taught fifth-grade math for a living. His eyes kept drifting to a basketball game on the muted television.

At some point, Marilyn and Caitlin started going out for dinner once a month, just the two of them, to a neighborhood brasserie run by a friend of Caitlin's, with tin ceilings painted white and small wooden tables set close together, and an extensive wine list, which they were determined to complete within the year.

When a new waitress asked if Marilyn was Caitlin's grandmother, Caitlin said, "We're friends," like it was a ludicrous question.

Which it wasn't. There were fifty-five years between them.

They looked at art together, and went to the movies. Caitlin invited Marilyn to join them for Thanksgiving. *Friendsgiving,* they called it. The apartment was full of young people, flirting and laughing and bouncing fat babies on their hips. She was older than anyone else there by half a century. Caitlin didn't seem to find this odd, so Marilyn decided she wouldn't either. She had a ball.

"Everyone loved you," Caitlin beamed the next morning.

They talked about everything—love, politics, art, progress, the planet. The invention of Botox. Girls Caitlin knew did it at house parties, the way they used to buy Mary Kay. Caitlin kept Marilyn current. She looked to Marilyn for guidance on how to live, which Marilyn appreciated. No one had wanted her opinion for a long, long time.

She told Caitlin about her two marriages, one good, one bad. Her career, which never got off the ground like she imagined it would, though it had its moments. None of it felt within her control as it happened, but when shaped into a narrative, her life became manageable, as if she had planned it exactly that way.

Caitlin had so many anxieties, such uncertainty about the future.

That was one aspect of youth Marilyn didn't miss. She had no fear anymore. The worst had already happened and she had survived.

Caitlin loved her job, but she worried about money. She and Josh both had student loan debt in the six figures, which seemed crazy to Marilyn. Caitlin feared they would never be able to buy a house or have children.

Marilyn reassured her—her first husband was a painter, her second a retired carpenter, and they had managed. But she knew things were different now. She felt sorry for them. The apartment building wasn't particularly nice. Marilyn only stayed because she was used to it. She had been on a fixed income for a long time. Now that she had money, she was too tired, too old, to move someplace new. And besides, she was saving that money for a reason.

Caitlin proposed that they call Marilyn's part of the show *Five Lives*. Because once, after several martinis, they were talking about reincarnation and Marilyn said she didn't believe in the concept as others defined it, but that she had lived five distinct lives in the span of her one lifetime. This was something she had often thought, but never uttered out loud until then.

The definition of a lifetime, as she saw it, was when the people most important to you wouldn't recognize the ones who previously filled their roles. *Make new friends but keep the old,* went a song from her childhood. But Marilyn had shed one batch of loved ones and then another and another and another after that. So much loss. So many new beginnings. Sometimes she thought strength had allowed her to be this way, and sometimes she feared it was hardness, a cold detachment with which she had been born.

In her first life, she was a doll. Blonde curls, blue eyes, white cotton sundress, and Mary Janes. Beloved only child of Ted and Minerva Torbert of Fairfield, Connecticut. Lionel, the boy next door, believed she was an actual princess because her father doted on her so. But her father had a terrifying temper sometimes, when no one else could see, and her mother was a coward. A bad combination, as far as being their daughter was concerned. They took her to the museum on Saturdays, gave her oil paints and an easel on her birthday, encouraged her to major in art history at Smith. And yet they were horrified when she wanted to become an artist. Her father forbade it.

Her second life: Becoming an artist anyway. Moving to New York. Developing her style. To pay the rent, she worked as a clerk in an art supply shop, where she met lots of other young people, starting out. Over the years, she swept the hair in an uptown salon and worked as a nanny, a bank teller, a salesgirl in the accessories department at Bloomingdale's.

She might have reconciled with her parents eventually, but when she was twenty-three, her mother died. Her father got remarried soon after, to her mother's best friend. Marilyn was appalled. She never set foot in her childhood home again.

She met Herbert at a party on the Lower East Side when she was twenty-six. He was a giant in every way. Six-foot-six, barrel-chested, broad shouldered. He had a head of thick black hair and a bushy black beard. Ten years her senior, with an MFA from Yale. His voice boomed and his laugh took over the room, but he did not strike her as arrogant, not then.

She wanted to know him; to matter to him. It turned out everyone felt that way about Herbert. That he chose her was a thrill. A shock too. Marilyn was used to having to reintroduce herself at parties to people she had met five times before. But, for some reason, Herbert seemed dazzled by her from the start.

They were married at City Hall, eight months to the day after they met.

Herbert grew up outside of Minneapolis, the youngest of five. His mother, a housewife, and his father, a plumber, had hoped he would continue on in the family trade. Herbert worked for his dad for a few years before telling them he wanted to go to art school. They didn't understand, he said, but they supported his decision and that was enough.

Herbert was an Abstract Expressionist. Everyone was then, besides her. Marilyn's work was not fashionable, but it was what she was called to do. Later, she would think maybe Herbert liked this about her because it made her less of a threat.

("Male fragility," Caitlin said upon hearing the story, with a know-ing roll of the eyes.)

Marilyn knew lots of women artists who tried to inject their work with masculinity, whatever that meant. There was an old story about Hans Hofmann praising something Lee Krasner had made as "so good you would not know that it was done by a woman." And Krasner was hardly ever mentioned without the detail about being Jackson Pol-lock's wife. Even though she taught him. Women carried knowledge of that sort of thing around, whether they wanted to admit it or not. It changed the way many of them worked.

Marilyn could no sooner choose to paint in abstraction than she could choose to sing opera. She made large-scale paintings of sun-light on glass. She bought interesting pieces at thrift shops and asked friends to lend her whatever glassware they had in their cupboards. She arranged the items on a table in front of a window, filled them with water sometimes, to see how the light bounced off of them. She might add a cut crystal vase of tulips, or borrow a goldfish in a glass fishbowl.

Later, she started painting glass and plastic bottles from the super-market. Whatever caught her eye while she shopped for dinner. She was endlessly curious about how daylight moved through a bottle of clear vinegar, say, versus a jar of honey. She painted apples and peaches wrapped tight in cellophane. She grew obsessed with clear packaging, how it managed to be both reflective and transparent.

People who saw her work sometimes mistook her as being primar-ily interested in the domestic object, but that wasn't right. She was interested in plastic and glass not for their own sake, but as a conduit to the light.

One gallery offered to represent her if she added a figure here and there. A woman seated in the midst of all those pretty things. Mari-lyn refused. Painting still life was a form of contemplation. She could not paint the human form because she didn't want to be in a room with another human while she painted. She didn't want to have to think about another person's needs. Herbert said he didn't think of models as people in that context. When he was at work, he cared as much about the needs and desires of a folding chair as he did the naked woman sitting on it. Perhaps she should have taken that as a sign.

They were each included in a handful of group shows in the years after they married. His work was met with praise. Hers was mostly ignored.

Herbert's signature was a swooping, layered effect achieved by coating a palette knife with multiple shades, then quickly dashing them onto the canvas. He would sometimes embed the paint with dirt from the streets, or dust collected from corners of their apartment. His titles were always a single word: *Renunciation. Desolation. Debris.* One critic called Herbert's work a response to the terrors of the atomic age. After that, Marilyn noticed Herbert himself sometimes used the same description. Really, she believed, he was interested primarily in color.

She didn't judge him for it. That's what art was—a person created a thing for his own reasons. Then others came along and said what it meant.

They had been together five years when Herbert got an adjunct teaching job in Albany. It didn't pay much, but they hoped it might lead to a tenured position down the line. They were offered an apartment downtown, near campus, but instead moved to the suburbs. For reasons she couldn't explain, even to herself, she wanted a house. They bought a three-bedroom Colonial on a street similar to the block Marilyn grew up on, but not as nice. They painted the house black, because they had never seen a black house before. In small ways like this, she believed, they would hold on to themselves.

CAITLIN AND MARILYN had been planning the show for a few weeks, looking through old press clippings and images of Marilyn's paintings, deciding which pieces to take out of storage, when Caitlin asked the inevitable question—why had she stopped? What was the reason for the gap of forty years between the prolific period in her thirties and the next time she picked up a paintbrush, at seventy-three?

Marilyn gave a vague answer.

She was still, as they said about people her age, *sharp*. Though lately, her memory felt like a canvas that had once been stretched taut but had come loose from its frame. There were holes in places. At other points, her mind overlapped onto itself so that she might be thinking of a time when she was shopping for a dress in Soho, in her thirties, with her mother. Even though she knew her mother hadn't been there then, couldn't possibly have been.

Sometimes she used this to her advantage, pretended not to recall what she didn't want to discuss.

Months went by. And then, a week ago, that woman, Jane Flanagan, started calling her, leaving messages about Lake Grove, making it impossible to think of anything else.

Marilyn ended up telling Caitlin the whole story over dinner. She needed to unburden herself of it. And she wanted Caitlin's advice as to whether she ought to call back.

"You asked why I stopped painting," she said.

She paused, unsure how to go on.

"Start at the beginning," she said out loud, to herself, then took a deep breath. "Something I haven't told you is that I had a little girl."

They were the last two customers in the restaurant. Caitlin listened with rapt attention. When Marilyn finished talking, Caitlin came and sat beside her in the booth and put her arms around her, and wept. Marilyn wasn't one for physical affection, but she appreciated that more than Caitlin would ever know. To see her grief reflected, even felt, after all these years.

STAR T at the beginning.

Marilyn's third life. The one she did not choose to leave, but had taken from her.

Soon after settling in Albany, she was shocked to discover she was pregnant. Later, looking back, she saw that this was what she had been driving at by insisting on that house in the suburbs. But Marilyn couldn't admit to herself that part of her craved a life so traditional.

Something seemed to change then, between Herbert and her. Some subtle shift in the formula she couldn't name. (Again, with hindsight, she knew what it was—he'd started up the first of many affairs, with an undergraduate named Betsy.)

Forlorn, Marilyn spent most of her time in bed, feeling nauseous and exhausted and alone. She thought often that what she missed most about her youth was not the loss of her beauty or her figure, like women usually said. She had never been all that pretty to begin with. What she missed was the capacity for love. That intense love, which she and Herbert felt for one another in the beginning, and for music and art. You couldn't ever love that way when you were older. Listening to the old songs or thinking hard on when she first met her husband, she could conjure up memories of how it felt. But remembering was not the same as feeling it.

When they lived in a cramped Manhattan walk-up, she sometimes dreamed that she had discovered a door in the apartment that led to more and more rooms they never knew were there. They thought they lived in a studio, when in fact they lived in a palace. This was how it felt when Daisy was born. Marilyn was ecstatic to learn that mother love was every bit as intense as the love she had known before, but more beautiful. Steadying. Love that didn't unsettle her, but instead made her comfortable in her skin, and in the world.

Contrary to what all the women artists she knew had warned her about, Marilyn found her creativity reawakened after her daughter was born. She wanted to paint, and did so as much as possible, fighting off the desire to rest, which was almost equally strong.

She and Herbert were both surprised when Marilyn pulled out ahead professionally, when certain critics they admired started crediting her with boldly reviving the still life when it wasn't remotely cool. For putting her own spin on it, making it feel new again.

Her first solo show coincided with Daisy's first birthday. The first of a million times she was made to choose.

Marilyn assured Caitlin this wouldn't happen to her. She couldn't believe the things young women expected now. It was glorious. They had it all, and still *The New York Times* seemed to print at least one article a week on the subject of their dissatisfaction. The other day she read one about "the mental load." Caitlin said her friends with kids talked about this concept all the time. It wasn't enough that their husbands did half the housework and child care, because they didn't have in their heads all the things a mother did—when to make dentist appointments and buy new shoes and what the third grade teacher's name was. Marilyn laughed. She had been born at the wrong time. In her day, Herbert was held up as a god because he had changed a diaper or two. She had visions of painting while the baby napped, or dutifully played on the floor at her side. She quickly realized how ridiculous an idea that was. But they made it work. Babysitters when they could afford them; college girls. Herbert's mother would come out from Ohio for a week at a time to help. Mostly, Marilyn cared for Daisy while Herbert worked, and he cared for her while Marilyn worked. Friends marveled at how egalitarian the arrangement was, though by then, only Marilyn was making any money. And really, only Marilyn was making art.

Herbert hadn't been asked back to the university after the first year. A very public fight with Betsy in the quad certainly hadn't endeared him to the administration, but the quality of his work had declined too. It didn't come easily anymore and he didn't seem interested in putting in the effort. To be young and fortunate was to believe in your own greatness. Not to understand the importance of the slog, the toil. The *work* of the work.

Years later, in New York, Marilyn stood alone before Lee Krasner's masterpiece *The Seasons,* seventeen feet wide and eight feet tall, hanging in the Whitney Museum. Krasner painted for two decades after Jackson Pollock descended into alcoholism and affairs, and one day drove his car into a tree and died.

During their marriage, Krasner painted in the small dining room of their house in East Hampton. Pollock worked from a barn behind the house, with sunbeams streaming in through the open doors. You could take a tour, even now. The paint splotches and streaks on the barn floorboards were viewed by some as works of art in their own right, and had been covered in protective plexiglass. But who could say which painter had made them? Marilyn heard that Krasner eventually emerged from her grief and claimed the barn for her own.

D A I S Y   W A S one and a half when they bought the house in Maine on a whim.

They hadn't been getting along, so at the suggestion of a long-married friend of Herbert's, they decided to leave the baby with Herbert's mother over Labor Day weekend and go away, just the two of them.

Another friend, the painter Jack Close, recommended the destination. They were at a party at Jack's place, and he was showing off his newly acquired statue of a Zuni war god, which, he said, was nearly identical to the one Warhol had purchased the previous year. The dealer he bought it from ran a gallery of Indian art in Awadapquit, Maine.

"It is the prettiest beach town you've ever seen," he said. "The name literally translates to 'beautiful cliffside views' or something like that."

Marilyn and Herbert fell in love with the town the instant they arrived.

The night before they were due to leave, they were eating mussels and drinking beer on the patio of a lobster shack in the cove, when they overheard their white-haired waitress chatting with a local guy passing by with his German shepherd.

They had been struggling to make conversation, to come up with anything to say that wasn't about Daisy. They both missed her. It was about all they had in common just then. But now, a shared interest in eavesdropping. A conspiratorial look exchanged, which awakened a certain fondness in her.

"He lives in California," the man said. "He's never set foot in the state of Maine and has no plans to start now."

"What I can't understand," the waitress said, "is why they left it to him in the first place. He never did a thing for those poor old birds."

"The numbskull nephew was next of kin, so he gets it," the man said. He had a strong New England accent, which made Marilyn smile for some reason. "Why does that stuff never happen to me? Closest I ever got was inheriting my cousin's collection of rusty snow shovels."

The waitress groaned. "Tell me about it."

Then, without saying goodbye, she turned away from him and back to Herbert and Marilyn.

"You folks all set?" she said.

The man walked on.

"What was that all about?" Herbert asked, overly familiar, like he too was a townsperson who passed by here every evening and had chatted with this woman a thousand times before.

Marilyn braced herself for annoyance, but the waitress seemed happy to tell them the whole story. There was a gorgeous house up on a cliff, just outside of town. A beautiful oceanfront property that had been owned for as long as anyone could remember by a pair of sisters, Ethel and Honey Troy.

The younger of the two had recently passed away, weeks after the first.

"They couldn't live without each other, I guess," the waitress said. "I never did see one without the other."

Their house had been handed down to a nephew out west, and word was he was eager to sell.

Marilyn met Herbert's eyes and could tell they were having the same thought. Even as the waitress said that Lake Grove had been a boardinghouse for years. That the floors were a mess. The paint peeling in every bedroom. That the bathrooms needed to be pulled out and replaced.

"They never took great care of the house," she said. "So many people traipsing through. A lot of seasonal help from overseas. And summer stock actors who came to do shows at the Playhouse. They were wild. Ethel told me once that after the Navy Yard opened, the house was filled to the rafters with sailors who stayed six months or a year, drank in the off hours, didn't exactly treat it like home. I remember once a fella passed out drunk right after he got in the tub. The water overflowed and flooded the whole second floor. Oh, and there was a fire. Someone passed out drunk with a lit cigarette in his mouth."

"I'm sensing a theme," Herbert said.

Marilyn smiled.

For the first time in ages, they were united on something: the unreasonable desire for a house on the ocean, in a town they hadn't known existed a week ago, two hundred and thirty miles from where they lived.

They called the real estate agent the next morning. He said he could get them in at noon.

They would only be the house's third owners. The real estate agent made a big deal of that.

"People who move into this house stay forever," he said, as he opened the front door.

"Someone told us a pair of sisters lived here," Marilyn said. "Did they grow up in the house?"

What she really wanted to know was if they had died in the house, but it felt rude to ask.

"No," he said. "But they were distantly related to the original owners. One of them, Ethel, was engaged when her husband-to-be bought the house from her great-uncle's children. The fiancé was from the Midwest someplace. A town called Lake Grove. In—Wisconsin? Iowa? He bought this house for cheap. Victorians were out of fashion then. No one wanted them. Imagine that? This was during the First World War. He was meant to ship out, but the night before, he disappeared. Went AWOL. Ethel had a breakdown. She couldn't handle it, so she pretended they had gotten married and he'd gone to war. Not like she lied about it. It was as if she actually believed it. She moved in, got the house ready for his return. But he never did come back. A lot of speculation about what he was running away from exactly and where he ended up. Ethel's sister Honey was your classic spinster who lives with the parents, cares for them until they die, only to realize she has nothing of her own. So she moved in here."

"How sad," Marilyn said.

"Not really. She was—simple. Wouldn't have married anyway."

According to him, the sisters only took in boarders occasionally, and none at all for the past decade or more. But it certainly had the look of a boardinghouse. A sign advertising the Lake Grove Inn hung from the front porch railing. Plywood walls had been nailed up in all but one of the original bedrooms, dividing each into three. Two sets of bunk beds were crammed into these smaller spaces. The mattresses were stained. The floors were warped. A jackknife had been stuck or flung into the wall in one bedroom and remained there, suspended by its blade.

Still, they loved the house. They saw all its potential. Herbert loved the ocean views. Marilyn loved the moody corners, and the dark, detailed wood trim everywhere.

They got a good deal. It was already September. The real estate agent advised the new owner that if he didn't sell now, the house was likely to sit until the following June, when summer tourists returned. He would have to pay property taxes, and those alone were an expense he couldn't afford, not to mention all the necessary repairs to bring the house up to code.

A portrait of the Troy sisters hung over the fireplace. Marilyn asked if they could keep it.

"I don't think that will be a problem," the real estate agent said.

The painting remained there as long as they did. Longer, most likely.

They kept the sign up on the porch too, until it blew off in a winter storm. Herbert found the sign in the grass months later and put it in the cellar, vowing to rehang it when he got the chance.

He never did rehang it. He didn't fix the wobbly banister in the upstairs hall or the broken sink in the bathroom. The restoration of Lake Grove was one more thing to which Herbert gave his all, before growing bored and moving on to something—or someone—else.

In the beginning, though, he worked nonstop, calling on the practical skills his father taught him. The house would perpetually need something, would always look a bit worn and shabby, but Marilyn didn't mind that. She was amazed at all he did to improve it. Sometimes, watching him, so capable, so strong, she felt like she was falling back in love, and maybe this was what marriage was supposed to be. Pulling apart, coming back together.

They started sleeping together again, with a frequency they hadn't had since before the baby.

But the mail got forwarded from home. The second summer, or maybe it was the third, she found love letters from a former student. Not Betsy. Another one. Marilyn burned the letters in the fireplace. She closed herself to him, but not to their beautiful life. Herbert was a lousy husband, but a good father. A great father. She believed then that he loved Daisy as much as she did. When Daisy was four, she asked him to paint the Maine house violet, her favorite color. Herbert did so, even though the house could have gone another five years without needing it, and neither of them would have picked that shade under any other circumstances. He painted the plain wooden barn violet too. Sometimes she wondered what the Troy sisters would have made of that.

Marilyn didn't fret much about Herbert. She thought of that part of her life as something to be figured out later, down the line. In the moment, they lived like two toddlers engaged in what the pediatrician had told her was called parallel play, side by side, each doing their own thing, and that was fine with her.

Summers were glorious. Daisy ran around naked, like some wild creature. She never went to bed. Friends came and stayed as long as they liked. Once or twice a season, someone swam out to the island in the distance, or they all took rowboats there and had a picnic, squealing with delight when a seal came near. A small monument detailed how the explorer Archibald Pembroke named the island Saint George's when he landed there in 1605. It became a game among their friends to guess what he might have looked like, to sketch various versions on a notepad they kept in the kitchen.

Once a sculptor friend of Herbert's brought his girlfriend, a poet, to stay for a week, and she wrote a funny sonnet about Pembroke on the notepad since, as she said, she had no talent for drawing. Late one night, after many strong cocktails, the couple retired upstairs. The next morning at breakfast, the poet told how just before climbing into bed, she looked out the window and saw a woman standing on the cliff's edge, gazing out at the sea.

"She was at the very end of that peninsula of land that juts out over the water," the poet said. "Standing right between those two tall pine trees. I ran outside. But she was nowhere to be found. I started crying. I swear, the air around me felt heavy. I worried she might have gone over the edge."

"What are you putting in those drinks of yours, Herbert?" the sculptor said, and everyone laughed, even the poet, swatting him with her napkin.

"Then I realized she was just a ghost and I went back to bed," the poet said.

"Let's not scare these two into thinking they've bought a haunted house," the sculptor said.

"Ghosts aren't generally scary," the poet said. "I've seen plenty of ghosts before."

"Have you now?"

Marilyn chalked it up to a dream. But she didn't think she'd mind having a ghost. Somehow the possibility made her like the place even more. They told everyone the story from then on. A badge of honor.

THEY ARRIVED each year at the end of May, intending to stay through August. It was usually October before they packed up the car and went home.

Marilyn did the best work of her life at Lake Grove.

A junk shop on the side of the road sold old blue glass medicine bottles. She bought them by the dozens. One morning, she popped in and found a glass milk bottle full to the top with marbles in shades of green, red, and blue. She took it home, where Daisy begged to be allowed to play with the marbles, and was told that she could not, that they were for her mother's work.

Marilyn set the bottle on the highest shelf in the butler's pantry off the kitchen, a space she had nearly filled with her glass objects by then. A few of the pieces had been there when they moved in, remnants of the Troy sisters and their boardinghouse. Cheap, chipped brandy snifters. A small collection of Depression glass. Mason jars for canning. The rest Marilyn acquired along the way. She had fans now. Patrons who commissioned her work. They sent her delicate champagne coupes and thick-cut crystal punch bowls and everything in between, hoping their gifts might appear in one of her paintings.

In time, the house offered up other treasures. When Herbert went to hang a heavy painting in the upstairs hall, he discovered that the wall behind it was hollow. At Marilyn's request, he left it alone for some time, but one day curiosity took over and he decided to knock down the wall and see what was on the other side. A most satisfying discovery—a hidden door, wallpapered over and sealed shut. Behind it, a tiny corner room with windows on two sides.

Immediately, Daisy said she wanted the room for her own. The idea of a secret passageway was irresistible to her, and her imagination won out over any argument about its relative size. She lugged her stuffed animals and her dolls and her crayons in there. She slept on the floor for three nights before Herbert finally got around to moving her bed.

In that room, Daisy found a wooden box that contained letters Hannah Littleton had exchanged with her brother during the Civil War; a silk bonnet, slightly crushed; a photograph of Samuel and Hannah Littleton; and a gold ring with a lock of hair pressed in glass, engraved with the words NOT LOST BUT GONE BEFORE.

Daisy wanted to keep the ring, but Marilyn told her it wasn't theirs to keep.

She knew Hannah Littleton had lost her husband at a young age. They were both buried in the charming family plot not far from the house, which Marilyn could see from her bedroom window. The ring must have been a reminder of him, of a love cut short. Absurd, but Marilyn envied this woman long dead, for having had such a love. She stared at that photograph of the two of them, studying Hannah's smile.

Marilyn suggested to Daisy that they bury the ring between Hannah's and Samuel's graves. Daisy was seven then and in love with fairy-tale romances. She liked the idea. They wrapped the ring in blue silk, and buried it deep. Daisy placed a yellow dandelion on the turned earth, so they would know just where they put it. The letters and the bonnet and the photograph, Marilyn kept, intending to give them to the local historical society.

She and Daisy both loved the old cemetery. They tended to it, placing flowers on the graves on birthdays. They planted pink beach roses around the perimeter, where once there must have been a rope or a chain of some kind, but now there were only four rusted black metal stakes in the ground. The scant information on each tombstone begged to be filled in. They made up stories, especially about Sister Eliza. Who was she? they wanted to know. Why was her grave different from the others? It was just a large rock that looked as if it had been pulled straight from a quarry and plopped down there. It had no decorative carvings, no engraved dates of birth and death. Only those two words. *Sister Eliza.* Was she Hannah's sister or Samuel's? Or was she their daughter? ("Or was she a *nun?*" Daisy asked once, making

Marilyn and Herbert laugh.) Herbert posited that the stone was so unusual and informal that perhaps Sister Eliza was the family dog.

Sometimes they sat there all afternoon and read books to keep the dead company. Daisy worried about the children. Marilyn told a half lie, explaining that in the old days, children did die sometimes, but not anymore. Daisy seemed satisfied with that. She talked to them, tried to comfort them. She told them they were lucky because they would be forever at their mother's side. Marilyn's own mother would have punished such behavior, accused her of being morbid. What a gift that her girl was as strange and curious as she had always been. She vowed to nurture these parts of Daisy. She never once called her pretty without also reminding her that she was smart or creative or kind.

Their fifth or sixth summer, a woman appeared at the door to ask if they would like to purchase a historic plaque for the front of the house. They were going up around town, on the homes of the town founders and other important figures. That was when they learned the story of Captain Littleton's sad fate, a shipwreck that claimed the lives of everyone on board and left Hannah alone with two small children.

Daisy asked the woman if she knew anything about Sister Eliza. She was so well informed about Samuel, after all. But the woman said no.

THE SUMMER Daisy turned eight, they arrived in Maine in early June, the very first day of her school vacation.

As he did every year, Herbert went directly into town for groceries. He was gone for three hours. Upon his return, he told Marilyn about a widow he met in line at the deli. She cleaned houses for a living, he said. Maybe they should have her in once a week.

A widow. Marilyn pictured an old lady. She wasn't sure she could let such a person clean for them without feeling guilty. But she didn't think much of it beyond that.

Two weeks passed. Herbert was gone a lot, without explanation, which wasn't unusual. Marilyn noticed. Her whole job was to notice. But she never said anything.

Then one day Mary Flanagan, the widow, turned up to clean and

Marilyn saw that she was young, her own age, give or take. She was curvy, with a big, open smile and enormous breasts. One would not look at her and think *widow*. Not in a million years. It took all the strength Marilyn had not to ask her outright if she was one, really.

It didn't take long, though, to realize that the smile was a fake. Mary was such a sad woman. She did a good enough job around the house, though she reeked of gin no matter the hour. She often seemed to have tears at the corners of her eyes, as if she had been crying or was just about to. She told Marilyn, the one time they had a conversation at some length, that she had a daughter too. That they had only moved to the area a year ago, after her husband died. She didn't know many people around here. Marilyn felt sorry for her. She understood then why Herbert had wanted to help.

Around this time, late June, Marilyn was invited to do a five-week residency at the MacDowell colony in New Hampshire, starting at the end of July. She was dying to accept, and yet her first thought was that it would be impossible for her to leave Daisy for that long.

Herbert seemed eager for her to go. He and Daisy would be fine, he said. Marilyn should absolutely do it. At some point, he mentioned Mary would be willing to babysit while Marilyn was gone.

She felt a familiar, nagging feeling when he said this, but she pushed it off. She was so happy to be free.

Her second night away, she called the house at Lake Grove and heard voices, laughter, when her husband picked up.

"Who's there?" she asked after saying hello.

Herbert said Mary and her young daughter had stayed for dinner. Mary's little girl, Shirley, was an only child, like Daisy, and she liked playing at big sister.

Marilyn hung up with a sense of unease. She never should have left.

What sort of mother was she? She was bowled over with love for her daughter, always. She told Daisy she loved her every day, something her own parents never did. She made Daisy paper dolls, intricate and beautiful. They had tea parties with real petit fours, and snuck jelly beans during bedtime stories. But Marilyn was distracted. She had no knack for discipline. Her approach to parenting was the path of least resistance. Daisy got away with murder. She screamed when Marilyn brushed her hair, so Marilyn just let it go. Once, waiting for her to come out of school, Marilyn heard one stuck-up housewife say to another, "Poor thing. Doesn't she have a mother?"

Mothers were supposed to rise early, before their children. To greet them with a smile and a kiss, to have breakfast waiting. But Marilyn was often working when Daisy woke up, and had to fight off a sense of irritation at being interrupted. Marilyn would try to convince her, or bribe her with cookies, to play with her dolls or look at a book alone for thirty minutes, to give herself more time.

A real mother would have gone back to Maine that first night, after that strange phone call. Returned home to her child. But Marilyn didn't do that. Marilyn stayed.

IN ONE CORNER of her MacDowell studio was a single bed, neatly made. In another, a small bathroom with a toilet, sink, and tub. That was all. She had ample space for her canvases. Natural northern light streamed through the windows.

Enough of her friends and acquaintances had been here through the years that she knew how it went. If you were young and single, or even not-so-young, maybe just married and bored, you might spend the entire time flirting and sleeping with people and creating drama everywhere but your studio. You'd lose every scrap of creative energy to this soap opera and then it would be time to go home.

Marilyn intended to avoid all that. At communal breakfasts and dinners, she spoke amicably to her fellow artists, but between those hours, she worked. Or else, she wandered through the woods and thought about her work, which was sometimes the most important part, and the part she could never quite manage to make space for in her real life. She hardly slept, wanting to use every second. A man named Petey arrived to her studio each day at noon with a picnic basket containing lunch. He didn't knock, just left it on the doorstep. One day Marilyn met him there as she was returning from a walk. She thanked him profusely.

"It's what we do," he said. "Our mission is to take care of you as no one has since you were a child, so that you can focus on your work."

An astonishing gift. She wanted to stay forever. At the same time, she missed Daisy to an unbearable degree. They spoke on the phone every other day. They wrote to each other. Daisy reported that Herbert had painted a mural of the ocean, the view from their yard at sunset, right onto the wall in the foyer. She said they were eating a lot of cold spaghetti, even for breakfast, and both agreed it was wonderful. She said Mary and Shirley came over most nights.

Dad and Mary talk, and me and Shirley play checkers, Daisy wrote. The next time Marilyn spoke to her husband on the phone, she asked him what he talked about with the cleaning lady, and he said she was surprisingly well read.

She found that odd, since Herbert wasn't, particularly, and had never seemed to value this trait in others. Anyway, she had only been poking at him. She didn't believe for a minute that the two of them were spending their time discussing literature.

Precisely what they *were* doing, she did not know. She couldn't imagine Herbert coming on to their despairing housekeeper. In any case, Marilyn found she could turn her mind away from such thoughts with ease, just shut them out, in a manner she could not when she was younger. She didn't really care.

It was, however, impossible to abide how much she missed her daughter.

As Daisy's eighth birthday approached, it seemed more and more unforgivable that Marilyn should not be there for it. Technically, she wasn't allowed to leave MacDowell. But she was an adult; she could do what she liked. She snuck off early that morning. It was only a two-hour drive. She would be back before anyone could miss her.

When she reached Awadapquit, she stopped at a bakery and bought a chocolate cake and pink candles. At the house, she found the key they kept under the porch mat and crept inside, not wanting to wake them and ruin the surprise. She placed the candles in a circle around the edge of the cake. She lit a burner on the gas stove, and used one candle to light the rest. As she did so, she noticed two wineglasses perched on the edge of the sink.

Marilyn tiptoed upstairs and into her daughter's bedroom, where she held the cake forth in two hands, and softly sang "Happy Birthday." Her own mother had done this once and the image stayed with her forever. She hoped the same would be true of Daisy. That when she was a grown woman, she would remember it.

No doubt, there would be other memories, far less wonderful. A mother who was always distracted, late, disorganized. Who never volunteered to be scout leader or to chaperone a field trip. A mother who committed the sin of loving her work as much as she loved her only child.

Waking to find her there, Daisy shrieked with joy. She came to Marilyn and hugged her around her waist, and Marilyn had to lift the cake in the air so Daisy's hair wouldn't be singed.

"Blow out the candles," she said. "Make a wish."

Daisy did, but first she said, "My wish already came true. I wished that you'd come back."

An arrow through her heart.

She could hear Herbert scurrying around in the hallway and down the stairs, and then returning up to them.

"What's all this?" he said. "You couldn't have told me you were coming?"

"Thanks for the warm welcome, darling, I've missed you too," she said.

"Can we have cake for breakfast?" Daisy said.

In unison, they answered yes.

Daisy wanted to spend the rest of the day at the beach.

All day, Herbert was twitchy. Defensive and on edge. Marilyn thought about the wineglasses. She almost asked him if there had been someone with him in the bedroom that morning. It was entirely possible. But for Daisy's sake, she decided to leave it alone.

After dinner, when it was time to go, the leaving felt physically painful. She held Daisy so long and so hard, as if she knew they would not see each other again in this lifetime.

TWO NIGHTS LATER, Marilyn was up working in her studio when she heard a soft knock at the door. It startled her. She opened it to find Petey there with an apologetic look on his face.

"There's a telephone call for you in the office in Colony Hall," he said. "There's been an emergency. An accident. Back home."

She had to follow him up a long path, lit only by the flashlight in his hand.

Herbert was on the line. He was at the hospital in Winston. He said the doctors did all they could. But they couldn't keep Daisy alive.

"What are you talking about?" she said.

He was drunk, she decided. He was insane. Daisy was right by his side. A sick joke, for which she would give them both hell when she saw them.

But Herbert barreled on. He needed just to say it, he said. Once and then never again.

After he had put Daisy to bed that night, Mary Flanagan came over for a nightcap.

"One thing led to another," he said, as if it had never happened before. As if there was any reason to lie at this point.

"Fucking shut up and get on with it," she said, her words hard-edged.

From the corner, gentle Petey looked at her through startled eyes. Marilyn hadn't realized he was still in the room.

"You had a glass jar of marbles in the closet off the kitchen," Herbert said.

She stiffened. "A milk bottle. Yes."

"All day she kept asking me to take them down and I told her no," he said. His voice trailed off into a wail.

Marilyn stood very still and closed her eyes, hand gripping the receiver.

He sniffled, exhaled, forced himself to go on.

"She must have snuck downstairs and taken them after I put her to bed. I guess she carried them to the upstairs hallway but she tripped in the dark. The marbles went everywhere, the bottle shattered. Mary wasn't thinking. She ran out of our room, wrapped up in a sheet. I don't really know what happened next. If Daisy recognized her or not. But when Mary called out to her, she ran. Only, it was dark, I guess she got disoriented. She went right into the railing and——" He stopped speaking. He wheezed, as if hyperventilating. "Fuck. Sorry," he said. "Marilyn, the railing collapsed and she went with it. She broke her neck."

There. Having said it, he dissolved into sobs.

"Herbert," she said. The quality of her voice surprised her. It was soft, slow, as if coaxing the truth from him. "Are you absolutely sure she's dead?"

"I'm sorry," he said.

"Let me talk to a doctor," she said.

A few minutes passed and then a man confirmed it, in a kind but rushed manner.

"I'll hand you back to your husband now," he said. "I'm so sorry for your loss."

"Thank you," she said, and hung up. She fell to the floor.

Petey came and held her while she shook.

She stayed at MacDowell three months longer than planned, because she had nowhere to go. She didn't work, didn't bathe, didn't sleep. She just lay there in darkness. Petey continued to leave her lunch in a basket outside her studio. He brought breakfast and dinner too. She rarely ate, rarely opened the door.

Marilyn had no interest in returning home. She had no interest in ever seeing Herbert again. He came to MacDowell, banging on doors, hysterical, thinking he could force his way in as usual. But he was mistaken.

Eventually, Marilyn had to leave. She decided to move to Philadelphia, because she didn't know anyone there. She subsisted on sorrow and a hatred for Herbert that burned so bright it could light up Atlantic City. If he hadn't been such an insecure narcissist. If he hadn't been a vile liar. If he had fixed the fucking banister, like she had asked him to a thousand times.

Daisy's death was ruled an accident by the coroner. There were never police involved, no mention of any criminal wrongdoing on Herbert's part. Much as she hated him, in those early days, Marilyn often found herself overcome with relief about this. What would Daisy do if her beloved father was in jail? That was no way for a girl to grow up. Then Marilyn would remember that Daisy was gone. That was the whole point.

Things went on like this for quite some time. The forgetting, the disbelief, the remembering again.

FROM THE FIRST voicemail Jane Flanagan left, Marilyn had wondered about the name.

"It's fairly common," Caitlin said. "Maybe a coincidence."

Seeing the doubtful look on Marilyn's face, she said, "Or maybe there's something she wants to tell you about Mary. Her—mother? Grandmother?"

A few years after Daisy's death, Mary Flanagan had managed to get a letter to Marilyn, through her divorce lawyer. She wrote that she was newly sober, doing a twelve-step program, and wanted to make amends. To explain herself. At the time of her affair with Herbert, she said, she was grieving her husband. She was drinking too much; she was in a fog. She wrote that she had been there the morning of Daisy's birthday, when Marilyn came home unannounced. She knew then what a wonderful mother Marilyn was, and tried to end it with Herbert. She would regret for the rest of her life that she didn't try harder. She loved Daisy, she said. *Such a bright light.* The memory of the night Daisy died would be with her forever. Mary reminded her that she was the mother of a daughter too and could only imagine what Marilyn was going through. She made a point of saying Marilyn was a far better mother than she had ever been. And that every time she laid eyes on her own daughter, she thought of Marilyn's. This had caused a lot of suffering. Mary had punished herself and her poor child for her sins, blah blah. She vowed to live honorably from then on. She could never say how sorry she was.

The letter was self-indulgent in the extreme. No doubt, writing it made her feel better. But it only cemented Marilyn's loathing for the woman.

Marilyn ultimately returned Jane's call because she had to know Jane's reason for reaching out.

Caitlin sat beside her as she dialed.

"Remember, you can keep the call as short as you want," she said. "You don't owe her anything."

To Marilyn's surprise, Jane Flanagan didn't even mention Mary.

She said the new owner of Lake Grove hired her. She seemed interested in the Littletons, in the history of the house itself, like she had said in her messages.

But then she asked about someone whose name began with the letter *D.*

Marilyn went cold.

Was it cruelty? Curiosity? Coincidence?

In any case, she hung up. She had no intention of speaking to Jane Flanagan ever again. She was furious at herself for speaking to her in the first place.

Marilyn had her reasons, all those years, for keeping Lake Grove. She was happy, at least, that she hadn't told Jane all the truth. When Jane asked, she said that when her marriage ended, it was the last time she ever saw the house. But in fact, Marilyn did go back once, on the first anniversary of Daisy's death.

At Marilyn's request, Daisy was buried in the Littleton family plot. That beautiful spot on the ocean, Daisy's favorite place, with other children she knew, in her way. Herbert's mother handled the details, but for the headstone, which Marilyn said she would provide, though she couldn't bring herself to do it. Nor did she visit.

She couldn't do much of anything then. Nothing mattered anymore. All she wanted was to be with her daughter again. A doctor prescribed sleeping pills. She took them constantly, needing to be awake as little as possible.

One year to the day after Daisy died, Marilyn drove straight to Awadapquit, starting out before sunrise, not stopping for gas, or to look at the beach one last time. When she arrived, she did exactly as she planned. She had written a note, which she set on the dashboard, instructions for anyone who might find her. She wanted to be buried next to Daisy. In her mind, she saw their two bodies becoming one with the dirt and stones and with one another, as they had when Daisy lived inside her, and Marilyn didn't have to do a thing to keep her safe.

Who knew when some poor soul would ever look in the barn. She still owned this property, and it was tucked away. But someone, the super back in Philadelphia, maybe, or the mailman, might notice she was gone and notify the authorities. Perhaps they would come searching for her here. She worried about getting eaten by wild animals or simply decomposing beyond recognition. But it was a risk she had to take.

Herbert, in absentia, had surprised Marilyn once more during their divorce proceedings, when the judge raised the issue of debt from the mortgage they had taken out on Lake Grove in order to buy a second house in Awadapquit, at an address she had never heard before.

"It's a mistake. We own Lake Grove outright," she said.

"You did, but then you borrowed against it," her lawyer said, gently, as if Marilyn might just not understand finances. "You signed the papers, right here."

He held something up and then, seeing the look on her face, he said, "Oh God. He forged your signature."

The house Herbert bought, with Marilyn's money, was Mary Flanagan's.

Ashamed to be caught, he agreed that Lake Grove would be Marilyn's alone, and that he would pay off the debt. She had heard by then that Herbert was already engaged, to one of his former students. It brought Marilyn a small degree of pleasure to think of the inconvenience those monthly payments would be in the establishment of his new life.

Not that she could ever bear to sleep at Lake Grove again, or even set foot inside. The property would be for her and Daisy now, returned to the earth. Let the rest of it crumble. She didn't care.

On that final visit, Marilyn could not stop herself from glimpsing through the kitchen window. A year since anyone had been there. The room looked undisturbed. She could see through to the butler's pantry. A chair set against the shelves. She knew immediately why it was there.

She went to the cool patch of earth where Daisy was, and put her hand there. She told her without words that they would be together soon.

Marilyn got in her car and slowly pulled it into the barn. She closed the barn doors tight, then sat in the driver's seat with the engine running, listening to classical music on the radio. She took the last few sleeping pills from the bottle in her purse, washed them down with red wine from a thermos. Soon she would be reunited with her girl, or else she would be nothing. Either way, she would be free of her pain. Eventually, she fell asleep, expecting never to wake up.

But she did wake up. She had no idea how or why.

Some force she couldn't name stopped her, shook her awake. It said she would be dead soon enough, and then forever.

Marilyn got out of the car.

SEVERAL YEARS LATER, she read about a heist at the Gardner Museum in Boston. A newspaper article offered details about the stolen masterpieces. The one that stuck in her mind was Rembrandt's *A Lady and Gentleman in Black*. A couple, looking in different directions, a gap of maybe three feet between them. Something not quite right about the composition. X-ray technology had revealed that there was once a child in that empty space. The child died and the couple asked Rembrandt to paint him out of the portrait, not wanting to be reminded of him every time they saw it.

Preposterous to imagine it might be as simple as painting him out. As if that blank space between them on the canvas wouldn't also conjure his memory, their loss. And yet Marilyn understood the impulse. Maybe that was why she never went back to Lake Grove after that day, even though Daisy was there.

She never told anyone about what she'd done, except Lionel, years later.

He just held her and said, "I'm so glad you found the strength to stay alive."

He was a treasure, her Lionel.

Over time, Marilyn had grown, increasingly, all right. She taught art. She had friends she could call up for dinner. She wasn't close to anyone, though. In the most intimate ways, she was alone. She never talked about what happened. She didn't paint. That part of her life was over.

At seventy-three, she fell down the stairs and broke her hip. She had almost gotten old then. If Lionel hadn't come along. Her childhood neighbor, recently widowed and, by chance, seated beside her in the waiting room of her physical therapist's office in Philadelphia. He had married a girl from the Main Line. He and Marilyn had lived a few miles apart all these years and never known.

For a decade, they had such adventures. They went to China, where his son lived at the time. They went to New Zealand just because she had always wanted to see it.

When Lionel died three years ago, Marilyn left their Craftsman in the suburbs to his children and moved back into her apartment downtown, which she had never given up. She was lonely, a feeling she didn't enjoy but was familiar enough with at that point in her life. Some days she didn't speak to anyone. She might go to the drugstore just to hear another person say hello.

Her daughter would be a grown woman now. The grief never abated. Each chapter of life brought fresh pain. Things happened and still, her first thought was that she wanted to tell Daisy. Daisy would take care of her if she were here. Daisy would have given her grandchildren.

Instead, Caitlin appeared to see Marilyn through the end. Her fifth and final life.

Plenty of prospective buyers had inquired about Lake Grove over the years. Marilyn always said no. Not for sale. These most recent people had been lucky, reaching her when they did. They thought their annoying persistence and negotiation skills sealed the deal, but it was really just timing.

One morning, not too long from now, Caitlin would get a surprise phone call like the one Ethel and Honey Troy's undeserving nephew received back in 1959. Telling her that Marilyn was gone, and a small fortune was coming her way.

It still stung when she thought of leaving Daisy's body there. Marilyn's possession of the house had felt for so long like the last form of protection she might offer her child. But Caitlin was the closest thing Marilyn would ever have to a granddaughter. Sometimes Marilyn pretended that's what she was. That Caitlin was Daisy's little girl. Every now and then, she did more than pretend. She wondered if, through a loophole in time, a trick of the universe, it might somehow be true.

8

Jane

A T T E N to five on Saturday, Jane set out for Genevieve's.

She was excited, had put on a dress for the first time in weeks. She even wore lipstick. Not for Genevieve, but for the house. For the occasion.

In her purse was a folder containing all the information she had collected about the Littletons. She felt like an eager kid, hoping to dazzle her teacher with her findings.

Halfway there, Jane braked at the stop sign in front of Chambers Park. A group of boys were playing catch in the parking lot, even though they were surrounded by green grassy fields on all sides. Were they in high school? College? She had reached an age where she could no longer tell the difference. Every last one was tall and lean, hormones having burnt off any hint of baby fat, and youth staving off the round bellies and creeping hairlines that would come later. They had such confidence about them. None seemed to have that feeling, so common to girls their age, that they were being watched, judged, always. Somewhere some lovesick teenager was writing in her journal about one of these oblivious giraffes. And here he was, entirely focused on a ball rising into the air and falling toward a glove.

Jane drove on, down Shore Road, until she came to the tree-lined dirt path that led to the property. It looked the same as ever, but for a new mailbox. She was relieved that they hadn't paved over the path. The car bumped along the uneven, rocky earth below, just as she remembered.

She missed David. He had been her companion all those times she came here to explore. Jane hadn't done a thing, big or small, these past ten years that he didn't know about, until now. She wondered what he was doing at this moment. If he missed her too, or if it was ultimately a relief to have her gone.

Days had passed since their last exchange, which had been entirely unsatisfying—a text from him to alert her that he was forwarding some mail to her mom's place. It was all starting to feel too real, this slipping away from one another.

The house came into view. Its more elaborate decorative elements had been toned down. The ornate moldings on the wraparound porch were replaced with a clean, basic white railing. Where once there were three exterior colors—purple, with blue and green trim—now the entire thing was painted gray. Otherwise, it looked much as it always had, but spruced up—a new roof, new windows. They had gotten rid of the barn and added a circular driveway, with a border of blue hydrangeas.

Tamed was the word that came to mind. Jane missed the wildness of the tall grass, yellow and unmowed. The old pebbled driveway, shot through with dandelions and buttercups.

She parked at the end of the driveway and got out. Only from this angle did she see that the back of the house had been extended by maybe twenty feet, with an enormous, garish two-story addition, full of windows. It looked all wrong, like two houses had crashed into each other.

Jane felt, suddenly, deflated.

Genevieve met her at the front door. She wore white pants and a silky sleeveless top and her hair was pushed back from her face with a headband. Were headbands a thing again? Had they ever stopped being a thing?

"Welcome!" Genevieve said with a smile. "Thank you for coming. Please. Come in."

She was friendly, if overly formal. Jane thought they must be around the same age, but Genevieve spoke as if she were Jane's elder. She reminded Jane of someone, though Jane couldn't think of whom.

With one straight arm, Genevieve pushed open the screen door.

Her son stood behind her, clutching a plastic truck, looking warily up at Jane.

"You've done a lot of work on this place," Jane said.

Her mother once told her and Holly that if you couldn't think of something nice to say, you could always just state a fact with enthusiasm, and it would be received as a compliment.

"Thank you," Genevieve said.

Jane smiled.

"I wish we could have done more outside," Genevieve went on. "We were able to make the porch more attractive because it wasn't original. I'm not the biggest fan of the scalloping and the gingerbread trim and all. It's so—busy. Not my style, but the town won't let you touch the front of a house this old. It's on the Historic Register. Thank God you're allowed to do whatever you want with the rest of it."

Stepping inside, where memory promised an entryway with a mural of the ocean and doors leading into various rooms, Jane felt a shock upon finding that the entire first floor was wide open. Genevieve had painted over the mural in white. The whole place was white, and all the furniture was white, beige, or navy. Jane could see clear through to the back wall, made up almost entirely of glass sliders overlooking the ocean, where once there had been a row of leaded windows, a curved window seat.

Jane was not a crier. She could go years without shedding a tear. But at this moment, she felt like she might weep for the second time in a week.

"It doesn't even look like the same house," she said, unable to stop herself.

"We put in a lot of blood, sweat, and tears," Genevieve said.

Jane wondered who she meant by *we*. Genevieve did not seem like the DIY type. Jane couldn't picture her demoing the old pine kitchen, or refinishing the hardwood floors, or even changing a lightbulb in the ten-foot ceilings.

It was pointless to say that she had loved the house as it was. That she never would have treated it this way. Devotion had no value in real estate. This was Genevieve's house and she could do with it whatever she wanted. But why buy a historic home and take the history out?

Genevieve insisted on a tour.

They went upstairs, all three of them, into several bedrooms and two baths, where everything was tasteful and tidy. No dirty T-shirts or stray toys on the floors. No unmade beds or damp bath mats. The whole place looked like it had been staged for an open house.

Jane knew they had just returned home from a long stay at the Saint Aspinquid Inn, because Allison had texted her a few hours earlier: Genevieve checked out. It's official. I'm freeeeee!

But there was no sign of that either. No suitcase waiting to be unpacked or put away. No pile of unopened junk mail.

The last time Jane had seen these rooms, they were in a state of decay. The transformation was extraordinary.

Once they had gone into every room on the second floor, they stood in the upstairs hallway and Benjamin, pointing at the wall, said, "That's my room."

"Where?" Jane said.

"Here," he said, placing his hand on the wall.

Jane noticed what she never had before. A door, painted the same color as the wall, completely flush, no hint of its existence but the faintest sliver of light coming through at the bottom.

"That's so cool," she said, in all sincerity, her inner Nancy Drew flaring.

This was what was great about an old house, she thought. There were details you'd never find in a new build. Thrilling, unexpected, and worth the lack of central air. (Though of course Genevieve had added that.) *Character.* It was nice to see it hadn't all been swept away in the name of updating.

"I can show you how the door works," Benjamin said.

"Yes please," Jane said.

But Genevieve was already steering them in the other direction.

"Let's go down to the patio," she said. "It's a gorgeous evening. I put out some nibbles."

She took Benjamin by the hand on her way down the stairs.

"I don't sleep in there anymore anyway," he said.

ON THEIR WAY OUTSIDE, Jane excused herself to use the new bathroom on the first floor. (*The powder room,* Genevieve called it.) She didn't actually need the bathroom. She just wanted a moment to herself. The space was small and windowless, with ridiculous wallpaper—black, with a pattern of hot pink flamingos that made her dizzy to look at. Jane supposed it must be fashionable or else Genevieve wouldn't have chosen it, but to her it felt off.

Two pages from *Maine Coast Magazine* hung on the wall, matted side by side in a gilded frame. It took her a minute to comprehend why the cover shot was familiar. She was looking at a picture of the house she was standing in. That open kitchen, all that white. *History Meets Modernity When an 1846 Beach House Gets a Makeover.*

Jane read the opposite page, which contained a lot of quotes from Genevieve and her decorator about the many lengths to which they had gone to honor the house's legacy. Perplexing, she thought, given that they hadn't, really. There was a sidebar about Genevieve's purchase of a Native American basket, presumed to have been made in the middle of the nineteenth century, right here in southern Maine. (*Mrs. Richards bought her treasured Abenaki basket from an Awadapquit-based antiques dealer. "I saw it and fell in love. It was so beautiful. I had to have it," she recalled.*)

Jane thought of the baskets she had seen at the exhibit in Portland a few days earlier. Created by people who each came from a long line of basket-makers, intent on preserving their traditions. This house, as designed by Genevieve, didn't feel like a satisfying final destination for such a creation.

She understood completely now why Genevieve irked Allison so much.

Even so, Jane couldn't quite believe she was here, in this place she once knew so intimately. Not trespassing onto some stranger's land now, but invited in, going up the stairs without fear of falling through them. Flushing a toilet. About to enjoy some nibbles on the patio. (Honestly, who said "nibbles"?)

Jane took a deep breath. She opened the bathroom door and went toward the back patio, where Genevieve and Benjamin were waiting.

Passing through the big open space between the white kitchen and white family room, Jane saw the basket, sitting on the coffee table.

She went right up to it. The braiding had a pattern of dark blue birds around the rim. To Jane, the basket radiated story. She wondered where it had been these past two hundred years. Where exactly it was made and by whom.

The sound of the sliding door opening made her stiffen.

"Jane?" Genevieve called. "Come on out."

Jane did as she was told.

Stepping into the sun, she said, "I was just admiring the basket on the coffee table."

"Hmm? Oh, yes. It's an antique," Genevieve said.

"It's beautiful," Jane said.

Genevieve shrugged.

"You don't think so?" Jane said.

"No, no, I like it. It's just. It's a basket. If my husband knew what I paid for that basket, he'd die," Genevieve said. "That's what I think every time I look at it."

Jane immediately wanted to know how much the basket cost.

Strange how every marriage had its secrets, its compromises, that seemed untenable to an outsider. It never would have occurred to Jane to ask David's permission to buy something; nor would she ever have hidden a purchase from him. Swiftly, her mind went to judgment. But then, Genevieve still had a husband. Jane herself did not.

"I bought it from an antiques dealer in town. Thomas Crosby," Genevieve said.

She looked at Jane expectantly, like she might recognize the name.

"He specializes in tribal art," Genevieve said. "I think he had a big gallery here in the sixties and seventies, but now he just works with clients one-on-one. Less public that way. Plus, he must be a thousand years old. Wine?"

She held up a bottle.

"No thanks," Jane said.

She wanted to linger on the basket longer, to ask what Genevieve meant by *less public*.

"Sit," Genevieve said firmly, then added, "Please," perhaps so Jane wouldn't feel quite so much like a golden retriever.

On a weathered wooden table with a blue canvas umbrella staked in the middle, Genevieve had arranged crackers and prosciutto and cheese on a slate cheese board, three small white plates, blue and white cloth napkins in a chevron print, and two empty wineglasses.

"Are you sure I can't tempt you with some pinot grigio?"

"No. Thank you. I don't drink," Jane said.

She was trying the words on, given this rare opportunity to use them on someone who didn't already know her, and whose opinion did not matter to her in the least.

"Oh!" Genevieve said. "Sorry."

"Not at all," Jane said.

"Let's just have sparkling water," Genevieve said.

"Please, have wine. It's fine by me," Jane said.

"Are you sure?"

"Absolutely."

"Pellegrino for you then?"

"I'll just have a glass of tap water if you don't mind," Jane said.

Genevieve nodded and went back inside, calling over her shoulder to Benjamin, "You stay where Jane can see you!"

Jane found this odd. Genevieve didn't really know her. But then, Jane was that least threatening of creatures—a middle-aged woman. Perhaps that was credential enough.

She breathed in, the ocean so close she could feel the moisture on her cheeks.

The view, at least, was the same. As magnificent as she remembered. Maybe even more so, because the extension on the house meant that she was that much closer to the water.

As soon as that thought passed through her head, she noticed. Off to the side, where there had once been a cluster of majestic pine trees, there was now a swimming pool.

It looked out of place. A pool on the ocean was a Hamptons thing. No one around here, even the wealthiest summer people, had pools.

Benjamin came up beside her, toy truck still in hand.

"Aren't you lucky to have a pool," Jane said.

"Yeah but we don't swim in it," he said.

"Why not?"

"It's not safe."

He was a slightly spooky child, Jane thought. But maybe he only meant that it wasn't safe for him to swim on his own.

There were no seals out on the island now. Jane could no longer look at it without thinking of the men kidnapped by the explorer, Pembroke. Had he ever really landed at that spot? She thought briefly of telling Genevieve about it, but she doubted Genevieve would be interested.

Genevieve returned, holding a glass of water with a perfect lemon slice on the rim. She handed it to Jane. The glass was surprisingly heavy. The ice cubes inside clinked together pleasingly.

Genevieve filled one of the preset wineglasses on the table for herself.

Benjamin sat with them. Genevieve handed him her cell phone, with some cartoon playing, and he stared at the screen, lost to it.

As she surveyed the spread before her, a vase of blue hydrangeas at the center of the table, it occurred to Jane who Genevieve reminded her of—the Schlesinger's benefactors, well-mannered, wealthy house-wives who were smart and educated and refined and mostly in their mid to late seventies. Women who had been raised to entertain; who did everything more elegantly than Jane ever could, even serve a glass of water.

Coincidentally then, Genevieve said, "I have a tiny confession to make. I looked you up on Facebook. I only mention it because that's how I learned we have a friend in common. Priscilla Bingham."

"Priscilla," Jane said. "Oh yes, she's on the alumnae advisory board at the library."

"That makes sense because I know her through the Seven Sisters book club," Genevieve said. "Small world."

Jane nodded.

From there, the conversation turned to the previous season of shows at the American Repertory Theater, across the street from Jane's office. Like Jane, Genevieve had an annual subscription. They both agreed that Anna Deavere Smith's latest one-woman show had been incredible, that a new, experimental, puppet-heavy musical was not their cup of tea.

Then they got onto the subject of good restaurants in Cambridge that had closed, and a few new ones they liked. Jane said her most recent was an Italian place called Gianna and Genevieve said her husband was friends with the owner.

"He and his wife might come up here soon for a visit," she said. "You should join us for dinner if they do."

Despite what Jane thought of Genevieve, this exchange, this reminder of her old life and the people in it, felt so welcome. Sometimes it seemed like the world Jane had spent years building for herself had vanished these past few months, like she had flipped a switch that could never be turned back on. But here was someone who knew that world well, and yet knew nothing of Jane's transgressions. The perfect combination.

"So, tell me what you learned," Genevieve said. "I'm dying to hear!"

"I'm dying to tell you," Jane said.

She went through each member of the Littleton family, explained who they were and what became of them. Genevieve nodded at the names in turn, like she had heard them before and was checking them off a list.

"I saved the best for last," Jane said when she was done.

Genevieve leaned in.

Jane pulled her phone from her purse. "A photograph!" she said.

In it, Hannah Littleton smiled up at her husband. She wore a dark, high-collared dress. Her cheeks were gaunt. Her hair brushed back and pinned up, but not as neatly as one would imagine, as if she had been in a rush.

Marilyn Martinson had texted the image to Jane after they spoke, though she hadn't responded after Jane thanked her for sending.

Jane didn't mention where she got the photo. The call she made to Marilyn seemed now like a strange choice on her part. Certainly outside the purview of what Genevieve had asked of her. Best to keep that to herself. Especially considering that Marilyn had more or less hung up on Jane the one time they spoke and never returned any of her subsequent calls.

Genevieve took a brief look at the photograph. She showed it to her son, who seemed bored. "Look at the woman in the picture, baby," she said. "Really look. Does she remind you of anyone?"

When Benjamin had no reaction, Genevieve handed the phone back to Jane and said, "What about Eliza?"

Jane was confused. "Their maid?"

"No, I think she was somebody's sister."

"Hmm," Jane said. "There was an Eliza who lived with the family but she wasn't related to them. Did you know this used to be a boardinghouse? Later, I mean. It was called the Lake Grove Inn."

Genevieve appeared entirely disinterested in this bit of information.

"I heard the original sign from the inn was left in the basement. Maybe it's still there," Jane said.

"Definitely not," Genevieve said. "When the junk guy was done, there was nothing left."

She took a long sip of wine. "He dragged twelve dumpstersful out of here. Since the last owners were too lazy to do it themselves."

There had been beautiful rugs and furniture. Framed paintings on the walls. Dishes in the cabinets. A dollhouse. Those shelves in the butler's pantry behind the kitchen, stacked high with crystal. Surely some of it had been worth saving.

"Getting back to Eliza," Genevieve said. "You're absolutely sure she wasn't related to the Littletons?"

"Pretty sure," Jane said. "A descendant of theirs who lives here in town sent me the whole genealogical record, so I can double-check that if you want, but it would have been highly unusual for people to hire a relative as a maid."

"Do you think this descendant would have photos of Eliza? Or know anyone else in the family who does?"

"Photos of their long-dead distant relatives' maid? I doubt it."

"No need then," Genevieve said. "I was hoping for a photo of Eliza most of all."

"Why?" Jane said.

"To show Benjamin," Genevieve replied.

This answer did nothing to illuminate Jane's understanding of the situation, but rather than probing further, she said, "I think it's unlikely we'll find one, especially given the time period."

Genevieve looked disappointed, but then perked up. "Unlikely, but not impossible."

Jane laughed, exasperated. "You're very persistent, aren't you, Genevieve?"

"Guilty as charged," Genevieve said. "Are you ready to eat? I made salmon."

"We hadn't talked about having dinner," Jane said. "I don't want to impose."

"Please," Genevieve said, and she sounded slightly desperate. "Please, Jane. Don't go."

AT NINE O'CLOCK, they were still sitting on that patio, at that table.

A glorious sunset came and went. Dusk fell. The air cooled considerably. Mosquitoes flew out to feast on their blood. Then darkness. A sky full of stars. A crescent moon. Somehow, inexplicably, there they were. When Jane left home earlier, she had assumed she would only be gone an hour. She had set a lone, sad frozen chicken breast on the counter to thaw for her dinner.

Genevieve's salmon was perfect. There was fresh dill involved, which was enough to impress Jane. Afterward, Genevieve served blueberry pie, the best Jane had ever tasted.

The meal had ended an hour ago now. There had been several lulls in the conversation since. Once they had exhausted talk of cultural must-dos and the Littletons, once they'd reached the point where it was time to talk about themselves, neither of them had much to say.

Despite all her wealth and good manners, Genevieve was awkward, a feeling Jane could relate to, all too well.

But every time Jane tried to say goodbye, Genevieve was suddenly desperate for her opinion on the tile samples her decorator sent for the upstairs laundry room, or she had another question about Awadapquit. For once, Jane got to be the expert on the town instead of feeling like an outsider, as she usually did despite the fact that three generations of her family had lived here at one time or another.

Benjamin had not been sent to bed. He was inside now, watching the same cartoon as before, on an iPad on the couch.

Genevieve glanced over at him through the glass sliders every minute or so. She kept getting up to check on him. To bring him water or a soft blanket.

"So you work in Cambridge, but you live here in the summers?" she said, squinting as if to indicate that she was thinking extra hard.

"My mother lives here," Jane said. "Or, she lived here. She passed away just over a year ago."

"Oh no. I'm sorry."

"Thanks."

"She must have been young," Genevieve said. "How did she die?"

"Lung cancer."

Genevieve shook her head.

"My cousin died of the same thing," she said. "It was so unfair. He never even smoked."

Jane's mother had smoked constantly for as long as Jane knew her. It could never be said that she hadn't brought it upon herself, she supposed, and yet Jane still saw her as a victim. Of the tobacco companies that got her hooked when she was thirteen. Of the culture that taught her to worship thinness above all else.

"And your dad?" Genevieve said. "Is he still around?"

"He left when my sister was two and I was basically a newborn," Jane said. "That was that. Never even got a birthday card from the guy. I couldn't pick him out of a lineup, to tell you the truth."

Tears sprang to Genevieve's eyes. Instantaneous, as if she were chopping onions.

"Sorry," she said, wiping them away. "I was raised by a single mom too. I can't imagine losing her."

It seemed as though she wanted Jane, whose mother had died, to console her over the prospect of her own mother dying at some unspecified time in the future.

"I really should get going," Jane said.

"You can't go yet," Genevieve said. "You haven't even told me what your connection to this house is. Allison said something, that day we met. Remember?"

"Well," Jane said. "I discovered it in high school. Of course there was no one living here then, and I used to come all the time. By myself. I would just sit outside and read. Then later, I came with my husband whenever we visited Awadapquit."

"I didn't realize you were married," Genevieve said, placing a hand over her mouth. "You could have brought your husband here tonight. I feel terrible for not inviting him."

"Please don't feel terrible for not inviting someone you didn't know existed," Jane said. "Anyway, David isn't here. We're—taking some time apart."

She had not admitted this out loud to anyone besides Allison and Holly. It felt like such an unreal thing to say.

"Marriage is complicated," Genevieve said.

Jane thought it was a perfect response. Not pitying or overly familiar, or prying for more information. Just as when Jane told Genevieve she didn't drink, Genevieve had not asked why or for how long. The upside of Genevieve's formality, Jane supposed, was her discretion.

"It is complicated," Jane said. "You're right about that."

From this distance, though, she was beginning to see clearly how it all happened. There had been a whiplash-like quality to her life for the past year and a half. Things that seemed permanent just went poof. Jane didn't have time to process one bit of bad news before the next arrived.

In the span of six months, her mother got sick and was gone. It had only been a year since she died. Jane had worried many times that she wasn't sad enough. But looking back, she had started drinking more than ever right after the funeral, and showing up late to work. She even called in sick some days, too hungover to deal. That was a first.

Occasionally, after several glasses of wine, she would lash out at David for no good reason.

The next morning, when she apologized, he would say, "You just lost your mom. You've had a hard year."

Jane appreciated this, even as she understood that he was letting her get away with something he shouldn't. He suggested she try therapy, but when she refused, David didn't push it. Jane feared that if she kept on like that, eventually she would make herself unlovable in his eyes. And then what? David would never leave her. He was so loyal. He came from a big family, in which no one had ever gotten divorced. He was ashamed of the fact that his first marriage ended. He would do anything, Jane knew, to stay married this time. Even ignore what was right in front of him. That was why she left. Because she loved him, and she knew he was better off without her. That version of her, at least.

There was silence, during which Jane could almost see the wheels turning in Genevieve's head. Like she was searching for something encouraging to say about Jane's troubled marriage, but kept coming up empty.

Maybe all she could think to do was offer her own secret in return. Because after that long pause, Genevieve said, "You'll probably think I'm crazy, but I'm pretty sure this house is haunted."

Jane blinked. It was truly the last thing she had expected Genevieve to say.

"I know how that sounds, but strange things have happened since we got here. There's no other explanation for them."

"What kind of things?" Jane said.

"Marbles," Genevieve said.

"Marbles?"

Jane remembered there being marbles in the upstairs hallway, all mixed up with shards of glass, that one time she had dared to go to the second floor as a teenager.

"The house was professionally emptied and deep-cleaned before we moved in," Genevieve said. "There was absolutely nothing here. And yet marbles just appear. Oh, and one night, suddenly, there was this huge crack in the wall. Lights flicker. Objects fall off shelves for no reason. And there's a ghost."

Jane tried to hold back a smile. She almost said, *Next time, lead with the ghost.* But she wasn't sure Genevieve had a sense of humor.

"Benjamin saw her. A girl. She kept coming into his room. It was Eliza, I'm pretty sure," Genevieve said. "Sister Eliza."

"What makes you think that?"

Genevieve paused, as if weighing her response.

"Just a feeling," she said, finally. "After Benjamin told me, we went straight to the Saint Aspinquid. Tonight will be our first night back here since."

"I see," Jane said.

"I told him he won't be sleeping in that room ever again. That was the only place he saw her. And only when he was alone. I'm nervous, though. This ghost, she's angry at us," Genevieve said. "I'm afraid it's something I did."

"Like what?" Jane said. *A tasteless home renovation?*

Genevieve didn't answer.

"So that's why you wanted a picture of Eliza."

"Yes." Genevieve inhaled and threw her head back. With one syllable uttered, she appeared unburdened.

"My husband, Paul, is supposed to join us tonight and stay for two weeks. That was the only reason I felt comfortable coming back. He said he would be here at seven but he has no sense of time." Genevieve seemed like she was going to go a step further in her complaint, but then she said, "Paul just works too much. He barely gets to enjoy this place."

So Jane was more than company. She was a form of protection. She had eaten the salmon, the pie, the corn on the cob, that were meant for him. A bribe so that Genevieve didn't have to be alone. As if Jane could do anything should a ghost appear.

"The funny thing is," Genevieve said, "Benjamin isn't scared of the ghost. I think she's more like a friend to him. While we were at the inn, he told me she would never hurt us. She only wants to find her mother."

"Her mother?" Jane said.

"Paul had a field day with that. He was like, well, this is what happens when a woman indulges her child. He starts seeing ghosts who want their mommies."

"Genevieve," Jane said. "I have to tell you something weird."

"What is it?"

"How do I say this?" Jane said. "Okay. Well. Allison bought me a reading with a medium."

Genevieve's face was neutral. Jane had expected surprise. Maybe Genevieve didn't know what a medium was.

"This woman Clementine. She's like a psychic. She talks to the dead," Jane clarified.

Still nothing.

Genevieve just nodded. Did no one find this odd but Jane?

"When we met, Clementine said she had contacted the spirits of my mom and my grandma. But there was someone else with them. The spirit of a young girl whose name started with the letter *D*. She mentioned a place called Lake Grove." Jane gestured emphatically at the house. "*Lake Grove. The Inn at Lake Grove.* And she was trying to reach her mother."

"Oh my God," Genevieve said. "I just got an actual chill up my spine."

"Right? It can't be a coincidence, can it?" Jane said.

"I don't even believe in ghosts," Genevieve said.

"Neither do I," Jane said.

"Do you know who D is?"

"Not a clue," Jane said.

"Maybe Eliza's last name started with a *D,*" Genevieve said, for some reason unable to give up on this baseless theory.

"No," Jane said. "It was Green."

"We should reach out to your medium friend and see if she can tell us more."

"Good idea," Jane said. "I'll call her on Monday."

"Can't you do it now?" Genevieve said.

Jane had a flash of Allison's story about Chris making Genevieve a club sandwich.

"Clementine isn't my friend," Jane said. "Can you imagine some random person you'd met once calling you about work at nine o'clock on a Saturday night?"

Genevieve shrugged.

Jane wondered whether she had ever had a job.

At that moment, Genevieve's phone lit up with an incoming text. She smiled. "Paul just crossed the bridge into New Hampshire. He'll be here soon."

With that, it seemed, Jane was dismissed.

Genevieve sent her off with a Tupperware full of leftovers and copious thank-yous for the fascinating findings, and a white envelope with a check for ten thousand dollars inside.

BEFORE SHE DROVE HOME, Jane sat in her car in Genevieve's driveway, doors locked, looking up at the house.

Marilyn Martinson had said it was cursed. The women who lived here ended up alone.

Jane's had always been a family without men. It shocked them all when Jason was born. How could he belong to them? Beneath the basic truth of it lay an unspoken fear that they drove men away. No sense in getting too attached if that was to be your fate.

Every light in the house was on, and the porch light, welcoming Paul home.

Even the swimming pool, off to the side of the house, was illuminated from within, the wind-rippled water casting shadows on the lawn.

LATER, alone on the couch at her mother's place, Jane found herself googling the antiques dealer who sold Genevieve the basket, and once had a gallery in town. Thomas Crosby.

She had texted Allison first to ask if she recognized the name, but Allison just replied with a question mark. Allison's mother would know, Jane thought, before the inevitable recollection that Betty wouldn't, anymore. Her illness hadn't only robbed them of future experiences with her, but of all the wisdom she possessed. That trove of names and dates and stories and petty feuds that went back generations.

Allison asked how the night went, and when Jane responded, It was good! Genevieve's an odd duck, huh? Allison wrote back: That's putting it mildly.

Jane detailed the realization they had had about ghosts looking for their mothers.

Wait, do you think she stayed at the inn because of a ghost? Allison replied.

Definitely, Jane wrote.

Ahahahahahahahahahahahahaha. Okay, but actually for once, I agree with her, you have to reach out to Clementine.

Jane put the phone down and continued her search on her computer.

Thomas Crosby had no website, no social media profile. He was mentioned briefly in a *Boston Globe* article from 2004, as one of many examples of non-Indigenous individuals who had profited from the sale of Indigenous artifacts. His popular Maine gallery—built on a collection passed down from a great-great-uncle—had attracted customers from all over the country for more than three decades, the article said, until it closed abruptly in 1992. Crosby had since been embroiled in various related legal disputes.

Jane wondered if Genevieve knew about that.

Only three other articles referenced Crosby, all from the *Portsmouth Herald,* and all concerning a man from New Mexico who had battled for years to get Crosby to hand over four Zuni war gods that rightfully belonged to his tribe.

"Native Americans believe some objects have a spiritual life," the man was quoted as saying. "We mean it literally. We view sacred objects as living beings. This is more than theft. This is akin to kidnapping."

Jane went to her purse and rummaged around until she found the notebook in which she had written the names of the men kidnapped by Pembroke. *Amoret, Tahanedo, Mannedo, Saffacomoit.* Something had compelled her to write them down.

Four men, their names unknown to her until now, stolen from their home by a man whose name she had spoken hundreds of times.

Even in high school, giving her evening tours, pointing out the little island, Jane had had her doubts that Pembroke ever landed in Awadapquit. Now she thought: Suppose he had. It was possible that the kidnapping occurred right here. Or that those men had been dragged from wherever they started through this place, on their way to another world.

Jane sent an email to Naomi Miller, the Penobscot woman Evan had introduced her to at the historical society. He had said Naomi ran a consultancy, that she knew everything there was to know about

Native Americans in Maine. In the email, Jane asked if she could send Naomi a question about information she had acquired on four Wabanaki men who may or may not have lived in Awadapquit. She warned her that the information was disturbing, that she fully understood if Naomi didn't want to go there, and for good measure, added a Feel free to ignore me if you are too busy!

THE NEXT MORNING, Sunday, Naomi called her.

"I have a few minutes now. I'm in the car," Naomi said. "I always find it easier to talk on the phone."

"Totally," Jane said, though she hated talking on the phone.

"So tell me what you're looking into," Naomi said.

"Well, I've known forever that this English explorer, a very minor one, but still, landed in my hometown in the early 1600s. Maybe."

Naomi laughed. "Okay."

"Yeah, I kind of think his landing here is a made-up story. But I do know that he was real, and I just learned that he kidnapped a group of Indigenous men on one of his voyages. I have their names written down. Probably a long shot, but I thought maybe you would know or be able to point me in the right direction to find out whether the names match names of people who would have lived in this area."

"Hmm," Naomi said. "Probably not. I'm not a language expert. I have been trying to learn more of my own language, Penobscot. Which is very closely linked to Abenaki, which probably would have been the main language spoken in those parts at that time. The problem is those early explorers wrote down everything phonetically. They got more wrong than right. *Kwenitew,* for example. It means *long river.* They heard *Connecticut.* The names of the men that were written down were likely not their actual names."

"Right," Jane said. "Makes sense."

"Even the town you live in, Awadapquit. The tourist board says the word means *where the beautiful cliffs meet the sea.* Right? But actually, it doesn't mean anything. That's not a word."

Jane sat up straighter.

"I can't decide if I'm shocked or totally unsurprised by that," she said.

"I looked it up after I met you, because Evan said those words and then I kept thinking about it, and it was bugging me," Naomi said. "I'm kind of a weirdo like that. I never turn off the work part of my brain."

"Oh, I'm the same way," Jane said.

"If I had to guess, I'd say *Awadapquit* was someone butchering the word *Sawadapskw'i*," Naomi said. "Which means in Abenaki, *of the jutting-out rock*. No one's putting that on a postcard."

Jane wondered if Allison knew this, if everyone did. If anyone did. She had never heard it before.

"One of the main things I've been involved in lately is a communal mapping project with the Penobscot Nation," Naomi said. "We are trying to restore traditional place-names and create a new map of Maine. Our people's place-names were never arbitrary. They were given by our ancestors, to describe elements of the landscape, or provide information. When the names were changed, the information itself was often lost."

"Oh my God," Jane said, a lightning bolt of connection striking in her mind. "*Of the jutting-out rock*. So Awadapquit is all cliffs. And the cliffs *do* jut out in this one spot. The exact spot where I've been doing research on an old house. There's an island across the way, and that is where they say this explorer landed. So maybe it is true. And maybe they called this area that word because the men were kidnapped in this jutting-out rock location."

"No," Naomi said, dismissing this, though not unkindly. "A name wouldn't be given for something like that. It was more a way of letting people know where an important recurring ceremony or gathering was to take place."

"Oh," Jane said. "I see. The mapping project sounds interesting. I'd love to hear more about it."

"Every aspect of my work is about the restoration of what my people already had to begin with," Naomi said. "It's all about returning us to ourselves. People send me things all the time. Stories and family lore, objects and mementos. I try to get them to the proper descendants, for whom they hold meaning. But that's part of the larger battle to take back our language, our land, our true sovereignty."

"How did you get into this line of work?" Jane said.

She found Naomi totally fascinating. She could talk to her all day.

"It started sort of by accident," Naomi said. "When a guy named Trip, yes Trip, sent me a batch of photos of Penobscot ancestors that his grandfather had been holding on to for decades. Think about that. His grandfather—a white man who had passed through this area once—had seen our ancestors' faces, but we never had."

Jane's phone beeped then, another call coming in. She looked at the screen and saw that it was Genevieve. She sent her to voicemail.

Seconds later, Genevieve sent a text message reminding Jane to call Clementine first thing on Monday. A second text arrived, outlining precisely what Jane ought to say.

Genevieve really was very annoying.

"Jane?" Naomi said.

"So sorry," Jane said. "This obnoxious client of mine keeps texting and calling me."

"Oh dear," Naomi said. "What does she want?"

"She wants me to call a psychic medium I know who works out of a place called Camp Mira, to see if she will come here and give her a reading."

As soon as the words were out of her mouth, Jane felt stupid. But Naomi responded, "Camp Mira? I have always wanted to go there."

"Really?" Jane said. "I never even knew it existed until this summer."

Another text from Genevieve appeared, as Naomi said, "I just got to my brother's house, so I should get going anyway. Good luck with your obnoxious client. Let's have lunch one of these days."

"I would love that," Jane said.

9

In spite of herself, Jane found that she was deeply curious to know what Clementine would tell them. The more she thought about it, the more curious she became.

Jane called her at nine-thirty Monday morning to ask her to make another visit to Awadapquit.

"Remember how the girl kept interrupting when you did my reading?" she said to Clementine. "And she said she was looking for her mother, and not at Lake Grove anymore? What's crazy is this woman I met lives at a house called Lake Grove. And her son has been visited by a ghost who says she's looking for *her* mother."

Jane expected Clementine to be intrigued, to say she would come right away.

Instead, Clementine said she wasn't free to visit in person until the fall. Jane could make an appointment for a reading by phone, but Clementine couldn't even do that until mid-September.

"It's the busy season at camp," she said. "We're in full swing. Unless you and your friend want to come here? The weekend after next is a fair day. We are open to the public, no appointments needed. There will be lots of demonstrations and lectures and things. I'd try my absolute best to see you. If not me, someone else will be available, I'm sure."

Jane still didn't think she believed in any of it, and yet the thought of seeing anyone but Clementine was disappointing.

She called Genevieve to tell her what Clementine had suggested.

"The drive to Camp Mira is three hours each way, plus a twenty-minute ferry ride," Jane said. When Genevieve didn't reply, she added, "It's way too far, obviously."

Inexplicably, Jane felt disappointed.

Genevieve said, "No, no! I was just checking my calendar. I'm free that day, and Paul will be here to watch Benjamin. Road trip, here we come. You'll pick me up?"

Right away, Jane wondered if she had made a mistake.

She looked on the camp's website to figure out what it even was.

Welcome to the world of Spiritualism, the home page read. Located on a peaceful, pedestrianized private island off Bar Harbor, Camp Mira is a place where each of us communicates directly with God and the spirit world. Ours is a highly personal religion. We each define our faith in different ways. But we share a core set of beliefs, chief among them that bodily death is not the end of consciousness. It is merely the passing of the soul into another plane. The women of Camp Mira are honored to serve as conduits to your loved ones in spirit form. No one is truly gone.

After reading it, Jane still wasn't sure what to expect, and now she was a bit weirded out.

She called Allison. "I'm going to cancel."

"No way," Allison said. "We're going."

"Really? You can get the day off?" Jane said.

"For this, yes. And for you, I am willing to spend an entire day trapped in a car with Genevieve. Remember that."

"That's love," Jane said.

"It is."

"Apparently, I'm driving us, by the way. Genevieve told me so."

"Of course she did," Allison said.

WHEN THE MORNING ARRIVED, Jane drove to her sister's place at six o'clock to drop Walter off. She carried the dog to Holly's front door, and used the spare key to get in.

The house was dark, silent. Holly and Jason were both late sleepers. Jane had initially texted them to ask if they could come to her mother's house and let Walter out today while she was gone. Jason, never one to waste a word, sent back a thumbs-up emoji. Holly did not reply. So Jane figured she had better bring Walter to them, lest they forget about him.

She set him down in the front hall, patted his head, and closed the door.

Walter started yapping before she even reached the car. Jane couldn't help but smile as she imagined Holly in the position she herself was in every other morning. A hostage to the whims of an insane creature the size of a loaf of bread.

She picked Allison up first.

A few minutes later, they arrived at Genevieve's house.

"It looks different than I remember," Allison said.

"Yeah, but this part is nothing. The inside is unrecognizable," Jane said.

"Did she paint over all that beautiful woodwork?" Allison said.

"Yes, of course. It's white like everything else in there."

Allison shook her head. "That is a sin. That woodwork was gorgeous."

Jane half hoped Genevieve would invite them in so Allison could grasp the extent of it. But Genevieve was waiting outside.

She got into the car with an overly bright, "Good morning!"

She brought muffins in a wax paper bag, from a bakery in Kittery Point Jane had never heard of. Jane took one, blueberry, as soon as they were offered. She plucked off bite-sized pieces, as if she might not eat the whole thing, until there was nothing left but the wrapper. She immediately wanted another.

"These are amazing," she said to Allison. "Try one."

"I'm good," Allison said.

Jane wondered if she really didn't want a muffin, or if she just couldn't give Genevieve the satisfaction.

The first hour of the drive passed in near-silence. They listened to NPR in lieu of talking. Then they stopped for coffee. Once the caffeine kicked in, they started to chat.

Allison and Genevieve compared notes on having boys. Jane tried to be an attentive listener, so as not to draw attention to the way this caused a tiny ache in her. These last few years, she had lost several friends to motherhood. Not overtly. It was just that women with children were busy. And, in her experience, women with children preferred the company of other women with children.

This was one reason why Pearl and Melissa had been such a good match for Jane and David. They didn't have kids either.

"I don't know how you do it with two and a full-time job," Genevieve said. "And you're always so together."

"It's a zoo at our place when the guests aren't looking, believe me," Allison said.

"Chris seems like such a hands-on dad," Genevieve said. "I wish Paul were more that way. He doesn't know how to connect with Benjamin. Even today—it's a Saturday, but he insisted on having a sitter there with them while I'm gone. I can count on one hand the number of times they've been alone together for more than an hour."

"Don't you want to murder him?" Allison said. "How do you deal with that?"

"He works so hard," Genevieve said. "I shouldn't complain."

"Complain away," Allison and Jane said simultaneously.

But Genevieve took it no further.

Jane thought of David. How involved he was in the lives of his nieces and nephews. Jason had once told her that David was like the dad he never had, even though he did have a dad. Because David would drive all the way to Maine to see one of Jason's hockey games. He took Jason fishing every summer. They talked on the phone when Jason was having a hard time socially, and David would come up with some relatable story from his past that offered hope, or a bigger picture, or just made Jason laugh.

It wasn't fair that fatherhood should come easily to Paul, who didn't appreciate or know what to do with it. Meanwhile David, who would have been so good at it, had never gotten the chance. This, Jane knew, was her fault.

She was grateful for the distraction from her thoughts when Allison asked Genevieve if there had been any more ghost sightings at her place.

"I don't think so," Genevieve said. "But Benjamin hasn't said anything on the subject since the last time he mentioned his ghost girl and Paul blew up at him to stop telling stories."

"Why did Paul blow up?" Allison said.

"All the ghost talk drives him crazy and I can't quite figure out why," Genevieve said. "Sometimes I think it's that he doesn't believe it. Other times, I think he does believe and is mad that we didn't intuit this before we bought the house."

"I always assumed that house was haunted when we were in high school," Allison said. "Didn't you, Jane?"

"Uhh, no. What? You did?"

Was that a thing people believed?

"Don't tell me that," Genevieve said. She covered her face with her hands.

THEY REACHED the ferry dock twenty minutes ahead of schedule. Jane texted Clementine to say they had arrived, as Clementine had asked her to do.

It was a gorgeous day. Not too hot. Warm and windless, sun shining bright in a pure blue sky.

When the boat arrived, maybe forty or fifty people were lined up. Once they boarded, Jane noticed all but three of the passengers were women. Two of the three men were husbands, accompanying their wives: A couple in their fifties, each looking down at their phones. A couple in their eighties. She was knitting as he stared out a porthole at the sea.

The third man was middle-aged. He wore a suit and sat alone, reading the *Times*. He looked so out of place that Jane had to hold herself back from asking if he was on the wrong boat.

The ferry approached the island fifteen minutes later.

In front of them, across an expansive lawn, was an enormous old building, pale yellow, with a wide front porch. To the right of the dock was a small beach. A group of white-haired women bobbed about in the water, laughing uproariously. A wooden sign planted on the sand read WELCOME TO CAMP MIRA.

Clementine stood waiting for them at the dock. She wore purple, as she had the day they met. At Jane's mother's place, she had seemed strange. In this setting she looked regal, floating above the crowd.

Clementine hugged Jane like they were old friends. "I'm glad you came," she said. "I've got to do a reading in ten minutes and then I've got more, back-to-back until two. I'll have time to chat with you then. You can come to my cottage and visit."

Genevieve stuck out her hand and introduced herself. "I'm the one Jane called you about," she said. "The one with the haunted house. We made quite a journey to get here, so I've got my fingers crossed for a private reading."

Jane cringed. She was so pushy. She seemed to think the entire world answered to her.

"I'm afraid private sessions book up far in advance, as I told Jane already," Clementine said. "By the previous September most years. I was hoping maybe there would be a cancellation, but no. You should all go to the public demonstration at one o'clock. There will be a chance to ask questions. That's your best bet for mediumship today."

"But I thought if we came in person, you'd squeeze us in," Genevieve said.

"I can only do so many readings each week," Clementine said. "Energetically, I get depleted by it."

"We understand," Jane said.

"Don't worry," Clementine said, patting Genevieve's arm. "You'll still get plenty out of this day. You must go to the past life regression. Not to be missed. Come on. Follow me."

Clementine led them along a gravel path, past the yellow building with the big porch.

It had been a hotel with a hundred and twenty-five rooms in the camp's heyday, she said, but was now mostly used for storage.

Behind the old hotel, the land was craggy in places, grassy in others. In the far distance was a three-peaked tent beside the ocean. Nearer to them were two dozen or so cottages, painted in pastel shades, arranged in no particular pattern. They were crisp and pretty, with flowers in the window boxes and all manner of ornaments on the small square lawns—wind chimes and dream catchers and pink crystal fountains, statues of fairies and, in one yard, a statue of the Virgin Mary.

Women alone or in groups of two or three roamed about.

"Big crowd today," Jane said.

Clementine shrugged. "A hundred years ago, we had tens of thousands of visitors each summer. Ferries came out here on the hour from Memorial Day to Labor Day. Now there are two ferries a day. I shouldn't complain. We're still much busier than most camps. A lot have closed outright. And you're right, a fair day tends to draw a decent crowd. We're happy with the turnout."

She checked her watch. "I've got to get going. I'll see you all this afternoon. That's my house over there."

She pointed at one of the cottages. Dark purple with a white picket fence, knee-high. A border of sunflowers all around.

"Almost forgot," Clementine said. "Here you go."

She handed each of them a sheet of paper and was off.

Jane looked down. A schedule of the day's offerings. She took in a few:

CANDLE MANIFESTATION
led by Florencia

ENERGY CLEARING
(instructor TBD)

PAST LIFE REGRESSION
with Evangeline and Special Guest

HOW TO TALK SO YOUR
SPIRIT GUIDES WILL LISTEN
AND LISTEN SO YOUR
SPIRIT GUIDES WILL TALK
(All, Campfire Chat)

"Wowsa," Allison whispered. "This is a lot."

Jane agreed; it was too strange. She was about to ask if they wanted to leave, when Allison went on, "It all looks incredible, I want to do everything."

"What was the one she said was a must?" Genevieve said.

"Past life regression," Allison said. "With——" Her eyes scanned the page. "Evangeline."

Jane remembered Clementine telling her about this woman. She was the one who said parents and their children chose one another. She had said Clementine and her own mother were married in a past life.

"Notice not one of them is named, like, Jennifer or Kim," Allison said.

"Maybe they use fake names, like hairdressers," Genevieve said.

They had an hour to go before the past life regression, and couldn't agree on how to spend it. Allison wanted to try a session on art and mediumship. Genevieve had three text messages from her husband. ("We have friends coming tomorrow and he has no idea how to prepare," she said.) She decided to stroll to the beach and call him, with instructions for exactly which cheese and crackers to buy, since apparently such things were beyond his grasp.

Jane chose a lecture on the feminist history of Spiritualism. The location was listed as *HBT*.

She looked around until she saw a squat white building, different from the rest. Clearly not a house. As she walked toward it, she saw the words *Hattie Butler Temple* above the door.

Jane went inside. The space was dim and cool, with laminate floors and rows of folding chairs. Nothing about it conveyed the notion of a *temple*, other than its name. At the front of the room was a raised platform, a sort of stage or altar, completely unadorned. A woman of maybe seventy with impeccable posture sat there, in a pink armchair.

Jane took a seat at the back. There were only four other people in the room, all women. "Come closer, I don't bite," the woman onstage called to her.

Jane smiled apologetically and moved up a few rows.

The woman introduced herself as Reverend Cora.

She thanked them for coming, then started in on her talk.

Most people, she told them, considered the first public demonstration of Spiritualism in America to have been a performance by the Fox sisters, young girls from a poor family in Hydesville, New York, in 1849. These sisters claimed to hear rappings that came from a spirit called Mr. Splitfoot. The rappings contained messages only they could decipher. People came from far and wide to watch them at work.

"That was the start of it," Reverend Cora said. "And the world was never the same."

Never the same? Jane thought. *Really?* She had never even heard of the Fox sisters.

Cora said Camp Mira's benefactor, Hattie M. Butler, was a wealthy woman from Beacon Hill, who gave this island to the Spiritualist church in 1887, to be used as a summer retreat.

"Hattie received messages from spirit," Cora said. "She held séances in her parlor on Pinckney Street, and during those, she used her middle name, Mira. She was a suffragist, an abolitionist, like so many Spiritualists of the time. Spiritualists were among the presenters at the first women's rights convention in Seneca Falls. The women there were doing something extraordinary that most of them had never done, or even seen, before: speaking in public. By the time Hattie came along, some of the largest gatherings in this country were public demonstrations of mediumship performed by women, and at every one, the ideas of social justice and human rights got their due. In the early years, we had an annual suffrage day here at Camp Mira. Elizabeth Cady Stanton spoke. And Susan B. Anthony."

Jane opened an email in her phone and addressed it to herself, with the subject line Overlap between mediums/spiritualists and suffragists/abolitionists. It would make a fascinating exhibit at the archives. If she was ever allowed back. It occurred to her that Clementine had suggested she look into all this when they met and Jane had dismissed it.

Cora spoke at length about how the Civil War played a pivotal role in the popularity of mediums.

"The entire country was grieving," she said. "Everyone wanted to reach their lost loved ones. Ten years after the war ended, Spiritualism had over a million practitioners in the United States and Europe. It was the second most popular religion in America. We are still a recognized religion today, though our numbers are far lower. For centuries, men in power have endeavored to disprove what we do. We are, and always have been, a religion in which many of the leaders are women. That just terrifies the pants off the patriarchy."

Everyone in the room chuckled. "There are no other examples of a woman-led religion in postcolonial America, besides Ann Lee and the

Shakers," Cora said. "I've wondered why not. But then, women are in sync with nature. Our cycles are linked to the moon, to the tides. Like them, we change two dozen times over, every month. What do men do? They don't get to experience much of life. We gestate the babies and bring them into existence while the men try not to faint. It's why they're obsessed with extrinsic markers of success. And war! Taking life to feel some speck of the power we get from making life. You have to hand it to men, they've managed to convince us that the things that make women powerful are weaknesses. Motherhood is the most radical act in the world, and we've turned it into tapioca pudding. What's more toothless, more invisible in this culture, than a mother?"

Jane considered the notion that mothers were radical creatures, that the act of bringing life into the world contained some secret power that she would never know.

THE PAST LIFE regression was being held in the temple as well. Jane stayed in her seat and watched as women poured in through the open doors.

The room filled up fast. Apparently past life regression was a much hotter topic than the feminist history of Spiritualism. Jane claimed the two seats to her left by placing her purse on one and her phone on the other.

A woman and a man walked in and went straight to the platform. They stood before it talking among themselves, looking authoritative. He wore a suit, a crisp pale blue oxford shirt. Jane realized now—he was the one from the ferry. The only unaccompanied man. He seemed improbable here, on this island ruled by women. Jane imagined what role he might play. Accountant to the clairvoyant?

The woman with him looked to be in her early fifties. She was thin with the blonde, straight hair of a Barbie doll fresh from the box. She had on a flowing skirt, a tight black tank top, and thin gold bracelets stacked from her right wrist halfway up her forearm.

When Allison and Genevieve walked in, Jane waved them over and they came and sat beside her. Allison had a rolled-up piece of paper in one hand. She unrolled it to show a pencil sketch of what appeared to be a small old lady drinking a cup of tea.

"Jane, meet my spirit guide, Rita O'Shea," Allison said.

"Hello, Rita," Jane said to the picture.

"Florencia is magic," Allison said. "She sees your spirit guides and can draw you a picture, so that you know for sure whether you recognize them."

"Do you recognize Rita O'Shea?" Jane said.

"No," Allison said.

Jane nodded, trying not to laugh.

The man and woman at the front of the room perched on the edge of the platform, legs dangling, like a pair of cool middle school drama teachers. The woman introduced herself as Evangeline, a resident of the island and the medium who would lead them in the past life regression. But first, she said, they would hear from a visitor, Dr. Jon Abrams, the head of the University of Virginia's Division of Perceptual Studies.

The man in the suit waved to the crowd as they applauded.

The last thing Jane imagined she would find in this place was an academic. According to Evangeline's introduction, the center at UVA had been there since the sixties. Its founder, the university's then chair of psychiatry, had recorded over three thousand cases of young children with past life memories over the course of his career. He had been a mentor to the man onstage, Abrams, who had since taken over the role.

Dr. Abrams began by speaking glowingly of his predecessor, the first person ever to take a rigorous research-based approach to the study of past lives. The children he worked with usually described memories of another person's life, with enough specifics—names, dates, places—that an actual dead person had been identified whose story matched exactly.

"Primarily, he found such children in Asian countries, where a belief in reincarnation was common," Dr. Abrams said. "In Western culture, children who told stories of past lives were more likely to be dismissed as making it all up. They might even be punished for it."

Jane looked at Genevieve, thinking of what she said earlier, about her husband getting angry with poor Benjamin when he talked about his ghost.

"But in recent years," he went on, "we have seen a shift. There are more cases popping up in the US and Europe. Parents overall are more tolerant, maybe. Even if what's happening doesn't align with their beliefs."

Jane tried to imagine what her grandmother and mother would have said if she told them she had been a milkmaid or a Ziegfeld Follies girl in a past life. Depending on the day, they might have laughed or said a novena or sent her to her room. Certainly, they would not have pursued it further.

Dr. Abrams told a story about a boy in Oklahoma, who was not yet two when he started talking about Hollywood, and how much he missed LA. About his wife, Annabelle, and their son, Eugene. His name, he said, was Benny Jackson, and he didn't know why he was trapped in some suburban tract house with these people, when he should be in Beverly Hills. The boy's parents were fundamentalist Christians, and yet, with time, he grew more insistent, shared such specific details, that they couldn't dismiss what he said. They did the opposite. Exposed him to media about old Hollywood, hoping to find out more. One day, looking through a book about the history of moviemaking in America with his mother, the child pointed at a black-and-white picture of some unnamed, unrecognizable guy, standing beside Jimmy Stewart.

"That's Jimmy," the boy said. And then, pointing to the unnamed man, "That's me."

The parents did everything in their power to figure out who the man in the picture was. It took them more than a year. It turned out his name was Bennett Jackson. He was a B-list actor who had been killed in a car accident in his early thirties in 1949, when his only child was seven years old. That child, Eugene, was still alive. They brought the boy to meet him and Eugene Jackson wept, convinced that the five-year-old stranger in front of him was his father.

"Another boy," Dr. Abrams went on, "recalled dying in a plane crash during World War Two. In that case, again, he knew details no one else could. The names of fellow airmen in his unit, the type of plane he was flying when he died, the street he grew up on in Morristown, New Jersey. It's often very traumatic for the children. They want to know where their families are, why they can't see them. They want their old lives back. For around seventy percent of the kids we meet with vivid memories of a past life, the death in that previous life was sudden and violent. Suicide, murder, combat, a car crash. Means of dying that we might consider outside the natural order of things. These kids remember every detail. They often have connected phobias. For instance, a child who drowned in a former life might be terrified of water."

A three-year-old in Thailand told his family he was a teacher who had been shot while riding his bicycle to work. He begged to be taken home, naming the village where, he said, his relatives still lived. When the boy's grandmother brought him to that village, thirty miles away, he led her to a house, in which lived the family of a young teacher who had been killed riding his bicycle to work five years earlier. Perhaps the strangest part, Dr. Abrams said, was that the boy had two birthmarks—a small perfect circle at the back of his head and a larger, more formless one on his face. These marks matched the entrance and exit wounds left by a bullet on the dead man's body.

Onstage, Dr. Abrams pulled down a projector screen.

"That's not an isolated incident," he said. "Often, the children have birthmarks or defects that match the way the person from the previous life died."

He went through a series of slides. A boy born with no left ear, who remembered dying from a shotgun blast to the side of the head. A child with no digits, who could recall being a man whose fingers were chopped off by gangsters when he couldn't pay his debts.

During the question-and-answer session that followed, a woman pushed back. "But how do you explain it?" she said. "How does it work? My daughter was born with a hemangioma covering half her face. Do you mean to tell me that's something left over from a past life?"

"Not necessarily," he said. "As for the how, we don't know. No one has been able to figure out *how* it happens, but we know *that* it happens. None of this makes sense when you filter it through the lens of rational thought. But there's no denying the evidence. Getting to the bottom of how is a huge part of our work."

Jane was often astonished that there were so many worlds. Ideas and obsessions that meant everything to one person, to which he might devote his entire life, which the next person knew and cared nothing about.

Genevieve raised a hand. A tentative half raise, like she didn't want to be a bother. Her voice, at first, was an almost whisper. She had to force it to come.

"What is it about children?" she said. "Why are they the ones who have to carry this burden? My son hasn't remembered a past life, but he sees a ghost. They have conversations."

Jane tensed up, embarrassed by association. But not a single person in the room even smirked. Of course they didn't. She reminded herself where they were.

"There is certainly a connection between the two," Dr. Abrams said. "We don't know enough about the mechanics of it all to say exactly why, but it is a fact that young children tend to have these experiences with the other side and then, by the time they are six or seven, it fades away. I've always thought it's because that's when they become aware of their peers' opinions. They don't want to be the weird kid, so they force themselves to forget."

Genevieve nodded, though she looked wounded. Because of the *weird kid* bit, Jane figured. Dr. Abrams went on. "Of course it's also right around then that most children start forgetting early childhood."

Jane looked over to see Allison frantically scribbling on the back of an envelope.

"Why are you taking notes?" she whispered.

Allison blinked at her, as if being pulled from a trance. "I have no idea."

"Maybe you should ask Rita O'Shea," Jane said. "Does she know something we don't?"

Allison's tongue quickly darted out of her mouth and back in again.

"Our findings point to the idea that the brain and the mind are not necessarily one and the same," Dr. Abrams said. "We have a great deal to learn about consciousness. Take Evangeline here. A medium's work is done in an altered state of consciousness. How does she tune in to those frequencies the rest of us can't, or don't? And speaking of Evangeline, I should probably turn this over to you now for the hypnosis. That's what the people came for."

"I prefer to call it a *meditation*. You know that," she said in a teasing tone of voice, as she reached over and touched his arm.

Jane met Allison's eye and knew they were both thinking the same thing: *These two are definitely sleeping together.*

"My friend Jon here doesn't believe in past life regression," Evangeline said. "He thinks past lives are only real if they come to a person who can recall them while fully conscious and not seeking them out. But it is scientifically proven that meditation and mindfulness lead to precognition, clairaudience. We can agree on that. Right, Jon?"

He nodded.

"How many of you present have been meditating and heard a voice you didn't expect to hear?" Evangeline said. "Or been out walking in the woods and had a visitation from someone dear to you?"

At least half the people in the room raised their hands. Privately, Jane doubted them. But when Evangeline said, "And what about déjà vu? Who here has experienced that?" Jane had to admit that she had, many times. It was always something she couldn't quite get a hold of, like a dream half-lost upon waking. An itchy sensation that whatever was happening in a given moment had happened before.

Evangeline went on. "Jon and I have entirely different belief systems, but the one thing we both know to be true is this: after bodily death, energetically speaking, we carry on. Today, we are going to try to access past lives. This process can be illuminating, it can be exciting, even sometimes a bit frightening. But my hope is that above all, it's healing. Many of your faces are new to me. Some of you I recognize. Frida, good to see you again. And Pamela. You're an old pro by now. You've done this, what, a dozen times? Would you like to share your story with the group?"

The woman stood up. She was maybe in her mid-sixties, with glasses and short white hair. She beamed at the fact of being called on. *A dozen times?* Jane supposed you could get addicted to this stuff as easily as you could to anything else, but wow.

"I always had so much rage in my heart," the woman said, thoughtful, deliberate, as if she were being interviewed by Oprah herself. "I felt it especially toward my mother. She had four daughters. I was the oldest. She never liked me. From day one. All my life, I had this intuition that there had to be some explanation for it. But I didn't know what until I did my first past life regression and learned that my mother and I were once brothers. I murdered her and married her wife. I got away with it. No one ever found out. No wonder she hated my guts."

Jane willed herself not to look at Allison for fear that they would start laughing.

"That realization did more for my relationship with my mother than fifteen years of therapy," the woman said.

Evangeline nodded, like she heard this all the time. Which, perhaps, she did.

Jane thought of her own mother. Had Jane murdered her in some other life? Did that explain everything?

"The impact is often profound," Evangeline said. "And the effects immediate."

She herself had been a Rothschild, then a German pediatrician who hid Jews in his home during the Holocaust, then the twenty-one-year-old pilot who went down in the single-engine plane crash that killed Ritchie Valens, Buddy Holly, and the Big Bopper.

Jane wondered why she had found the academic convincing while this struck her as truly nuts. Were they really telling such different stories? Was she programmed to believe a man with the title of *doctor* and disbelieve a woman with the title of *medium*? Yes. Of course she was.

"A belief in reincarnation is as old as humanity itself," Evangeline said. "Hindus and Buddhists and Native Americans have believed in it for thousands of years. Most people in this country are just beginning to acknowledge it as a possibility, but we do tend to drag our feet when it comes to the obvious. Thirty-three percent of American adults believe in reincarnation. Thirty-eight percent of women and twenty-seven percent of men. Are you among the believers?"

Some in the room nodded vigorously.

"Even if you don't think you believe, or don't know if you do, I ask you today to be open to whatever happens."

Evangeline stood and walked to the door. She turned off the lights and returned to her spot onstage.

"Now. Get into as comfortable a position as you can. Take a few deep breaths. Close your eyes and focus on relaxing your body from top to bottom. Feel your head fill with a warm, golden liquid. Now feel the liquid flow into your neck, your shoulders, down your arms and into your fingertips."

Jane resisted for a moment, then gave herself over to the soft, soothing sound of Evangeline's voice. She dropped her shoulders. Let her head fall back.

Once they were relaxed and breathing in and out, muscles loose and light, Evangeline asked them each to access a childhood memory. Whatever came first to mind.

Jane was in the kitchen at her grandmother's house, five or six years old, a stack of Chips Ahoy! cookies on a saucer in front of her. She couldn't sleep. Her grandmother said they would have a midnight snack. It felt magical in the moment. Jane had forgotten all about that.

"Travel further back in time now, to your mother's womb," Evangeline instructed. "What does it sound like? What do you see?"

Jane saw red all around her, felt herself curled up, sensed her mother's fear.

"Now," Evangeline said. "You're being born."

A light, her mother sliced open, a doctor with dark curls in pale blue scrubs pulling Jane out. It couldn't be a memory. It was too much like every television scene in which a baby is born. But it felt like something Jane had lived, rather than seen.

She thought that next time she spoke to her mother, she would ask if her mother remembered what the doctor who delivered her looked like. Then came the recollection that her mother was gone, that Jane would never get to ask her anything ever again. Unless all this was real, which it wasn't.

Evangeline told them to picture a beautiful door. To imagine opening that door and finding on the other side a bright, bright light.

"I want you to pass through the bright light. Beyond it, you will find someone you used to be."

Jane's door was bright blue, in a high white stucco wall. She opened it, saw the light, and passed through.

At first, she searched for something to no avail. But then she saw an old-timey teenage girl and boy on a hillside, green as an advertisement from the Irish Tourism Board. There might as well have been a Cranberries song playing in the background.

Who was this girl? Jane's great-grandmother, maybe. Her great-great-grandmother?

"Are you in a body?" Evangeline asked. "What does that body look like? Look down at your clothing, what do you see? Are you wearing sandals? Furs? Animal pelts? Is there anyone there with you?"

Jane saw saddle shoes. Was that even historically accurate? She had, before leaving the archives, been working on a new acquisition, the papers of two Irish sisters who immigrated to Boston in 1910. Surely her brain was just borrowing.

Disappointed, she lost the thread. As Evangeline instructed everyone to visualize this other person's death, Jane kept her eyes closed but she wasn't in it anymore.

After the hour was up, Evangeline turned the lights back on.

"What did you two see?" Genevieve asked eagerly.

"Never mind," Allison said.

"I was a Viking," Genevieve said. "I had on a suit of armor. I felt *fearless.*"

Allison raised her eyebrows in surprise.

"I can see it," Jane said with a nod. "What did you see, Al?"

Allison shook her head.

"Come on."

"Fine," Allison said. "I saw Liesl."

"Who?"

"Liesl. And the Nazi mailman. In the gazebo in the rain."

"From *The Sound of Music,*" Genevieve said.

Allison nodded, ashamed.

"I saw my great-grandmother in Ireland, and she was on a very green hill and I really couldn't tell what kind of shoes she had on,"

Jane said. "What I'm saying is I have no imagination either, if it makes you feel better."

"It does," Allison said.

LUNCH WAS SERVED on the farthest edge of the island, in the white sailcloth tent they saw when they arrived.

"This reminds me of every summer wedding I've been to in the past few years," Genevieve said. "It's such a tired trend. If I see one more Chiavari ballroom chair."

"Yeah," Jane said, even though she didn't really know what Genevieve was talking about. She thought it was beautiful. It reminded her of an old circus tent.

Folding tables and chairs had been set up. Women sold sandwiches and soda and homemade cakes and cookies.

They ate quickly and then they waited. The public demonstration was happening here at one. This, Clementine had said, would be their best chance at getting the answers they came for.

At ten to the hour, the tent was full of people, standing shoulder to shoulder, taking up every seat. An excited, nervous energy hung in the air.

The medium arrived five minutes late, eating a granola bar, still chewing as she said, "Well! This is quite a crowd."

She had a cheery English accent and a baby face, with long, straight brown hair and blunt bangs that skimmed her eyelids. She was one of those young people who might be fifteen or twenty or twenty-eight. Impossible to say.

"For those of you who don't know me, my name is Camille," she said. "I'm a psychic medium and a Reiki healer. I first became aware of my gift for mediumship in high school. I know it's a cliché, but it all started for me with a friend's Ouija board."

Jane and Allison locked eyes. Ahh, the Ouija board. Present at many a freshman-year sleepover, where they asked spirits from the great beyond to answer life's deepest questions, such as *Does Matt Mitchell like me?*

"I'm also telepathic," Camille went on. "At first that might sound far-fetched, like something from the movies. But I'd ask you to think of ways that you might be as well. For example, mothers can often read their children's minds. They might get a start seconds before their baby cries or an older child gets hurt. Even adult children at a long distance from their mothers sometimes report a phone call coming in at the exact moment of crisis."

She looked directly at Allison and Jane.

"You two, you're smiling at each other. You've experienced this?"

"Yes," they said.

For years, they had been in a mind meld. That's what David called it. Jane would pick up the phone to text Allison the instant Allison was texting her. When they were together, they sometimes found themselves saying the same words at the same time so often that it seemed they hardly needed to speak.

"Are you mother and daughter?" Camille asked them.

Wait, who did she think was whose mother? They were the exact same age, born two months apart. Perhaps Camille looked generically young to Jane, and Jane looked generically old to her.

"Best friends," Allison called back.

Camille nodded, like she had known this all along. "Yes. And it happens for married couples sometimes too. Siblings. Twins, most of all."

"Nice pivot," Genevieve said quietly.

Jane and Allison laughed, perhaps more than was warranted. It was a pleasant surprise to hear Genevieve crack a joke.

"All right then, let's get started," Camille said. "There are a lot of voices wanting to come through. It's a full house today."

Camille paced back and forth, before saying, "I have a woman here in spirit. She was maybe sixty-five or seventy when she died of a heart attack. How many of you can take this information?"

Ten people raised their hands.

"She is making me aware that she was born in Maine and lived here all her life. She lived on a lake and she had three children, I believe."

All but one of the hands went down. It belonged to a heavyset woman in her forties, with thinning hair. Camille went up close to her.

"She wants you to know she loves you and she forgives you."

The woman let out a loud exhale that was almost a moan.

"Also she says you're using too much salt in your cooking, and that's why your kids don't like it. They're not picky eaters. It's just too much salt."

Camille walked toward the other side of the tent before the woman could respond.

"I have a message from a young person, for this person's parents," she said.

Jane saw the elderly couple from the ferry, looking eager, as if they knew they were about to be singled out.

But Camille went past them and stopped in front of another table, another man and woman.

"Hello again," Camille said. "May I come to you?"

"Yes," the woman said.

"I'm glad to see you brought your husband this time. Your son wants you both to be healed. He wants me to make you aware that it wasn't suicide. It was an accident. He wasn't trying to die."

The man burst into tears. His face went a shade of red that was almost purple.

His wife wiped tears from her eyes too.

"Thank you," she said. "Thank you."

Camille said, "You've had dreams about him, haven't you, sir?"

The man nodded.

"He is making me aware that those are not dreams. He visits you."

With that, the man put his head in his hands, overcome.

There had been moments today when Jane was willing to believe. But now her hackles went up. There were too many people suffering here. It felt exploitative. To tell a woman her dead mother thought she used too much salt in her cooking? Weird, but whatever. But to tell a man his son didn't really commit suicide seemed irresponsible. It seemed wrong.

Camille had many more messages for people in the crowd. From one woman's fiancé, who had been killed in a car crash. From dead parents and grandparents and even somebody's childhood dog. ("He is saying it was not your fault he got hit by that truck.")

Then Camille said, "I have a word of warning for someone going through a divorce."

Jane's cheeks burned but she did not raise her hand. No one else did either.

It wasn't her. It couldn't be her. They weren't divorcing. Not yet.

She had an overwhelming feeling that Camille was about to single her out, that she already knew it was Jane. And then Jane would have her answer. About all of this. About David.

Camille's tone turned irritable. "Look, I know one of you isn't putting your hand up, but this person should come see me later, in private. It's important."

There was no way Jane was going to present herself to Camille, now or later, and admit that her marriage was over. Though she very much wanted to know what Camille would say if she did.

"Let's see," Camille said. "I'm aware of someone here who lost a baby."

So many hands in the air. More than Jane could quickly count.

One of the hands belonged to the elderly woman from the ferry.

"This was not a miscarriage," Camille said. "This was a fully realized child, close to a year old."

Once again, most hands went down. The old woman's remained raised.

Camille zeroed in on her.

"May I come to you?"

"Yes, dear," the old woman said.

"You lost a baby girl," she said, and the woman nodded.

Did Camille have some means of knowing this? Or was it simply a 50/50 guess and she had gotten lucky?

"She sends you signs," Camille said. "Do you notice them? She says she leaves pennies from her birth year all around you."

Jane wondered how a one-year-old might manage to say, let alone do, that. She assumed everyone might find it as absurd as she did. A bridge too far.

But both the woman and her husband were nodding.

"That's her," Camille said. "That's your baby girl."

There had to be some explanation for the pennies. Confirmation bias or some other theory for why we notice what we do.

The couple cried and shook. Jane was amazed by how fresh the wound seemed. After so much time, they were still grieving. The question of what their life might have looked like if the child had survived would be with them until the end, she supposed. In that way, their daughter lived on. And in that way, they could never move past her death.

"Your loved ones will leave you signs, talismans," Camille said, to everyone now. "Keep an eye out. It could be an important date or some other significant number, like an address, that keeps popping up. Or you might suddenly smell a fragrance the person wore. If someone loved a certain flower, you might see it, even out of season or in places you wouldn't expect. It's a way they let us know they're with us. My grandmother leaves seashells. I once found one on a sidewalk in Columbus, Ohio, in the dead of winter."

Jane's mother had loved hummingbirds. Jane saw them all the time now when she was alone in the yard. They did remind her of her mom. Was it that much further a leap to believe her mother sent them?

It was as comforting and implausible as her grandmother's version of heaven, a place where old friends reunited and played golf in the clouds. Jane had never believed in all that, even as a child. So why was she entertaining this now? She supposed that for an atheist like her it was easier to imagine an afterlife that had nothing to do with God. Just humans, continuing to be something like themselves.

Camille told the audience there were only a few minutes left. She asked if anyone had a truly pressing matter. Almost everyone did.

Genevieve was the first to be called on.

"I was hoping to talk to someone named Eliza," she said. "I want to know if she's still at my house."

"I have Eliza," Camille said. "Yes, she's there. She's guarding your house. She was your—grandmother?"

"No," Genevieve said. "We aren't related."

"Right. She's telling me you were related once, but that was many lifetimes ago."

How convenient, Jane thought.

Genevieve hesitated, then said, "Is she angry with me? Does she want me to go away?"

Jane looked at her. Why was Genevieve so insistent that this long-dead woman was mad at her? Why was she so certain that Eliza was Benjamin's ghost?

"I'm not able to discern answers to those questions just now," Camille said.

A childhood Magic 8 Ball's most dissatisfying response: *Ask again later.*

"I want to know if Eliza knows who D is," Genevieve said. "Or, if the two of them are connected."

The medium closed her eyes and focused. "D hasn't crossed over yet. There's a lot of dark energy around D. Eliza is trying to help but nothing has worked so far."

Jane noticed the woman hadn't attached a name, or even a pronoun, to the letter. She was fairly certain Camille was full of shit.

Genevieve seemed to be about to probe further, when Camille said, "The woman beside you—what's your name?"

"Allison," she said, and her voice cracked.

"You've got the weight of the world on your shoulders, don't you, darling? Everyone expects so much of you. But what about what you need? Do they ever ask you that?"

Jane thought some version of these words would probably ring true to any woman on earth. It was so generic, so obvious.

But Allison was instantly in tears.

"Thank you," she said, gazing at Camille like she was a prophet.

THEY WERE ALL a bit dazed and quiet as they made their way along the path that led to Clementine's cottage.

She had said to come at two, and she was waiting at the door when they arrived.

Jane's first thought as she ushered them inside was that it looked like a cabin on a ship. Wood beams. A bloodred antique rug. Bookshelves painted the same dark shade of blue as the walls, packed with hardcovers and crystals and every imaginable bauble—snow globes and statues of the Buddha and miniature furniture. On a television in the corner, a game show was on.

Clementine went into the galley kitchen and reemerged a minute later with four mugs of tea on a plastic tray.

A gray cat lay on an ottoman. She scooped up the cat, put down the tray, then sat on the sofa, holding the animal under her arm like a football.

"Tell me about your day," Clementine said. "What did you think?"

"I had no idea about the history of it all. Fascinating stuff," Jane said.

"Isn't it? And what did you make of Dr. Abrams's talk?"

"Incredible," Allison said.

"It really was," Jane said. "Some of those stories were just—"

She didn't know how to finish the sentence.

"I'm glad you got to hear him speak. What a brilliant man. We're lucky Evangeline brought him to us."

"They're kind of an unlikely pair, huh?" Jane said, only noticing the judgment in her voice once the words were out.

"They've been friends forever," Clementine said. "They went to school together. Evangeline taught for years at UC Santa Cruz, in their History of Consciousness department. The scientific and the spiritual are far more connected than most people realize, Jane."

Having thus scolded her, Clementine kindly changed the subject. "And what about the public demonstration?" she said. "How did you find it? Be honest."

"I don't know," Jane said. "It didn't feel very specific. Some of what she said was so broad, it could have been about anyone."

"She was right about that old couple's baby," Allison pointed out. "The pennies! That was crazy."

"She thought we were mother and daughter," Jane said.

Allison laughed. "I chalked that up to her needing glasses."

"It seemed, I don't know, manipulative, what she did," Jane said.

"How so?" Clementine said.

"Maybe I just didn't anticipate the number of people who come here to alleviate grief."

The rest of them went silent. Jane didn't know what they were thinking, but she sensed it was about her, and that she had been inadvertently offensive.

"Grief is baked into the human experience," Clementine said. "People find different ways of coping. This is one way. Communing with the spirits can be extremely healing."

"I'm sorry," Jane said. "I guess I'm just a cynic. I can't help it."

"And that's fine. We don't consider it our job to persuade anyone of anything. That would be silly, and ultimately a huge waste of time," Clementine said. "A medium will never get it one hundred percent correct. That's asking too much."

Jane felt a prick to the chest, remembering how Clementine predicted that she was about to have a baby. How excited she had been by the prospect. How stupid she felt when it turned out not to be true.

"Think of how hard it is to communicate with the *living* and get your point across," Clementine went on. "It's even harder with the other side. The conversation between our two worlds is like a telephone call. Both sides have to pick up, or else you are just talking with no one to hear you at the other end of the line, or listening for a voice that isn't there."

"I see," Jane said.

"And mediums have off days at work, like anyone," Clementine said. "A medium can't be at her full powers if she's tired, for example, and you know people Camille's age. They're always exhausted, God knows why. My kids are that age. They sleep eleven hours straight, then call me and complain about being tired. It's something else."

"How many kids do you have?" Allison asked.

"Two."

"Are they into—all this?"

"My daughter is psychic, but she doesn't apply herself. Her abilities scare her," Clementine said. "My son just thinks I'm a weirdo. But hey, my readings kept a roof over his head and food on the table. He can't deny that. Though I'm pretty sure he tells people I'm a dental hygienist."

The others laughed. A burst of guilt shot through Jane for all the times she had lied in high school and college and probably beyond, when people asked what her mother did for work.

"I raised those kids on my own," Clementine said. "And I mean on my own. Their deadbeat father had nothing to do with them after he left."

"Jane's mother was a single mom," Allison said. "And her father was the same way. A deadbeat."

Clementine glanced at Jane, and Jane thought she was wondering if this comment had offended her. It had not. It was the truth. And Allison was Jane's family, too. She could say what she liked about Jane's relatives.

"My dad was too," Genevieve piped up.

It was the first thing she had said since they arrived at Clementine's door.

"He ran off with my mother's much younger cousin when I was two," Genevieve said. "This girl was just out of college. On their honeymoon a year later, there was a carbon monoxide leak in the condo they rented. They both died in their sleep."

Everyone gasped. Jane wondered why, if what went on at Camp Mira was real, neither of these people had surfaced with a message today.

"That is horrendous. I'm so sorry," Allison said.

Genevieve shrugged. "I have no memory of him," she said. "He never helped my mother in the year between leaving us and dying. Never once called our house or came to see me. He never gave us a cent. And after he was gone, his family pretended we didn't exist. It was almost like they blamed my mother for introducing him to his second wife!"

Jane thought of her grandmother's story of being widowed at a young age, how her in-laws were unkind to her too. And of her mother, who Jane mostly thought of as having procreated on her own, so absent and unknown was Jane and Holly's father. Jane had wondered whether maybe their mother didn't know who their father was, or if indeed they even had the same father. She never said this out loud to anyone besides David.

"Your poor mom," she said to Genevieve now, willing the thought to vanish.

"As far back as I can remember, she was nervous," Genevieve said. "Still is. Always bracing for catastrophe. There have been times when I've thought maybe if he hadn't died, she would have been different. But I don't think so. I think she only would have been different if he hadn't left us in the first place."

Clementine nodded. "She never remarried?"

"No. What happened with my father put her off men forever. But she was obsessed with the idea that I needed to marry well. She practically pushed me down the aisle when my husband proposed. She's always struck me as like a character out of Jane Austen. We had a gorgeous house, but no funds to keep it up. The paint was always peeling, the ceilings leaked. She had some beautiful clothes, three Chanel handbags. All the things she had when my father left. But we didn't have money to buy more. We were simultaneously rich and poor."

Jane wanted to ask why her mother didn't sell the gorgeous house and the handbags, buy a sensible apartment, and put the leftover money in the bank.

"I don't understand how someone could leave a child behind like that," Allison said.

"Neither do I," said Genevieve. "After Benjamin was born, I thought about that all the time."

"Speaking of your son," Clementine said. "Did you get any clarity while you were here on what's going on at your house?"

"Not exactly," Genevieve said. "Though Camille did hear from the dead woman I suspected of being there. Eliza. She made Eliza sound harmless. It's still scary, though. I don't know if we can carry on living in the house if her spirit won't leave."

"There's nothing scary about spirits," Clementine said. "The living are far more dangerous." She sighed. "I know I said I wouldn't, but— let's see what I can get."

Clementine closed her eyes. The rest of them exchanged a giddy look.

When she opened her eyes, Clementine said, "I think Camille was right. The first woman who lived in that place suffered after her husband was taken from her. I can see her there. She's stuck."

Jane thought of Marilyn Martinson's words. All the women who lived in that house ended up alone. "I see a boat pulling away from the coast, and this poor woman watching it. Devastated," Clementine said.

"Pulling *toward* the coast," Jane said.

"What?" Clementine said, like she did not appreciate being corrected.

"Samuel Littleton died in a shipwreck on his return voyage," Jane said. "But like you said, his boat was visible from shore. His wife, Hannah, saw the whole thing. How fascinating that you can see all that."

Clementine nodded. "The wife was left alone. She was pregnant with her first child. No one knows what she endured."

"So then your ghost is Hannah, not Eliza," Jane said to Genevieve.

Hannah hadn't been pregnant when Samuel died, though, had she? And she already had two children by then.

"Do you know why Hannah is haunting us?" Genevieve said.

"The woman I'm seeing is trapped," Clementine said. "Something's keeping her from moving on to the next realm. She's likely to be a nuisance to you until she does. But it doesn't make sense she would be talking to Benjamin. Earthbound spirits keep playing out whatever it was that got them stuck here in the first place. They don't tend to interact with the living. For the most part, they have no idea they're dead."

"This ghost interacts plenty," Genevieve said.

"Could there be two ghosts?" Allison said.

Genevieve shook her head. "There's only one ghost."

Jane almost laughed at how sure she was. As if any of this involved hard facts.

Clementine said, "This is New England. There is rarely only one ghost."

"What can I do to make it stop?" Genevieve said. She sounded like a whiny child.

"If I were you, I'd have someone come and perform a soul rescue," Clementine said, as if telling Genevieve she ought to have her rain gutters cleaned. "Sometimes they need help crossing over. Sometimes you have to explain to them that they've died. They may not know. They don't tend to see anyone else when they're in that state. They get caught in a loop, playing the same traumatic events out over and over."

God, the thought of being trapped for all eternity at the work event where Jane ruined her own life. Or no, the next morning in Melissa's office when she heard what she had done.

"Have you ever seen this woman? Does she always appear in the same spot? That might offer some clues."

"Only Benjamin has seen her, as far as I know," Genevieve said.

"Any repetitive sounds? Rappings, moaning, footsteps?"

"No."

"Do you notice particularly high humidity?"

"The house is on the ocean."

"Right. Well, some experts believe water can be a vessel for a kind of recording that happens, forcing the haunting to get trapped in a memory loop, as I said. I would keep an eye out for any of the things I mentioned."

Would one really need to keep an eye out for inexplicable moaning? Jane wondered. Wouldn't it rather make itself known?

"This figure your son sees, she's an Indigenous woman, right?" Clementine said.

"No," Jane and Genevieve answered at once.

Clementine shrugged. She seemed in this case to accept that she was off.

But Jane lingered on the idea. Was it possible Hannah was Indigenous? She didn't think so. Jane had a flash of the basket Genevieve bought. Was it the source of whatever Clementine was sensing?

"And then there's Jane's ghost. D. Is she the same one Benjamin sees?" Genevieve said.

"That I don't know," Clementine said.

"Could it be a coincidence that they both are looking for their mothers?"

"Yes," Clementine said. "Mothers tend to loom large, here and in the spirit realm. But then again, what is called coincidence is often just spirit guiding us in a given direction."

They stayed for another hour, until just before the five o'clock ferry arrived to take them back to the real world.

As they said goodbye outside Clementine's door, Clementine said, "Jane, I have a message from your grandmother. She wants you to know that your sister is in a lot of pain, missing your mom. Do you know if she talks to a photo of your mother sometimes?"

"I don't," Jane said.

"She must, because your grandmother says to tell her your mom hears her. To keep talking. You have to be gentle with your sister. Her grief over your mom is different from yours. More intense. They were so close. They saw each other every day."

"Okay," Jane said.

She hadn't expected this. She hadn't been thinking of her family at all. Of course the message from her mother was for Holly, not for her. Of course her mother couldn't be bothered to deliver it to Jane directly and her grandmother was forced to play intermediary.

There wasn't time to press on this thought. A moment later they were walking fast to the dock, boarding the ferry at the last possible second, pulling out into open water.

Jane glanced around and saw many of the same faces she had seen on the way here. They looked different to her now that she understood why they had come.

She wondered if any of them felt satisfied by what they had been told today. Even if the dead could somehow tell you they heard your prayers or that your cooking was too salty, what did that matter? You couldn't hold them or kiss them good night or take them to dinner. Even if they were here, they were gone.

Life was painfully, unimaginably brief. In some strange way, the thought filled Jane with courage. It made her want to act. The situation with David was bad, but at least they were both alive and breathing. So many people on this boat couldn't say as much about the ones they loved most.

Jane would call him and tell him she wanted to come home. Or maybe she would go to him in person tomorrow, let him know she was willing to do whatever it might take. They had no time for anything less.

IN THE CAR on the way home, they passed a cute little bookshop, which prompted Allison to mention that she was a member of a monthly book club she had managed to attend only twice in the past year. That got Genevieve talking about what she was reading. Jane was surprised to hear that Genevieve read at all. Popular novels and celebrity biographies, but still.

Jane told them about the exhibit she had seen at the Portland Historical Society, how she had purchased half a dozen books on Native American culture and history that day, and was now reading them all, simultaneously.

Every night since she went up to Portland, Jane had found herself dipping into these books, staying up later than she should. She was reading again, the most familiar occupation, which had left her during this troubled time. She was so relieved to have it back.

"I'm just about to finish this fascinating book on repatriation," Jane said. "*Plundered Skulls and Stolen Spirits* by Chip Colwell."

"I should probably know this. But remind me—what's repatriation?" Allison said.

"Basically it's a process by which stolen funerary objects and sacred items and body parts are returned to the proper Indian tribes and lineal descendants."

"*Body parts?*" Genevieve said, sounding horrified.

"Stolen by whom?" Allison said.

"The federal government, the Smithsonian, Harvard. Every major museum and university in the country and the world, pretty much," Jane said. "There are something like two hundred thousand skeletal remains and a million sacred objects in these places within the US."

"You're saying people dug up graves and stole the bodies out of them?" Genevieve said.

"Correct," Jane said. "It happened with alarming frequency. When the Pilgrims arrived at Plymouth Rock, one of the first things they did was come across mounds in the earth. Out of curiosity, they dug them up. They later wrote that finding buried there a Wampanoag man and child, they made off with 'sundry of the prettiest things.' Thomas Jefferson did the same. He sent his slaves out to excavate burial mounds and then displayed these Native people's remains and sacred items in the entryway to Monticello."

"Jesus," Allison said.

"In some cases, like at Sand Creek in the 1860s, US soldiers ambushed members of the Cheyenne and Arapaho tribes at dawn, and scalped them. Men, women, and children. Which brings the issue of repatriation into even sharper focus, because these were not people who died and were buried. They never got buried in the first place. And according to the beliefs of some Indigenous people, that means their spirits can never rest. Soldiers hacked off body parts and kept them as trophies—fingers, toes. They cut out labias and stretched them over saddles and hats. Scalps were kept, and handed down one generation to the next."

The book posed a question: How could modern members of these tribes ever heal from the atrocities committed against their people when the bones and scalps and body parts taken that day continued to circulate, in families and private collections around the country?

"Dear God," Genevieve said.

In the rearview mirror, Jane could see that her eyes were filled with tears.

Genevieve confused Jane. She didn't care about preservation when it came to her house, but she was obsessed with the house's history. She was crying over repatriation, but she had purchased a basket from a dealer whose shadiness took only a quick online search to uncover.

Jane almost spelled it out for her: *Thomas Crosby, the guy you bought your basket from, is one of the people I'm talking about.*

But that seemed too much like an accusation. Jane didn't think there was anything shady or suspect about the basket itself, just the man who had sold it to her. Should Genevieve be held accountable for that? Maybe.

"What do the tribes do when they get these things back?" Genevieve said.

Jane told them how she had read in the book by Colwell an account of Cheyenne tribal elders standing in a storage room at the National Museum of Natural History, with the bones and skulls of eighteen of their ancestors laid out on a table. The elders spent hours drumming, singing, talking. Burning sweetgrass as an offering to their ancestors trapped between worlds.

One of the skulls belonged to a young girl. When the remains were finally released, one of the elders held this skull gently. She kissed it before placing it in a coffin.

When they had returned to their home state of Oklahoma, a traditional burial ceremony took place. Eighteen pine coffins were carried in a procession. The elders were preparing them to go back into the earth. A job no one present had ever wished for, but still they faced it with solemnity and reverence. They were people for whom ceremony mattered a great deal, but there existed no ceremony for this. Many Native people honored and feared the dead in equal measure. Some believed just contemplating the idea of bodies dug up, disturbed, displayed could make them and their families sick, or bring harm to them.

Still, they took this on. They believed the ancestors would help guide them through it.

They chose a burial site only after seeking approval from the other side. They dug the holes by hand, and all in attendance made an offering or said a prayer. The ancestors were asked to accept the remains back into the womb of Mother Earth, completing the cycle of life.

"That's beautiful. But so upsetting," Genevieve said. "I can't even imagine."

She sniffled, pulled a tissue from her purse, blew her nose.

"You never did master the art of small talk, did you, Jane?" Allison said with a wink.

AN HOUR SOUTH of Bar Harbor, they passed a pickup truck flying an enormous Confederate flag off the back.

Jane wondered what the bozo behind the wheel thought he meant by it.

"Why," she said, "do you suppose that in past life regression, people always see themselves as being royalty or a hero who fought the Nazis or something like that? I bet no one ever does one of those meditations and finds out, hey, I was one of the millions of unremarkable people who lived through the Holocaust and just went about my business. When statistically, the heroic and the evil combined throughout humankind must be a fraction of the do-nothings."

"Maybe do-nothings don't get reincarnated as often because they're boring?" Allison said.

Genevieve took a call from her husband, who sounded highly concerned about whether they had ordered ribs and steaks for their barbecue tomorrow. She calmly replied that yes, she had done this weeks ago.

"Are you having a big party?" Allison asked after she hung up.

"No, he just likes things to be a certain way," Genevieve said.

Jane tightened her grip on the steering wheel in order to keep her mouth shut.

They passed a farm, green hills dotted with horses and cows. A huge red barn more impressive than the farmhouse. An outbuilding made of gray stones stacked one upon the other sat at the edge of the road. Smaller white stones had been layered in at the bottom corner to spell out the year it was built: 1902.

Such a human impulse. That even as we were living, we were telling future generations to remember us. Hadn't Jane and her sister had the same idea in mind when, as kids, they carved their full names and the date into just-poured cement in the basement of a two-family house they lived in for only a year?

They stopped at a seafood shack on the side of the road and ate lobster rolls at a picnic table for dinner.

Jane had ordered clam chowder too. When Allison reached for her spoon and took a bite without asking, Genevieve said, "I've never had a friend like you two are to each other. I've always wanted a friend like that. You're lucky, you know."

"We are," Allison said. "Speaking of lucky, right now, I'm supposed to be taking the minutes at the Awadapquit Beach Erosion Committee meeting. Thank you both for sparing me that."

Genevieve asked what the committee did, and Allison explained that while everyone in town agreed that the sand at the beach's southern end was disappearing, there was still debate as to why, and what to do about it. The monthly meetings were maddening. "At high tide, the beach is a foot below water," Allison said. "On a full moon, half the parking lot gets flooded. We need to act fast. People aren't going to pay thirty dollars to park at a beach when there's nowhere to sit. The town makes over a million a summer off that lot."

Global warming, the whole, overwhelming, terrifying idea of it, was a topic Jane was used to talking about all the time with her colleagues and friends in Cambridge. David had cried once, reading an article in the *Atlantic* that said there were three billion fewer birds in North America than there had been fifty years earlier. He cried, but what did he, or anyone they knew, actually do, besides make a donation here or there?

Allison was thinking about climate change from a parking lot revenue standpoint. Ultimately, she would probably be the only one of them who would take meaningful action, even if just in her own small corner of the world.

AFTER DINNER, back in the car, Genevieve called her husband again. While they were eating, he had sent several frantic texts about how to explain the turnoff for their house to the guests who were coming tomorrow.

Jane and Allison tried not to listen, or at least not to laugh, as Genevieve patiently made suggestions.

"I can email them a link to a map," she said. "Right. Well, if they do lose signal *and* get lost, they can drive back to town and call for directions. It's a five-minute drive. Yes, I understand. They're coming a long way as it is. A balloon? On the mailbox?" She inhaled deeply. "I don't think I will have time to pick one up tonight, no. I can do it first thing in the morning, when I go to buy corn and tomatoes at the farm stand. I'll pop into the toy store. I'm pretty sure they have a helium tank. Mmmhmm. Love you. Kiss Benjamin for me."

Immediately after hanging up, perhaps exhausted from this ridiculous exchange, Genevieve closed her eyes and fell asleep. She started snoring gently.

Allison said, "If you'd told me a month ago that you and I would be spending the day at a camp for psychic mediums, I'd think you'd lost your mind. Especially if you told me we'd be doing it with the lady Viking back there."

"It was definitely an experience," Jane said. "You know, sometimes I think Clementine might be the real deal."

"She is," Allison said. "She's certified by the Windbridge Institute. There's only a handful of mediums in that category in the whole world."

Jane fought the urge to roll her eyes.

"I guess it's a good thing no one at the two-cent sale auction was interested, so I got her as a result of your pity bid."

"Yup," Allison said.

A thought occurred to Jane then. "How did Clementine end up in the Awadapquit two-cent sale auction anyway?"

"Fine. I lied," Allison said, like Jane had been interrogating her and she could no longer stand it.

"About what?" Jane said, entirely confused.

"I read about Clementine in a magazine," Allison said. "All these people said she was the best medium in Maine, so I called her up and convinced her to do a session with you. She was fully booked for a year, but I talked her into it. I said it was an emergency."

"Huh?" Jane said. "I thought everyone just donated their services to the auction."

"She wasn't part of the auction," Allison said. "It was all a ruse. I wanted you to be able to talk to your mom. You two had a lot to sort out. But you would never have done it if I'd just given it to you as a gift. I had to turn it into you doing me a favor, and book it myself."

"Well. That is the sweetest, weirdest thing," Jane said. "Thank you?"

"You're welcome," Allison said. "What I wish for most in the world is the chance to talk to my mother. When I read about Clementine, I thought, huh, Jane's mother as a ghost might be more reachable than my mom, who I see in the flesh almost every day."

"Oh, Allison."

"You pointed out that I was writing stuff down today at Mira. Jane, I write everything down now. I have this pathological need to have it all on paper. What I've done each day, where things are in the house. The recipes I know by heart, because what if one morning I wake up and I don't know them anymore? I find myself recording conversations with the kids on my phone when we're driving home from school. In case a day comes when a basic conversation isn't something I can have. I want them to remember who I was to them."

For the first time, Jane realized what should have been clear much sooner: they had both lost their mothers. There were so many conversations they would never get to have.

"I'm so sorry," Jane said.

"It's okay. I've got my boyfriend, Zoloft, to help me through."

"You do?" Jane said. "Since when?"

"February. I've had such a hard time dealing with the situation. Last winter, I couldn't get out of bed I was so depressed, so I started taking it and it helps."

"Well, that's good," Jane said.

She thought of how that last medium of the day, Camille, had said Allison had the weight of the world on her shoulders.

"Maybe one night next week, you and Chris can go to dinner and I can hang with the kids," Jane said.

Allison smiled. "That would be nice."

"You deserve a break," Jane said.

When they got back to town, they stopped first at Genevieve's, shaking her gently awake.

As they watched her walk inside, Allison said, "That one grew on me a teeny bit today."

"Me too," Jane said.

She dropped Allison outside her door a few minutes later. Jane hugged her best friend tight.

IT WAS AFTER TEN when she pulled up outside her sister's house. Jane was exhausted, ready to climb into bed. Since it was a Saturday night, she assumed Holly and Jason would be out and she would take Walter home with as little fanfare as she had delivered him that morning. But there were several cars out front. When she opened the front door, she heard raucous laughter from the kitchen. Men's voices.

A strange blend of fear and excitement and curiosity arose in her. A sensation from childhood. Who was her sister entertaining at this hour?

The front hall was full of stuff. It reminded Jane of their house growing up. She had to maneuver her way past two large lamps set on the floor, only one of which had a shade, and a long dresser that sat atop a sheet, which her sister was apparently Mod Podgeing in magazine photos of fifties pinup girls. A pile of thrift store clothes sat heaped on a chair. Past that was a stack of unopened cardboard boxes.

Jane peeked at the return address on the topmost one. A PO box in New Mexico, c/o eBay.

In the kitchen, Jane found not Holly, but Jason at the table, with a handful of friends. Three guys and a girl with purple hair. The one with his back to Jane was speaking. He wore a tank top that showed off his muscled shoulders. His greasy brown hair was up in a ponytail. A red star had been tattooed dead center on the back of his neck.

"I'm telling you," he said. "Pallets are gonna make me rich. Richer than I already am. I'm taking all the money I made and putting it into pallets."

"Bullshit," one of the guys said.

"Think about it. Amazon takes all the crap people return and sells it off to liquidators. The liquidators sell the returned shit by the pallet. So you spend two hundred bucks and the pallet full of random crap you receive might be worth five thousand."

"Or a hundred," said the purple-haired girl.

"Extremely unlikely, these things are huge."

"What's in the pallets?" Jason said.

"Could be anything. You don't know until it arrives. Then you sell it all. It's called the reverse supply chain."

"I'm in," Jason said. "What do I have to lose?"

"Everything?" the lone female in the group said. "Jason, you're drunk. Give him an answer tomorrow."

They all noticed Jane as Jane noticed the one thousand empty beer bottles on the table in front of them.

"Hi, Jason," she said.

"Hey," he said. "Everyone, meet my aunt Jane."

"Hi Aunt Jane!" they called, and laughed at how clever they were.

"I came for—"

Jane stopped talking as she heard Walter's paws click-clicking toward her from the hall.

She turned to see him. Her sister trailed behind in a green silk pajama set, a glass of white wine in her hand. Walter gave Jane a look like she imagined a child might give his mother after the babysitter threw a party while she was gone.

"Closing time, everyone," Holly said. "You don't have to go home but you can't stay here."

She turned to Jane. "How did it go with the witches?"

"They're not witches," Jane said. Though maybe some of them were? She wasn't sure exactly.

The purple-haired girl perked up.

"What about witches?" she said. "My friend Gloria and I, when we were in high school, we used to take the bus down to Salem, Mass, like, every other weekend. We thought we were Wiccan. They've got these shops there where you can buy potions and spell books and all that. I got a voodoo doll. I used to torture my algebra teacher with it."

Jane had driven through Salem once, when she and David were in the area to admire the foliage and take a tour of the House of the Seven Gables. She noticed the shops this girl was talking about. That, and a banner hanging over the main street that read *Witch City.* She remembered thinking it was ironic, considering the whole point of the Salem witch trials was that the girls and women accused were not witches.

"You'd better not try that shit on me," Jason said as they all got up to go.

"One spell we learned could shrink a guy's left nut," the girl said. "Just the one. Worse than both in a way, right?"

"What the fuck, Erika?" Jason said.

They left the room.

Jane said, "Is Erika Jason's girlfriend?"

"What? No," her sister said. "She's gay. She's a friend of his from high school. That girl is crazy smart. Her parents are assholes. They kicked her out when they found out she had a girlfriend. She's staying here on the sofa for now."

Jane's eyes landed on a photograph of their mother attached to the fridge with a magnet. She looked so young and pretty. She was laughing, a little-boy version of Jason on her lap.

"Do you talk to Mom?" Jane said.

"What?" Holly said.

"Like, do you ever talk to that picture of her? Or any other picture of her?"

"I don't know. Why?"

"The medium said to tell you she hears you."

"Oh."

Next to the photo was an article clipped from the *Portsmouth Tribune*, with the headline EVERYTHING OLD IS NEW AGAIN. It was dated the previous August. Jane started reading.

Holly Flanagan is a second-generation thrifter. Her mom, Shirley, who passed away last month, started the family business three decades ago. Holly joined her right after high school graduation. The pair were ahead of their time, focused on sustainability and the need to keep possessions in circulation and out of landfills, long before others jumped on the bandwagon.

Was that true? Jane wondered. She was almost positive her mother had never given any thought to such concepts.

"Holly," she said, pointing at the article. "Why didn't you tell me about this?"

"It never occurred to me," Holly said.

"Why not?"

"You've literally never taken an interest in what I do," Holly said. "I love you, but face it, you're a snob."

"That's not true," Jane said, as proof to the contrary flooded her mind.

"It is," Holly said. "And it's fine."

"I'm proud of you," Jane insisted. "This is so great."

"You're proud of me because I was in the paper."

"Yes," Jane said. "Is that a bad thing?"

"Mom used to say it was funny that you were so embarrassed by what she did for work, considering it was the reason you ended up with the job you did," Holly said. "You're in the family business too when you think about it."

"Really?" Jane said, her tone revealing how absurd an idea she thought this was.

"She used to bring home antiques from garage sales when we were kids and you'd be there, making up elaborate stories about the people who owned them before."

"I don't remember doing that," Jane said.

"Well, you did."

"The medium, Clementine, she said Mom's death was harder on you than it was on me."

"Yeah," Holly said, practically spitting out the word.

Though she knew this was probably true, Holly's reaction upset Jane. She wasn't even sure why. Conversations with her sister—and her mother, when she was alive—so often veered in unintended directions, loaded as they were with a lifetime of resentment and shared memory and unspoken longing for things to be different this time.

"The end was brutal," Holly said.

"I know. I was there." Jane's words came out harsher than she meant them to.

"She was sick for months, Jane," Holly said. "You were there for the last week."

There it was. The reason Holly felt entitled to make Jane alone deal with their mother's house, the reason Holly always seemed slightly pissed off at her.

Maybe Jane should have apologized then, but instead she felt her own sort of righteous anger rise up. Of the two of them, only Holly ever got any warmth or understanding from their mother. It was only right that she should be the one to see her out of the world.

Jane had done all the grunt work after the fact, planned and paid for the funeral, made the necessary phone calls. David spent two months canceling her mother's credit cards and phone number and various accounts. Returning her cable box, contacting the Social Security office, and the mortgage company and her health insurance provider.

Jane started to speak just as the front door slammed.

Jason came back into the kitchen alone.

"I thought you'd be headed out with your friends," Holly said.

"Nah," he said. "Keith is bugging me. I can't listen to him brag about his newfound riches anymore tonight."

"He win the lottery or something?" Jane said, changing her tone, pretending everything was fine, for her nephew's sake.

"Kind of. Some crazy rich lady paid him to dig up an old cemetery in her yard."

Holly shook her head, a gesture that told Jane she already knew this story and disapproved, but she wasn't going to lose sleep over it.

"Is that legal?" Jane said.

"Uhh, no. And on top of what she paid him, the lucky bastard dug up some buried treasure in the process. A ring from, like, the Revolution? It had hair in it."

"Hair?"

"Yeah. I don't know the details, but I know Keith sold that ring for a shit ton and he hasn't stopped bragging about it since. Hold on, I have a picture."

Jason scrolled through his phone for ages, then held it up.

The ring was rusted, with the words NOT LOST BUT GONE BEFORE carved into the metal, and a flat, circular viewing window at the top where one might expect to find a jewel.

"That's where the hair is," Jason said. "I guess the ring belonged to a dead sea captain's wife."

"Keith came to me and said he had some old jewelry to sell," Holly said. "He didn't say anything about how he got it. I think he thought I might make him an offer, but no. Some fancy antiques dealer did, though. I don't know why on earth someone would pay good money to buy the ring of a dead woman that had been sitting in an old cemetery forever."

"Why on earth would someone dig up a cemetery in the first place?" Jane said.

"Keith said it happened to be right where the lady wanted to put a swimming pool," Jason said.

"A swimming—"

Oh dear God. Genevieve.

Jason produced before and after shots Keith had sent him. In the first picture were a few old tombstones. Jane zoomed in on the shot and could make out the word *Littleton* on one, the word *Eliza* on another. In the second photo there was just a flat piece of blackish dirt, like a small garden patch tilled for winter.

Yes. There had been a cemetery. Right there, under that cluster of trees Genevieve had cut down. Jane had forgotten all about it.

"I've got to go," she said.

She picked Walter up and went toward the front door.

As she opened it and walked out, her sister called after her, "The dog hasn't been out since noon!"

"Why not?" Jane said, annoyed.

"He didn't want to go!"

"Right."

She got in her car and drove straight to the cove.

She thought about the ring. Jason had said it dated back to the Revolutionary War, but that couldn't be so. The Littletons' house hadn't been built for another seventy years after that. Unless—and this was entirely possible, perhaps more likely than not—Jason had the wrong war. A ring with hair in it was a Victorian sort of thing. Jane rattled with anger. Genevieve had pretended to care about Hannah, and Samuel, and Eliza. Poor Eliza, who died and was buried with her employers, not her loved ones. Another story lost to time.

So this was why Genevieve was so certain she was being haunted by her house's original owners. Because she had paid some dumbass kid to dig up their graves. It was revolting. It was criminal. How could anyone do such a thing? How could Genevieve have left this part of the story out, even as she dragged Jane into it?

Easy, Jane thought. Because she wanted Jane's sympathy and her help and she knew she'd never get either if she told the truth.

She had acted horrified by the idea of bodies dug up not five hours ago.

Jane parked her car and walked Walter around the empty parking lot. The shops and restaurants had been closed for two hours. The cove was silent, but for the sound of the waves hitting the rocks.

She took her phone out of her purse to call Allison and tell her what she had learned.

There was a message waiting from Melissa.

Before she even heard it, Jane knew. She just knew.

"*Jane, I'm so sorry to have to deliver this news, and I'm sorry to call on a Saturday, but word just reached me that the board has made its decision,*" Melissa said into her voicemail. "*They voted unanimously for your permanent removal. Several of us spoke in your defense. But they think it's best to part ways. They are still willing and able to pay for any kind of treatment you might need. Call me. Let's talk about next steps.*"

It suddenly became clear to Jane that until this moment, deep down, she did not really believe she would lose her job. It was the part of her life she could always just *do*. The part that wouldn't fail her.

Her knees went wobbly. She had to sit down on the pavement.

Jane called David. She needed him now. David would know what to do.

His phone went straight to voicemail. Was it turned off, she wondered, or had he seen her name and declined the call?

She texted him. Can you talk?

No response.

Instinctively, Jane toggled over to his Facebook page for reassurance. David's profile picture was the usual one from their wedding. His bio still described him as *married*. But there were two new photos on the page. David hadn't posted them. His ex-wife, Angela, had. In the photos, the two of them were seated at a table covered in a white tablecloth, a bottle of red wine between them. They were smiling. Her arm was around his shoulder. Angela had tagged him, and captioned the photo Dinner date with D. Never say never!

Jane tried to gulp down a chestful of air. It felt hard to catch her breath. She thought maybe she was hyperventilating.

What happened next was something she would wonder about for a long time after. What if Jane hadn't heard Melissa's message just then? What if she hadn't learned the truth about Genevieve? What if she had called David, and he picked up? What if she hadn't called David at all?

What if Jane hadn't had to walk the dog, hadn't decided to walk him in the cove, hadn't noticed a light on at Charlie's Chowder House long after closing, hadn't made eye contact through the window with Abe Adams, who beckoned her inside, dog and all, and when she came, offered her a drink, which she accepted, because what was a drink in the grand scheme of things?

10

Eliza

B U T   F O R   T H E dirt road that has since been paved, this
village looks the same as it ever did. Two thousand acres of farm and
forest on the banks of a tranquil lake. Nineteen thousand apple trees.
The white meetinghouse, which I saw built in 1846, the year I turned
twelve. The schoolhouse, now a research center, rarely used. The
Brick House. The dwelling houses. The Sisters' Shop.

Nearly all the village's inhabitants, though, are gone. Only three
Shakers remain at Sabbathday Lake and in all the world. In my
youth, we numbered one hundred and fifty here. Across the country there were other communities like ours, home to six thousand
Believers. We never saw one another, but on a Sunday we might sing
the same hymn at the same time, a bridge connecting us.

Great men visited to learn what they could from our ways. George
Washington. Ralph Waldo Emerson. Thomas Jefferson wrote of the
Shaker faith, "If their principles are maintained and sustained by a
practical life, it is destined eventually to overthrow all other religions."

We believed the world was coming undone. War, greed, suffering.
Lust. All were signs that the end was near. And yet we gave every bit
of ourselves to our work. To the weaving and sewing and washing,
to the gardening, the farming, the creation of buildings and bonnets
and bottled herbs.

While we worked, we told the stories of our founder, intent on
preserving her memory. Mother Ann Lee started out a blacksmith's
wife in Manchester, England, an unremarkable member of the Ward-
ley Society, which had broken off from the Quakers in 1747. They
called themselves the United Society of Believers in Christ's Second

Appearing. Outsiders, in mockery, called them Shaking Quakers, or Shakers, because of their ecstatic way of worshipping. In time, they reclaimed that name for themselves. They believed in spiritualism and messages received directly from God. They believed the second coming of Christ would arrive in the form of a woman.

Mother Ann was just one of many followers then, as I have said. It was her tragedy that lifted her to greatness, that let them know she was the one they had been waiting for.

MY FATHER BROUGHT my sister and me to Sabbathday Lake when we were three and five years old, months after our mother died. He wept as he handed us over and signed the indenture that said we would live here, as Shakers, until we were eighteen because he could no longer manage on his own. Even so, he promised he would return for us as soon as he was able.

For the first few years, he visited every so often. I recall him bending down to embrace me, his coarse beard against my cheek. Each time he left, he vowed that next time he would take us away with him. Until he came on my seventh birthday. He left in tears. After that, we never saw nor heard from him again. We were led to believe he was dead.

My sister and I went from living in a cozy house, with a mother who tucked us in at night and made us dresses in our favorite colors and knew the names of our dolls, to sleeping in the Children's Order at Sabbathday Lake. A long bare room with nothing remotely frivolous allowed. No rugs or mirrors. Certainly no dolls to sleep with.

Sister Florence instructed us each night to rest in the fear of God and lie straight. She was kind and patient, but firm, and nothing like a mother. Emily and I were two of fourteen girls in her care.

Late, after everyone else was asleep, Emily would creep into my narrow bed or I into hers, and we would take comfort in the familiar warmth of one another, for a short while.

Our lives were ruled by order. Hands to work, hearts to God. We woke at 4:30 in summer, 5:30 in winter, at the ringing of a bell. We did hours of chores each day. As a child, I helped make three thousand perfect poplar boxes a year for hotels. I made baskets and palm leaf bonnets. I filled paper packets with garden seeds until my fingers cramped, and still I was made to keep on, without so much as a penny earned.

We attended school, boys in wintertime, girls in summer. At some point, the world's people began sending their children to study with us. The Shaker schools were considered excellent. I recall being proud of that. And because sometimes there were a great many spectators at Sunday service. Once Emily and I counted the carriages. They numbered one hundred and seventy-two. When I saw girls from school there with their mothers, their fathers, their families, it stung. Emily and I had been told to think of one another as we would any other girl in our dormitory. Family bonds, like all the rest of life's comforts, were forbidden.

Life at Sabbathday Lake was full of contradictions. All individuals were provided for, but none was allowed to have money of his or her own. Men and women were considered equals, yet lived entirely apart.

There was no rule I did not dream of breaking. I was obedient most of the time, but I had a natural inclination to ask why, which the elders did not approve of. Sister Florence said she couldn't understand how a child with no memory of life before the Shakers could be so headstrong. But I wasn't sure I didn't remember. My sister did, and maybe it was only that she told me things and my mind claimed them for its own. But I think I can conjure an image of my mother. Her hands, lowering a bowl into mine.

A few of the other children had arrived at Sabbathday Lake as part of intact families, all the members of which remained in the Society. But upon signing the covenant, those ties were dissolved. Husband and wife no longer, parent and child no longer. The formerly married became brother and sister. Their children would be raised by the community.

I felt sorrier for those children than I did for myself. I watched them and the women I knew to be their mothers for any hint of affection exchanged.

———

I WAS NINE when word came to Sabbathday Lake that four girls in the Shaker village at Watervliet had been visited by the spirit of Mother Ann. Within months, girls and women in several Shaker villages were having visions. Mother Ann, we knew, had heard voices from the other side. Spirits sent by God to instruct her on her mission. She never wanted to marry, but her parents forced her to. All four of her children died in infancy. She herself nearly died giving birth to them.

Later, she had a vision of Adam and Eve in the Garden of Eden, and understood that her struggles had been sent down as divine punishment. Concupiscence was the source of evil in the world. Therefore marriage must also be against God's will. Jesus spoke to her. They became one in body and spirit. She was the second coming, the female half of the whole. The Shakers made her their leader. She could read anyone's past or future. She could heal broken bones and cancers with her mind. Mother Ann called on her flock to confess their sins, to give up worldly possessions, to renounce the lustful gratifications of sex and marriage and live as celibates.

The Shakers were condemned in England. Accused of heresy, sorcery, witchcraft. Mother Ann was twice imprisoned for her beliefs. The second time, her jailers intended to starve her. They didn't give her a drop of water for two weeks. She might have died had her followers not snuck into the jail each night, fed her milk and wine through the thinnest pipe stem, run through the keyhole in her cell. Upon her release, Mother Ann had the vision that changed everything: she saw that in America, land of religious liberty, the Shakers would flourish.

It was the dawn of a revolution in this new land. Some suspected the Shakers of being British spies. Upon arrival in New York, they were imprisoned for six months for refusing to swear an Oath of Allegiance. After that, they undertook a two-and-a-half-year journey across New England, proselytizing to all who would listen. Wherever the Shakers went, they gained followers but violent crowds gathered too, accusing them of witchcraft and treason.

Mother Ann's skull was fractured in 1781 at Petersham, when she was dragged down a flight of stairs feetfirst. At Ashfield two years later, she was accused of being a man in disguise. A vicious crowd tore off her clothes and forced her to allow them to inspect her naked body before they would let her go. By the time the mission trip ended, Mother Ann was depleted. She died soon after.

The faith she had created lived on.

I never doubted that she had been every bit as clairvoyant as Joan of Arc. But I couldn't bring myself to believe it when girls with whom I spent my days and nights claimed that they too had been visited by spirits. If such things were possible, surely my mother would have come to me before, say, the ghost of Benjamin Franklin came to visit Holly Dean. I spent many wordless hours toiling in the bakeshop with Holly. Under the supposed power of inspiration, she grew fatigued and had to rest for days on end. Her work fell to me.

Olive Collins, who slept three beds from mine, claimed to channel Christopher Columbus and Chief Tecumseh. Most importantly, Olive said she was visited often by Mother Ann, who wanted her to pass along instructions. We were no longer to eat pork at Sabbathday Lake, nor were we to drink coffee or tea. This was met with pushback from the brethren but the Ministry took the message on its face and these luxuries were banned.

Those girls had such influence over the rest of us. Believers were sometimes singled out and expelled, based on alleged spirit messages accusing them of this or that offense. Some adults seemed terrified that they would be next, especially those who voiced doubt. I once heard Sister Florence whisper to Sister Phebe that she did not envy the elders; that in this hurricane of gifts, it was impossible for them to say what was revelation and what was not.

Diana Abbott was one of many Shaker girls who produced gift drawings, works of art that defied the girls' own artistic abilities, and as such were believed to be gifts from God. These too were understood to contain messages from spirit, interpretable only by she who had created them. Watercolor masterpieces, ornate and inspired, adorned with images of Mother Ann, of flowers and fruit and golden chariots and intricate lacework. Of biblical and Shaker stories alike. Of the Savior dressed in Shaker garb.

At any other time in Shaker history, the drawings would have been forbidden. Understand this was a place where decoration, excess was never allowed. Gift drawings were not displayed or shared with outsiders. Most ended up in the kindling bin near the ovens. Only a handful survived, and those by accident—tucked away in a book or forgotten in a drawer.

I thought it was all the girls' invention, a product of their wild imaginations, or maybe the devil's work. Holly, Olive, and Diana had not the abilities of Mother Ann. Of that, I was certain. As a result of all this, outsiders were banned from attending our worship services and school, for fear of how they might misunderstand the moment of spiritual ecstasy that was upon us.

After that, the only visitors to Sabbathday Lake were those who came seeking help in various forms. Another contradiction: how separate we made ourselves, and yet how charitable we were. When poor neighbors stole our vegetables, the brethren planted more. Sister Florence said, "We plant some for the Shakers, some for the thieves, and some for the crows. Thieves and crows have to eat too."

People came fleeing all sorts of persecution—escaped slaves came, abused wives, families who had lost every penny. We were told to embrace them as kin. Some stayed for days or weeks, others all their lives. There were Winter Shakers, who came and went with the season. There were children adopted out of orphanages or collected from poorhouses, and once even a newborn baby left on the doorstep of the women's dwelling house.

If a child had a living parent on arrival, as we did, the parent signed an indenture, swearing that in exchange for stability, food and shelter, education, a trade, they would not interfere with their children's upbringing by the Shakers, nor would they try to take a child back. But not everyone could keep these promises. It was not so unusual for a mother or father to change their mind.

When I was eight years old, Sarah Ogden's mother came to see her with a constable and a burly young man, intent on taking her away. They did not succeed, but for many weeks after, the case was in court, with the elders traveling to Portland each day, and Sarah going on among us as normal, like she didn't care how the whole thing turned out. Three young brothers were kidnapped in the night by their father and uncle. Another boy's father marched into the schoolhouse mid-lesson and carried him away, though he left the boy's sister, his daughter, behind.

I dreamed of my father coming to take Emily and me.

Sister Florence told me once that in her youth and all generations of Shakers that came before, most children who entered into the Society came with their families and were not separated from them. We were the first generation to come alone. Perhaps that is why nearly half of them stayed on for their entire lives, while almost all of us left as soon as we were able.

I don't think there was ever a day when we were not in some fashion reminded that our decision whether or not to stay would influence the ability of the Shakers to go on existing. It weighed heavy on us.

I DID NOT SEE the world until age eleven, when I accompanied Sister Florence to the hotel at Poland Springs for the winter sale of fancy goods. As we set up our tent, I gasped at the sight of two Indian women in their costumes, selling baskets a few tables away. They wore dresses made of buckskin, with beadwork decorating their necks and fringe at the sleeves and hem. On their heads, tall pointed caps. Their baskets were printed with patterns of flowers and sunbursts and birds, dyed red and blue.

"Don't stare, child," Sister Florence said, but I couldn't help it.

People giggled nervously as they approached the pair, as if on a dare. They whispered and pointed. I felt sorry for them.

But then those who bought our wares seemed amused by our old-fashioned homemade clothes. We were something of a spectacle too.

I tried to focus on the task at hand, but I couldn't stop noticing people in the crowd. A mother and two daughters, around my age, walking hand in hand. A married couple with a baby in a pram, the man's arms loaded down with Christmas presents. A younger couple, talking excitedly of a sleigh ride later that day.

When we got back to the village, I wept.

On the first Saturday of every month, we children went to confession and told our sins to Sister Florence. That week, I confessed my longing to flee, confessed that I was not as good as a Shaker ought to be. There is no penance in Shaker confession. Rather, the confession itself is an act of humility. In Sister Florence's kind silence, I saw all my failings reflected. I knew I would not stay.

From then on, at night, my sister and I whispered of our plans for liberation. How, when I turned eighteen, we would leave together and be free. Emily would wait two years after her own eighteenth birthday, rather than go ahead without me. She wanted to marry and have lots of babies. A home of her own. Emily talked about her wedding day—the dress and the white silk gloves she would wear.

I never much cared for the world of men. I wanted something else. Something indescribable. A life that was only mine. A place where I made my own decisions, though what those might be I had no idea.

At sixteen, like my sister before me, I left the Children's Order and moved into the women's dwelling house.

Emily was eighteen then. She had reached the end of her indenture. As our plan had it, she waited two more years for me. But something happened to her in those two years. I've never understood what or why. Somehow she realized that after all, she was a Believer. When the time came for us to go, Emily could not do it. Instead, she signed the covenant, vowing to spend the rest of her life at Sabbathday Lake.

The greatest heartbreak I have ever known was leaving my sister behind.

I TRAVELED an hour south to Portland by train and, through the kindness of a former Shaker sister, found work as a hand-stitcher in a straw bonnet bleachery, where I was to make four dollars a week, plus boarding. The owner liked to hire former Shakers for our discipline, our work ethic, our attention to detail. I did not know until I arrived that he would hold back my first month's pay, expecting me to work on trial. Nor did I know that my bedroom would share a wall with the one in which he and his wife slept. The two of them had shouting matches at all hours. The sound terrified me. Never in my life had I heard a raised voice from the people with whom I lived.

He praised my speed and dexterity. Before long, he assigned me to work Saturdays in his milliner's shop, and to trim hats at home in my own time. I had no life outside of work. On Sundays, most of the girls went to church, but I wasn't sure which one to attend, so instead I stayed home and read my Bible and wrote to my sister, and slept a great deal. The stench of petroleum coming off the wharves as I walked to work each morning at seven was an unpleasant new addition to my life. As were the swearing and singing of sailors in the pubs as I walked home alone at nine or ten at night, petrified.

In the shop on Saturdays, two local girls worked alongside me. Their friends and customers often stayed for hours, gossiping. I had never seen such a thing. I told myself this was what I had craved. This lack of rigidity. But I couldn't see it as anything other than a waste of time. And it often seemed cruel.

Once, a woman with a black eye entered the shop. She had fallen in the night, she said, while trying to get to her crying baby in the dark. They fussed over her, said it might have happened to anyone. But when she left, they talked at once, with too much excitement, about the wretched drunk of a husband who did it to her.

I thought of the women who came alone to Sabbathday Lake, covered in bruises, intent on escaping such circumstances. And the widows who had been left destitute. A sense I had long before I could put it into words: that men were a danger to women. That women must find or build spaces of our own in order to be safe. The Shakers promised respite. Stability. Peace. Nonjudgment. Standing there in a hat shop in Portland, I felt intensely proud of the Shakers, as if they were still mine to be proud of. I thought of the true kindness I had known all my life.

A WOMAN NAMED Agnes Foster came into the shop twice a month before a meeting with an editor at the *Eastern Argus,* in which she had a semi-regular column.

Agnes fascinated me. She was taller than any woman I had ever seen, and as straight and narrow as a lamppost. She seemed to have a strong opinion on every imaginable topic. She was always on her way to a lecture at the lyceum, or a temperance meeting at the New City Hall, always with a book in her hand. When she learned that I was raised by the Shakers, she at once tried to engage me in a debate. She had, she said, attended the Women's Rights Convention in Syracuse, New York, one year prior, where the activist Harriot Kezia

Hunt cited the Shakers as some of the earliest proponents of equal rights and the advancement of women. That got Agnes looking into it more. And while she admired the Shakers, she wanted my thoughts on whether they could rightfully be called Christians, given that they did not believe in the Holy Trinity, the immaculate conception, the resurrection of the body, and so on.

I had never been asked such a question. I felt my face grow hot, unable to properly defend myself. But defend myself against what? I had never felt that I was a true Shaker in the first place. And the Shakers called other forms of Christianity the Antichrist. They were not shy about proclaiming themselves the only true Christians, so why should it surprise me that others felt the same way?

"Shakers seek to rebuild the primitive church as Christ himself designed it," I said.

"I'm suspicious of sects. I often wonder if they're merely calling themselves religions in order to avoid paying taxes," Agnes said.

"The Shakers pay taxes," I said. "They feel it is their duty as members of this nation and the only real way to separate church and state."

At this, Agnes cocked her head. "Interesting," she said. "I did not know that."

The shopgirls giggled. "I've never seen you cede a point," one of them said.

"True," Agnes said. "Bravo, Eliza."

Later I would feel foolish for crying, but in that moment, tears came to my eyes.

Agnes seemed to understand before I did. "You miss home," she said.

"No," I said. "I just don't think the city is for me. It's too loud, too chaotic, too fast, too severe."

"Dear girl," Agnes said. "Forgive me. I must be more sensitive. My sister is always telling me so."

At the mention of a sister, I started crying all the more, causing her to exclaim, "What have I done now?"

She came behind the counter then, and hugged me.

We laughed. The first laugh I'd had since I got to Portland.

———

A WEEK LATER, Agnes burst into the shop and said, "Eliza, I've a proposition for you."

The others flung their heads in her direction, eager to learn if they were missing out on something that was rightfully theirs.

Her sister, Agnes said, was in need of a hired girl.

"Impossible to find anyone decent locally, down where we're from. The ones who want to work all run off to the mills in Dover as soon as they can."

I had seen signs advertising these positions. ASSIST IN THE PRO-DUCTION OF THE FINEST PRINTED CALICO . . . EMPLOYING GIRLS BETWEEN THE AGES OF 12 AND 25 . . . ROOM AND BOARD PROVIDED, GOOD MANNERS A MUST.

"It's a quiet house by the sea," Agnes went on. "All the modern conveniences. I daresay you'll be happier there. My sister, Hannah, is lovely. Sweet and dear and shy. But fierce in her way. She's used to being head of household much of the time. Two years back, she came upon a wolf with one of her chickens in its mouth down in the root cellar of her house. She went right down there and beat the thing with a broom until it dropped the chicken and ran off. She's a better shot than either of our brothers. She used to go on hunts with them and our dad, and the boys would always come home so frustrated because Hannah got a buck and they didn't."

Agnes smiled, lost in her thoughts. Then she looked at me.

"Hannah never wants to be a bother to anyone. She wouldn't dream of having help, usually. But she's expecting. She's had a hard time of it. The doctor's just ordered her to stay in bed until the baby comes. Two months hence! She'll need someone to do the cleaning and so on. Do you know how to cook?"

"Of course," I said.

She nodded. "Of course."

I asked if Hannah had other children for whom I would be responsible, and Agnes answered quickly, "No." She went on. "Samuel, Hannah's husband, is an officer on a ship and won't be back for several months. You'd have to give me your word you'll stay at least until he returns. Hannah has our brother Charles's wife, Alice, to help some, but Alice has her own household to run. And she gets dreadful headaches. She's been put on a rest cure herself, but good luck resting with five children. It might be hard at times. It's a big house. Samuel built it for my sister as a wedding present five years ago."

At this, the other girls cooed.

"Samuel is a dreamer," Agnes said. "Some men build their grand home having made their fortune. Samuel built his in expectation of it. His great-great-great-great grandfather, or some such, was one of our town founders. Some of the men in his family are as rich as Croesus. Not his father, sadly, but Samuel expects that he himself will be. He insisted on a butler's pantry, though they have little hope of ever employing an actual butler. My sister thought that was so silly. Eliza, I'm guessing you don't mind hard work."

"Not at all."

And so it was settled. A new chapter begun. All my life until I had come to Portland, the weight of whether I would leave Sabbathday Lake, and what that choice would do to the people I loved, gnawed at me. In Portland, I simply left. The city churned on the same as ever, without even a ripple where I'd stood.

I took a train to a place called Winston and a surrey from the railroad station to the town of Awadapquit, two miles south. It was November then. Gray and rainy. The only people I saw as the carriage passed through town were fishermen in waders and a mass of faceless bodies hauling timber at the docks. There was a hotel on the main street. A grocer. A handful of other shops, all closed for the season.

The driver took a long carriage road that ran through the middle of a dense wood. For some time, I worried he had veered from the path and planned to do something terrible with me. The area did not look populated at all. It was a wonder there was even a road. After a while, we crossed paths with a hay wagon pulled by a white horse. The farmer sitting on top gave a wave. The sight made me think of my old home at Sabbathday Lake.

A few moments later, we turned down the long driveway that led to Hannah's house. The sound of horse hooves coming up that drive was one I would soon come to recognize as the sign that visitors were approaching. I saw then that the road we were traveling was not out in an endless wood, but just a few minutes' walk to the sea.

The house was far too big for a couple with only one child. It was stately and elegant and modern, painted pale yellow. Tall pines surrounded it on three sides, and the ocean on the fourth. A beautiful spot. I wished my sister were there to see it.

Alice, the sister-in-law, greeted me at the door. She was plump, with brown hair that wisped in a crown around her lined face.

Hannah, she said, was resting. "Poor thing. She's all nerves," she whispered. "About the baby."

"I suppose that's understandable, being as it's her first?" I said. From the look on her face, I could tell it was not the right thing to say.

"Agnes should have told you," Alice said. "But then, I don't even know how much Agnes knows. She just comes and goes as she likes. Hannah isn't well. It's all been too much for her. I'm only telling you this because Hannah is fragile just now. You should be aware of that."

I nodded, though I wasn't sure what she was telling me exactly, or how I ought to respond.

Alice offered me a bowl of soup, which I gladly accepted. She watched me eat, and talked about her husband Charles's family as if she had known me forever.

"I've always thought Samuel built this house way out here, away from town and Hannah's people, because he's jealous. He knew he'd be gone for long stretches and didn't want anyone else's eyes on her. But that makes it all the harder for me, you see."

"Of course," I said.

After she left, I spent the rest of the day getting acquainted with the house, and with the bedroom Alice had told me was mine. The room was peculiar. It stood behind a door, perfectly flat, that when closed disappeared into the wallpaper pattern of the second-floor landing. The room was tiny, but it had windows on two sides, which let in a good deal of light, and a spectacular ocean view. There was just enough space for a single bed, a small desk, and a chest of drawers. I didn't know how I'd be able to sleep. I had never had a room of my own before.

I didn't lay eyes on Hannah until later that evening, when I brought her dinner. I knocked gently on the bedroom door in case she was asleep, which I hoped she was. But she said softly, "Come in."

Hannah had sunken cheeks, a tired smile.

The bulge beneath the bedsheet seemed unreal. I could not stop staring. I had never known a pregnant woman before.

"You're Eliza," she said.

"Yes, Mrs. Littleton."

"You must call me Hannah," she said.

She thanked me for the food, inquired politely about my journey, and begged my pardon for not saying hello sooner. She asked if I had everything I needed. I kept my answers brief. When no further questions came, I regretted that. Not knowing what to do, I left her there to eat. In the days that followed, when I checked on her or brought her a plate of food, she said she was sorry for being of no help to me.

She apologized at great length when I brought her a towel and a pitcher of hot water and set it on the marble-topped washstand in her room. It was one of the tasks Alice had laid out for me, but Hannah went red with embarrassment and said, "You shouldn't have to do that."

I told her it was no trouble, and left her to her washing.

Another day, she said, "This house. It's so much work, I know."

I told her that I liked hard work. I was accustomed.

"My sister said you were raised by the Shakers," Hannah said. "I suppose you are used to much harder."

The truth was, the Shakers had sinks and pumps and stoves beyond anything the world's people had yet incorporated into daily life. The brethren erected mechanical lifts that hoisted our heavy wet clothes and bedsheets into an attic to dry.

At Hannah's house, the first time I hung laundry on an outdoor line, I spent half an hour hanging and pinning each piece—and at the last second, the entire line came down and all the clean clothes landed in the mud.

I washed every Monday, unless it rained or the pump froze. I hauled heavy buckets of water into the house and onto the stove. I scrubbed and wrung each bedsheet and tablecloth, every article of clothing, then placed them in a tub and hauled them back outside, hanging them one by one on the line until my arms shook and my wrists ached. The next day, I heated six irons on the stove and alternated their use as one by one the heat went out of them. I burned my fingertips, and they swelled up red. I stood beside the hot stove sweating, praying no one would knock at the door and come upon me in that state. Every day, I polished and swept and mended. I washed windows. I piled wood in the bitter cold. I fed the sheep. I fed the chickens and slaughtered the chickens and dressed the chickens. I collected the eggs. I cooked everything we ate over the coal stove.

Entire days passed with only the sound of the ocean outside the window for company. I wrote letters to my sister every evening, and when she replied with news from Sabbathday Lake, the events she described played out before my eyes. I missed her. Sometimes I wondered if it would be my fate to return to her. But I had promised Agnes I would stay until the husband came home.

Hannah barely ate. Most mornings, when I brought her toast and tea, she was sitting in a chair by the window, in her white nightgown. She always had a book in her lap, though she was never reading. She was looking out. At the sea, I imagined. Thinking of her husband far away. Until one day, I followed her gaze and saw: off to the side of the house, where the trees began, four metal posts had been hammered into the ground, a chain connecting them in the form of a square. A burial plot. Later that day, I went to investigate more closely and saw two bright white child's headstones, the letters freshly carved:

IN LOVING MEMORY OF POLLY,
BORN JUNE 6, 1851
DIED DECEMBER 12, 1851

OUR WILLIAM,
BORN SEPTEMBER 17, 1852
DIED SEPTEMBER 9, 1853

I knelt down and prayed for them, and for her. The poor woman must be terrified. At Sabbathday Lake, we were taught that Mother Ann's children were lost because of some sin she herself committed. I never questioned this until that moment. Nothing Hannah could have done could have brought about an outcome so tragic. I wanted to tell her it would work out as God intended. But I couldn't muster the courage to say anything on the subject.

Weeks later, in the middle of the night, I awoke to the sound of Hannah screaming my name. I ran to her side. There wasn't time to call for the doctor. Already, I could see the top of the baby's head emerging from between her legs. Round and impossible, yet there it was. The sheets were soaked through with blood. It pooled on the hardwood floor. Hannah let out a groan, a wail, the likes of which I'd never heard.

The child did not cry. Hannah said she could tell he wouldn't survive. I had no idea whether or not it was true. I'd never seen a newborn baby. Little Alfred lasted two days. Afterward, Hannah sat rocking him for another day and night. As she did this, she told me about the other children she had lost. William was one year old. Spotted fever. Polly was just six months. They never knew what it was that took her. An infection, the doctor said. She was sickly from the time she was born. Hannah told me she had been pregnant seven times.

When Alice came, she screamed at the sight of the dead baby in Hannah's arms. She insisted we call for the doctor. "Why did you let her do that?" she demanded, but it made all the sense to me. He was her child.

I was sent from the room when the doctor got there, but I heard him and Alice pleading with Hannah. The doctor left soon after with a cloth-covered box. It reminded me of a woman I had seen on the train from Portland, who kept two lovebirds in a cage on the seat beside her, and would throw a bedsheet over the top when she wanted them to be quiet.

Alice told me she would return in the morning, but the next day brought with it a blizzard so intense that you could not see the ocean for the wall of white snow outside the window. Alice didn't come. No one did.

I could not bear the sound of Hannah's weeping once they had taken the baby away. I had never witnessed a grief that deep or a love that intense. On the second night, I brought her dinner, placed it on the side table, and was about to slip out when she said, "Please. Stay."

She patted the edge of the bed and I sat there, rubbing her back as she cried. This went on for hours, until at last, exhausted, I yawned, and she said, "I'm so sorry, Eliza. You're tired. Lie down."

And I did. That night I held her, just as I'd held my sister when we were young.

HANNAH COULD BARELY take a bite of food or lift her head from a pillow, the pain was that severe. I helped her bathe, gently pulling off her cotton nightgown, dipping a towel into the basin of warm, soapy water, and running it gently along her back, her arms, her neck, her legs.

The weather didn't help matters. It was midnight-dark by late afternoon. The cold came inside, and the wind shook the windowpanes. One night I was awakened by the sound of glass shattering. The inkstand on my desk had frozen and burst.

That winter, it seemed the snow never stopped falling. We hardly had any visitors.

When Hannah went four days without eating, I baked an apple pie, using the recipe we made for breakfast at Sabbathday Lake, sweet and delicious and enough to fill up a hungry farmer who had been toiling in the fields before dawn. I brought her a slice and fed it to her, one small forkful at a time. She ate every bite.

HER HUSBAND RETURNED the third week of March.

Samuel was handsome—tall and broad-shouldered. You could easily see how the two of them made a pair. At night, I heard Hannah crying behind the closed bedroom door. And him pleading, telling her he hated to see her this way. He insisted she get dressed; that she eat meals with him in the dining room.

"Please, Pet, I only want you to be happy," he said. "I won't be home for long. Let's make the most of the time we have."

He wasn't a bad man. He loved Hannah, that was clear. But he was out of his depth. He wished her to be *happy*. He wished her to be the girl she was when first they met. He may as well have wished her to be a deer traipsing through the woods, so grotesque and impossible was his request.

Samuel brought Hannah two trunks of gifts from the voyage, the most beautiful of which was a set of Staffordshire china in a brilliant shade of jade green, with a border of what looked like lacework, painted on in gold, and flowers, pink and yellow, sprinkled all across. There were eight full place settings. I unwrapped each piece, taking great care, and displayed them on the middle shelf in the otherwise empty butler's pantry, remembering Agnes's joke about the lack of an actual butler.

Every time I passed through the space, I admired those dishes as if they were hung in frames upon the wall. Hannah had no interest in looking at them, or at the silks he brought her, or even the jewelry. I could see how it hurt Samuel. I felt sorry for him.

Before he went away again, Samuel made Hannah pose for an ambrotype of the two of them together, a keepsake for his voyage. She insisted on wearing all black, as was proper. She was still mourning the loss of her child. Samuel grew cross and said Hannah looked lovely in the green dress he bought her, and he wished to remember her in something more cheerful. She was crying even as the photographer set up his camera.

"Come now," Samuel said, with the sternness of a father. It made me jump. "Smile, Hannah."

And so she did.

"Look into your husband's eyes," the man with the camera said.

And so she did.

They were made to hold the pose for a good two minutes. I counted the seconds in my head. The moment it was over, Hannah returned to bed, exhausted.

I felt relief when Samuel was gone again. I don't know how Hannah felt. She cried, but she was crying already. She said one morning that it was awful having him away so often and for so long. But then, why marry a man who made his living at sea? Like most things I could not understand, I attributed my inability to comprehend it to my upbringing. I had never been taught a thing about romantic love. Certainly I had never seen it with my own eyes.

Perhaps love required some element of difficulty. Perhaps in order to be true, love must also be inconvenient. The girls in the hat shop in

Portland were forever complaining about their beaus—their short-comings and betrayals. But none of this deterred them from carrying on. None of them ever decided instead to be alone and free from such intensity of feeling.

SOON AFTER SAMUEL LEFT, a letter arrived from my sister. As was my habit, I tucked it away in my room, saving it to read at bedtime. Usually, Emily wrote to me about the weather and her work on the farm. She wrote of the health of the elders. The content of her letters was never thrilling. The letter itself was the thing.

This time, though, her words shocked me. She had recently learned a secret from our past. After our father left us, she wrote, he met a woman and married her, and never let on that he had been married before. Their daughter had come to Sabbathday Lake in search of my sister and me. She explained to my sister that her father—our father—had recently died, and had told her on his deathbed about the two daughters he left behind.

I told myself I had no reason to despair. I had believed for as long as I could remember that my father was gone, and now he was. What difference did it make? But I could not stop crying. I didn't realize how loud I was until I heard a knock at the door.

"Eliza?" Hannah said. "What is it?"

I told her. Afterward, she sat beside me on the bed and held me.

She said, "When I was small, I thought I'd have eight children. Now I would do anything if God would grant me one."

I assumed she had turned her thoughts back to her own troubles. But in fact, she was thinking of me. "How could he?" she said. "Leave his precious children like that?"

We talked for hours that night. Certainly the fastest way to forget one's own troubles is by helping someone else face hers, and that evening, I saw Hannah as she must have been before all her losses. The sun was rising in the sky when at last she said we ought to get some sleep. She kissed me on the cheek and returned to her room down the hall.

————

THE FOLLOWING WEEK, Hannah felt well enough to do the spring cleaning with me, and—the work halved—we got through in good season, talking all the while. She exclaimed over the fact that I had lived in Maine all my life, but had not seen the ocean until I was eighteen. For two weeks, we scrubbed the house from top to bottom. We went through countless rags and brushes that turned black with soot that had accumulated from the stove and lamps. We hung rugs and drapes on the clothesline and beat every speck of dust and dirt out of them. We moved every piece of furniture out of the room in which it belonged. The parlor chairs and sofa went on the lawn to air out. The beds got pushed into a single upstairs room. There was no inch of wall or floor or ceiling we did not touch. We oiled and polished the woodwork and wood furniture and wood floors. We dusted. We mopped.

At the end of each day, we collapsed into our beds, exhausted.

It was during this time that Hannah started eating in the dining room again by choice. She insisted I join her at the table. One night, I told her about the beautiful hats we made at the shop in Portland where I first met her sister. She said she adored hats, and hadn't had the occasion to wear one for so long.

I got it into my head that Hannah might like a silk drawn bonnet, and started rising before dawn to work on one in secret. I made the wire frame and the silk lining by hand, stretched the ivory-colored taffeta over layers of muslin and netting. When I at last presented Hannah with it, her smile was so genuine, so radiant. She hugged me. A soaring feeling shot through my body. The sense that making her happy was the most satisfying thing I could ever have the good fortune to do.

That time marked the beginning of joy in the house. The lifting off of gloom like fog over the water. I thought then that it was mostly down to the change in the season, the arrival of blossoms and warm air and long afternoons with the windows thrown open. The true reason eluded me.

When I told Hannah one night that I missed Sabbathday Lake, even though I had always intended to leave, she asked me to tell her about it. I told her that among the Shakers I was called Sister Eliza and she said she would call me that too if I liked, for I had become something like a sister to her.

We shared a warmth and a closeness that I had never known before, not even with my sister. Agnes remarked on it when she visited. "I knew you would care for my Hannah and be kind," she said. "But I never imagined you'd become such friends! Thank goodness for you, Eliza. You've brought her back to life."

We did not know yet that Hannah was carrying a baby, who would be born healthy and strong. Who would live for more than a century. Frances Constance Littleton. Our Fannie.

FOR SEVERAL MONTHS after Fannie was born, Hannah couldn't stop checking on her, waking her to make sure she was breathing. She didn't believe she might get to keep her daughter. She expected the bright light in our lives to vanish, as had happened every time before. I worried about Hannah's health, her frailty, her exhaustion. Most nights I'd get up and keep her company while she nursed Fannie in bed. Once, all three of us fell asleep there, and from then on, we went to bed that way on purpose every night.

Much of Hannah's fear seemed to melt away when Fannie turned one. Those were dreamlike days. I never saw Hannah so happy as she was then.

On Fannie's first birthday, Hannah kissed me on the lips in the darkness of early morning. A thing no one had ever done before. I received it as a form of ecstasy, a word I had heard in my childhood but never understood until then.

SAMUEL RETURNED HOME three months later, ahead of schedule, when Fannie was fifteen months old. He fell in love with the baby, and she with him. I tried not to be jealous as I made the silent return to my room. I found myself furious at Hannah, even as I knew it was absurd. He was her husband. Of course they would sleep together, and hold hands as they walked the cliffs, leaving me with the baby. They were in love, that was clear.

I spent an inordinate amount of time thinking about the kiss. I replayed the memory of it so often that I came to wonder if perhaps I had invented it. In Samuel's presence, Hannah was as kind to me as ever, but I sensed a distance there that left me drenched in sadness.

He went away again after four months. I didn't know what to do with Hannah's tears. I was so glad to see him go. This next voyage was to be his first as captain and would last three years.

"Three years feels like eternity," Hannah said.

Three years went by in an instant.

I felt bashful around her for the first week or two, but then she asked me to please come back to bed with her and Fannie. So I did and, despite all confusion, was happy again.

Nine months later, like his sister before him, James came bounding into the world, fat and healthy and howling.

Samuel sent letters home, asking for details of the boy, thrilled to have a son. Hannah never invited me to read these letters, but she left them unfolded on the nightstand so it didn't seem too much a violation to look them over when I was alone. Samuel wrote that he could not stand the distance. He would take Hannah and the children along with him on the next voyage, a four-year journey to Indonesia.

Hannah did not mention a word of this to me. I was left to wonder whether she really would go, and what would become of me if she did. I wanted more than anything to know what she wrote in her replies to him, but I could never bring myself to ask. I thought of the promise I made Agnes at the start, to stay as long as Hannah needed me. No one had promised me anything in return.

EXCEPT FOR THE odd unpleasant reminder of its impermanence, our life was one of simple pleasures. Hannah's kisses became a regular occurrence. The children felt like ours. We both mothered them, as well as managing the house together. We never quarreled, we were such a peaceful pair. On summer nights, we sat on the porch and I read to her until the sun set. Hannah told me she loved me, as easily and freely as she said it to the children.

Sometimes we held hands and listened to the waves, and I felt filled to bursting from my blessings. The children in their own rooms now, we continued to sleep together every night in her bed. The candle blown out, we ran our hands gently, softly under one another's thin cotton nightgowns. Her fingertips like bursts of sunshine on my skin. I held my breath. Neither of us ever said a word.

TRULY, I HAD ALMOST forgotten Samuel existed when a letter reached us in October of 1860. His ship, homeward bound from Spain, was due to arrive in Awadapquit one month hence.

Hannah began to take greater care with her appearance. She kept mentioning how plump she had gotten. She refused to eat even her favorite foods. Taking in her reflection, she fretted over her hair, which was not as full as it once had been, and her arms, which were fuller. Agnes called on us for a visit and Hannah asked her to bring a perfume Samuel liked from a shop in Portland on her next trip home.

I asked Hannah for no assurances. Where I was raised, no one ever showed a hint of discontent, no matter what roiled beneath the surface. I was well practiced. And I knew there was no point. I believed Hannah loved me and I believed that when her husband returned, she would have no choice but to leave me. My greatest hope was that she might convince him to keep me on to run the house while they were away so that I could see her again in four years, the moment she returned.

For days in advance, we prepared for his homecoming lunch.

Hannah asked me to bake my apple pie. "The pie that brought me back to life," she said with a happy smile, and I smiled back though I wished I could say the pie was only for her, not him. I said no such thing, of course. I made the pie.

We baked bread and roasted four chickens and chopped vegetables and polished the silver.

Finally one morning word came that the ship had been spotted, three miles out, and would arrive within hours. We set the dining room table with the green Staffordshire china Samuel brought back the first time I met him, when Hannah was too sad and sick to even unwrap it.

"These are lovely," she said, admiring the dishes.

"They are," I said.

"And my favorite color," she said. "So thoughtful."

Hannah's dress for the occasion had been hanging on the back of the bedroom door for two weeks. I helped her into it, pulling her corset as tight as I could bear to, and still she told me to make it tighter. I tried not to care that she wanted to look beautiful for him.

We brought the children to the beach, scrubbed and dressed in their finest, each of us taking one by the hand. It was a cold day, but Hannah refused a coat, wanting him to lay eyes on her in that pale green dress, adorned with a silk collar. I made it myself, spent weeks cutting and basting the sleeves, shaping the waist, because I knew how much she would admire it, and how beautiful the dress would look on her. She wore the silk bonnet I made her as well, and she looked so pretty, I thought I might cry.

The ship was already visible from shore when we arrived. A crowd had gathered to welcome the men home. There was a sense of excitement among them but also, I thought, of trepidation. The mouth of the river was known to be perilous. Powerful currents collided there with ocean waves. On the best of days, it made for a difficult entrance into the harbor.

That day, the seas were rough, and strong winds whipped the waves.

Fannie shouted to James, "That's our dad out there. He's come to meet you."

Everyone laughed and Hannah said that indeed he had.

God forgive me, all I could think was that I would give anything to see the ship turn back.

We all watched as it entered into the tidal passage at the mouth of the river, seeming to strain against the rising waves. The vessel rocked back and forth, like a toy in the grips of some indifferent child in his morning bath.

A rumbling among the men in the crowd.

"What is it?" I asked one of them.

He looked deadly serious. "There is a sandbar out there, and it's made into the sea considerably these last two years. Littleton won't be able to pass it in these conditions. I don't think he has any idea."

Strong headwinds threw the ship back. A massive wave washed over the top. Later we would learn that the sternpost hit bottom, breaking in two, destroying the rudder, and with it any hope of steering the ship to safety. Everyone on land screamed as the boat was tossed onto its beam ends, its topmasts ripped clear away. Some of the men on the beach tried to get the women to leave, but the wives were adamant. I wanted to stay with Hannah, but she begged me to take the children away, out of sight. She looked like she would faint. I would have given anything to hold her then, but I did as she asked. One of the men made her sit down on a blanket.

I pulled Fannie and James away, though they fought me, unaware of precisely what was happening, but smart enough to sense that something not to plan had occurred. I'm sure the truth seemed impossible to them. It did to me. I looked back only once, and saw men clinging to the wreck. The next wave simply ripped them away, and tore the ship to bits.

I listened as a teenage boy explained to a child, his brother maybe, that there was nothing to do but wait. The child pleaded—he could swim out and save them, or take the rowboat, he said. To me, it didn't seem impossible. I understood hardly anything about the ocean then. But the older boy looked at him pitifully. He said the water was too cold to swim, too violent to row out into.

Nothing to do but wait. No one could bear to admit they had nothing to wait for. The more time passed, the clearer it became that the men were not going to emerge from the water or swim victorious to shore. And yet we waited. Hours later, at home, Hannah took the children to bed. The table was still set for Samuel's welcome lunch. In a frenzy, I put the dishes back in the pantry he had built for her, as if doing so might make Hannah forget.

Bodies kept appearing in the days and weeks that followed. Not a single person aboard survived. The ship's officers and six of its sailors were local boys. Ten others were foreigners, picked up in Italian and Spanish ports. There was no one to identify them when their bodies washed ashore. No list of their names. A woman had been on the ship as well, her provenance completely unaccounted for. She and the anonymous sailors were buried on a hill near the beach, a simple wooden cross to commemorate them all.

Samuel was found freshly shaven and dressed in his finest clothes, in anticipation of his reunion with Hannah.

We laid him out in the parlor for two days. Never had we had so many visitors. The sound of horse hooves on the drive was near constant. The mourners wished to pay their respects, of course, but I suspected that in many cases, their motives weren't entirely pure. They wanted in on a tragic tale, to be part of it in their way. People have such a strange attraction to the misery of others. I felt more protective than ever of Hannah just then.

Early that second morning, I found Fannie and James side by side in the doorway to the parlor. My heart broke to look at them, children who had not known until then that life was finite. It was the first and only time James would ever be in his father's physical presence.

Samuel was buried in the family plot, alongside the three lost children.

At the funeral, the minister spoke of Samuel's courage. Of his ever-present knowledge that the mission could be perilous, even fatal, and his determination to see it through, even so. I thought of Hannah, how many times she nearly died attempting to bring a child into the world. If she had been taken in that pursuit, would he have spoken of her mission with such reverence?

When it was over, Agnes found me in the crowd and took my hand.

"Please don't leave," she said. "She'll need you."

I answered honestly, telling her that I had no intention of going anywhere.

I WROTE TO MY SISTER about what happened, but I could not say half the things I would have needed to paint an accurate picture of how our world had changed. One could spend a lifetime trying to make sense of the bare facts of what transpired before our eyes that day on the beach. But what was inside me could never be told, to her or anyone.

The house once again became a somber place, but that only lasted so long.

For the rest of my life, I carried the guilt. A fear that I had willed

Samuel to die, to vanish. But the feeling was a small price to pay for what became mine as a result. Twelve more years with Hannah and the children. A life unlike any I had ever seen or heard about. Sometimes I walked around the house in Samuel's old clothing, liking the feel of the comfortable, baggy pants, the three-button linen shirts. His overcoat when it was particularly cold. Hannah called me *Husband* then, laughing.

If Alice was right, poor Samuel had hid his bride away in that secluded house by the sea so that no one else could have her. But our seclusion was what allowed us to be. The children went to school and made friends. I don't believe they ever told anyone about our arrangement. I liked to think that was because they saw nothing unusual in it, but I know that wasn't true. In any case, they knew they were fiercely loved. Even now, I can see the four of us sitting at the fireside in the kitchen, reading aloud from *The Eastern Argus* or *The Christian Mirror,* or from our favorite Bible passages. Later, James and Fannie read us Shakespeare and Poe and Henry Ward Beecher.

Had Samuel not perished when he did, he might very well have been taken a year or two hence. So many men we knew went off to war and never returned.

Hannah's brother, Charles, enlisted with the Maine Twentieth Infantry. He wrote letters home to Alice and their five children, and to Hannah too, at least once a week. When five weeks passed without word from him, the family feared the worst. I prayed to God that it not be so. They had suffered too much already.

Agnes came to the house early one morning. We were still asleep. She let herself in and climbed the stairs, came right into the bedroom. "My darling," she said. "Wake up. It's Charles. Oh, Hannah, he—"

Realizing then that there were two of us in bed, Agnes fled.

Hannah ran after her. Downstairs in the kitchen, they cried in each other's arms and ignored what Agnes had seen. It was never mentioned again.

TWO YEARS LATER, in 1864, Agnes brought a man named Leonard Crosby, a colleague from the newspaper, to our house in the forenoon on a Monday. The governor had declared it a fasting day, and they had it off from work.

"Call me Crosby," he said.

Crosby was as short and plump as Agnes was tall. He was bald, but for a ring of bushy brown hair that reminded me of a monk's.

He told a story of a man they'd seen at the train station earlier, shouting about how it was time for war to end, time for Lincoln to bring our boys home now that he had won reelection. Crosby called him a traitor to the cause of emancipation. I understood that. And yet I thought that he didn't understand how tired people were of war. How much it had taken from them. One of every five local boys who went to fight had died. It was impossible to walk through town without seeing a new black wreath on someone's door. There were men home on furlough, missing an arm, a leg, a hand.

As time went by, recruits got older and older. Walter Farnham, the sixty-two-year-old town postmaster, went to Louisiana and died on the battlefield within a month. Many others died at home, after long and violent illness contracted in those swampy southern climates, so foreign to their New England blood.

Every Friday, Hannah volunteered at the Ladies' Aid Society, rolling bandages and packing provisions to be sent to the front. Each week she returned with what felt like a lifetime of heartbreaking stories. She told me more than once how grateful she was that James was only a child, and wouldn't be sent to war. Were he old enough, she would have to let him go. But the anguish of mothers whose sons were killed felt senseless. It broke her heart. She swore that had she known how troubled the world was going to become, she might not have brought children into it at all.

Crosby said he was at work on a long article about the United States surgeon general, William Hammond. I had never heard the name before.

"He's a genius," Crosby said. "The man has saved countless soldiers' lives. His mind is always at work. Wants to write a novel, and a book of nonfiction debunking Spiritualism."

"Why?" Agnes said.

"*Why?*"

"Yes, why? I went to a séance once," Agnes said. "It was entertaining. There was no harm in it."

"You did?" Hannah said.

"No harm?" Crosby said. "At this very moment, a woman is on trial down in Cambridge for murder. She was working as an attendant to a lady in her sickbed, and as her personal medium, until she fed her arsenic and ran off with her husband. Now she claims evil spirits made her do it. No harm."

Crosby scoffed.

Agnes rolled her eyes. But she smiled. She seemed to enjoy sparring with him.

"Hammond says," he continued, "that any woman who believes in all that suffers from a form of nervous derangement. The First Lady has mediums *living* in the White House, so that she might contact her dead sons at any moment. Lincoln should put a stop to it, if you ask me."

No one asked you, I thought, but did not say.

I hardly had time to wonder why I had taken offense at what he said before he went on.

"Hammond's establishing a medical museum of human specimens in the Capitol. He's instructed military doctors to collect and send to him amputated body parts from the front. He's got six thousand specimens already. Bones and brains and hearts. Legs and arms with the bullets still in."

"That's barbaric," Hannah said, clutching her throat.

I knew she was thinking about her brother, whose body arriving home had been her only solace after he died. And Samuel too, perhaps. I wished I could squeeze her hand.

"Not at all," Crosby said. "It's in the name of research. There has never been anything like it."

No one seemed to know how to respond. Agnes told us about a column she was writing, denouncing the deserters who were hiding out in the woods around Awadapquit and all throughout Maine, and those who paid three hundred dollars for a substitute, rather than go to war.

Privately, I wondered why Crosby had not gone.

I told them my sister had written to tell me that Shaker elders had traveled to Washington to plead with Lincoln that as pacifists, they should be exempt from military service. The president agreed. Shaker villages still felt the impact of war. Union and Confederate soldiers alike turned up there for food and shelter, and the Shakers— though they sympathized with the Union—provided for all.

Agnes couldn't understand how what the Shakers were doing was any different from the Copperheads she so despised for their cowardice.

"People like that don't care enough about freeing Blacks to fight," she said.

At this, I felt indignant. I told her of the runaway slaves taken in by the Shakers when I was a child. How, from the start, Blacks and whites lived together in our communities.

I could have taken this a step further. I could have pointed out that though Maine was established specifically to be a free state as part of the Missouri Compromise, and people like Agnes took great pride in this fact, it was also true that Agnes and Hannah's family and almost all the others in Awadapquit were very much involved in the slave trade. The slaves in question were laboring in the Caribbean, out of sight. But the sugar and tobacco they harvested came back to America on the ships of New Englanders. No one wanted to discuss this.

Somewhat chastened by what I had said, Agnes wrote it up for the paper. She praised the Shakers for their vision of what was just and true, and said in the years she had known me, I had been a shining example of how a Shaker upbringing shaped a person. In the piece, she referred to me as "my sister's longtime housekeeper," which delivered a shot to the gut, though I knew it shouldn't.

It wasn't unlike the way Samuel's mother called on the children sometimes and I was made to blend in, like the door to that upstairs room that, when closed, could no longer be seen.

Hannah and I went to prayer meetings together every Tuesday. I once heard a woman there whisper to another that it was strange, how Hannah brought along her hired girl. The woman's companion replied that it wasn't as strange as it seemed because Hannah and I were cousins. I've no idea where she heard that. People believe what they want.

I suppose the hearts of others are always a mystery. I couldn't have been more surprised when Agnes married Crosby a year later. Agnes told Hannah she knew how he seemed, but he was, in private, a good, decent man. The only one she had yet to meet who did not want her to become some other kind of woman, but accepted her as she was.

They moved back to Awadapquit, though Crosby often traveled for work. He became obsessed with that surgeon general, who, a few years later, began hunting the skulls and body parts of Indians. Eager to impress him, Crosby went on hunts around Awadapquit, hoping to stumble upon some interesting human artifact. He even employed James to help, though as far as I know they only ever discovered a few dozen arrowheads in the forest.

Crosby spoke of Hammond's exploits as if he was telling some swashbuckling adventure story. Army officers sent Hammond detailed letters of how they came to find the bodies they sent him. On one occasion, Crosby read one to us. The officer said he had watched a grieving Indian family at a burial, then snuck out from his hiding place after they left the grave site, and beheaded the dead man.

Hannah looked at Crosby like he was mad to think this was what passed for pleasant conversation.

"The Indian's way of life is disappearing," he said. "They're primitives. There are hardly any of them left. They'd be close to dying out by now even without our help. They carry disease. They scalp and enslave one another. There's no loyalty among them at all. Collecting these artifacts is a kindness. It means proof of the savages' existence will be preserved."

HANNAH FOUND CROSBY unappealing, of course. She was baffled that her sister had married such a man. But of the two of us, only I seemed unable to let go of what he had said. To approach a man just buried and cut off his head? What could be more savage than that?

Nor did Hannah seem overly troubled when Crosby started building his own collection of Indian skulls and scalps and pottery shards.

Whenever Indians came up in conversation, Hannah spoke of her ancestors, killed in bloody raids. Her great-great-grandparents were victims of the Candlemas Massacre, murdered in their own bed just south of Awadapquit in 1692. Their house and the houses of all their neighbors in York were burned by the Abenaki, she said. Their two oldest children, Hannah's great-aunts, were among the 260 towns-people kidnapped and force-marched to Canada in the dead of winter.

One of the great-aunts was, at the time, a young woman who had given birth to her third child three weeks earlier. The Abenaki kept complaining that she was too slow on the trail, and when she pro-tested, pointing out that she was nursing an infant, one of the men snatched the baby from her arms and killed it right in front of her. Now, he said, she no longer had any excuse for slowing them down. The woman was ransomed. Eight years later, she made it home to tell the tale. Her sister stayed on in Canada, becoming a nun in the order of Saint Joseph.

Samuel was descended from Ephraim Littleton, one of the first set-tlers to this part of Maine. The land on which our house was built had once been the site of his home—a humble one-room cottage made of logs, with a dirt floor. It was burned to the ground by Indians with Ephraim sleeping inside.

All this had put a fear of Indians into Hannah and Samuel for life, though it happened long before they were born. A fear and a sort of disgust. A sense that they were not fully human.

Savages. That is what the Shakers were called in the early days too. Our way of life so unlike that of so-called civilized people.

I never did say this to Hannah. I don't know why. Perhaps out of cowardice. Perhaps out of fear that she wouldn't understand my posi-tion. That she never could have loved that former version of me.

She told me once that the secret room I slept in when first I arrived was meant as a hideaway should Indians ever return.

AGNES AND CROSBY never had any children of their own. Even so, the *Argus* wouldn't allow a married woman to write a col-umn. Agnes had to give that up. She surprised us by getting involved with the temperance movement, devoting her whole life to it. She went all over New England giving lectures on the evils of liquor. Hannah and I wondered, between us, if part of the appeal was that this gave Agnes an excuse to leave home, to travel by coach and stay overnight alone in a hotel somewhere. To be independent again. A means of putting some money away, in case.

Hannah and I worried a great deal about money through the years, but we survived. We took in mending and bleaching and spinning. We made bayberry candles and sold them in town. Hannah received a regular stipend from a fund set up for widows of men lost at sea. It helped, but not enough. Some years we took in a boarder or two to manage the cost of keeping up such a large house.

We were always talking about how we ought to move someplace more manageable, closer to town. The house was too much work. It was too big. But we never left. Hannah said Samuel had built the house intending for it to be hers. She wanted to stay. Privately, perhaps self-servingly, I believed it wasn't about Samuel at all, but rather that she would not leave because her babies were buried there. Hannah visited with them often, went out and sat alone among the gravestones and talked to them. Or maybe to Samuel, but I prefer to think it was the children to whom she whispered.

In her letters, my sister fretted over my future. She thought I had stayed too long. It seemed to her an arrangement that offered no benefit to me. It was one thing to keep working for Hannah, she wrote, but why should I take on outside work to help my employer make ends meet? If Hannah let me go, what would I have to show for the time put in? I had no home of my own. I had hardly any experience working at a trade.

I worried about Emily as much as she worried for me. The Shakers were by then at the beginning of the end. An American war had been the backdrop of the group's formation and another American war now seemed to be the backdrop of its demise. The country was changing. Shakers could not compete with mass production. They could not retain young members, who wished to seek better, more exciting opportunities, far from home. Of more than a hundred children brought to Sabbathday Lake over the next thirty years, not one would remain there into adulthood.

The Shakers prepared me well for the life I lived. I owned nothing, could claim no one, legally. But I had family. I had all the riches I could want. I could think back to the girls in the milliner's shop in Portland, where I met Agnes—they were always going on about how things were supposed to be, and how the people in their lives had fallen short. A beau refused to make a marriage proposal fast enough, and so must be parted from, despite one's feelings. I never had an image in mind for how life ought to look. I believe that to be the most freeing fact of my existence.

THE MORE TIME PASSES, the more I remember only the best and worst of what happened. I remember ice-skating with Hannah and the children on a frozen pond a mile from home, where now there is a golf course. I remember the first Christmas tree I ever had, erected in the parlor by the window seat, where I sat with James in my lap and we both stared in amazement. I remember cake and ices on our birthdays. Walks with Hannah at twilight, side by side, the backs of our fingers brushing every now and then.

I regret only the complications we made for ourselves. The silly things we fretted over. Like we did not know our time together would be devastatingly brief. Briefer than I ever imagined. From the day we met to the day I died, just seventeen years. A speck of time. A grain of sand.

Do all your work as if you had a thousand years to live and as you would if you knew you must die tomorrow.

Those words from Mother Ann, repeated daily when I lived with the Shakers, though I didn't comprehend their meaning at the time. They echo through me now. Mother Ann lived only ten years longer than I did and look at all the people she touched. More than most who live twice as long.

I was thirty-eight and just beginning to think about the next spring cleaning when consumption took me. Life was that way. What next, what next, what next, until one day it was over, and I found myself hovering near the bedroom ceiling, looking down on my own body in our bed. As the shock of it hit me, Agnes stepped into the room. She came to my side. She cried. She touched my cheek. She pulled from her pocket a pair of scissors. I watched her snip a lock of my hair. It is even now in the ring Agnes gave Hannah soon after, inscribed with the words NOT LOST BUT GONE BEFORE.

Hannah wore the ring for years, but eventually the sight of it made her too sad, and she placed it in a box of keepsakes, along with letters from her brother and the bonnet I made her, well-loved and worn from use, and the ambrotype of her and Samuel. She put the box in my old bedroom, intending to tell the children about it one day, but she never did. A point came when she did not want to think of me at all. She asked James to seal up the doorway and paint the wall around it so that it blended in with the hall, and no one would ever know it was there.

Hannah had my body buried in the family plot. It would have been unthinkable for her to give me a gravestone like the one Samuel had. To hire a stonecutter, to pay all that money, to have to see the pastor and ask for his approval on the text. I was just her maid in the eyes of the world. It would have raised too many questions.

I had anticipated this. I told her I never wanted one. Shakers should die as they lived, without adornment or pride.

"But you're not a Shaker anymore," Hannah said.

In the end, they memorialized me with a simple fieldstone, on which, at his mother's request, James carved the words *Sister Eliza*. As anonymous as she could bear to let me be. It was intimate too, though. At the end, as in life, Hannah called me by my Shaker name.

As LONG AS HANNAH and the children lived in the house, I lingered there in spirit, wanting to be close. But after they were gone, I had no reason to stay. I found myself at Sabbathday Lake. I have been here for more than a century now. I stop in at the house in Awadapquit from time to time, hoping to find Hannah there. But I never stay for long. I don't much like the place without her in it. I've liked it even less since they put Samuel Littleton's name by the door. Preposterous. That was more my house than it ever was his.

There is one who lingers there, refusing to go. She was there when I crossed, and when the pair of sisters crossed in 1959, weeks apart.

She was there when the young girl, Daisy, crossed, and when Daisy's mother went into the barn to die, but did not die, as it was.

The one who lingers has never left that patch of land on the sea for an instant. She stands on the promontory, watching, waiting. For whom, I do not know. She doesn't say a word to anyone. She doesn't seem to see us at all, neither the living nor the dead. She's lost in a world between worlds.

Sweet Daisy is the opposite. She talks to everyone, or tries to, desperate to get a message to her mother. No doubt, she will be reborn in the form of a bouncing, happy baby, some delighted couple's miracle child.

Daisy is sometimes by herself when I pop in, sometimes with the old woman who watches over her. She doesn't seem to get frustrated that no one understands her. She keeps trying.

On this side, a hundred years, a minute—all the same. It's not unlike the place you travel to in dreams. In spirit, we are thoughts. Pure energy. Vibration. In dreams, there might be trees and buildings and oceans and rivers. But the dreamer is not bound by them. She can jump from one to the next in a blink. She can walk right through a tree and come out on the other side, or in another city. So it is for us.

Sometimes I am preoccupied with the thought of what would have happened had all Hannah's babies lived, and Samuel too. Had Hannah gotten the family she dreamed of as a girl. There would have never been *us*. If Mother Ann's babies had lived, there would have been no Shakers. She would likely have remained an illiterate blacksmith's wife and died anonymous, as most people do. In every graveyard in every town in all the world, there lie buried stories more remarkable and strange than a name, a date, a designation on stone could ever in a million years convey.

11

Jane

SHE WOKE with a banging in her skull.

No, not that. A banging at the door. An actual sound. Alarming in its intensity.

Jane was in bed, on top of the covers. The lights were on.

Pain radiated from behind her eyeballs. At her temples—the squeeze, release; squeeze, release of a pumping heart. Her head felt like it would burst.

From outside, a man's voice shouted her name. He sounded angry. Insistent.

Jane put a pillow over her head.

She knew well this morning-after moment when all must be surrendered to the hangover. She had once gotten out of bed for a glass of water after a night out and vomited all over the dishes in her kitchen sink. She had been horrified, but resolved to ignore the mess until some later hour, when she would be able to deal.

Had the man at the door come to tell her she left her purse at the bar? Or had she offended him, harmed him, in some way? Jane had no idea. Nor did she have the wherewithal to do anything about it whatever the case.

The man's voice quieted, and with it the banging. He had gone away. At least there was that.

Now. What the hell happened?

Think. *Think.*

She had been at Charlie's Chowder House with a crowd. Maybe twelve or fifteen locals, most of them old-timers like Abe, and Charlie himself. The kitchen was closed for the night; the waitresses and busboys and cooks had been sent home. The dining room lights were off, the floors swept clean. Everyone congregated in the bar area, a spontaneous gathering of friends. Jane remembered Abe coming to work after nights like that with hilarious stories when she was a teen-ager. She felt some old thrill in being invited to join.

The last thing she recalled was Lydia Beazley talking loud and close about a book she had just read on Edgar Allan Poe. Poe, she said, was a curmudgeon about progress, furious about beautiful old buildings in New York City being torn down so they could put up unsightly new ones.

"It tickles me," Lydia said, "Considering how I've practically chained myself to the door of houses built when Poe was alive, be-cause of their historical significance."

Lydia started laughing, and couldn't stop. Jane thought, *This fellow nerd is very drunk.* But she herself was not. She was proud of that.

Everyone was drinking Dark and Stormies when she got there. Somebody put one in front of Jane and she told herself she would have just that one—maybe even half—and then she would go home and watch TV and never drink again, nor tell anyone that she had. There would be no need. She wasn't wrecking her sobriety. She was simply taking a break from it after a tumultuous night. A night when she officially lost her beloved job, her husband wouldn't take her calls because he was on a date with his ex-wife, and she learned that she had accidentally been an accomplice to grave desecration. Nobody could begrudge her that.

Jane remembered watching one drink turn into two and then three for everyone else, and who knew how many they'd had before she got there. Meanwhile, she sipped her first, making it last, feeling virtuous. She remembered Charlie saying he was out of ginger beer, maybe they should pack it in, but instead everyone switched to some-thing else. Jane asked for seltzer. Lydia wanted chardonnay, but Char-lie didn't have any uncorked, and she didn't want him to open a whole bottle just for her. She asked Jane to split it with her, and Jane agreed, thinking that there was no harm in having a glass in front of her for show. She wasn't going to drink it. She didn't even like chardonnay.

The bottle was perched right on the bar between their glasses so that they could reach over at any time and add more without having to ask.

At some point, a man came by to say hello to Lydia, and she introduced him to Jane as Teddy McCarthy, manager at the Lake Grove Country Club.

"Teddy!" Lydia said. "Jane and I were wondering where the club got its name. Do you know?"

He told them the country club was named after the Lake Grove Inn. The owner liked the ring of it, and didn't realize until all the signs were made and hung that there was no such lake nearby. So that answered that. It was something she might have texted Genevieve about right then had things not taken the strange turn they did at her sister's house earlier that night.

After talking for half an hour, Jane wanted more seltzer, but by then Charlie was circulating, no longer behind the bar, and so, just to wet her throat, she took a sip of wine. Then Lydia refilled both their glasses. Then—what?

Had she told Lydia about Genevieve digging up the old cemetery? What *had* she said?

The banging resumed. Closer now. The man hadn't left. He was right outside her bedroom window, knocking on the glass. Jesus.

Jane's heart raced. Fear overtook all other feelings. Without removing the pillow from her head, she felt around for her phone on the mattress in case she needed to call 911. Finding the phone there, she turned her face, peered at the screen. Seventeen missed calls and fourteen texts from David.

David.

David was the man at the window.

Jane got out of bed and went over, pulled up the shade. He was standing there and it was still dark outside and he looked furious.

She held up one finger, then went to the front door. She was wearing her clothes from the night before, shoes and all.

Jane turned the porch light on. Moths flew out from all corners like confetti tossed into the air. She switched the light back off.

David came around the side of the house, but instead of walking toward her, he went toward his car in the driveway.

Jane's car wasn't there. Had she been in an accident? Had David been with her?

"David?" she said. "What are you doing here? Where are you going?"

He didn't come closer.

"It's four-thirty in the morning," he said. "I drove here at three because after calling me some insane number of times in a row, you then proceeded to ignore all my calls to you and I was worried you were dead."

"I'm sorry," she said. "I fell asleep."

"Whatever. I came to make sure you were alive, and you are. Now I'm leaving."

"Wait," she said. "Please. I'm confused."

"What are you confused about?" he said. "Clearly, you got drunk. That's what you do."

"It isn't," she said. "I haven't had a drink since——"

"So you weren't drinking last night?"

"No, I mean. I was. I did. Besides that."

He buried his face in his hands, then pushed back his hair.

"I hadn't looked at my phone all night. I came out of a restaurant, and I see you've called me a thousand times. You screamed into my voicemail, I don't even know how many times, that you knew my secret, you'd found me out."

She winced.

"That was the least of it," he said.

"What else did I say?"

"What else did you say? Here, go ahead and listen to it." He pulled his phone from his pocket, a violent gesture that made her go cold. He pressed on the screen a few times, and there was her voice, screaming, *You're a coward, David. Pick up! I fucking hate you. You never loved me. We've both always known that. Haven't we?*

Jane's mind went to Allison's mom, Betty, in the dementia ward, who often acted out and yelled, and had twice struck an orderly in the face. Behavior so incongruous with everything Betty was—kind and calm and composed. Jane had heard before that a dementia patient could take on a personality far different from her own. Where had all that anger come from? Where did it live when Betty was still herself?

Some people believed that anything you said or did while drunk was what you wanted to do or say, deep down. Your truest feeling. But Jane knew this was not true. Everything she had said on that recording was the opposite of what she meant. The opposite of what she had so carefully planned to say to him when next they spoke.

"Please delete that," she said pitifully. "I was out of my mind. None of that means anything."

"I tried reaching you for three hours," he said. "Then I thought, well, she's either passed out or she's dead. I'd better go there and find out which."

This was a nightmare.

"You were with Angela," she said, in some strange attempt at defending herself. "I saw the pictures on Facebook. Are you seeing each other?"

"You saw——" He sighed.

She thought he would deny it, or provide some explanation. But David said, "You're the one who gave up on us. You're the one who left. I don't owe you an explanation."

No, *this* was a nightmare.

She wanted to beg him to pretend these last several hours hadn't happened. Because she was better than she had been, she was. And she wanted him back, and had planned to tell him so. But there was no way she could say any of that now.

David opened his mouth to speak, just as an eighteen-wheeler rumbled past.

Jane's body braced for the usual overreaction from the dog.

When no sound came, she realized. The dog wasn't there.

"Walter," she said.

FOR THE NEXT several hours, they searched. At first, they walked up and down the street, calling Walter's name, shaking a bag of treats, promising turkey and toys and bacon if he would come out of hiding. They combed through the yards of neighbors who were still asleep, and even walked up Shore Road for a mile or so with flash-lights in hand, both thinking, she assumed, that if he had gone this way, he was probably dead. The road was full of sharp curves, and drivers just flew down it.

They didn't talk about anything other than where to look next. Jane felt like garbage. She wanted nothing more than to go back to bed, but she did not dare say so out loud.

At some point, David suggested they cover more ground by driv-ing for a while. In separate cars. He made that clear.

"Where is your car?" he said.

Jane told him she had left it in the cove the night before. She hoped that was true. The thought of being unable to find her car, of having to admit that to him, was too humiliating. Luckily, the car was there, right where she left it when she stopped to walk Walter the night before. The keys were in the small pocket of her purse, put there by some saner version of herself.

She slid into the driver's seat, grateful for this, at least.

Taking in her reflection in the rearview mirror, Jane saw the mas-cara she hadn't bothered to wash off, pooling beneath her eyes. Her hair was everywhere, like she had been riding around in a convertible for hours. She had imagined reuniting with David as a new, better version of herself, but here was the same old shitty version, greeting them both.

She found Abe at his boat, as usual, before seven. He looked bright as ever.

Jane choked back tears. This was usually when she took her morn-ing walk with the dog. Had she done that for the last time without knowing it?

"You feel okay, kiddo?" Abe said. "I was worried about you."

"How did I get home?" she said.

"You walked. I offered to drive you, but you were quite insistent that you didn't need anyone's help."

The memory of her sister, belligerent in the driveway not so long ago. Had she been as bad as that?

"I'm embarrassed," she said. "Did I do anything exceptionally stupid? Last night is a blur."

"Embarrassed? Nah," Abe said. "Don't worry about it. Welcome to the club."

Jane wished she were that person he saw, that good girl, for whom such behavior was an anomaly. She did not need to be welcomed to the club. She was president, vice president, secretary, and treasurer.

Abe said she had Walter with her at the Chowder House. He was roaming around, having a ball, getting belly rubs from everyone. When Jane left, Abe was almost positive, Walter went too.

David went to the library as soon as it opened to make flyers. He texted her and told her to meet him at the entrance to the beach parking lot so he could give her half.

Jane imagined taking his hand and saying she was sorry, she would do anything if he would just love her again, and be as kind to her as he always was before. If he would give her one more chance. She wanted to tell him that she spent yesterday in the company of people in mourning, willing to believe their lost loved ones could be brought back via the help of psychic mediums. And she had realized that their challenges were nothing, compared to that. But clearly this was not the time. So instead, she got them each an enormous iced coffee and a muffin at Millie's Bakery.

She had often had the feeling, after a night she couldn't remember, that every person she interacted with the next day knew what an ass she'd made of herself. She felt it as the girl behind the counter handed her the change. That familiar paranoia. That shame.

The beach parking lot was already full. Tourists unloaded sand chairs and toys and tents from the backs of minivans, debating where to sit, unaware of the many-tiered crisis on display right in front of them.

When they still hadn't found Walter by noon, David said he was sorry but he had to get home. He didn't say why. It was a Sunday. Jane wondered if he had left Angela at home in his bedroom—*their* bedroom. Which, come to think of it, had once been his and Angela's. She understood he was exhausted. But she wished he would stay. Take a nap on her mother's sofa. Go have lunch with her and talk. David had been Jane's person for ten years. But not anymore. He didn't even hug her when he left.

Jane watched him drive off. She thought she might cry again or puke or both.

She called her sister to tell her about the dog and ask if she would come help search.

"You *lost* Walter?" Holly said, as if he were her child. "How, Jane? What happened?"

"He just—got out," Jane said.

"Jason is going to be devastated," Holly said.

"Really?"

If they had bothered to take the damn dog for a walk the day before, then maybe Jane would never have gone to the cove, would never have fallen off the wagon, wouldn't have called David one thousand times and ruined any chance she had of persuading him she had changed.

"Are you going to help me look or not?" Jane said.

"Of course!" Holly said, indignant. "Well, not me. I have to work. But Jason will, for sure."

JANE LOOKED everywhere.

She got Allison and Chris and their kids to help. Allison called up their babysitters, the staff at the inn, and what seemed like half the people in town and asked them to search too. Walter might have been the Lindbergh baby.

Stopping by the inn to drop off flyers, Jane told Allison everything that happened the night before, except the part where she got drunk. She couldn't bear to disappoint her friend. Allison had made it clear that she didn't think Jane should drink, that she was proud of her for quitting. She didn't need to know that Jane had slipped. So Jane told the story minus that part. That she'd lost her job. That she had argued with her sister, and made this shocking discovery about Genevieve. That she tried to call David and ended up seeing photos of him and his ex-wife, then called to confront him, fell asleep, and woke up to find him at her door, furious.

"I think I've officially succeeded at driving him away," she said.

"What part of him coming in person from another state in the middle of the night to make sure you're okay qualifies as him being driven away?" Allison said.

"He admitted he had dinner with his ex-wife."

"What does that mean?"

"I don't know. He seemed so *annoyed* by me."

"You have to admit, you've put that man through a lot this year, but he clearly cares about you. He loves you. It's just——" Allison trailed off.

"What?"

"I'm guessing he's trying to protect himself."

Why did that land on Jane like a body blow? It was true. Maybe that was why.

IN EVERY SHOP, at the fire station and the cafés and the art galleries, when Jane asked to hang a flyer about a lost dog, people asked what happened. Jane lied and said the backyard gate wasn't latched properly and Walter escaped. The truth was too awful to tell. And it seemed less believable that this middle-aged lady in capri pants had gotten so drunk that she couldn't remember what happened.

She kept passing by Lydia's toy store, but it was closed.

Around three, Jane finally spotted her from across the street as she arrived. Lydia wore sunglasses and carried a large travel mug.

"My partner in crime!" she called when she saw Jane in the cross-walk. "I'm paying for it today. How about you?"

"I feel like death," Jane said. "What even happened? I don't remember drinking that much."

"I think we had two bottles of white between the two of us," Lydia said.

"God. Really?" Jane let this sink in, then added, "And now my mother's dog is missing."

She handed Lydia a few flyers.

"Not that little fluffball!" Lydia said. "He is so cute. You don't think coyotes got him, do you?"

"I hadn't until you mentioned it," Jane said.

"Never mind, I'm sure it wasn't that. He'll turn up."

Lydia looked toward her store. A gaggle of school-age kids were rattling the doorknob.

"Hey!" she snapped. "Cool it!"

"I gather they're not there to visit the Historical Society," Jane said.

"They look like the Nerf gun type to me," Lydia said. "Speaking of the Historical Society, I loved your idea for incorporating more Native American history. We should talk more about that."

Jane didn't remember bringing the topic up.

"You were funny about old Tom Crosby," Lydia said.

"Was I? What did I say about him?"

"You were calling him a thief and a liar and saying he had to close up shop and go underground because of it."

Jane put a hand over her mouth. "I don't even know him," she said. "I never should have said any of that."

Lydia shrugged. "I do know him. You're not wrong." She looked toward the kids outside her shop. "I guess I'd better get a move on, spreading joy to the children of Awadapquit like I do."

Jane laughed.

Lydia held out her travel mug. "Here, take this. I haven't had a sip yet. You look like you could use it. I have more in the shop."

Jane thanked her for it, and walked to her car.

She was driving along Main Street, unsure where to go next, when she took a big sip from Lydia's mug. She nearly spat the liquid out all over the steering wheel. It tasted cold and briny and not at all like what she was expecting. It took her a second to realize that Lydia had not handed her coffee, but a strong Bloody Mary.

Jane laughed ruefully, thinking of how Lydia hadn't even thought to mention what was in the mug. And at the thought that maybe she drank Bloody Marys all day behind the counter of that sweet toy store and no one was the wiser.

Having searched every other inch of town, Jane pulled over in front of the small cemetery on Main Street, where Allison once hunted for baby names on tombstones. She got out, Lydia's mug in hand, calling softly for Walter, imagining him emerging from behind a tree or the monument engraved with the names of Awadapquit's Civil War dead, even as she sensed that he was not here.

There was no one else around. The people buried in this cemetery had been gone so long that anyone who might have visited them was long gone too.

Jane sat on a bench and regarded the drink in her hand.

The vodka would help her headache, her general feeling of having been run over by a bus. True, she had told herself last night was a one-off, but it could be argued that today was an extension of last night.

Jane took a sip, then another. Decision made.

She liked cemeteries, the older the better. She found them soothing, and capable of bringing about in her a sense of perspective. Sort of like the mediums at Camp Mira had. On vacations, she sought out old cemeteries. In Paris, she spent hours wandering around Père Lachaise. In London, she visited churches where kings and queens were buried in tombs beneath the flagstone floors.

In the before times, she and David sometimes took a morning run through Mount Auburn Cemetery in Cambridge, stopping every so often to take note of who was buried there. The graves meant to celebrate great men of the nineteenth century were usually adorned with figures of women. Angels. Goddesses. Or else by some phallic obelisk, jutting out above the rest.

Women's graves always listed them as *Wife of.* There was one couple at Mount Auburn who broke with tradition. His grave said *Husband of.* Jane had always been curious about them.

Newer graves didn't hold the same appeal. They were too close to the living. Tacky and overdone, like people. Some of them even had the deceased's photograph laser-printed onto the stone now. It was undeniable how human they had been. You couldn't romanticize them. The more recent the death, the more often visitors came. They left Mylar balloons or brightly colored carnations. Fake plastic lilies that sat out in the rain for months, until the next birthday or anniversary.

Jane never went to the cemetery where her own family was buried. Most people didn't anymore, did they? Her grandmother had taken her once, to plant daffodil bulbs at her grandfather's grave in the nowhere town in Massachusetts he was from. Having never met the man, Jane didn't think she'd feel much, but then she saw her grandmother's name carved into the stone beneath his, alongside her date of birth and a dash, which was a sort of question mark—*When?*

Its existence felt rude, among other things. Jane wanted to shield her grandmother from it. When she actually died, Jane was indignant. Why should she be buried so far from them, and forever with her husband's family, who had treated her terribly? Jane's mother took a more practical view—the reason was, they paid for that plot, so they might as well use it.

Jane had recently read an article that said this was the first time in modern history that most people did not plan where their bodies would go after they died. Did this mean they were removed from the reality of death, or hoping to avoid it? Was it down to a lack of kinship, tradition, religion? All of these? Jane didn't think she cared what happened to her. There would be none of her self left. But then, she would not dream of throwing away her mother's ashes. They felt sacred, though she couldn't say why.

Jane drained her drink. She felt a welcome sort of buzzing in her head.

After a while, she stood up and walked back toward the gates, pausing in front of a small statue of a lamb, with the epitaph *Our Georgie* carved on a stone so old the dates could no longer be read.

Children's graves always made her melancholy. The loss of a stranger's three-year-old one hundred years ago put the same pit of sorrow in her gut that it would have had it happened yesterday. How did people bear so much loss?

Samuel and Hannah Littleton had buried three young children. Genevieve had torn their graves up along with their parents'. That made the whole thing seem so much more gruesome. How could she live with herself, after what she had done?

Jane sat with it a moment, contemplating. She wondered if the Littletons' ghosts really were haunting Genevieve. She certainly deserved it if they were.

Was Genevieve so scared of their graves that she couldn't find a way to let them stay in what they thought would be their final resting place? Did she not know there were dead bodies buried everywhere? Boston Common hid a thousand beneath its green fields of picnickers, its cheerful skating rink and carousel. They were a previous century's poor, the sick, the ones hanged from trees in that same park for being criminals, pirates, witches, natives.

In Portsmouth, New Hampshire, fifteen miles from here, construction workers discovered human remains the summer after Jane graduated from college. The bodies belonged to eight Africans from the eighteenth century—men, women, and children—laid to rest in the only African burial ground of the period in all of New England. The graveyard contained the remains of nearly two hundred additional freed and enslaved people.

An artist rendered an image that Jane would never forget. A modern-day picture of the buildings that lined Chestnut Street, with a white rectangle added for every wooden coffin that lay below the paved road, mobbed with traffic.

The City Council and the citizens of Portsmouth raised funds for a memorial park. At the dedication, the bodies exhumed were reburied. The whole city came out to celebrate the memorial erected to remember another, earlier memorial, wrongly covered up somewhere along the line.

The response was beautiful. Some people understood the importance of such things. Not like Genevieve, afraid of ghosts.

No, Jane remembered now. It wasn't even about fear. It was, according to Jason, all down to Genevieve's plan to install a swimming pool. God, what a monster she was.

Jane left the cemetery, got back in her car, and continued the search for Walter. She drove slow along Shore Road, aware that she was tipsy. She didn't think she had a destination in mind. But this anger, this sense of injustice burned beneath her skin, and when she approached the turnoff for Genevieve's house and saw the white balloon tied to the mailbox, bobbing in the wind, Jane wondered if coming here had been her plan all along.

She remembered the horrified look on Genevieve's face, when

Jane told them about the remains of Indigenous people being dug up. *Bodies?* she said, seeming so innocent, so disturbed.

Jane got out of the car and went to the front door. It was open, and she could see clear through to the back of the house, where people were sitting on the patio.

She went around.

"Hello," she said, and they all looked up.

Having unknowingly set off the avalanche of the previous night, Genevieve seemed genuinely happy to see her.

"Jane! What a nice surprise. I'd love for you to meet our friends the Davenports. We were just about to have steaks. Are you hungry? I bought extras."

The couple at the table both wore pink. They smiled wanly at Jane. They were thin and pale and Jane's only thought was that they had a lot of money and needed an iron supplement.

A handsome older guy stood at the grill in a white collared shirt and khaki shorts. He too had that look of wealth about him. Those straight white teeth that came only at great expense.

"I'm Paul," he said. "Good to meet you. Genevieve speaks highly of you."

"Jane works at Harvard," Genevieve said to the Davenports, who nodded their approval of the institution, if not Jane herself.

She had forgotten that she looked like shit. She had never gone home to change or take her makeup off. She was wearing the same clothes as yesterday, which she had subsequently slept in.

"My dog ran away," she said.

"No!" Genevieve said.

"Yes, so I am just out here looking for him."

"Here?" said Paul.

"Well, everywhere. All over."

"Have you thought of consulting Clementine?" Genevieve said. Then, turning to the Davenports, "Clementine is Jane's psychic. We went and saw her yesterday."

"What fun," said the woman dryly.

"It was," Genevieve said. "That's not my thing usually, but I figured what the heck."

Jane wanted to smack her.

"Genevieve, can I talk to you for a minute?" she said, in such a way that all their eyes went wide.

"Umm, sure," Genevieve said. "Come on inside. Can I get anyone anything while I'm up?"

No one spoke. Jane followed Genevieve through the sliding door and into the gleaming white kitchen.

"Jane, are you okay?" Genevieve whispered. "Have you been drinking?"

"There's a rumor going around about you," Jane said.

Genevieve's cheeks flashed red. "What do you mean? Is it something bad? People think the addition is too showy, is that it?"

"No. The rumor is you dug up an old cemetery to make room for your pool."

Genevieve froze. Making it clear that she had never imagined this was what Jane was about to say.

"The kid you hired to dig up the graves won't shut up about it. No wonder they're haunting you, after what you did."

Genevieve looked at her with a crooked smile, as if to assess whether Jane was joking.

"Everyone in town knows," Jane said.

Genevieve sat down at one of the white French bistro chairs that surrounded her round white kitchen table.

"Oh God," she said.

Because as scared as she was of ghosts, Genevieve was even more terrified of being disliked.

"Now you've implicated me in this whole mess," Jane said. "You know what you did is a felony, right? You can't just disturb a grave."

On this point, she was not one hundred percent sure, but it sounded correct.

They both jumped when Paul spoke up. Neither of them had seen him and Mrs. Davenport come inside.

"Gen," he said. "You did what now? What the hell is going on?"

12

AT HER MOTHER'S HOUSE later that evening, Jane sat out on the back deck and sobbed. The sight of Walter's organic kibble set her off. That and the stupid set of felt-covered stairs her mother bought for him years ago, so that he could get up on the couch without assistance. Her sadness over Walter gave way to thoughts of her mother, her grandmother, David. Even her boss—her former boss—Melissa. A montage of her bad luck and bad choices played out before her eyes.

Jane let the shame spiral unfurl for a long time, her thoughts jumping from one lousy life decision to another without any particular pattern. It occurred to her after a while that maybe if she wrote it all down, she could make sense of it, contain it somehow. She got a notebook and a pen from inside, returned to her spot, and began to write the story chronologically.

She started all the way back at the beginning, freshman year of college, before she had taken so much as a sip of alcohol and believed with a certainty possessed only by the very young that she never would. She wished she could bend time and return to the start, follow that good impulse.

Her best friend at Wesleyan was a kid from Ohio named Matthew. They bonded over their shared love of Elizabeth Bishop poems and their mutual crush on Jared Leto. Matthew's dorm room closet was essentially a well-stocked bar, available to anyone who asked.

For the first half of their first year, Jane did not drink. Matthew was always trying to tempt her. She told him the truth—her mother's drinking had turned her off the stuff forever.

Second semester she was enrolled in a class on Chaucer, required for her major.

Jane felt in over her head from the beginning. A sensation she wasn't used to. In high school, she aced every test, she was every teacher's favorite. In college, given the course, she was either middle of the pack or, as with Chaucer, unable to keep up with her peers.

When the professor handed back the first papers, hers had no grade written on it, only the words SEE ME in red ink on the last page.

Jane went to his office hours later that afternoon. She waited in the hall while he laughed with a senior for whom he had written a glowing grad school recommendation.

When it was finally Jane's turn, the professor's voice turned from jovial to stern.

"It feels like you didn't bother to try," he said.

Jane protested. She had worked hard on that paper.

"Maybe you're not up to the task," he said, the only thing worse she could imagine than his guessing that she hadn't tried.

Jane looked around the room, with its sloped ceilings and books piled everywhere, and wondered if he was right. Her intellect was the only part of herself that she had never doubted, never despised. But right then she questioned whether she was as smart as she had always believed.

Jane left that professor's office and went straight to Matthew's room.

"I need to get drunk," she said.

He whooped and hollered and made her a vodka tonic.

"Not too strong!" she said.

Jane, responsible always, found a box of saltines and filled a water bottle. She wanted to get drunk, but not too drunk.

Matthew paraded her around like a new puppy.

"Jane's drinking!" he told everyone.

Their fellow students were used to hoarding their booze because it was expensive and hard to come by—getting to the liquor store required a car, and most of them were underage. But that day, they were drawn in by Matthew's enthusiasm. Jane was given a beer here, a shot of tequila there, welcoming her into the fold.

She felt light, unburdened in a way she never had before. Every-thing struck her as hilarious. She couldn't stop laughing.

The next morning, she was mildly hungover. She drank again that night, a few beers. It did not occur to her that having started, she could stop.

Her first blackout came two months later. A dazzling spring had descended on that cold gray corner of New England. The trees burst forth with lush green leaves and cherry blossoms. Yellow daffodils lined the pathways. All over campus, young people shed heavy parkas and wet woolen hats like cocoons.

In late April, Matthew received a check from his grandfather for his nineteenth birthday. He told Jane he wanted to use it to test a theory.

Three years earlier, before their time, a freshman had gotten into one of the dive bars downtown with a fake ID and ended up drink-ing himself into a coma, from which he never woke up. After that, the local bars cracked down. Students had nowhere to go and drink off-campus. Matthew surmised that the one fancy cocktail bar at the one fancy hotel in town was so expensive that the staff would never suspect anyone who could afford it of being a student. He was positive they wouldn't check IDs.

Of course the flaw in the plan was that they *couldn't* afford it. But when his birthday money arrived, the two of them dressed up one Saturday night. Jane bit down on her lip as Matthew spoke to the hostess, asked for a table for two. The hostess didn't blink. Nor did the waitress when they ordered Long Island Iced Teas. They ordered a second round and then a third. Everything was so much nicer than they were used to. The glasses felt heavy in their hands; the cocktail napkins were trimmed with gold. The waitress kept refilling a bowl of warm, salty nuts. Brazil nuts and cashews and nuts neither of them could name.

"A peanut wouldn't dare come into this establishment," Matthew said.

Jane started laughing so hard her drink came out of her nose.

The next thing she knew, she woke up on a sofa in the common room of a dorm, not her own. She had no idea how she had gotten there.

She was still wearing her black dress. Her high heels lay on the carpet. Beside her slept a girl named Stacy Shields, who was nice enough but talked too much. They had a few classes together.

Stacy's mouth was open. A strand of drool hung from the corner of her lip.

Jane felt desperate for a glass of water. She reached for her shoes.

Stacy opened her eyes.

"Jane?" she whispered.

"Stacy. What happened last night? How did I get here?"

"I don't know. You were at the party."

"What party? Was Matthew with me?"

"Don't think so. You were making everyone laugh with some story about a waitress. Do you remember what I told you about Jonathan Mills? The RA?"

"No. I don't remember anything."

"Good," Stacy said, nodding. "Good."

She closed her eyes and went back to sleep.

Jane walked home barefoot, shoes in hand, stopping twice to vomit in the grass. She couldn't find her keys. Birds tweeted, cheerful and incessant overhead, mocking her.

She kept trying to access some shred of memory, something she had been able to do before on nights when she drank too much. But it was like she had time-traveled directly from one place to the other. Absolutely nothing in between.

Later that morning, Matthew showed up at her room, in the clothes he'd been wearing the night before. He collapsed down beside her on the bed.

"*What* the hell happened?" he said.

"I don't know!" Jane said.

"I woke up in a bush on some professor's front lawn," he said. "Did we have Chinese food? My hair was full of white rice."

They laughed so hard then. Just laughed and laughed.

BY THE TIME Jane graduated, she had developed a certain polish, having studied not only her coursework, but her classmates— she started listening to NPR, as they all had since kindergarten. She subscribed to *The New Yorker*. She had yet to travel, but she no longer got shocked when her dormmates flew to Aspen for the weekend, or spent spring break in Capri. She felt like a different person from the one who arrived at orientation with half her belongings in Hefty bags.

She drank like her peers too. She drank to feel charming, smart, outgoing. She drank to feel more like them than she actually was.

This continued after college.

In her twenties, every night, she had a glass or two of wine out to dinner with friends, or a couple of beers at home alone while she read a book or watched TV. On the weekends, she might have one or two drinks more at a party or a bar, but nine times out of ten, she switched to water before she did anything too regrettable. The problem was she could never tell in advance when things were going to go further. It always caught her off guard.

On a weekend trip to the Cape with Matthew and some other friends from college the summer she was twenty-three, Jane was drinking a gin and tonic, playing Monopoly in their rented cottage one minute and coming to in an emergency room the next. Matthew was at her side. A young doctor was administering stitches in her wrist. They had to tell her she had put her arm through a glass coffee table.

Matthew was confused. He said she had seemed fine, she was talking like normal. Repeating herself a lot, clearly drunk, but fine. The doctor explained that a blackout was the result of the brain's long-term memory center shutting down. You retained nothing from one minute to the next. But no one around you could tell when you were in that state.

"To the uninitiated, blackouts sound made up," he said. "An excuse. We've all had fuzzy memories or nights we'd like to forget. People think it's that. But it's not, as you know, Jane. You have to be careful."

That whole episode scared her, but not enough to make her think of stopping. Most people her age she knew drank as much as she did, or more. She wasn't her mother; she was just young and having fun. She would just have to be more careful.

On several occasions after that, Jane woke up in some stranger's bed with no idea how she had gotten there or what had happened between them. And yet she kept expecting things to improve. As if drinking was like playing the violin, and one needed ten thousand hours of practice to master it. She learned the patterns of other people's drinking. She befriended the ones who drank as much as she did or more. She knew which friends would want to stop after one drink, and only ever saw them on a Tuesday.

As time passed, she got used to performing a certain morning-after litany of remorse and regret, and, when needed, apology. She became a detective of her own bad behavior, searching through text messages and photos on her phone to piece together where she had been, what she had done. Examining her body for bruises, then trying to determine who or what had left them.

On the mornings after the worst nights, sick and weighed down by shame, Jane briefly pondered sobriety, in a ritual that involved reading certain pieces of writing, all of them by women who had been there, and stopped.

Caroline Knapp: *If I am an alcoholic, I shouldn't drink and if I'm not an alcoholic, I don't need to.* And: *People who aren't alcoholics do not lie in bed at two-thirty in the morning wondering if they're alcoholics.*

A Cambridge-based novelist Jane knew socially had written an acclaimed book, thinly veiled, about her own drunken escapades and eventual path to sobriety. On the darkest mornings, Jane composed emails to her, confessing her desire to get sober, asking for help. She never sent a single one. Soon enough—often by dinnertime that same night—she was having a glass of wine, laughing it off, listening to anyone who would tell her not to be so hard on herself.

She was forever lowering the bar. She created firm, if arbitrary, lines and then she crossed them. *I'll never do anything that hurts anyone other than me. I'll never drive drunk. I'll never mess with someone else's marriage.*

Jane kept drinking because, she told herself, the upside was so much fun. She had spent countless delicious nights in bars, flirting and laughing and telling stories. She loved sharing wine with friends over dinner, or visiting Allison and strolling down the beach with coffee mugs full of rum and lemonade. Some of the best times she ever had, she had drinking. It was the only way to lose her self-consciousness.

She couldn't give it up. She just needed to find a means of stopping on any given night before things got bad.

Jane did so, with varying degrees of success, through all sorts of agreements with herself. She tried drinking only on weekends. Drinking only after eating a full meal. Stopping at eleven. Switching to seltzer after the second drink. Swearing off hard liquor and sticking to white wine. These things worked until they didn't.

As she got older, Jane lost days to pounding headaches and online "Are You an Alcoholic?" quizzes.

Have you ever decided to stop drinking for a week or so, but only lasted a couple of days? Yes.

Have you ever switched from one kind of drink to another in the hope that this would keep you from getting drunk? Yes.

Do you have blackouts? Yes.

Get drunk when you don't intend to? Yes.

Have you had to have an eye-opener upon awakening during the past year? There it was. No! No, she had never done that. Not in the past year. Not ever. Which proved there were people far worse off than she was. And so she carried on.

Hangovers got worse with age. Consequences became more serious. Jane had been stupid, cringe-inducing drunk in front of her mother and her sister, in front of Allison. In front of countless friends and men she never saw again. A drunken argument eventually ended her friendship with Matthew.

Yet through it all, she excelled professionally. The morning after one of her all-time worst nights, she walked into her office and was given a promotion. Her work was the one sacred space that she managed to keep separate.

Melissa didn't know that side of her. Had she known, she never would have set Jane up with David. By the time Jane met him, her drinking buddies were mostly slowing down and so was she, or so she thought. Booze was still present everywhere she went, but in a more adult way. Where once alcohol had been hard to come by, now the wine flowed at conferences, at baby showers, at book parties and gallery openings. At every brunch and dinner out. The drinking was less frenzied, less intense, but it seemed essential to take part.

David appreciated good wine. He might have two beers if they went to a Red Sox game. But he had no compulsion about alcohol. He could take it or leave it. That was how Jane wanted to be, more than anything.

In their early days together, she tried hard to manage her drinking, just like she tried hard to manage all the other unappealing parts of herself, like maybe falling in love could change her into a better person if she willed it to be so.

Blacking out after a night with some guy she met once and would never see again was one thing. But David was her partner. When she drank too much around him, her thinking got twisted. She felt like he was out to get her, out to kill her joy. Because unlike all the random guys she'd met in bars, David didn't think it was funny when Jane started slurring her words or belting out Madonna in a cab before puking out the window. He got concerned, scared. Annoyed.

She developed a certain sneakiness around booze in their apartment, throwing empty bottles away in public trash cans and replacing them with full ones immediately, so he wouldn't know how much she drank.

Four years after they met, they eloped, with only Allison and David's younger brother as their witnesses. Jane couldn't imagine having to have a bunch of people looking at her, wearing a white dress in front of a crowd. As she had told David many times, she wanted to *be* married to him, but she did not want to *get* married to him. David understood. Plus, he had already done the fancy two-hundred-person wedding the first time around.

Jane didn't eat a thing that day, it was such a whirlwind. They drank a lot of champagne. The next morning, when David said, "That was a night I will never forget," she looked into his eyes and said, "Me too," having no memory of how it ended.

WHEN THEY WENT out for their first wedding anniversary, a seven o'clock dinner reservation at her favorite restaurant in

Cambridge, Jane ordered a bottle of wine for them to share. Once it was empty, she knew she'd had far more than half, but she ordered one more glass.

David frowned. "You sure?" he said.

She found his tone condescending.

"Yes," she said. "I'm sure."

Jane was eating dessert and laughing at nine. The next thing she knew, it was midnight and she was alone on the sofa at home.

David entered the room with a wet washcloth and a box of Band-Aids. That's when she noticed that her knees were bloody.

She gave him a confused look.

"You fell down the stairs coming back from the restaurant bathroom," he said. "You don't remember?"

He told her the rest the next morning. That she had also made a scene about driving home in the restaurant lobby, swearing she was fine, shouting at him. They never did return to that restaurant, much as she loved it. Jane had a whole list of places she could never return to.

She didn't drink then for six months. She never came out and said she was quitting, but it was the longest she had gone without drinking since she started. From September to February, through holiday parties, through New Year's Eve and a long weekend at a friend's house in the Berkshires, everyone else gobbling down apple cider doused with whiskey and Jane drinking her cider with nothing in it but a cinnamon stick.

She decided somewhere in there that they needed a trip. She booked five nights at a luxury resort in Turks and Caicos, the cost of which gave her a small panic attack, which she tried her best to ignore. She watched a video on the hotel's website over and over again to cheer herself up. In addition to the award-winning spa, the three swimming pools, and the tree-house yoga studio, the video mentioned a complimentary welcome drink. A glass of rum punch handed to each guest at check-in. She thought about that glass of rum punch every day until they left, weighing whether or not she would take it, knowing on some level that she would.

"Is it okay with you if I have a drink when we get there?" she said on the plane. "They hand out rum punch at check-in, apparently. But if you don't want me to drink, I won't."

David looked at her. "That's not my decision to make," he said.

Did she sense disappointment in his voice? Or resignation? Jane couldn't be sure.

She spent the trip on good behavior. A glass of wine at dinner. A single piña colada by the pool each afternoon. Feeling virtuous, but never sated. Thinking every minute about when she would drink again.

David never commented on this, one way or the other.

A few months of sensible drinking followed. Then she met up with Tanya, a grad school friend she hadn't seen in ages, who was in Boston for the night. Tanya drank like a fish. So had Jane when they knew one another. To nip any possible bad behavior in the bud, Jane told her she could only have one drink, claiming to be on antibiotics.

Despite her precautions, they got soused. They ended up at some scuzzy dive bar near Downtown Crossing where they flirted with a couple of Englishmen in town on business. Jane woke up in the bathroom there, sitting on a toilet, with her jeans around her ankles. Tanya and the Englishmen were gone.

On her phone were several missed calls and texts from David, wondering where she was, if she was okay. Just as she went to call him, her phone's battery died.

When Jane got home, he was pacing the apartment.

"I was about to call the police," David said.

"Honey!" she said. "I'm sorry I worried you. We went to dinner and I left my phone at the restaurant. Then we went back to her hotel and talked forever, and then I realized, and had to go back to the restaurant and beg the hostess to let me in, since they were closed. And after all that, my phone was dead."

Jane heard the lie flow so smoothly from her lips. She could tell he didn't believe her. He looked angry, and just over it.

"I'm going to bed," was all he said. "I'm glad you're okay."

The next morning, Jane found her phone charging in the kitchen. David had plugged it in for her, which wasn't unusual. But to her horror, she saw that Tanya had texted photos from the night before: In one, Jane was kissing one of the Englishmen on the lips. In another, she was kissing Tanya. She didn't remember kissing either one of them.

Her heart raced. She frantically deleted the pictures, and prayed David hadn't seen them.

David, for his part, acted like nothing had happened.

Jane was relieved at first, but then she recalled how once, very early on in their relationship, they had confessed to one another their deepest fears about themselves. Hers: that she was not as smart as she thought, and everyone knew it. His: that his first wife's infidelity, their divorce, made people think there was something wrong with him.

"Divorce nearly killed me," he said. "I'd rather do anything than be back there again."

AFTER THAT, Jane had things under control, mostly. She had maybe one or two bad nights a year, when she drank more than she should have and picked a fight with David for no reason, or chatted too much with a cute bartender while they were out to dinner. David, she knew, was hurt by these occurrences. But he always let them go, and Jane always told herself it wouldn't happen again.

Sometimes when she drank, separate and apart from David, she confided in someone she shouldn't, or told a secret that wasn't hers to tell. The next day she agonized over whether to apologize sincerely or make a joke or just let it go. Usually she did say something, in search of every drunk's favorite reassurance: *Don't worry. You were fine.*

After her mother died, Jane started drinking more than ever.

Actually, it began even earlier, when her mother lay dying. But that felt like crisis management more than a problem. Jane drank all through the wake and funeral, but no one seemed to think that was anything other than a means of survival. Then she kept drinking that way once they were back home.

Jane didn't notice how bad it was until David suggested they both take a month off from drinking. Considering he hardly drank, Jane understood this was about her. When she didn't take him up on it, David came out and said he was worried.

"You're trying to get pregnant," he said.

"Yes," she said. "I'm not going to drink once I am, obviously."

"So this is some kind of last hurrah?"

"No," she said. "It isn't anything. I'm fine."

He crossed his arms.

"You never run in the mornings anymore because you're too hungover," he said.

"That's not why," she said, offended.

"You've missed work four or five times this month because you were hungover," he said. "I've never seen you do that before. I think maybe you should talk to someone."

Jane reminded him she was under a ton of stress at work. She had no time to find a therapist, let alone go see one on a regular basis. She promised she would think about it after her big spring event.

She had planned every detail of the night herself. Written the program, decided what to order from the caterer, perfected her speech. Gone through it moment by moment in her head dozens of times.

The archive held the collection of the outspoken second-wave feminist Arianna Randall. Part of it was comprised of detailed notes taken for a book begun and never completed, co-authored with Carolyn Molloy, a titan of commercial real estate, at Molloy's family cabin at Cranberry Lake, New Jersey, in 1992. In that book, Molloy and Randall intended to expose explosive secrets of misogyny and corruption in the world of politics. But for some reason, it was never published. The notes for the book were included in Randall's archive, with instructions not to open them until after her death, fueling much speculation.

Arianna Randall had been dead for six months the night of the unveiling.

The event took place at the home of their wealthiest board member, a mansion just outside Harvard Square. Specifically, in her showstopper of a library, with vaulted ceilings and books tucked into every corner of the built-in bookshelves. There was a balcony overhead, full of still more bookshelves. A wrought-iron spiral staircase leading to it.

They never had so much press for an event, or so many donors in attendance. Everything went perfectly. Jane was so relieved.

After the program and her speech, which happened while everyone else was eating dinner, she rewarded herself with a glass of champagne from the open bar. It hit her after just a couple of sips, and she told herself she needed to eat something sooner rather than later.

She got to talking, one person after another telling her what a great job she had done. It seemed like half of them pressed a new drink into her hand as they did so. Jane relaxed. She was so happy. She remembered David kissing her on the cheek, giving her a glass of tonic water and lime. She drank it, but then there was more champagne, more wine.

Eventually, David said they should leave. It was getting late. He had an early morning the next day.

Jane was annoyed at him. She was having fun. She had earned this. She told him to go; she would take a cab later. She walked him to the front door, but did not lean in when he tried to hug her goodbye.

"You were amazing tonight," David said.

"I should get back," she said.

Jane remembered turning in the foyer, stumbling on her high heel, looking around, grateful no one saw. And then the doors to the party opened and out walked Tim, the assistant librarian Jane worked with on a few projects. He was the only male on staff. A sweet, funny twenty-five-year-old kid whose fiancée had gotten him interested in female poets of the Victorian age.

"Are you heading out?" Jane said.

"Yeah," he said. "I am officially overserved."

She laughed.

"Aww, come on. The night is young," she said, surprised at her flirtatious tone, as if she were not the one speaking. "Come back inside."

"If you insist," he said.

They ordered two champagnes and then two more. They laughed and Jane had the drunken thought that she wanted to kiss him, but of course she would not.

Then, nothing. Fade to black.

She woke up in her own bed at seven the next morning, naked under the sheets, pain in her head like someone had hit her with a brick. She was full of dread.

Rain pelted the windows.

She was alone, but before long she heard the sound of the apartment door opening, Walter's leash hitting the hardwood floor. David came in, handed her a coffee in a white paper cup.

"Hi," he said. "Thought you might need that."

"Thank you," she said.

"I'm sorry I left the party without you last night," he said. "I feel like a jerk."

She didn't say anything.

"You were so drunk," he said. "I kept trying to get you to go."

"I'm sorry," she said.

"I didn't want you to embarrass yourself in front of your friends and colleagues," he said. "Not to mention, my friends and colleagues."

He sounded pained.

"How was the rest of the night?"

"Good," she said, because to say she didn't know was a level of indignity she didn't think she could survive.

Feeling like death, she got up and got ready and went to the office. Once there, Jane ducked into the bathroom and puked before washing her mouth out at the sink and heading toward her desk. She felt paranoid. It seemed like every person she crossed paths with looked away as she approached. She had expected them to congratulate her on a job well done.

No sooner had she sat down at her desk than Melissa flew out from her office and said, "Jane, please come in here."

Jane went toward Melissa, feeling like she was moving through cement.

She could smell the alcohol coming through her own pores.

Melissa closed the door, which was unusual.

"I'm surprised to see you here," she said, her voice ice cold. Jane had never heard her sound that way before. "I think it would be best if you go," Melissa said.

"What?" Jane said. "Why?"

"People are really upset about what happened, Jane. *I'm* really upset."

"I'm so sorry. I don't remember."

Melissa hung her head. "You've got to be kidding."

"I wish I were. Please, can you tell me?"

"Jane, you were fully making out with Tim at the end of the night. He had his hand up your shirt."

Jane froze. "Jesus. Did anyone see?"

"Everyone saw. All the donors, the honoree's family, the *Globe*. You had gone up to the balcony, like you thought that made you invisible or something. When really it was the opposite. Pearl and I ran up there when we realized what was happening, but we couldn't reason with you. It was like you were having some kind of breakdown. You were belligerent. You actually told us to fuck off. Then the two of you left together."

"Oh my God."

"I convinced the *Globe* not to run a story about it."

"Oh my God."

"Someone was taping you on his phone, Jane. I got him to erase the video before he posted it anywhere, I think. I had the assistants look online to make sure, and they didn't see it. Not yet, anyway. But there were a few references to what you did on Twitter. You should go home," Melissa said. "Let's see what the weekend brings. Maybe this just blows over. I don't know. I've honestly never experienced anything like this. I need to think. I'll call you."

The bottom dropped out of the world then, and Jane was falling, falling, falling.

"How did this happen, Jane?" Melissa said. She sounded so disappointed.

Jane kept trying to find an answer, but none came.

"Did you tell David?" was the last thing Jane said.

Melissa shook her head.

"That's your job, Jane. I suggest you do it soon. He's going to hear about it either way. Probably best if he hears it from you."

HAVING TO TELL him was the worst experience of Jane's life.

Her husband looked thoroughly horrified. His face crumpled. It seemed beside the point to say that she had never had an ounce of interest in Tim, though it was true. She had no idea why she had done it. Did she really hate herself this much?

"I swear to you, I will never drink again," she said.

David stared at her, disgusted. She hadn't seen that look before.

"Did you sleep with him?" he said.

"No," she said. Though she was not one hundred percent sure. She couldn't bear to call Tim and ask; nor did that seem like a good idea. "I am so sorry," she said. When David didn't answer, Jane added, "Should I leave?"

"I don't know," he said. "No, no, of course you shouldn't."

He sounded pleading, like he wanted guidance. This was worse than fury.

Jane could not believe what was happening. Three days earlier, they were holding hands, walking along the Charles, making summer plans. Last night, they had gotten ready for the party together in this room, Jane tying David's tie, David fastening the clasp on her necklace, gently pulling her hair back, kissing her neck.

They were trying for a baby.

THE FOLLOWING MONDAY morning at six o'clock, Melissa called. She said Tim had confessed everything to his fiancée and she in turn had written to the dean, demanding an investigation into Jane.

"They will likely bring you up on sexual harassment charges," Melissa said. "I talked them out of pursuing sexual assault. It wasn't that. Tim's not even saying that."

"What?" was all Jane could manage to say.

"He told me himself it was consensual, just a stupid decision on both your parts. And no actual sex. Still. You are his superior."

No actual sex. That at least was a relief.

"So what happens now?" Jane said.

"We put you on unpaid leave for a while. We can't have this turning into a huge, explosive thing. I don't want it ending up in the press and overshadowing all our hard work."

Jane had marched in rallies against sexual harassment in the workplace. She had sat on panels, read every op-ed on the subject. This was a turn so improbable, so unexpected, that she went numb. She left her body.

"Harvard is willing to pay for you to go to rehab," Melissa said. "I will email you all the information."

"Thank you," Jane said, but she knew she wouldn't go.

Rehab was for the true fuck-ups, she thought. People who put vodka in their morning Cheerios. Rock-bottom people.

Though what was this if not rock bottom?

In the weeks that followed, Jane missed her office. She pictured it like Pompeii. Abandoned unexpectedly in the middle of things. Her plants on the windowsill, in need of water. Her papers neatly arranged on the desk. She always wanted things to be just so. Orderly. Sometimes, to mess with her, Melissa snuck in while Jane was in the bathroom or at lunch, and set one or two pages askew.

JANE AND DAVID slogged it out for several weeks, but things were not the same. She doubted they ever would be.

They had an emergency session with a couples' therapist. The woman's voice was calm and gentle, all wrong for the situation. She asked Jane to tell her version first.

Jane came out with it then, the whole sad tale of her drinking life and the bad choices she had made that she had no memory of the next morning. Especially when it came to men.

When she finished talking, the therapist asked David if he believed her when she said she couldn't remember.

"I do, mostly," he said.

Mostly.

"My first wife was unfaithful," David said. "I never thought I'd be here again. It's not the same. Jane's nothing like Angela and this was a one-time, drunken mistake. Jane's grieving. I know that. But it doesn't feel like that."

"My mother died nine months ago," Jane said. A cheap excuse, she thought at the time. The two things had nothing to do with one another. But David had opened the door by saying Jane was grieving, so she walked through.

"I've been mixed up ever since," she went on. "But I can promise that I will never drink like that again. I'll stop. Believe me, there is nothing I want less than to drink alcohol now. I'm done."

"There have been some issues around alcohol in our marriage before. For Jane," David croaked out, clearly feeling guilty for saying it, as mild as it was. He was the most loyal partner. He would never want to make her look bad to a stranger, even now.

"Do you have anything to say in response?" the therapist asked Jane.

Jane thought the best solution might be for her to go out to Mass Ave. and walk in front of a bus.

"Have you gone to any twelve-step meetings?" the therapist said.

"No," Jane said.

The therapist suggested that she do so, and that the two of them come weekly. But after that first appointment, neither Jane nor David brought it up again.

Their apartment, usually full of banter and laughter and conversation, turned silent. They stopped having sex.

They still slept in the same bed. One night, lying there, staring at his back, certain he was wide awake, Jane wondered if this was just how they would be from now on. David would never leave her, but would he ever love her again? Would he forgive her? Would he be okay if she allowed him to pretend they could chalk what she did up to grief and nothing else?

He was such a good man. He had done so much for her, and in return, she had trampled on his heart. Jane was broken. After everything she had put him through, she thought, maybe the kindest thing she could do for the man she loved was leave.

"I think we should take some time apart," she said, trying the words on. "This isn't working anymore."

She wanted him to protest. The idea of either of them leaving terrified her. But David didn't push back. He just shrugged, without turning to face her.

"If that's what you want," he said.

Jane left for Maine the next day.

13

ON THE WEDNESDAY after Labor Day at six o'clock in the morning, Jane woke to the sound of scratching at the screen door. The dog had returned home. Walter was filthy and smelled like a swamp, but he seemed otherwise fine.

As soon as she let him in, he went straight to the leash hanging by the door, and nosed at it. Wherever he had been for the previous three weeks, he was back and, absurdly, still expecting his morning walk.

"You can't be serious," Jane said as she picked him up and held him close, relief coursing through her. "God, you're an asshole."

She put on shoes and took him out, texting everyone a photo to let them know he was back. Allison replied with a dozen heart emojis. Holly wrote Thank you Jesus! Jason sent his usual thumbs-up. David was the only one who didn't respond. Jane hadn't heard from him since the day Walter disappeared.

Her head ached. Yesterday, as had become her custom since that night at Charlie's Chowder House, Jane sat on the back deck and drank a bottle of white wine by herself while the sun set. Each evening, she seemed to start her secret solo cocktail hour a bit earlier than the last. Sometimes she followed up the wine with a gin and tonic or two. She never felt satisfied. She was like some boozed-up version of that book about a very hungry caterpillar Jason loved when he was a toddler. *On Tuesday, she drank half a bottle of tequila, but she was STILL thirsty.*

The previous weekend had been the vacationers' last hurrah, the town packed full of people and cars. For three days, wanting to avoid them, Jane barely left the house. Not until seven p.m. on Monday did she go farther than the end of the road. She wandered then to the

Cliffwalk, and found it close to empty. On the stretch of sand in the distance, not a single umbrella could be seen. All the tourists were sitting in traffic on 95, homeward-bound. The people of Awadapquit had their town to themselves again. This was her favorite time of year here. It had been her grandmother's favorite. Her mother's too.

Tuesday broke beautiful and hot, a perfect beach day. By then, children were back at school, their mothers and fathers back to work, suntans and freckles the only proof that they had recently experienced some other, better form of existence.

This morning, the sky over the cove was dark and ominous. As soon as Jane and Walter got home from their walk, it started to pour. Walter jumped up on the sofa and passed out immediately. Jane looked at him and felt like she might cry from the relief of having him back.

She wondered if she would ever get to the bottom of where he had gone. There had not been a single sighting reported, except for a woman who saw a flash of orange in her yard that turned out to be her own cat and a call from the police about a small dog killed in a hit-and-run two towns over. Jane was so relieved when they sent a description and pictures of the dog's collar and she saw that it wasn't Walter.

She had grown accustomed these past three weeks to sleeping in until ten or eleven, even noon some days, feeling gross and guilty for wasting so much time. Jane had blamed poor Walter for the fact that she did not run in the mornings anymore. It turned out Walter had been her reason for getting out of bed.

Now, as the rain came down outside, Jane sorted through the last few boxes of stuff in her mother's room, which would be picked up in the afternoon and taken to Goodwill, along with dishes and small kitchen appliances. The further into the move she got, the more tedious it became, as she sifted through plastic bags and cereal bowls full of nonsense. Used double-A batteries, an old pair of promotional sunglasses, a fistful of pennies, a CD case with no CD inside, remote controls that she was fairly certain served no purpose, a dozen plastic bottles of cleaning supplies, each with only a drop or two of liquid left.

At lunchtime, she made herself a turkey sandwich and poured a glass of wine, then sat on the sofa and turned on a home renovation show. It was entirely pleasant, and so, on the commercial break before the big reveal, Jane dashed back to the fridge and poured herself a second glass.

As she did this, through the window, she saw Allison's car turn into the driveway.

Swiftly, as though she had done it a thousand times before, Jane opened the cabinet beneath the sink and stuck the wine bottle in behind the jug of Clorox and the Windex and the ant traps. She almost poured the full glass down the drain but that seemed like such a waste, she couldn't bring herself to do it.

Jane put the glass of wine in the cabinet too, and shut the door.

Allison knocked a few moments later.

Walter flew off the couch and started barking.

"Hi," Jane said, letting Allison in. "It's so peaceful having him back."

Allison bent down and petted the dog's head.

"You scared us to death, young man," she said. She wrinkled her nose. "Does he need a bath?"

"Yes," Jane said.

"Should we give him one?"

Jane was slightly irked by the question.

She herself had not bathed in days. She felt sluggish, depleted. The simplest tasks were beyond her. It was all she could do to pack up a box or two before collapsing on the couch. She had taken to ignoring all incoming calls and emails, even those from people she liked. When Naomi Miller, the consultant she met at the Portland Historical Society, reached out to say she had a meeting in Portsmouth and would Jane like to meet for lunch afterward, Jane didn't even respond.

She was well aware that she was imploding. She didn't need Allison to point it out.

"I'll do it later," Jane said.

Allison held a bakery box in her hands. "Can you believe this weather? Seemed like a good day for cookies," she said. "I got the ones you like, from Millie's. They're still warm." She kicked off her shoes. "It's dreary out, isn't it? They say it will stop by three, but I'm not so sure. And then tomorrow there is going to be fog. The weekend looks nice, but you know as well as I do how reliable those online forecasts are around here."

Something was off. Allison never just stopped by in the middle of the day. Certainly not to talk about the weather.

"Are you okay?" Jane said.

Her mind went to Betty. Had she died? Had Allison come to tell her? No, that couldn't be it. Thinking Allison would arrive with cookies to soften that particular blow was probably proof that Jane was a raging narcissist.

"I'm fine!" Allison said. "Things are finally slowing down at the inn. And the kids are back to school. So I thought I'd come visit my bestie."

Bestie too rang of false cheer, even coming from Allison, who was a generally cheerful person.

"What are you up to today?" Allison said.

"Actually, I'm really busy," Jane said.

Allison glanced at the TV. "Yeah?"

Jane wanted more than anything to be left alone with the sauvignon blanc. Why did she have to explain what she was doing in the privacy of her home?

"I'm tackling the last of the clean-out," she said. "The Realtor plans to list the house tomorrow. People will start coming through later this week."

"Did you end up going with Lauren Murphy?"

"Yes. Holly insisted."

"Good. She's good." Allison looked around, took in the space. "Wow, Jane. This place looks so different."

At the Realtor's urging, Jane had paid Jason and his friend Erika with the purple hair to paint the whole interior white—walls, ceilings, even the green cabinets that had allegedly offended her grandmother. Jane purchased new white rugs at the Crate & Barrel outlet in Kittery.

She had bristled at this suggestion at first. It reminded her of what Genevieve had done to her house, taking out all the specificity. But Jane had to admit the space looked ten times brighter than it ever had.

The Realtor also said to rid the house of personal details—family photographs and such—so that potential buyers could have a blank canvas onto which they might project themselves. Jane had done this, for the most part. But when Lauren told her to take down the small sign outside the front door that read FLANAGAN, she couldn't do it. Jane left it right where it was.

"I feel like a cup of tea. Do you?" Allison said now.

She went to the sink and filled the kettle before Jane could respond. As Allison stood there, Jane panicked, unlikely though it was that Allison would reach down and open the cabinet below.

"You're acting weird," Jane said.

"Am I?"

Allison opened the fridge, took out the milk. She unscrewed the cap and sniffed it, then made a face. She looked closely at the bottle.

"Jane, this is expired," she said. "And you have nothing in your fridge." Allison sighed deeply. "I'm really worried about you. We need to talk."

Oh God.

"We are talking," Jane said, playing dumb.

Allison turned off the kettle, and came and sat by Jane's side. "You've been through a lot this past year," she said. "Especially lately. It makes sense that you might slip."

"What do you mean, slip?" said Jane, who knew exactly what she meant.

"We're pretty sure you're drinking again."

"Who's we?"

"Chris and me. His cousin said he saw you at the liquor store in New Hampshire."

"His cousin?"

"Yeah, the one who lives in Kittery. His name is also Chris. He said it looked like you were loading up your cart for a party."

The irony of this was that on the first night she went to buy wine three weeks ago, Jane had gone to the wine shop in the center of Awadapquit. She was standing at the register, next in line, when Chris passed by the window with Amelia and Ollie. Jane turned around, put the wine down, and drove forty minutes away, just over the state line, to avoid seeing anyone she knew.

She had forgotten how small this part of the world was.

"Also," Allison said. "I heard from Lucy Samuels that you were at some party at the Chowder House the night David showed up in town and Walter ran away. She said everyone was hitting it pretty hard, including you."

Exasperated, Jane said, "Who is Lucy Samuels?"

"She owns that pottery place in the cove. You know her. I'm not trying to be big brother, or whatever. But I'm your best friend, Jane. I don't understand why you'd keep this a secret unless you felt in your heart that you shouldn't be doing it."

Jane's first instinct was to lie. She would simply say that both Chris's cousin Chris and Lucy from the pottery place were mistaken.

Her second instinct was to say that yes, sure, she'd had a few drinks at the Chowder House and every night since, but Allison was correct—this was a horrible time in her life. She would revisit the idea of total sobriety when things felt better. And was total sobriety even healthy? Wasn't that just as severe an addiction as drinking too much when you thought about it? She had stopped drinking as part of an effort to save her life from falling apart, but it fell apart anyway. Given that, why not have a drink every now and then?

Certainly she had needed a few glasses of wine before calling Melissa back. Liquid courage. It was practically medicinal.

For days, Jane could not bear to respond to Melissa's message. What was there to say? Jane worshipped Melissa and yet had let her down on every possible level. Melissa gave Jane her dream job. Melissa introduced her to the man she married. Jane had squandered both these gifts.

When they finally spoke, the conversation was so tender and kind that Jane felt even worse. She told Melissa she was sorry for everything, that working for her had been the greatest honor and the greatest joy.

"Have you thought about rehab?" Melissa said. "I don't mean to harp on this issue. But it could be helpful with future jobs. It might be good to do, from the standpoint of next steps. Rehabbing your career, so to speak."

Next steps. Right. Jane would have to find another job now, and the field was small. Everyone in it probably knew what she'd done.

Before they hung up, Jane asked how Pearl was.

"She's good," Melissa said, but that was all.

Jane wished she would say more, suggest that they should all get together soon, even if it was a lie.

Now here was Jane, with her best friend, about to be told again that she needed to get help.

She knew she should apologize for worrying everyone, for messing up again and again, but instead her stupid pride won out and she said to Allison, "I didn't realize you had spies all over town keeping an eye on me. I know you're practically the mayor of Awadapquit, but that's next level."

Allison looked surprised, hurt. "I wrote you a letter," she said. "Is it okay if I read it to you?"

"Now?" Jane said.

She assumed Allison had googled how to do an intervention and this had come up.

Jane had planned and executed no fewer than three interventions for her mother over the years, and one for her sister. If anyone knew how to try to get someone to quit drinking, it was her. She knew all the places she might go. Other families passed around recommendations for restaurants or vacation spots. Her family was fluent in the language of New England's finest detox centers and rehabs.

Allison's letter was, like Allison herself, loving and encouraging, a remembrance of who Jane was at her best. She practically gave a eulogy before going in for the kill. Jane was the smartest and funniest person she knew. She had accomplished unbelievable things. Allison's children adored her. Allison was worried, so worried about how out of control the drinking had gotten. And she feared that by not saying this sooner, she had enabled the worst of Jane's behavior. So now she was saying it, even though it was one of the hardest things she had ever had to do.

Jane held back from asking if she wanted a medal. She knew Allison had her best interest at heart, and yet, wasn't it easy for her to say what constituted appropriate behavior? With her perfect family, her perfect life? Wasn't there a hint of smugness in the way she made it known that she had eyes everywhere?

Jane half wanted to tell her that Chris's cousin Chris might have seen her buying booze, but no one had seen her drive up on the curb in front of Scoops ice cream parlor two nights ago after midnight, drunk and on her way to the all-night Walgreens for boxed macaroni and cheese. No one in Awadapquit knew about how Jane picked a fight with some scholar on Twitter last week that ended with her calling him a douchebag and getting suspended from the site for forty-eight hours. Allison might have her spies, but she didn't know everything.

Never had Jane been so annoyed by the open-concept floor plan of this house. The kitchen, the dining area, and the TV room, all one. Had there been walls and doors, she could have excused herself to go get that glass of wine under the sink and chug it. She felt like a drowning woman who could see a life raft in the distance, just out of reach.

"I know this feels like a lot. But think for a minute, okay?" Allison said. "The bottom line is you've lost way too much to alcohol and it has given you nothing in return. I watched you go through this with your mother for so long, Jane. You know how addiction works. It kills me to see you falling prey to it anyway."

Having delivered this speech, Allison looked like she might pass out from the stress.

It was too much. An overreaction.

Jane waited for an ultimatum, but that wasn't Allison's way.

"Look," Jane said, in her calmest voice. "I appreciate your concern. It means a lot to me that you care this much. But really, I'm fine. I'd tell you if I wasn't."

"Bullshit," Allison said.

"Excuse me?"

"I have been holding my tongue for so long because I love you, and I know you've been through a lot. But I can't keep watching you blow up your life, and just sit by," Allison said. "That's not even being a good friend. And besides, it's taking a toll on me too. You don't know how many nights I'm up talking to Chris about how worried I am for you, and how sad I am about what you did to David, and what I can do to fix it all."

Allison was angry.

Jane felt a flame of anger rise up in her now too.

"I'm so sorry to have kept you up," she said. "It must be really hard to have such a perfect life that you have to spend your time worrying about your fuck-up friend."

Allison scoffed. "Jane. My life is so far from perfect. Sometimes I feel like you don't even register what's going on with me, you're so focused on yourself."

"I think we've established that I'm an asshole," Jane said. "I need to get back to what I was doing. You should probably go."

The dejected look on Allison's face when she left brought Jane a strange sort of pleasure. Allison hadn't even backed her car out of the driveway before Jane was drawn back to the glass of wine under the sink. A homing signal. A beacon. She drank it down in one glorious gulp.

Allison's bakery box, that cookie-filled Trojan horse, was still on the countertop, tied up with red string. Jane ate all six cookies inside, letting herself sink into the specific private shame to which she had grown accustomed. No one could see her; no one could stop her. When she was done, she brought the box to the outside recycling bin, which was full to the top with wine bottles. She got in her car and drove to Portsmouth for more.

THE GUYS FROM Goodwill came just before five o'clock. It felt cleansing watching them load the truck. When they were done, the house was down to a few pieces of furniture. The shelves and the closets and the cupboards were bare. All the boxes were gone.

There was more of Jane in this house now than there was of anyone else. Her clothes hung in the closet. Her facewash and toothbrush and several anti-aging products she had bought but never used covered the bathroom counter. Her books about Native American history, opened and piled and filled with Post-its, sat atop the kitchen table. She imagined what it might be like to live here alone the way her mother and grandmother had. How this house, which seemed claustrophobic when she was young, could be a refuge for a woman on her own.

FOR THE NEXT THREE DAYS, Allison didn't call or text. This was unprecedented. Jane was thinking about it, wondering if she would have to broach the subject of their last conversation and apologize or if they could somehow pretend it never happened, as she went through a tote bag full of her mother's important papers. The last of what remained in the house.

At the liquor store on Wednesday, there had been a promotion on rum. KEEP SUMMER GOING THIS SEPTEMBER! a sign read. Jane took it as an order.

Now, at two p.m., she was drinking her second Captain's and Coke, a favorite of her mother's.

She was in a good mood, the taste and smell of the rum transporting her to various Caribbean vacations and summer days on the beach.

She texted her sister: Our mother kept her most important documents in a tote bag.

Holly wrote back: Of course she did.

Jane ripped to shreds old medical bills and insurance statements. She came to a smaller piece of paper, which she nearly ripped too, but noticing her grandmother's signature, she took a closer look. It was the mortgage for the house. Jane had seen it once before, when she was a teenager. But now the names on it meant something to her. Marilyn and Herbert Martinson.

What on earth.

Without hesitation, she called Marilyn.

Someone answered. That alone surprised Jane. It wasn't Marilyn, but a young-sounding woman. A woman in her early thirties, maybe even her twenties.

When Jane introduced herself and asked to speak with Marilyn, the woman's tone turned chilly. Marilyn, she said, wasn't available.

"If you could tell her Jane Flanagan called," she said, repeating her name. "We spoke not too long ago about a house she used to own in Maine."

"I know who you are."

"Okay. Well. I just learned that Marilyn and her ex-husband helped my grandmother buy her house and I'm curious why, when we spoke previously, Marilyn didn't mention it. Maybe she didn't make the connection."

"No, she knew."

"I guess I was hoping to find out more about that," Jane said. "My mother told me this nice married couple helped my grandma. That they were people whose house she cleaned. But I never realized which house they lived in. It's odd because well, clearly, I have some connection to the house. I was very close with my grandmother but didn't know she knew the people who lived there."

When the woman didn't reply, Jane said, "Sorry if this sounds crazy. Could you pass the message on to her?"

"Marilyn's in the hospital," the woman said. "She had a stroke. She isn't conscious."

"I'm so sorry," Jane said. "Are you a relative?"

"A close friend," the woman said.

"I'll keep her in my thoughts," Jane said. "I'm sorry to bother you at a time like this."

Again, no reply.

Jane knew she should say goodbye and hang up but instead she asked, "Have I done something to you? You seem hostile and I'm not sure why."

A sigh at the other end of the line.

"Marilyn was—she *is*—an old woman. Why did you have to bring this all up again? Your grandmother didn't do enough to destroy her all those years ago? You had to come along and finish the job?"

"I have no idea what you are talking about," Jane said.

"I have to go now," the woman said.

"Please, I'm so confused," Jane said.

"No you're not."

After they hung up, she sat there, stunned.

Jane's instinct led her to her laptop. Half an hour and one more rum and Coke later, she was deep in the online records. She found Herbert Martinson's death certificate, then an obituary. The latter said he was survived by his second wife and their two children, preceded in death by his parents and a daughter from his first marriage. Daisy.

According to Daisy's death certificate, she had died in Maine in 1967. She was eight years old. Her cause of death was listed only as *accidental*.

That was the same year Marilyn and Herbert co-signed for Jane's grandmother's house.

"Holy shit," Jane said out loud.

Daisy.

D.

She had to be the one Clementine saw, the girl in Jane's grand-mother's lap who wanted Jane to give her mother a message. Marilyn was D's mother.

Jane might have known all of this sooner had she looked at Mari-lyn's records, but instead Jane took her at her word. Usually, for Jane, piecing together the history of a life was some mix of dry documents full of dates and names and addresses and DNA findings, as well as the far less clear-cut stories people told about themselves. That was at the crux of everything she had ever done, professionally.

Jane searched for articles about Daisy's death, but did not find a single one. What sort of accident, she wondered, had taken the life of such a young girl? When Marilyn spoke of her time at Lake Grove, her divorce, she had never mentioned a child.

Had Daisy died in the house? Was that why they abandoned it?

Without thinking, Jane got in her car and started driving toward her sister's place.

She called Holly to say she was coming. She was about to tell her why when Holly said, "Jason just told me you were wasted the other day when he and Erika came to Mom's to paint."

Jane felt her face flush. It was true, she had been wasted. But she didn't think Jason could tell. It had been his birthday a couple of days before, and he told her casually that day that David had emailed him a gift card to his favorite local restaurant. Jane had felt touched by that, and a bit encouraged, and then deeply sad.

She braced herself for Holly to mention this, to say her feelings had been entirely transparent.

But Holly said, "He said you were slurring your words and talking gibberish, asking him all these questions about Keith."

"Who's Keith?" Jane said.

"The kid who dug up the graveyard."

Jane remembered asking about that, but she thought it had been in the course of normal conversation.

"You wouldn't let them leave," Holly went on. "You freaked Jason out."

"You didn't freak me out," Jason said in the background.

"You're on speaker," Holly said.

"I'm sorry, Aunt Jane," Jason said.

His voice was a portal to all they had put him through as a kid, and all they had been put through themselves. The cycle of this stupid addiction, the boring tedium of it.

Jane remembered how vulnerable Jason looked when he was eleven and Holly went to rehab for the second time, and Jane drove up here to spend the weekend. They told him Holly was "away on business." Jane was the one who said it first, hoping he believed it. Like he hadn't seen the worst of Holly's drinking when the two of them were alone together. Like Jane was protecting him, when really she threw him to the wolves every time she drove away.

"You didn't do anything wrong, bud," she said now.

"You're coming over?" Holly said.

"No, never mind," Jane said.

She hung up and turned the car around. It all still seemed crazy to her, but she wondered now whether Daisy, who died while staying at Lake Grove, was the little girl Benjamin saw in his bedroom. On the one hand, it stood to reason that she must be. On the other, if that was the case, why would Daisy have insisted that she wasn't at Lake Grove anymore?

Jane supposed that if Lake Grove really was haunted, Benjamin's ghost could be the maid, Eliza, as Genevieve suspected. Or perhaps, like Clementine said at Camp Mira, the ghost was Hannah Littlefield, crying over her husband's ship as she watched it meet a tragic fate. Or none of them. Who knew how many others lay in the ground beneath their feet?

As the car reached the center of town, Jane drove by the Saint Aspinquid. All the lights were on inside. The warm glow of the inn depressed her. Since high school, Jane had envied what came naturally to Allison. A family made up of people who loved one another, and actually enjoyed being together.

Next came the inevitable guilt for feeling this way. The great good fortune of being loved by Allison and her family was something Jane hadn't earned.

She promised herself she would make things right with Allison. She would go see Allison's mom in the morning, as she had been meaning to all summer.

JANE DIDN'T DO IT. Every day lately brought some unexpected detour, and that morning there were two, both arriving in the form of phone calls. The first was from the Realtor—they had a buyer, a couple offering just over the asking price, before even seeing the house in person. They owned a few properties in town, all of which they rented out by the week in summer.

Jane was excited while they talked. The moment they hung up, she started to cry.

She barely had time to process the news before the phone rang again. David's name flashed across the screen.

Jane felt a surge of hope at the sight of it. But as soon as she answered and he said, "Hi, Jane," it vanished. His tone reminded her of a doctor on a TV drama, about to tell his patient she has two days to live.

David asked how she was, and apologized for not replying sooner about Walter. He was so relieved to hear that the dog was okay.

"I just found out we got a buyer for my mom's place," Jane said.

In her dream scenario, this would be his cue to ask when she was coming home. But David didn't ask.

"That's great," he said. "Congrats."

Jane had a knot in her chest. She sensed in his voice a purposeful sort of distance, a formality. She knew that if she didn't say what she needed to now, she might not get another chance.

"David, I realize this probably sounds ridiculous, but just before you came up here, I had decided to tell you that I want to come back. I am so sorry for everything. Please, let's try again. I know it can be different this time."

There was a pit of sorrow in her belly because nothing was different, not really. And she had no idea how to make it so. But Jane wouldn't say this out loud. She would simply go home and find a way if he'd have her.

David didn't speak for a moment. Then he said, "Do you remember that church in Harvard Square where we used to see signs for Al-Anon meetings on the way home from work?"

"Yes," Jane said. She had always meant to go. She would go now, if he wanted her to.

"After you left, I started going," he said.

"Oh."

"It's been really helpful. I think you could get a lot out of trying a meeting too."

"Al-Anon or have I graduated to the big leagues of AA now?" she said. It was a stupid attempt at a joke.

"Some people do both," he said. "Alcoholism is a family disease. I don't have to tell you that. You know how it's handed down."

"And here I thought I hadn't gotten an inheritance," Jane said.

She was deflecting, but he didn't laugh. He just kept going, as if he were reading from a script. Maybe he was.

"The main thing I've learned is that I need to focus on myself," David said. "I can only be responsible for my actions, no one else's. I'm sorry too, Jane. I played a part in everything that happened. I enabled you all these years. I regret that."

She opened her mouth to speak, but could not think of what to say.

"I love you, Jane. But I can't be with you anymore," he said. "I want to be, I've tried to just get over what happened, but I can't."

Here it was then. The final blow. Jane felt all her defenses flare. She almost accused him of never wanting to be with her in the first place.

Desperate, heart racing, she said, "I made a mistake. A huge one, I realize. But David, don't you know how much I regret it?"

"The fact that you think it was a one-off is kind of the whole problem," he said. "We both know you've been trying to hide the truth about your drinking from me for years."

"That makes it sound so much worse than it is," she said.

"It wasn't just you. I hid the truth from myself," he said. "I buried my head in the sand, because it was easier. I want to explain that picture you saw of me and Angela on Facebook. There was nothing romantic about it. I asked her to meet me for dinner because I'm trying to take a moral inventory of myself. Trying to find out what it is about me and my lack of self-esteem that makes me think it's okay to be with women who lie to me."

Jane started to protest, to defend herself—Angela had had a full-blown affair. Jane's offense was nothing like that.

But David wouldn't let her interrupt.

"I needed to look Angela in the eye and ask her the questions I was too afraid to ask before."

"Was it helpful?" Jane said.

"It was."

"But why did she post a picture of the two of you on Facebook?"

"Because she's an idiot," he said.

They laughed, a sad sort of laughter, encompassing as it did the knowledge on both their parts that their connection wasn't gone, but it wasn't enough to keep them together.

Jane started to cry.

"I'm sorry," she said, and she meant it.

"I'm sorry too," he said. "You don't deserve this."

"Me? No, *you* don't deserve this," she said. After a pause, she added, "Well, I guess now we know what it's like when polite people end a marriage, huh?"

"We make a pretty pitiful sequel to *The War of the Roses*," he said.

Jane smiled.

"I should go. I'm sure we'll talk again soon," David said. "Take care of yourself, okay?"

Jane moved quickly from despair to panic. This was actually happening. She wasn't going home to him. Soon this house would belong to someone else. She had nowhere to live. No job. No partner.

Once, when they had been together maybe two or three years, David had a flare-up of insecurity about cheating. Jane took his face in her hands and said, "I would never want to be with anyone else but you. It's that simple."

And it was.

Now what. She would be alone for the rest of her life.

Take care of yourself. Take care of yourself. Wasn't that what Jane had always done? But how, after all this. How?

14

A FEW MORNINGS LATER, Walter started barking as if a murderer with a hatchet had entered the house, which meant the UPS guy was outside.

Jane had walked the dog early at his insistence and was now back in bed, with no plans to get out anytime soon.

She hadn't been able to sleep since David's phone call. All night, her mind looped around and around, as if there might be an outcome she hadn't considered yet, some secret path back to life as she once knew it.

Things had gotten very, very bad. None of the possible paths forward seemed appealing. None of the possible paths forward even seemed possible. Everyone wanted her to stop drinking, but if she did, then what? David wasn't going to take her back. Her job was gone. Her colleagues. White wine was the only friend Jane had left.

She couldn't bring herself to tell Allison what had happened, knowing Allison's reaction would inevitably contain some element of "I told you so." Even though she wouldn't say it out loud.

Jane wanted her mother. More than she could recall ever wanting her when she was alive. Jane interrogated this longing and remembered that when the one other big breakup of her life occurred, with her ex-boyfriend Andre, her mother had swooped in.

She drove down from Maine. She brought ice cream and tequila and a month's worth of *People* magazine and *Us Weekly*. She filled Jane's fridge with groceries and took her out for dinner, making an exception to her usual diet so they could both stuff their faces full of garlic bread and chicken parmesan. They got drunk on red wine, and Jane's mom narrowed her eyes and said in a deep voice, "Mark my words, Jane. Men. Is. *Dogs*." And then they both laughed so hard Jane thought she might throw up.

That visit had been so unlike her mother, who never stepped into her life generally. Jane had loved it. Then she had forgotten about it. She wanted some version of it now, more than anything.

Before Walter interrupted her thoughts by barking at the UPS guy, Jane had been thinking about Clementine, and working herself into a lather. She figured now that Clementine must be a researcher by nature, like she was. A deep dive into public records could have led Clementine to piece together that Jane's grandmother knew the Martinsons well enough for them to help her buy a house, that the Martinsons owned Lake Grove at the time, that they had a daughter who died there. This, Clementine spun into a story about the ghost of Marilyn and Herbert's daughter, sitting in the lap of the ghost of Jane's grandmother. It was despicable that someone could profit off strangers' grief in this way, but it made sense. Jane pictured Clementine and her fellow phonies at Camp Mira, sitting around counting their money and laughing at gullible idiots like her.

The only pieces of the story Jane couldn't make fit were Benjamin's ghost, a girl who wanted to reach her mother, just like D did—there was no way Clementine could have known about that when they met—and the fact that Jane had felt pulled to Lake Grove since she was a teenager, without ever knowing her grandmother had anything to do with the place.

Just before noon, Jane got out of bed and went to the kitchen to make coffee. She saw a cardboard box on the driveway and walked out in bare feet, crossing the lawn, to pick it up. The return address was in Philadelphia.

She brought the box inside and opened it.

It was stuffed with white tissue paper. A handwritten note lay on top, signed *Caitlin Rogers*.

Jane,

Here are the items from Marilyn's old house in Awadapquit. She did intend to send them to you. They are fragile. I've wrapped them as carefully as I could. There is a photo here of the Littletons, a hat that Marilyn said

*belonged to Mrs. Littleton, and letters she received from her brother during
the Civil War. Marilyn always wanted to see these go to the local historical
society, and I think she hoped you would get them there. As I believe you
are aware, her daughter Daisy died at that house in Maine. She is buried
there. Which made it too painful for Marilyn to ever return.*

Buried? Jane froze. *I'm not at Lake Grove anymore.* Had Daisy's remains
been dug up along with the Littletons? Is that what she wanted to
convey?

No sooner had this thought landed than Jane noticed the PS:

*PS As I write this, Marilyn is still in critical condition. You said you
had no idea what the connection between your family and hers was.
I've included a letter your grandmother sent Marilyn after the death
of her daughter. Since you're so curious about personal histories,
I thought this bit of your own might be of interest.*

Jane's heart sped up. Her chest fizzed with nervous energy. She
reached past the bonnet and the Civil War letters and the photo in
its brown paper sleeve, all of which would have thrilled her under
any other circumstances, until she came to a small white envelope
addressed to Marilyn Martinson, courtesy of a law office in Albany,
New York. The return address was for the house she was standing
in now.

Jane gently removed the pages of stationery, yellowed from age.
Her grandmother's handwriting was so familiar. Before she read a
word, Jane ran a finger over it.

She took a deep breath and began.

Dear Marilyn,

*I want to say from the bottom of my heart how sorry I am for the loss of
your beautiful Daisy. She was such a bright light. In the brief time I knew
her, I came to love her very much. Three years later, I still think of her
every day. I am certain I always will.*

*I regret everything that happened leading up to the night she died. In
my right mind, I am not the sort of woman who commits adultery. I hope*

you can believe that. This is no excuse but shortly before I met Herbert, as you know, my beloved husband passed away quite suddenly. In my grief, I found myself practically living at the bottom of a bottle of gin. That whole time is a blur. I barely remember anything.

I do remember when you came home to surprise Daisy for her birthday. She was delighted. I understood that morning that you were a far better mother than I. My own poor daughter was afraid of me. Shirley got the worst of my drinking. My husband's family had stopped speaking to me altogether because I was so far gone with the alcohol, and they couldn't stand to see what I was putting her through. I didn't understand that then.

I knew that morning when you showed up with a birthday cake that the affair with Herbert must end. It wasn't fair to you and Daisy. I did try to end it. I only wish I had tried harder.

I didn't think it possible that I could sink lower than I sank after losing my husband. But after Daisy died, I did. I thought of ending my life, but I couldn't leave my daughter behind. And yet, I made her life a living hell. When I drank, I became another person. I was neglectful. I yelled. Every time I saw my daughter, I thought of what I'd done to yours, and how I didn't deserve her. I think that is why I treated her like I did. Because I believed then that what might be best for us both would be if she was taken from me.

Eventually, she was. Shirley told her father's sister about our home life. My former sister-in-law did not come to me about it. She went to the police. I lost Shirley for close to a year. When I saw her again, she was a different person. Not a child anymore, really.

While we were apart, I started going back to church. The church of my youth. That has saved me.

Several months ago, I confessed all this to my priest. He recommended Alcoholics Anonymous meetings, to which I now go three times a week. I am one of two women at these meetings, an extra layer of shame on top of the rest. No other woman I know has tried to make her problems go away by drinking, a choice so particular to foolish men. Part of the program I am in is about making amends to those you have harmed. I can think of no one I have harmed more than you. I cannot imagine how devastated you still must be. I hope time has brought some measure of healing. This is probably a foolish thing to say, but if there is ever anything I can do to help you, even in some small way, please tell me.

And please forgive me if this letter causes you pain. Words will never be enough to convey how sorry I am. I pledge to live a more honorable life from this point forward. I have started taking classes toward my degree, in the hopes of becoming a teacher. I want to be a force for good in this world. The memory of Daisy, and of you, will never be far from my mind.

Yours,

Mary Flanagan

Jane was shaking when she finished. There were tears in her eyes.

So this was why her mother told her not to go near Lake Grove when she was a teenager. And why she told Holly that their grandmother must have told Jane the whole story. Because why else would Jane be so interested in that house?

She called her sister.

"You were right," she said.

"About what?" Holly said.

"Can I come over? There's something you should see."

Jane went straight to Holly's house with the letter.

Holly was waiting on the front stoop when she arrived. Jane thrust the letter toward her without introduction.

"Shit," Holly said, when she had finished reading.

She didn't seem as shaken by it as Jane was.

"Why aren't you as freaked out as I am?"

Holly shrugged. "Mom always said something terrible happened with the married guy Grandma was with. Like maybe a hit-and-run or something. She was pretty sure someone got killed that night."

"Seriously? Jesus, Holly."

"I told you all this."

"Did you know Grandma had a drinking problem?"

"Yeah."

"Why didn't Mom ever tell me?"

"She didn't want to burden you with it," Holly said. "You were the golden child. You were the one who was just going to waltz in and break all the shitty patterns. Mom knew a lot of that was down to you believing you had one sane, stable person in your family."

"Basically everything I thought about Mom and Grandma was a lie," Jane said.

"No," Holly said. "Grandma *was* sane and stable, when we knew her."

"Mom's childhood was so much worse than ours," Jane said.

Holly nodded. "That's definitely true."

"All the times I bitched about how much better a mother she had than we did. She never said a word to me."

"She spared you, Jane," Holly said.

"Why am I finding this out now?" Jane said. "When there is nothing I can do about it, when it's too late?"

Holly came over and hugged Jane, awkwardly. They were not a family of huggers.

Still, Jane tried to accept her sister's embrace.

TWENTY-FOUR HOURS LATER, Jane drove through the center of Awadapquit and out the other side. A month ago at this time of day, it would have taken her twenty minutes. But there was no traffic now. She zipped along in a quarter of the time, stopping at a farm stand to buy a mason jar full of sunflowers, cut short and tied with a purple ribbon.

A few miles more, and the buildings that lined the road turned over from cute motels and surf bars to the bland essentials of everyday life. Dentist offices, dry cleaners, gas stations.

Sunny Days Memory Care was down a small side road, but you could see the building from Route 1. The lot was nearly empty. Jane parked in a spot close to the door, as if she might need to make a quick escape.

Memory Care. Such a strange term for what went on here, she thought as she walked inside.

The woman behind the front desk wore pink scrubs. She was squinting at a computer screen and did not look up until Jane said, "Excuse me," at which point she met Jane's eye but didn't say a word.

"I'm here to see Betty Anderson. She doesn't know I'm coming."

It was clearly a stupid thing to say about a dementia patient, but the woman's expression remained fixed.

"Third floor. It's a locked unit. They'll buzz you in."

Jane rode the elevator up alone. She was nervous.

Through a small window in the locked door, she saw a woman talking on the phone at a desk. She too wore pink scrubs, though she was younger than the one downstairs, probably in her thirties. Jane rang the bell. The woman unlocked the door by pressing a button.

As Jane approached her, she smiled at Jane and held up one finger. Jane nodded in response. The woman sounded irritated as she explained to whoever was at the end of the line that the coffee machine was still broken and the last two guys they sent to fix it had no idea what they were doing.

Off to the side was a lounge with big, beat-up orange couches and a large fish tank. A dapper silver-haired man in a suit paced the floor.

"I don't even know him!" he shouted, to no one in particular.

A small old lady sat in the corner of one of the sofas, gently crying. Jane ached for her. Why was no one helping this person? She wanted to do it herself, but she was ill equipped for a thing like that. She wouldn't know what to say.

Another woman walked in from down the hall, holding a blue balloon.

"Balloon," she said to Jane, in a manner that made that one word sound like it was the funniest joke she had ever heard.

Jane smiled back.

"Can I help you?" the woman at the desk said finally, hanging up the phone.

"Hi," Jane said. "I'm Jane. I came to visit Betty. I'm her daughter Allison's friend. I hope it's okay that I came. I should have called ahead. I can come another time."

She actively wanted this woman to turn her away.

The woman clicked around on her computer screen, then said, "Jane Flanagan?"

"Yes."

"You're on her list of approved guests."

"Oh," Jane said. "That's great."

The woman smiled wide now. "You're the one who sends Betty flowers every week. I always tell her I'm jealous."

"It's the least I can do, given how good Betty has been to me," Jane said.

"Come on back. She's having a good day today."

Jane followed her down the hall.

"We're big fans of Allison's around here," the woman said over her shoulder.

"Me too," Jane said.

"She's so good to her mom. You wouldn't believe how many people in here never get a visitor. And she's wonderful to all of us too. She's always bringing us treats, keeping our spirits up."

"Sounds like Allison," Jane said.

"She was in this morning. Richard, too. Such lovely people."

They passed a room with a small wooden altar at the front and two pews on either side, a piece of stained-glass suction-cupped to the window. At first, Jane thought it was a real church of sorts, like the one-room chapels you sometimes found in hospital lobbies. Then they passed a room set up like a classroom—a chalkboard up front, three rows of two desks each, picture books on the shelves, and a map of the world on the wall.

As they approached yet another room, with the word NURS- ERY written on a piece of lined paper taped to the open door, she clenched. Jane didn't want to go any farther, but she did. Inside, an elderly woman sat tenderly rocking a baby doll. There were other dolls scattered around, in old playpens from the eighties. On a chang- ing table with real diapers. In a tiny doll-sized high chair.

Jane felt so uncomfortable, she forgot about her own problems for a minute.

The nurse stopped in front of a room that looked like any hospital room—linoleum floors, fluorescent lights, two adjustable beds with guardrails, one of them empty and neatly made. In the other bed, the one near the window, Betty lay, propped up on pillows, watching *Judge Judy* on a TV that hung high on the wall.

"Betty, love," the nurse said. "You have a friend here to see you."

Betty looked over at them. She smiled politely, then turned back to the show.

"Go ahead in," the nurse said. "I'll come check on you two in a bit."

Jane went toward her. Betty looked fearful, and that made her want to run.

"Hi, Betty," she said. "It's me, Jane."

Betty didn't seem to register the words.

"I'm your daughter Allison's friend. It's okay if you can't remember. I brought you some sunflowers. I know they're your favorite."

Betty gave her a suspicious look, like Jane was one of those guys who squeegees your car at a red light without asking and then expects you to pay him for it. She turned back to the TV.

The nurse had said Betty was having a good day. Jane wondered how she could tell the difference. Then she remembered stories Allison had told her about Betty throwing fits, throwing objects, screaming at people. She was still so young, hardly even any gray in her hair. She didn't look all that different, but a light was missing from her eyes. Her expressions were no longer hers. She looked like someone wearing a Betty mask. Jane wanted to hold her hand but she was scared this might set Betty off, or frighten her. She pulled a chair to Betty's bedside and pretended to be engrossed in what was happening on TV. They sat that way together for close to an hour.

There were versions of death that existed inside of life, Jane thought. Her drunken blackouts, that time unaccounted for. The state Betty and the other patients here were in, almost the opposite of being ghosts—a body with no awareness, no memory. The shadows of past lives all around in graveyards, in old houses, in Jane's work as an archivist. In stories.

Allison told Jane once that a person's oldest memories were the last ones the brain held on to, and that every so often, her mother would come out with some story about playing tetherball or going to the Sadie Hawkins dance, even though she had no idea who the president was or who her own husband was, for that matter.

On Betty's nightstand were framed photos of her children and grandchildren, and a shot of Betty and Richard on their wedding day.

Jane wondered if these were meant to jog Betty's memory, if they brought her comfort or confusion or no feeling at all. Maybe the pictures weren't even for Betty, but there as a reminder to the doctors and nurses that she had once had a life every bit as full as theirs.

A memory came to Jane, something she hadn't thought about in years. School picture day. An agonizing annual occurrence. Jane was acutely aware, even in elementary school, that the photographer took everyone's picture, including kids whose parents couldn't afford to buy them. Jane's mother never bought. Jane pretended otherwise, getting dressed up like her classmates. She did this all the way through high school. When, senior year, a packet arrived in the mailbox with the return address of the local photo studio, she felt a rush of gratitude. Her senior picture. Finally, she thought then, her mother understood how much it mattered.

Jane couldn't recall how she learned that it was Betty who ordered and paid for the images of her stiff smile in eight-by-ten, four-by-six, and wallet-sized glossies.

Betty never once said a bad word about Jane's mother. Jane looked hard at her now, asking a question in her head, since there was no reason to say it out loud: *Did you know? Did everyone know?*

How could all of Betty's kindness turn to this? Watching *Judge Judy* alone when she should be traveling the world with her husband, reaping the rewards of her hard work?

Suffering was relative. Jane had the luxury of knowing she could start again, even though she had no idea what that meant. The not knowing felt terrifying, but she was certain any one of the patients here would give the world to trade places with her.

At some point she took her phone from her purse and texted Allison. I'm so sorry. You were right, as usual. I love you.

Jane stayed with Betty all afternoon.

They didn't say much. Sometimes Betty responded to something on TV—she repeated the words in a toothpaste ad as if agreeing: "Minty fresh." She murmured pleasantries, like "Nice day out there," as if she was trying to recall how to make small talk.

Jane nodded and smiled and said, "Yes."

A nurse brought Betty's dinner in on a tray at five-thirty. Jane asked her if she should leave, and the nurse said, "No, I think she likes having you here, don't you, Betty?"

So Jane stayed another hour. At which point, she stood up and told Betty, "I've got to get going. I have somewhere to be. I'll tell you all about it next time."

She kissed Betty on the cheek.

Betty gave no sign of how she felt about the gesture, just continued staring at the TV.

The nurse who brought her dinner was in the hall.

"It's good you came," she said. "You don't know what it does for these patients to have visitors. Even if it doesn't feel that way. I read in the newspaper the other day, a woman was in a coma for four years. When she finally woke up, she said she heard every word the people around her said during that time. Can you imagine?"

Jane was still thinking of this as she got into her car, and when she started driving. She turned the idea over in her mind at the red light at the entrance to town, and as she turned onto Shore Road, and then, as she passed by the long driveway that led to Lake Grove.

Jane pulled over to the side of the road, car still running, and dialed Marilyn's number.

She knew Caitlin had most likely only sent her grandmother's letter out of anger, but in a way it had been the greatest gift. A message from her favorite person, a person she never thought she would hear from again. A confession. It was possible Caitlin had saved Jane's life.

Marilyn's phone went to voicemail, as Jane knew it would. She left a rambling message. She relayed what happened with Clementine, how Daisy—or anyway, D—wanted desperately for her mother to know she was at peace.

"Do with this what you will," Jane said. "I know it probably sounds completely crazy to you. It does to me too. I'm just passing it along in case it might bring you comfort, or, I don't know. Closure, maybe."

Jane thought about the terrible thing Genevieve had done. She doubted they would ever speak again. She thought of the basket Genevieve bought from Thomas Crosby, and wondered about its provenance, whether the hands that made it had belonged to someone who suffered, or survived, or both.

Human beings did so much damage to one another just by being alive. To the people they loved most, and to the ones they knew so little about that they could convince themselves they weren't even people.

Jane kept driving. Past her mother's house and all the way to the Presbyterian church at the corner of Shore and Main. She got a parking spot right out front. The meeting started at seven. The door was wide open.

TWO YEARS LATER

15

Naomi

NAOMI WAS IN her home office, working late, digging out from under what felt like a million letters and emails that had come in while she was away on her honeymoon in Niagara Falls.

An hour ago, a heavy rain had broken the day's heat. Now a strong breeze was blowing through the window screens, rattling the blinds. She liked the sound. Out back, Gerry was grilling salmon and corn on the cob. The smells wafted up to her, making her hungry.

Naomi took hold of a manila envelope, saw her cousin Barbara's familiar return address in the top left corner, and felt a jolt of curiosity. She pushed everything else to the side. In the envelope, on the topmost page, was a crude map, a photocopy of a line drawing. A stretch of land with a natural curve that poked out in the middle, like the nose on a face in profile. The nose pointed at a little uneven circle, meant to represent an island.

The map was marked up with familiar symbols. Arrows pointing east. A sun with seven lines beneath it to indicate the number of days spent there. The word *Sawadapskw'i* was printed on the page. Beside it, Barbara had stuck a pair of hot pink Post-it Notes, on which she had written: *The sender claims this is re-created from a birchbark map, which was in his family for centuries, but ultimately lost. No idea where this place was located, if it ever existed. He is Canadian, Abenaki, from Odanak, but he thinks (as you'll see) that the family originated in what is now southern Maine. Maybe northern New Hampshire? No such place-name exists in present-day Maine or NH as far as I can tell.*

Sawadapskw'i. The word was familiar, but Naomi couldn't put her finger on why.

She did a quick Google search. *Sawadapskw'i, Maine.* Nothing.

Sawadapskw'i, New Hampshire. No.

At the bottom of the envelope was a small, flat cardboard jewelry box. Naomi lifted the lid, peered inside. Two polished purple quahog shells sat on a square of cotton, each with a clean round hole drilled through the top. On a folded-up piece of lined paper, like the notes girls used to pass back and forth in high school, Barbara had written *Best wishes to the bride and groom.*

Naomi smiled, touched. Receiving wedding gifts for this, her third marriage, felt somewhat embarrassing, but she was trying to resist that reaction in herself. She was older now, wiser. This one was going to stick. Maybe people thought all newlyweds felt that way, but it wasn't so: the first two times, she had known on some level, even as she walked down the aisle, that they would not go the distance.

Anyway, she appreciated Barbara's well wishes. She appreciated Barbara, period.

The two of them were second cousins. They had met only a handful of times in their lives, but since they started working together a year ago, they texted and called one another several times a month.

Their mothers, first cousins, were raised together on Indian Island. Barbara's mother married a white man, during the period in the late forties when doing so meant giving up one's citizenship in the Penobscot Nation, and barred any future children from enrolling. Barbara's mother moved to California, where her new husband was stationed in the army. That branch of the family had remained out west ever since.

Barbara told Naomi that there were no outward symbols of their Penobscot heritage in her home growing up. When someone said to her mother, "You're so exotic-looking, what are you?" her mother would answer only, "I'm from Maine." (Fair enough answer to a stupid question, Naomi thought.)

She did hold on to certain private rituals, Barbara said. Her mother spoke to her ancestors daily, burned cedar and sage to bring them close. She told her children stories from Wabanaki mythology. About Gluskabe. About Azban the Raccoon, who challenged a waterfall to a shouting match and, receiving no reply, jumped into the waterfall to show he could shout louder, and was swept away. Every story contained a lesson. The moral of that one was: don't get too cocky.

Barbara had been to Indian Island only once, when their great-grandmother died. Naomi remembered meeting her then, this cousin from across the country, ten years her senior, so cool in her Levi's and boots.

Barbara had learned then that their great-grandfather, who had worked as a guide for wealthy tourists, showing them the best places to hunt and fish and set up camp in the area, had died young, under suspicious circumstances, from a gunshot wound to the head.

Their great-grandmother raised five children, all of whom had their struggles, on her own. Like most of the women on Indian Island at the time, she made a living selling baskets. She specialized in miniature sweetgrass baskets no bigger than a woman's thumbnail, but she made them in all shapes and sizes, at all hours.

Barbara had never been to a Catholic wake before then. Had never seen the way they laid the body out in front of everyone. She hadn't even known her mother's people were Catholic—baptized, confirmed, married, and educated at St. Anne's, buried at the southern tip of Indian Island in the church cemetery, which dated to 1668, the year French missionaries arrived.

Barbara said she remembered hearing on that trip that their great-grandparents spoke fluent Penobscot when they were young. But the language was gone from their kin now. She never heard her mother speak it. She herself didn't know a word.

She had never before felt the presence of her own large, close-knit family until then, how they teased one another and all knew the same stories, which had been told a hundred times. She loved baseball, but did not know until then that the first Indigenous player in the major league, Louis Sockalexis, grew up right there on Indian Island and joined the Cleveland Spiders (later called the Indians) all the way back in 1897.

Barbara said she remembered her mother crying on the flight home to California. They never returned to Maine.

On one of their long phone calls in recent months, Barbara said, "Mom never talked about what she was forced to give up when she married, but I know it crushed her. That policy was a form of genocide. The blood quantums they use now to establish membership are just a slower way of accomplishing the same goal. So many tribes only have another generation or two left. I've been reading about it. It's all rooted in eugenics, you know."

"Yes," Naomi said. "I know."

After Barbara's mom passed away two years ago, Barbara had gotten obsessed with learning more about this half of her heritage. She found Naomi on Facebook, read about her work, asked if she could be of assistance.

She had watched Naomi deliver a few lectures via YouTube. She said she loved the way Naomi introduced herself in front of a crowd. As "Naomi Miller, citizen of Penobscot Nation, daughter of Lucille, granddaughter of Beatrice, great-granddaughter of Rosie, mother of Wren."

That connection to family, Barbara said, the idea of them all as one unbroken chain, was what she had longed for all her life.

At first, Naomi was wary of the offer. She was used to working alone. But Barbara was a recently retired librarian. She turned out to be a tremendous asset. She could track down anyone or anything. She was a fast learner and understood online communities much better than Naomi did. There, she found stories and made connections Naomi never would have.

The Internet was terrible for many reasons, but in this way, it was magic. It brought people together who wouldn't otherwise have found one another. Naomi could have saved so much time had it existed when she first started this work thirty years ago.

WHEN SHE WAS TWENTY-TWO, a friend who worked for the tribal council helped her get a job in local government, working as the chief's secretary. Naomi's direct phone line was listed on all literature related to the Penobscot Nation, and in the phone book. She got every kind of call. People wanting a reference for an emergency plumber or a personal injury attorney or someone to talk sense into their teenage son, who refused to go to school. People angry about a neighbor's bamboo creeping into their yard, or worried about a particularly skinny stray cat they kept seeing around. A rotation of four elderly ladies who were lonely and just wanted to chat.

Naomi's parents raised her in a house ten miles east of the Penobscot River. She grew up near the reservation, but not on it. Through this job, though, she got to know what felt like everyone.

Two years after she started, she was getting itchy, planning her escape, applying to Teach for America, because she couldn't think of what else to do, when a package arrived on her desk. It contained several old black-and-white photographs of men in turkey-feather headdresses, standing together, looking straight at the camera.

A note said the sender, a man named Trip Baker, had found them while cleaning out his recently deceased grandfather's attic. The grandfather had been an anthropology professor and an amateur photographer. He must have visited the reservation sometime in the twenties or thirties. On the back of the pictures, he had written by hand, *Penobscot Men in Traditional Attire*.

The grandson wrote that he had recently seen and been moved by the Kevin Costner movie *Dances with Wolves*. He felt wrong being in possession of these photos, and considered it his duty to return them to the tribe.

"Good boy, Trip," Naomi said out loud at the time. "Here, have a cookie."

But a knowing crackled within her that told her this was something important, there was something here.

She only had to show the pictures to a handful of tribal elders before she got answers. One of them recognized his two great-uncles. They were able to piece together who most of the other men were too.

The tribe hadn't had camera equipment until the sixties. Any photos taken prior to that time were taken by outsiders, who possessed them, put them on display, but had no awareness of the stories attached to them, or the people in them. The photos were stripped of all context, meant to symbolize some idea of the exotic other. This went for recordings as well. Of their language, their songs, their traditions. Made by white visitors, and taken away from the people to whom they would matter most.

This had become her life's work. To locate all sorts of items, to reunite them with their stories and their descendants. To help outsiders and tribal citizens alike tell a richer, fuller version of events. It pleased her that in recent years the tribal council had voted to pro-hibit outsiders from taking photographs on Indian Island, without the express permission of the chief.

NAOMI HEARD GERRY's footsteps on the stairs as she looked again at that word, *Sawadapskw'i*. It was bugging her now, like a seed caught in her teeth that her tongue could not manage to wriggle out.

She decided to look it up, found it easily in Henry Lorne Masta, saw that she had underlined it, though she had no memory of doing so.

Gerry knocked gently at the office door, then came in with a cold beer for her.

"Dinner in fifteen?" he said.

"Sounds good."

He kissed the top of her head, sending a current through her.

Definitely going the distance.

After he'd gone, Naomi took a sip of beer. She set the green glass bottle down on a book on her desk, with silent apologies to the book for using it as a coaster. It was quite boring, but still.

Beneath the map Barbara had sent were several pages stapled together, printed in an old typewriter font. Or maybe someone had actually typed this up on a typewriter and it had been photocopied some untold number of times since. It was dated and signed at the top: *As told to Francois by Grandpa, and translated from French, October 3, 1987.*

Who was Francois? she wondered.

Another one of Barbara's pink Post-its here, marked up with her familiar looping handwriting: *Noteworthy because we never get anything this old.*

Naomi frowned. *This old? 1987?* But once she started reading, she understood.

As told to Francois by Grandpa, and translated from French, October 3, 1987.

This is a story of our ancestors, passed down through generations, to those who are worthy of hearing it. For centuries, it was told in longhouses throughout Wabanaki

Country in Winter when families gathered around their camp fires in the evening.

We have only an educated guess that our people started out in what is now called Maine, or perhaps in New Hampshire, and were forced to travel north. We do not know if, originally, they were Abenaki or Pennacook or something altogether different. But we are Abenaki now, living on the Odanak Reserve. This is the story of how we got here.

It began one summer, somewhere on the coast, in a place called Sawadapskw'i, on a cliff overlooking the sea.

It was there that a young man named Manedo—our twelfth great-grandfather—kissed his wife, Kanti—our twelfth great-grandmother—and told her: "Wait right here."

This was nearly four hundred years ago, when you could stand on that cliff, turn right, left, and backward and see only trees. Long before there was a house, a sawmill, a shipyard, a town, though all of that would come.

The spot on the cliff held great meaning for the couple. Their people camped by the nearby river each summer. It was tradition that on the night of a marriage ceremony, the elders led the newlyweds to that promontory, where a small wigwam had been erected. According to custom, a bride and groom would go there together for a time, just the two of them. Only then would they truly be married. They could always find the spot again because of the way the gentle curve of the land was interrupted there, jutting out like a fat finger into the sea, pointing toward a small island.

Those first nights with her husband were the happiest of Kanti's life. Before they left the cliff to return to their people, Manedo gave her a necklace of quahog shells he had made into beads, white with flashes of purple. The women in our family still wear these today. They receive them as wedding gifts.

A year after they were wed, Kanti and Manedo were once again on that cliff. He said goodbye, then left her there and went to the nearby beach to meet his friends. It was only supposed to be for a short time, but Kanti was worried.

From her spot, she watched the four men get into a canoe and glide across rippling water to a massive ship, anchored on the edge of the small island. They were dressed in deerskin. Their faces tinged red with ochre, bright blue lines added above their chins, lips, and noses—for protection, to draw the ancestors close.

Two weeks earlier, when the ship first appeared, they had taken it for an island itself. A floating island, unlike anything they had seen before. They couldn't understand how it didn't sink. From their neighbors, they had heard stories of fair-skinned fishermen who appeared and then were gone. But they had never seen them—maybe not quite believed in them—until then.

The men on the ship dressed strangely, smelled odd, had black fur covering their white cheeks. They erected a white cross on the island's rocky shore. For many days, they paddled around in canoes, exploring the nearby river, marshes, and creeks. When at last they came ashore to introduce themselves, they smiled. They offered gifts of tobacco pipes, jewelry, and rainbow-tinged peacock feathers. Around the council fire, the tribal elders decided to receive these strangers as friends.

It was early summer, the easiest and sweetest time of year. Planting was done. The weather pleasant and warm. The trees abundant in their green, green beauty. The ocean twinkled in the sunlight. The visitors praised the place. A land of plenty. The strawberries, they said, were twice the size of any they had seen and better tasting. They thrilled over a mussel with fourteen pearls inside, a sturgeon the length of two boys, salmon jumping up out of the water, as if begging to be caught.

They wanted to know the Indigenous people's words for everything. The white men would point to a tree, to the ocean, to a rabbit and ask what they would call it. One man wrote down the answers in a book. The white men asked their name, and were told that they were called People of the Dawn, because the sun rose on that coastline before it rose anywhere else, and for thousands of years, they had been there to greet it each morning.

Every night, our ancestors invited these visitors onto
the beach for celebrations. Just before sunset, they spread
deerskins on the sand around a fire—pots and kettles boiling,
venison and duck roasting on a spit. They danced and sang and
drummed. They brought enough tobacco to fill the men's pipes,
even though it meant depleting their own supply.

The ancestors could give those men nothing for which the men
did not offer them something in return. The men brought biscuits
and cloth. Glass beads, which all the women coveted for their
beauty, even if they were wary of the men's loud voices, and their
guns, something no member of that tribe had seen before.

After several nights, the visitors said they wanted to
repay the Native people's hospitality. They invited four men,
including Manedo, to come aboard the ship the next day for a
meal, and an exchange of gifts.

Someone lowered a ladder down as the canoe approached. One by
one, the men climbed up, took hold of a hand when they reached
the top, and were swallowed into the belly of the ship. Manedo
was last to board. Up the ladder he went, turning his head in his
wife's direction, where he knew she would be, before the stranger
pulled him over the edge.

From her spot on the cliff, Kanti kept watching the ship, even
when there was nothing to see. For hours, she sat there and wove
a basket for their home. The warp was a plaited bark base, the
wefts made of wool and cornhusk. She twined one and then the
other, again and again, to form a pattern that resembled birds
flying in formation. This skill was a gift from her ancestors,
which she would soon pass along to her own child. She was half
done when finally she sensed movement on the ocean. Relief
filled her body. But what she saw when she looked up was not the
men descending, returning, as she expected.

The ship itself was moving. Turning around. Relief drained
away. Terror took its place. She screamed, but no one heard. She
got to her feet, using her hands to support the new, strange
shape of her. She ran as fast as she could.

––––––––––

After Manedo was taken, Kanti went to the cliff early each morning and sat in that same spot, completely still. She heard the voices of ancestors in the waves. They told her he would come back. It was only a matter of time.

Her sisters took turns sleeping in her husband's place beside her at night until the baby came. Nuna. A beautiful girl, born with thick black hair.

Their people had a feast to celebrate the birth. They sang and danced. The drumbeat sounded out like a heartbeat, steady beneath it all. But Kanti felt full of poison. She did not love her daughter as she should. Her kin said the child resembled Manedo. Kanti wondered if this was why she felt that she had been made to trade him for her.

The feeling did not leave her, much as she wished it would.

Kanti begged her ancestors to help her love her child as she harvested the beans, dried and stored them for winter, carrying Nuna on the cradle board Manedo had made from split ash. As she carefully saved the seeds from the best plants to be planted a year hence. As she dried the corn, ground it to be eaten in leaner months, when they traveled inland for winter. All this preparation for a future she had no desire to live.

Terrifying possibilities filled her head. She thought of nothing else. Was her husband in pain, was he hungry? What were they doing to him? What would they do? Rumors flew. That Manedo and the others had been murdered. That the white men had gone upriver and captured five more Native men, and all nine captives had been sold to the Iroquois as slaves.

The not knowing drove her to near-madness. All night long, she wandered the cliffs alone.

The air turned cold. One morning the people heard the sound of wild pigeons flapping their wings, beginning their migration. This made clear that it would soon be time for them to leave as well.

Kanti begged her mother and sisters to take her child and let her stay behind. She had promised her husband she would wait. He would need her when he returned.

The elders said that in her grief, she could not see clearly. That she would die if they left her there alone.

Pebonkas, the winter-maker moon, appeared in the sky, a signal that they must go.

On the marriage cliff, Kanti left Manedo a basket of food—dried fish and venison and squash, and the sweet acorns of a white oak tree. She left a trail of quahog shells, pointing in the direction they would take the next morning.

The food was devoured by animals. The shells were soon covered in snow.

Every spring thereafter, Kanti went straight to the cliff each time her people arrived at Sawadapskw'i. She looked out toward the little island, half expecting her husband to appear. Some years, she brought their daughter with her and told her stories about him. Some years, she went alone, intending to jump, imagining her body smashing against rock, putting an end to her despair. But what if the moment she died, Manedo came back?

Two of the four men did return, which gave Kanti hope. The first arrived a few years after they vanished, aboard a ship from England, carrying a hundred men, women, and children who planned to settle there. He moved back in with his own people, but visited the English every day, to negotiate on their behalf for food and furs. His position as a close relative of two chiefs made him the ideal man for the role, and he seemed to take pride in wielding his power on both sides, the single person who spoke both languages and understood the intentions of all involved.

One can only imagine how Kanti felt, watching this. How certain she must have been that Manedo never would have helped those people, his own kidnappers. Watching his friend do so must have seemed to her like a betrayal, though perhaps he only understood earlier than the rest that this would be one way to survive.

————

The winter that followed was brutal. By the time Kanti's people returned to the coast in the spring, many of the English had died from sickness and starvation. A fire had destroyed their houses and what remained of their supplies. Those still alive got back aboard their ship and sailed home.

Three summers later, the second man returned. N'tahanada. Manedo's cousin and dear friend. He told Kanti that they had been held together in a place called London, where they lived in the household of a man with great wealth and influence. They were at once this man's captives and his guests. Fed and kept warm, given their own spacious quarters. But they were not allowed to go anywhere alone. They had to perform on command—they were put on display in skins and face paint, made to demonstrate skills with bows and arrows. They were paraded around, shown as curiosities from a faraway land.

London, N'tahanada said, was like nothing he had ever seen. There were longhouses as big as mountains. Some people had beautiful jewels and furs, enormous homes with more rooms than there were bodies to fill them. But most people had nothing. They begged for food and slept exposed to the cold and rain, on footpaths, where strangers walked past them as if they were not there. The English, he said, were a brutal people. He had seen men hanged for their crimes in a public square. When they were close to death, they were taken down, still conscious, and disemboweled, beheaded, their penises chopped off, their hearts removed, and what remained of them hacked to pieces. Throughout it all, a crowd gathered to watch and cheer.

From the start, their captor assured Manedo and N'tahanada he would send them home when his needs had been met. But first, he wanted every detail of life in the Dawnland. Their names for every bird and berry. The location of each island, river, and safe harbor. Lists of their enemies and their friends. Their ways of making decisions, of choosing leaders, of shaping their days and years. He wanted to know all this, N'tahanada said, even though much of the time, their most basic ways of being made no sense to the English.

N'tahanada told Kanti those men could not comprehend what it meant to see and honor what Creator provides. Only the possibility for what it could become. He and Manedo had heard one sailor talk about the oak trees in the Dawnland, except he didn't call them trees. He called them masts for ships of 400 tons.

Those men never meant to go to Sawadapskw'i. They were looking for someplace else. But after they arrived and saw how plentiful the land was, they came to believe their god led them to discover it, and must want them to stay. They did not understand that the land was not place alone. That the land was kin.

After one year, Manedo and N'tahanada's captor said they could go home. Their ship made it as far as Puerto Rico, where they were intercepted by enemies from Spain. All aboard were taken captive and hauled there, in chains. N'tahanada and Manedo were separated and sold into slavery. Years passed. N'tahanada had resigned himself to the thought that he would die a slave in a land where he knew not a soul. And then one day somebody came for him. He was free. When at last freedom was granted, though, Manedo could not be found. No one was able to account for where he ended up, or if he was even alive.

Soon, Kanti's people once again saw ships on their horizon. They never had any peace after that. What happened next is well established. The English came in droves, intent on staying, no matter the cost. They believed their god sent illness to erase the Native people from the new world they were making. In the first wave of disease, three out of every four of them were killed. Yet even as the English killed them, the Native people came to depend on them. The metal the white men brought could be fashioned into spearpoints, fish hooks, knives, and needles so that all their work could be done in a quarter the time. They traded iron pots, and guns, changing their ways.

At the trading post, the English introduced the local men to rum. The tribal elders believed they did it so they could trick their men and cheat them out of what they deserved. The men stumbled home out of their senses, as they had never done before. The white men's cattle roamed all over the Native people's land, destroying their corn. The pace at which the English took down trees made so many parts of their lives impossible. Much of the woods where their men had hunted for thousands of years was destroyed. The planting grounds beside the river were forever altered. Food no longer grew there. Congested with the output of the sawmills, the river itself ceased to be a feasible highway, as it had been for thousands of years.

When they arrived at the coast the thirty-seventh spring without Manedo, as she always did, Kanti followed the path through the woods that led to their spot on the cliff. She no longer expected to find her husband there. But she could feel him present in that place, the last place they ever touched, in a way she didn't elsewhere.

Before the ocean even came into view, she had a shock. Where once there had been a thick canopy of trees, she found a clearing. In the middle of it, a house, built of logs. She got close enough to see a leather bucket by the door, a pile of firewood.

A man appeared from inside, and pointed a gun at her. He yelled, but Kanti couldn't understand what he said.

She ran back to her people, just as she had run for help all those summers before, the day they took Manedo away, though she was the head of the family now. She found N'tahanada, told him what had happened. He went into his wigwam and emerged, knife in hand.

She led him back to the house.

The man was still outside, gun aloft, as if waiting for them.

He and N'tahanada shouted back and forth in English. When at last, the man went back inside, Kanti asked N'tahanada what he said.

"He said you were trespassing on private property. That he was given a grant to build a sawmill on the river, and as part of the agreement, he got this land as well, for his home, and he pays a tax of four pounds to prove it."

None of this made sense to her. This house was built on a cliff that was sacred to her people. Sacred to her. Why did he think it belonged to him?

Before the English arrived, even war had its season. After, attacks could happen anytime. The two sides went through periods of bloody fighting and periods when they simply coexisted, or attempted diplomacy. Things would seem to have improved and then, without warning, another attack. This went on for decades. There was so much loss that no band looked as it once had. Instead they were made up of fragments, survivors thrown together, turned into something new.

Squandro, sachem of the Sokokis tribe on the Saco River, was known to have coexisted peaceably with the English in the fifty years since they came to live on his people's land. He was a good man. Given a white child as a slave, he found her family and returned her to them.

One day, English sailors came upon his wife and baby out in a canoe. One of the sailors had heard that the Native people's infants knew how to swim from birth. The other didn't believe it. They tipped the canoe over to see who was right. The baby drowned, despite his mother's best efforts to save him.

Squandro had no choice but to seek retribution. An uprising began that would last three years. Tribes banded together, united against a common enemy. The white men murdered Weetammo, chief of the Pocasset, chopped off her head, and displayed it on a pike. The white men stretched nets across their rivers to stop fish from swimming up to their villages. They banned trade of shot and powder, making it harder for Native people to hunt. They wanted them to starve, to die from hunger, with plentiful food not far away. Many did.

Is it any wonder that one day, when the Englishmen were busy in the fields and fishing boats, Kanti's people cut off access to their village, where the women and children were waiting, and burned everything, their men going from one cabin to the next in a fury?

That day, for the first time in many years, Kanti went to the marriage cliff, to watch from a distance, unafraid of the man in the house. Old age had freed her from fear.

The man was gone. The house was gone. Burned to the ground earlier that morning. The ash pile still smoldered. Later, her daughter's husband told her that the man's sawmill had been burned as well, a message that their people would no longer tolerate the English way of life, which had made their own nearly impossible.

Her daughter's husband not only spoke English, but could write in it. Kanti felt like they were from a world that had no place for her. They were born into all this suffering. Had the mothers of her generation known what was coming, would they ever have brought children into existence?

By the time a peace treaty was signed, six thousand English had been killed or driven away. A few, taken captive, tried to escape. As punishment, their noses and ears were cut off. They were burned at the stake.

The Native people were almost all dead, or else had been sold into slavery in Barbados, Bermuda, Jamaica. Spain. A place Kanti could not picture, but which always felt familiar because it was where her husband was, most likely, whether alive or dead.

She had long since stopped talking about Manedo. She knew no one could understand how much she missed him. How often she imagined how different life would have been if he had stayed. In a place teeming with murder and violence, illness and death, what value could one man's life hold? Except that he was her world. Impossible to comprehend how a love so strong as theirs had no power to save him.

The few who survived that fight went north, to Canada, where it was said, for some time, the French had been friends to their people.

Nuna and her husband and children wanted to go, but they would not leave Kanti behind. She begged them to. She had heard the French were far kinder than the English. The English wanted their land. The French wanted their souls for Christ. Up north, she was told, Catholic missionaries helped with food and shelter.

The day Kanti died, she made her daughter promise that she would leave. They would be safer in Canada. Another place Kanti had never seen, and never would.

She was happy to die. She had lasted far longer than most.

In her final seconds, Kanti closed her eyes and she was back on the cliff, with Nuna still in her belly, and Manedo walking away to meet the others. She saw him appear on the beach and hug his friends hello. They were about to depart in the canoe, when Manedo suddenly decided not to go. He walked away, down the beach and into the woods. He was nervous, he came back to tell her so. Later, when they saw the unimaginable sight of a stranger's ship taking their friends away, they were together, at least.

Her daughter buried her on the marriage cliff. In her grave, beneath a blanket of birchbark, Kanti wore her wedding garments, the necklace of quahog shells around her neck. Such kindness from a dear child to whom she was never kind enough. Nuna understood without being told that this was where her mother belonged. Where all her memories resided, as etched into the earth as the quartz that ran like veins through the cliffs.

Kanti would wait right there. Manedo said to wait.

There was a third pink Post-it on the final page, on which Barbara had written in all caps, DO YOU THINK THERE COULD BE ANY TRUTH TO THIS STORY? SEEMS LIKE A MAJOR FIND IF SO!

Naomi touched the quahog shells on her desk.

She looked at the map. Again, she stared at the word. *Sawadapskw'i.*

Was there truth to it? As for all the brutality and destruction in general, yes, of course. As for the kidnapping of those four men in particular, perhaps. Such things had happened many, many times in those terrible years.

About the woman, Kanti. Well. No one ever wrote down what

women did, let alone how they felt. Naomi had no idea if there ever was a Kanti, if there truly was a marriage cliff someplace. She hadn't heard of such a tradition. She would have to ask certain elders who knew such things if they ever had.

The story felt vaguely familiar to her, like déjà vu, or something left over from a dream.

She was about to call Barbara to discuss. Naomi had so many questions. Where had the story come from? Where did Barbara find this family?

But all that would have to wait. Downstairs, Gerry had put on a Lucinda Williams album she loved. He called up to her that dinner was ready.

MANY HOURS LATER, long after they had gone to sleep, Naomi woke up in the stillness of their bedroom and had her answer. It was as if someone whispered it in her ear. *Sawadapskw'i*. She recognized the word because she had underlined it for Jane Flanagan, suggested maybe it was the original place-name of the town where Jane lived, the one called Awadapquit now. And hadn't Jane mentioned a story out of that area, of men kidnapped by some early explorer?

Jane had opened a little museum down there. She was eager to include stories about Wabanaki people. She asked Naomi for advice sometimes; hired her to consult on certain projects.

Naomi wished she could call Jane now. She had a feeling Jane was going to be all over the story Barbara had sent. But it was five in the morning so she tried to sleep instead.

When that didn't work, she looked over at her husband. She allowed herself to imagine that there really was a woman who had been waiting four hundred years somewhere, on a cliff, for her love to return. Naomi was not a romantic by any stretch. But in this moment, at this hour, in the light of the almost-dawn, she believed.

16

Jane

THE SOUND OF tires on the long driveway made her pause at the window. The first guests of the day had arrived, thirty minutes ahead of the museum's opening. Jane would let them in early if they wanted. She was excited to show off the new exhibit on the lives of Shaker women in Maine.

As on most days, the baby had been up at five. Now, at eight-thirty, she was likely down for her morning nap at home with the sitter. Jane wished she could join her. She had never known such exhaustion in her life.

Three weeks from now, Mary would turn one. On the two-year anniversary of Jane's sobriety, as fate would have it. These twin miracles, her not drinking and the birth of her daughter, were linked. Impossible to imagine one without the other.

Jane watched the car park off to the side of the house. A couple, maybe sixty years old, got out and walked across the lawn. Jane had set up two picnic tables several feet from the cliff's edge. The couple sat at one of them, side by side.

They would be the first to see the exhibit. Jane had spent weeks putting it together. She visited Sabbathday Lake several times, poring over detailed records of every day spent in that village over two hundred years, marveling at the farm's beauty and its strangeness.

She looked at pictures of so-called gift drawings, made there in the nineteenth century. They were beautiful, brightly colored images that, the story went, far exceeded the abilities of the young women who made them. Messages from spirits, working through young girls. The drawings weren't meant to be seen outside the community. Most had been destroyed. But those that survived now sold for tens of thousands. They hung in museums, showcased in a way that would have mortified Shakers of the time.

There were only three Shakers left on earth, and they all lived at Sabbathday Lake. The oldest, a woman brought there as an orphan, was ninety-four. The other two, men in their fifties, joined as young adults. One of them, Brother Michael, spoke with crisp matter-of-factness. He was a sort of self-appointed spokesperson for the group.

"Most of the people here from day to day are tourists now," he told Jane. "This is a place to visit once, on vacation, the day it rains. The visitors know about the furniture the Shakers made and they know one song out of ten thousand we sang, and they know that Shakers were—are—celibate. On the way back to their cars, they joke about how this was a bad plan, in terms of keeping a religion afloat. Each thinks he is the first to make the joke."

Jane smiled at this.

"But it is rare," he went on, "that any of them deeply considers our beliefs—revolutionary at the start, and revolutionary still. Pacifism. Equality of the sexes and races. The goal was utopia. Imagine what the world could have been had they listened."

Instead, one by one, the villages closed. And yet he remained optimistic. Mother Ann Lee, the group's founder, had, he said, prophesied that the Shakers would get down to fewer members than a child could count on one hand and then a revival would come.

Jane knew nothing about the Shakers prior to this. She had no clue such a place existed in Maine. It was her assistant, Jessie, who discovered that Eliza Green, the Littletons' maid, had been raised a Shaker at Sabbathday Lake. That's where the idea for the exhibit began.

The idea for the museum itself had started to form a few weeks after Jane's first AA meeting two years earlier, though she did not realize it at the time. Lydia had just hired Jane to help make sense of all the papers kept by the town historical society and to revive the idea of finding a permanent place to display them. The pay was a fraction of what Jane made in her previous job, but she was grateful for it. For now, she told herself.

At the last minute, she had told Holly she wanted to back out of selling their mother's house. Jane swore she would find a way to buy her sister out officially, in time. To her relief, Holly was happy about this.

Allison was elated. "You're staying!" she said.

"For now," Jane said, those two words becoming a sort of mantra.

That following winter, during the town's annual Christmas stroll, the final weekend before stores and restaurants shut for the winter, Jane ran into Priscilla Bingham, who served on the alumnae board at the Schlesinger when she was there.

"Jane!" she said. "How nice to see you."

Jane resisted the urge to run away, to sink down into her shame. She took a deep breath.

"How have you been, Priscilla?" she said.

"Good. My sisters and I are here for the weekend, doing a bit of holiday shopping. You too?"

"Actually, I live here now," Jane said, even though it didn't feel quite true.

"I'm jealous!" Priscilla said. "We just went to look at a house a friend of a friend is selling. Gorgeous place. It's the talk of our social circle back home. The woman who owns it wanted a pool but there was no room, so she dug up an old *cemetery* in order to put one in."

"Genevieve," Jane said.

"Yes, you know her?"

"I do."

"Strange woman," Priscilla said, and shook her head.

Jane remembered then how Genevieve had told her they knew each other. She had said kind things about Priscilla at the time.

"I didn't realize she was selling," Jane said. "Are you thinking of buying the house?"

"No, no. I just wanted to see it. My friend Leslie Davenport found out about the cemetery thing when she was up visiting Genevieve last summer. She told a few people. It's all just taken on a life of its own. So now they're selling. And from what I hear, no one wants to buy."

Immediately upon saying goodbye to Priscilla, Jane looked the house up online. There it was, Lake Grove, listed for three million dollars.

Genevieve had only owned the house for a little over a year, most of which she had spent renovating. She barely got to live there.

Jane couldn't get that exchange with Priscilla out of her head. She had not yet reached the making amends stage of AA, but she felt a need to do so with Genevieve, sooner rather than later.

It was March before Jane worked up the nerve to call her. She was surprised when Genevieve answered the phone.

Jane explained that she was sober now and so sorry for the distress she had caused.

"It was horrible that I barged into your home and accused you of those things in front of your friends," she said. "I never would have done that if I hadn't been drinking."

Genevieve didn't respond.

"I hope that isn't why you're selling," Jane said.

Genevieve sighed. "I just want to move on from the whole situation," she said. "I wish I had never seen that house. I am sorry for what I did, Jane. But you should know, I've paid a price for it. Everyone thinks I'm nuts. Even my own husband. I've been shunned by some of my closest acquaintances."

My closest acquaintances. Allison would have laughed at that. But Jane thought of the time they went to Camp Mira and Genevieve said she wished she could have a friend like Jane and Allison were to each other. Despite everything, she felt a little bad for Genevieve. The silver lining of being a total fuck-up was that you could sometimes find the grace to give others a pass for their failings. Or if not a pass, at least some understanding.

"We're probably being shunned by some of the same people, come to think of it," Jane said. "We should compare notes."

Jane told Genevieve about why she had been in Awadapquit the previous summer. She told her her marriage was officially over, and that she had lost her job.

"I'm sorry," Genevieve said. She sounded sincere. "What will you do now?"

Jane explained that she was trying to raise money and find a place for the local historical society.

They hung up on good terms, Jane thought, agreeing to keep in touch.

Lake Grove sat on the market through the end of the following summer, even after they lowered the price twice. There weren't many buyers who could afford such a house in this area. A good number of those who could probably knew why Genevieve and Paul were selling, and wanted no part of it.

A year after they listed the house, Genevieve surprised Jane by calling her with a proposition: Lake Grove could be the location of the new historical society.

Her husband had agreed to sell it at a cut rate if the town would purchase soon. There were a few other financial stipulations, which would benefit Genevieve and Paul tax-wise. And one more thing: they wanted the place to be named in their honor.

Jane understood that this was likely the only way they could think of to save face. Throw money at the problem, like they always did. She told Genevieve she would call her back.

Lydia was crazy about the idea. Antique houses were her great love. Such a backdrop, she said, would give the historical society a warm feel and, at the same time, imbue the objects on display with heightened meaning.

The town council rejected their proposal for funding to buy the property, even at a reduced rate. But simultaneously, Jane had submitted the idea to Historic Homes of New England, the organization where her friend Evan once worked, which bought up old estates and farms and houses for this very purpose. She wrote an impassioned pitch, beginning with a quote she had never forgotten, from that professor she had studied with for two seconds at Bates when she was in high school: *Most lives will be lost to time.*

Jane detailed how the museum's focus could be the real women who lived in the house, in the context of their historical moments.

HHNE loved the idea. They hired Jane to be the museum's director.

She felt grateful to Lydia, and in a way, to Genevieve, for giving her a purpose again. Though certainly Genevieve tested the extent of her gratitude. When Genevieve showed up unannounced one day with a television crew from the local New England show *Chronicle,* to film a segment some paid publicist had arranged about her extreme generosity and commitment to preserving the past. When an article appeared in *The Boston Globe* with the headline AFTER WORKERS

MADE A GRIEVOUS MISTAKE, A HOMEOWNER RIGHTED THEIR WRONG. And when, as agreed upon, Genevieve had a plaque hung directly above the one honoring Samuel Littleton, with the words MADE POSSIBLE BY PAUL AND GENEVIEVE RICHARDS. It was gross and ridiculous, but it felt to Jane like a reasonable price to pay for what they got in return.

Jane repopulated the house with the belongings of its former inhabitants. The town provided the funds to buy back Hannah Littleton's mourning ring. At an antiques shop on Route 1, Jane tracked down the sign from the Lake Grove Inn that Genevieve swore had gone in a dumpster.

John Irving, the junk guy Genevieve hired when she emptied the house, gave Jane three boxes of random items he hadn't been able to sell, including a portrait of the Troy sisters, the same one that hung over the fireplace for decades. And twenty glass bowls and wine goblets of unusual shapes and sizes, which Jane now knew were a hallmark of Marilyn Martinson's work. These Jane arranged in the butler's pantry, where they had always lived. In the center, she placed a crystal vase and kept it full at all times with daisies.

Jane looked further into Samuel and Hannah Littleton's children. James became a school principal in New Hampshire. Frances moved north, close to the Canadian border, having married a furrier from Montreal. She lived to be a hundred and two. Her obituary listed ten children, nineteen grandchildren, and thirty-five great-grandchildren. It also said no one ever called her Frances. For as long as anyone could remember, she'd been Fannie.

Rose Littleton, Samuel's distant relative who still lived in Awadapquit, put Jane in touch with one of Fannie's great-granddaughters, a doctor in Toronto named Mabel. Mabel donated two jade green china plates and one bowl to the museum, with a note explaining that they were what remained of a set that Samuel Littleton brought back from a voyage to Europe. Mabel also told Jane that Hannah Littleton's only sister had been an unusual woman for her time. Agnes Crosby, a newspaper writer and temperance movement leader, was, in the way of small towns, connected to Thomas Crosby, the collector of Indigenous artifacts who sold Genevieve her basket. Agnes's husband, Leonard, was Thomas Crosby's great-great-uncle, and had passed along both his own dubiously acquired collection and his passion for such things when he died.

Agnes had a place in the museum now, in a corner of the former dining room, the room dedicated to Hannah.

Jane decided early on that in addition to the permanent collection, the museum would have one or two rotating exhibits, all of which were tangentially related to one of the women of Lake Grove. Ideas for such exhibits cropped up in the strangest ways. Upon learning the museum existed, elderly locals and history buffs and amateur geneal-ogists came with mementos and stories. The Troy sisters in particular were the subject of fascinating rumors. An old woman who grew up in Awadapquit and now lived two towns away told Jane that Ethel's fiancé had not abandoned her or dodged the war, as the story had it, but that in fact he was an abusive drunk, and she and her sister Honey had killed him, hiding his body in the small secret bedroom upstairs and, one night, under a full moon, tossing it off the cliff.

"Another ghost," Allison said when Jane told her.

"Yes, this place is crawling with them," Jane said.

In fact, there had been no further sightings of the ghost Jane had decided was Daisy after Benjamin left. But then, whenever Jane brought Walter to work with her, he would run straight to the edge of the cliff and stop at the farthest point out, where the land jut-ted into the sea. He barked and barked and danced around in circles on his hind legs. Always in that spot. As if greeting someone. Even though Walter barked at everything, when he did it there, Jane was reminded of something Clementine had said: *Animals can sense the pres-ence of spirits.*

Sometimes she wondered if her grandmother lingered here. Jane thought of the women who had spent time in the house as being in conversation with one another. They had so much in common, when you thought about it. Her grandmother and Eliza Green had washed the same windows and polished the same floors, a hundred years apart.

Once, at an AA meeting, Jane met a woman in her eighties who had known her grandma.

"Not many women in AA back when we started," she said. "The two of us were pioneers."

At Jane's first several meetings, she fought the urge to leave. She kept thinking she didn't belong. Everyone else was so much worse off than she was. One woman had spent years in prison, after a drunk driving accident that left three people dead, including her own brother.

But when Jane told her story to the group, no one said, *AA seems like an overreaction,* as she imagined they might. She got the same sympathetic nods and knowing winces as everyone else.

She now went four times a week. She ran there and back on nice days, sweating on arrival, heart pumping hard. There were moments when Jane thought of how her mother and grandmother once sat in that same room and told stories about their lives that she would never hear. She missed them both. She thought she would do just about anything to have the chance to introduce them to her daughter.

Jessie's car pulled up in front of the museum at a quarter to nine. She came in through the kitchen door, which they referred to as the staff entrance.

"We've got a couple of live ones out there," Jessie said. "Are you pumped to give the first official tour? I know how excited you are to geek out on the Shakers."

Jane smiled. "I am," she said.

Most days, it was just the two of them here. Jessie was twenty-four. When they met, she was working at the fancy coffee shop in the cove. As she handed Jane her latte across the counter one morning, Jane noticed she had a line from Emily Dickinson tattooed on her wrist: *That it will never come again is what makes life so sweet.*

Jessie had recently graduated from Emerson, with a major in gender studies and a minor in American history. She wanted to be a writer. She had celebrated her ninth, tenth, and eleventh birthdays by visiting Louisa May Alcott's Orchard House in Concord, Massachusetts.

Jane was thrilled to know the world was still producing girls like this. Or one of them, at least. When Lydia said they had space in the budget to hire an assistant, Jane thought immediately of Jessie. Throughout Jane's own career, at every stage, women who saw something in her had given her a chance. They were often the ones who had made it on their own. It was like the opposite of an old boys' club. Women connected by their lack of connections, helping one another rise.

In the early days, Jane and Jessie traveled around New England to various museums for inspiration.

There was one exhibit that moved Jane to tears, on the subject of Native Americans and epigenetics, the newish field of study that said the effects of mass trauma—genocide, slavery, colonialism—got passed down from one generation to the next at the cellular level. Native Americans referred to this as the soul wound. Some believed it played a role in high rates of addiction, mental illness, suicide, and sexual violence in their community today.

If trauma could be passed down from the cells of one body to another, Jane wondered, was it so much further a leap to imagine that trauma might infect the land on which it happened? Was that a form of haunting all its own?

New England was bursting with signs and statues commemorating firsts—America's oldest weather observatory or chocolate factory or pub. But how many firsts came before the ones this country celebrated? How many went unrecognized? In this place she was building, Jane wanted to make clear that the beginning of American history was Indigenous history. As much as she thought of the women who had lived in the house at Lake Grove, she was keenly aware of the ones who came before them.

With consultation from Naomi Miller, she created an exhibit on Awadapquit's Indigenous women, and what their lives might have been like. Jane was trying to learn more about the language, since Naomi had taught her that was an essential piece of understanding how the story got told. The Abenaki word for history was ôjmowô- gan. Rather than a static event from the past, it conveyed an active, ongoing collective practice. Something ever-cycling, ever-evolving, building upon itself.

Here too Jane found overlap. She was delighted to learn that for a few years now, there had been an annual festival of Wabanaki crafts and music held at Sabbathday Lake, the Shakers and the Wabanaki having established kinship and commonality between them.

Jane was far from alone in her desire to tell a bigger, more complicated, more complete story of America. Things were shifting in her field. Because she was on the lists for various news alerts pertaining to Native American culture, one day a press release appeared in her inbox announcing an Inclusive and Reparative Language conference at the Schlesinger.

She was pleased and not surprised to see that Melissa was trying to navigate the same terrain she was. The Schlesinger had formed a committee dedicated to assessing and shaping the library's descriptive practices with an eye toward recognizing bias, replacing inaccurate, insensitive language, and bringing more voices in. Had the conference been anywhere else, Jane probably would have gone. But she wasn't ready to see Melissa. Not yet.

JANE GLANCED OUT the window and saw the couple at the picnic table. She assumed now that they knew the museum opened at nine and weren't going to attempt to get in any earlier. They were rule followers. She liked them already.

The man reached for the woman's hand. Jane felt a twinge of envy. She looked away. She thought of David.

He came to visit every few weeks. More often lately, Jane had noticed, though she didn't say anything about it, not wanting to upset their delicate balance.

Shortly after she moved into her mother's house officially, David brought some of her belongings from their old apartment. They were cordial to one another. They had nothing left to fight about. Divorce proceedings were underway and the whole thing was going to be quick. Neither of them wanted anything from the other. It was a bit shocking how easy it was to end their marriage. Nothing had tied them to one another except for their mutual desire to be there.

He wanted her to have her things, especially her grandmother's wing chair, which Jane had taken from every home she ever lived in to the next. David offered to deliver it all himself. She imagined him dropping everything on the porch and running away. But to Jane's surprise, he rang the bell. She invited him in and they sat together in the living room and talked.

Eventually, David said he had to go. But instead of leaving, he kissed her. They ended up having sex on the sofa. Strictly speaking, unprotected sex with one's soon-to-be ex-husband was not the recommended course of action at three months sober. But Jane would always feel lucky that things happened the way they did. Mary was conceived that day.

She and David hadn't slept together since. He was in the delivery room when Mary was born, along with Allison. In the early weeks, he sometimes slept on the sofa in the nursery and did the night feedings so Jane could sleep. At that point, with hormones raging and what felt like a whole new language to learn, Jane cried after he left, every time, wanting him entirely or not at all.

But she had gotten the hang of her new life, mostly. She and Mary had it down. It was hard to imagine someone else being there with them all the time. When David visited now, it felt comfortable. The two of them would bask in the delights of their daughter and after she went down for a nap, they'd sit together on the back deck and catch up. He kissed Jane goodbye on some occasions and not on others. She could never predict when it would happen.

She sensed David still moving through it all, trying to figure out what he could forgive, what he could live with. They loved each other, and said so. They had made a perfect baby girl together. Even if that was all they could ever be, it was enough. When they were married, it felt impossible to imagine settling into the expected family dynamic—husband, wife, kids. The only plausible scenario, then, was for them to break apart. Jane never thought to imagine them settling into something unexpected instead.

THE GRANDFATHER CLOCK in the foyer struck nine. Jane opened the front door.

The couple walked toward her. She waved.

In the kitchen, her cell phone rang. She thought Jessie must have switched it off, because it went silent right away. But in fact, seeing the name of the caller, Jessie had picked up.

"Jane!" she called out moments later, her voice full of excitement. "It's Naomi on the phone. There's a story she wants you to hear."

Acknowledgments

Here, at the end of the years-long process of writing my sixth novel, I feel overwhelmingly grateful.

To my agent, Brettne Bloom, and my editor, Jenny Jackson: Dear friends and brilliant collaborators. What a privilege to have spent the last decade and a half telling stories with you.

To Reagan Arthur, Emily Reardon, Maria Massey, Sara Eagle, Lisa Silverman, Jason Gobble, and everyone at Knopf and Vintage. To the Book Group. To Jenny Meyer and Heidi Gall at the Jenny Meyer Literary Agency. To Josie Freedman at CAA. To Christie Hinrichs and the team at Authors Unbound.

To Charlotte Gordon and Christina Baker Kline, whose kindness and desire to help astounds me still.

Thank you to my early readers, all of whom provided invaluable feedback: Maris Dyer, Tiara Sharma, Louisa Skerry, DJ Kim, Ann Napolitano, Jami Attenberg, Kate Sweeney Regan, Michael Johnson, and my husband, Kevin Johannesen.

To all who gave so generously of their wisdom, time, and expertise. Donna Loring and Jenn Ashton were indispensable in helping shape my thoughts and words about Indigenous history and culture, weighing in on the text with great care. Phil Deloria provided additional insight and encouragement at just the right moment. Sara Pitman was my medical advisor, as usual. Lucie Prinz is always at the heart of it and I'll never forget. Ken McAuliffe at the Old York Historical Society and Bryce Waldrop at the Historical Society of Wells and Ogunquit were knowledgeable, helpful, and wise. Sharon Seelig's seminar on early women writers at Smith College twenty years ago provided inspiration, as did her book *Autobiography and Gender in Early Modern Literature*. Another source of inspiration came from hours spent researching my third novel, *The Engagements,* at the Schlesinger Library back in 2012. I've wanted to put this special and essential place in a book ever since. (With apologies to the real staff for Jane's entirely fictional bad workplace behavior.)

This book enters into several historical chapters from Maine's past. *History of Ogunquit Village, with Many Interesting Facts of More Recent Interest* by Esselyn Gilman Perkins was the first book I read as I dove in, and it led me down a surprising path.

For helping me construct the sections about Clementine and Camp Mira, I am in debt to my friend Mira Ptacin, whose breathtaking nonfiction book *The In-Betweens* transports readers to the real-life Spiritualist gathering place in Maine, Camp Etna. Mira and her son Theo were kind enough to bring me to Camp Etna one summer day, to experience it for myself. The documentary *No One Dies in Lily Dale* also helped me imagine what the world of Camp Mira might look like, as did Peter Ross's series of photographs *Spiritualists, psychics, mediums, and healers* taken at Lily Dale and Cassadaga.

Where Two Worlds Meet by Janet Nohavec was a fascinating behind-the-scenes look at how mediumship works. *Boston in the Golden Age of Spiritualism: Seances, Mediums and Immortality* by Dee Morris offered a great local history. Leslie Kean's brilliant and exhaustively researched *Surviving Death* was a tremendous resource, which led me to learn about the work being done at the University of Virginia's Division of Perceptual Studies. (That group's website provided extensive additional information.)

To help me construct Eliza's world, I read *Women, Family, and Utopia: Communal Experiments of the Shakers, the Oneida Community, and the Mormons* by Lawrence Foster; *The Diaries of Sarah Jane and Emma Ann Foster: A Year in Maine During the Civil War* edited by Wayne E. Reilly; *"Dear Friend Anna": The Civil War Letters of a Common Soldier From Maine* edited by Beverly Hayes Kallgren and James L. Crouthamel; *The Pearl of Orr's Island* by Harriet Beecher Stowe; and "Harriet Beecher Stowe and the Loss of the *Hanover*: Transforming a Maine Shipwreck in *The Pearl of Orr's Island,*" an article by Susan F. Beegel, published in *American Literary Realism,* vol. 50, no. 2 (Winter 2018).

The Maine Maritime Museum's online resources about the *Hanover* provided additional information. As did the Ken Burns documentary

The Shakers: Hands to Work, Hearts to God and videos and digital archives from the Sabbathday Lake Shaker Village. An in-person visit to Sabbathday Lake helped add dimension to physical descriptions of the place.

The story of Archibald Pembroke's voyage and the kidnapping of four Indigenous men in what is now called Maine was very loosely based on accounts of the 1605 voyage of George Weymouth, as recorded in *The Beginnings of Colonial Maine 1602–1658* by Henry Sweetser Burrage; *Rosier's Relation of Waymouth's Voyage to the Coast of Maine, 1605* by James Rosier and Henry Sweetser Burrage; and *Transatlantic Encounters: American Indians in Britain, 1500–1776* by Alden T. Vaughan.

Plundered Skulls and Stolen Spirits by Chip Colwell is an essential look at repatriation and museum culture. It was so important to my understanding that I had to include it in the body of my novel, even though in reality it wasn't published until two years after the events in this book take place. Likewise, the Penobscot Nation did not grant personhood and citizenship to the Penobscot River until 2019, but I included this detail in these pages because it so beautifully signifies the respect and kinship Indigenous people feel toward their natural surroundings.

My education in Indigenous history, culture, and the fight for tribal sovereignty in the part of the world where I grew up is ongoing— a lifelong practice of learning and unlearning, which was vastly expanded by several incredible books. Among them: *Dawnland Voices: An Anthology of Indigenous Writing from New England* edited by Siobhan Senier; *Abenaki Indian Legends, Grammar and Place-Names* by Henry Lorne Masta; *In the Shadow of the Eagle: A Tribal Representative in Maine* by Donna Loring; *Women of the Dawn* by Bunny McBride; *The Life and Traditions of the Red Man* by Joseph Nicolar; *Indians in Eden* by Bunny McBride and Harald Prins; *The Common Pot* and *Our Beloved Kin* by Lisa Brooks; *Memory Lands* by Christine DeLucia; *The Voice of the Dawn: An Autohistory of the Abenaki Nation* by Frederick Matthew Wiseman; *Notes on a Lost Flute: A Field Guide to the Wabanaki* by Kerry Hardy; *Playing Indian* by Philip Deloria; *Night of the Living Rez* by Morgan Talty; *Notable Native People* by Adrienne Keene; and *The Age of Homespun: Objects and Stories in the Creation of an American Myth* by Laurel Thatcher Ulrich (with gratitude to Jenny Gotwals for recommending that last one).

Donna Loring's radio show *Wabanaki Windows* was an invaluable resource. As were the following documentaries: Alanis Obomsawin's *Waban-Aki: People from Where the Sun Rises,* Sunlight Media Collective's *This River Is Our Relative,* and *Dawnland,* directed by Adam Mazo.

During the first year of Covid, when museum visits were impossible, I did a huge amount of research and learning through online resources provided by the Maine Historical Society and the Abbe Museum. Last month I was lucky enough to visit the Abbe in person as well, a fascinating and moving experience.

Larry Ravelson and Erin Curtiss have let us borrow their beautiful Maine home for a week or two each summer for the past thirteen years. Time spent there has now provided inspiration for two of my novels. The weekend the seed was planted for *The Cliffs* was eight years ago now. Michael and Melissa Johnson were there, along with Stuart Nadler and Shamis Beckley. Thank you, Melissa, for trespassing with me. Thank you, Shamis, for saying something that you probably forgot about a minute later, but which stayed with me and provided part of the foundation for this story.

Thank you to my mother, M. Joyce Gallagher, to my father, Eugene Sullivan, and to my sister, Callie Sullivan. To the extended family of Joyces, Gallaghers, Sullivans, Troys, and Hickeys. And to Cynthia Biron.

My husband Kevin is a source of daily laughter, encouragement, conversation, and strong coffee. There is a line from a Jason Isbell song that floats through my mind sometimes: "This is how you help her when the muse goes missing / You vanish so she can go drowning in a dream again." Kevin knows just when to vanish so I can drown in a dream, and he takes our children with him when he goes.

Speaking of our children, the biggest thank-you is to them. Leo and Stella, you were no help at all in writing this book, but you infuse our days with joy.

A Note About the Author

J. Courtney Sullivan is the *New York Times* best-selling author of the novels *Commencement, Maine, The Engagements, Saints for All Occasions,* and *Friends and Strangers.* Her work has been translated into seventeen languages. Sullivan's writing has appeared in *The New York Times Book Review, The Washington Post,* the *Chicago Tribune, New York, Real Simple,* and *O: The Oprah Magazine,* among many other publications. In 2017, she wrote the forewords to new editions of two of her favorite classic novels—*Anne of Green Gables* and *Little Women.* She lives in Massachusetts with her husband and two children.

A NOTE ON THE TYPE

The text of this book was set in a typeface named Perpetua, designed by the British artist Eric Gill (1882–1940) and cut by the Monotype Corporation of London in 1928–30. Perpetua is a contemporary letter of original design, without any direct historical antecedents. The shapes of the roman letters basically derive from stonecutting, a form of lettering in which Gill was eminent. The italic is essentially an inclined roman. The general effect of the typeface in reading sizes is one of lightness and grace. The larger display sizes of the type are extremely elegant and form what is probably the most distinguished series of inscriptional letters cut in the last century.

Composed by North Market Street Graphics, Lancaster, Pennsylvania

Printed and bound by Berryville Graphics, Berryville, Virginia

Designed by Anna B. Knighton